LEVIATHANS
ARMORED SKIES

———◆———

EDITED BY JOHN HELFERS

LEVIATHANS: ARMORED SKIES
Edited by John Helfers
Cover art by Douglas Chaffee
Design by Matt Heerdt and David Kerber

Printed in USA.

Published by Catalyst Game Labs,
an imprint of InMediaRes Productions, LLC
7108 S. Pheasant Ridge Drive • Spokane, WA 99224

TABLE of CONTENTS

FOREWORD

In 1986, two pivotal events occurred that would lead to this foreword over three-and-half decades later.

The first was discovering the *Dragonlance Chronicles* trilogy by Margaret Weis and Tracy Hickman—*Dragons of Autumn Twilight, Dragons of Winter Night,* and *Dragons of Spring Dawning.* I read them voraciously, and then re-read them over the years. Even now, *Dragonlance* remains my favorite of all of the *Dungeons & Dragons* settings.

The second occurred at the very end of that year, as I biked with my friends to a game store in Tempe, AZ and bought the *BattleTech Second Edition* box set. I've played inordinate amounts of that game over the decades while reading every scrap of fiction published. What's more, through some hard work and wonderful luck, I joined the Adventure Game industry in 1996 and have been working with *BattleTech* ever since.

In both instances, the vistas of my imagination exploded to distant, previously unknown lands and ideas. Specifically, the concept of a living, breathing and changing universe crafted by a multitude of talented authors and artists. And that the universe would not only wax and wane, excite and terrify: but that as gamers you could directly immerse yourself into that experience. When you finished reading the harrowing exploits of a character just trying to overcome and keep their head high, you could take your own creations, and slide them in next to those events—the dice tumbling and pieces moving around the board. All the while laughing with friends, and discussing if said character would raise a salute to you across the field of battle, even as they raised their weapons. Those tabletop miniatures and roleplaying games wedded to dynamic settings turned a passive experience into a call to action!

I'd fallen in love with that experience from a young age—and most of my writing and game development experience interwove with such active universes. As such, it's no surprise, then, that when I had the chance to create my first original game design—and to help craft the setting that would enmesh it—of course it would be brimming with all the depth that the best fiction can bring to bear.

The game, art, and fiction of *Leviathans* crafts a larger-than-life, alternate history image of clashing empires at the dawn of the technological age. Yet heroes still make the difference, whether in the palaces of far distant lands as political machinations bring a knife in the dark, or on the deck of a ship fighting for its life in a raging storm as hellfire from 12" gun batteries try to obliterate it from existence.

While *BattleTech* will always remain my first love, *Leviathans* will also remain that first love as well—as I worked to forge a great game, John Haward, Blaine Lee Pardoe, Jim Rapkins, and I built around it a universe filled with possibilities that draw out that call to action.

I'm incredibly humbled and grateful that storytellers of the caliber found within these pages were eager to embrace my creation, and make it our creation. And you, as the reader—and hopefully player of the game returning via Kickstarter—can also make it *ours*. Every time you read, and every time you toss the dice: you join a community that is always so much greater than the sum of its parts.

Thank you! To these amazing authors that continue to build upon our foundation; to the long-time fans whose kind words and enthusiasm year after year have always been infectious; to Bryn Bills, the current Line Developer, whose love of the game and universe always kept the ships aloft and is taking that vision far beyond my own; and to you, the new reader. Welcome.

Stoke the fires, batten the hatches, and prepare to leap into the action!

—RANDALL N. BILLS
FEBRUARY 2021

INTRODUCTION

$\blacklozenge$

I love alternate history.

The infinite possibilities that can spiral out of a simple question: "What if..." can lead to incredible explorations of what might have been. Many authors and game companies both have made handsome careers out of exploring these alternate histories...and now it's Catalyst's turn to enter the field.

Or rather, re-enter it. Many folks are aware of the first iteration of *Leviathans*, and I'm not going to rehash the past, but look to the future instead. Randall N. Bills and Bryn Bills have retooled and updated the *Leviathans* tabletop game to create a fast-paced tactical war simulation where the navies of this alternate early 20the century no longer sail the seas, but have taken to the air.

With the game soon to be released, we thought what better way to celebrate the triumphant return of *Leviathans* with a start-studded anthology exploring this alternate universe. We set our own sights on inviting some of the biggest names in science fiction and alternate history, and at the end of it all, we've assembled an amazing roster of authors writing gripping tales of combat and courage as massive iron warships do battle high above the ground.

Accomplished and acclaimed author Steven Mohan Jr. leads off with an early tale of leviathan combat that ushers in a new age of warfare. Then bestselling science fiction master S. M. Stirling brings us a story of East meeting West, as Japanese student engineers journey to a far-away land to study the strange craft known as leviathans...and gain valuable information for their homeland at the same time. Military science fiction bestseller and naval veteran William H. Keith is up next with a story of political intrigue and skullduggery over African skies, culminating in one of the most unusual operation ever attempted by a leviathan. Then we have a double shot of naval adventure by Blaine Lee Pardoe, first with the Japanese testing the bounds of the Monroe Doctrine in the South Pacific Ocean, and then a story of honor upheld as the French and English duel for supremacy of the skies over northern Africa. Last, but definitely not least, the grand master of alternate history fiction, Harry Turtledove, closes out the volume with his story of a German leviathan assigned to raid airship commerce in the South Pacific whose captain discovers a dangerous plot that could destabilize the entire region.

In between these grand stories of flying ships, courageous captains, and cunning tactics and strategy are interspersed several vignettes that reveal more details about this alternate timeline, from the discovery of the lighter-than-air element electroid, to the gradual destabilization of the European continent, ending with a shocking event that threatens to plunge several nations into all-out war.

It is the dawn of a new age…an age not of sail or steam…but the age of the leviathan. We hope you'll join us as we take to the skies in celebration of their reign of iron.

—JOHN HELFERS, EXECUTIVE EDITOR
CATALYST GAME LABS
FEBRUARY 2021

GRAND REVELATION OF LEVIATHANS AT THE GREAT EXHIBITION!

Daily Telegraph, London, 7 May, 1890

—

**Stunning New Practical Use
for Electroid Brought to the Fore**

—

**Britain and France Reveal the Existence
of Leviathans, a New Type of Airship**

—

**Concerns Raised by Existence
of New Technology with War Applications**

◆

The entire world was shocked today with the unveiling of a spectacular new technology at the Great Exhibition in London, England. In competing presentations, both the British and French national contingents stunned the assembled crowds with the launching of a spectacular new type of aerial vehicle, capable of transporting material through the air with safety and stability. These new vessels, called 'leviathans' by their creators, have apparently been developed in secret over the last several years as competing scientific programs to provide an alternate to sea travel.

Capitalizing on the work of the esteemed Polish scientist Frances Rychnowski, who famously developed the existence of the intriguing 'electroid' from eteroid, the lighter-than-air fluid allows for immense vessels to be constructed, and allows for transportation between the continents with great speed and safety, unburdened by the fickle nature of the tides or sea-going hazards. Utilizing the exciting potential of this new element, the scientific teams had created several prototype airships with the potential capability for transatlantic crossing, allowing for a new and exciting era of transportation.

The primary spokesperson for the British team, Dr. Edgar Cariss, was thrilled to extol the virtues of the new leviathans program. "Thanks to the boundless potential of electroid, mankind can now claim the skies as the next great frontier! We are now able to fly safely above any conceivable danger, no longer at the mercy of the winds or the waves, soaring above the clouds as we travel the world in unmatched luxury. Thanks to our new leviathans, we can cross previously unfathomable distances in complete safety and comfort."

Although the technology that has been developed to take advantage of electroid is still relatively new, Dr. Cariss was quick to cite several studies that have shown the reliability of the new technology, highlighting its preliminary use in a variety of different lifesaving fields, including medicine, energy production, and communications.

Unfortunately, not everyone shares the excitement over the existence of such a revolutionary form of travel. Professor Aloysius D. Semfeld, a professor of Political Science for the University of Caledonia, was on hand with a small group of his students, protesting the ramifications of such a revolutionary new technology. While clearly some of the first to raise the point, already there are questions that the mere existence of such airships might lead to a whole new type of warfare between nations.

"The seagoing ship was instrumental in revealing the world to us," Professor Semfield stated during a brief interview. "It helped to breach the previously-insurmountable barrier of the oceans and took us down the first steps towards becoming a global community. When armed, however, it also brought death and destruction to the four corners of the Earth."

Semfield continued, "The automobile, in and of itself, was one of the most revolutionary forms of transportation in the last century, instrumental in making mid-range continental transportation both affordable and time-efficient. However, when armored and armed, they became the predecessors to the tanks and armored vehicles of our time. It is our concern that the very same situation will happen again, leading to unprecedented levels of destruction. Despite the loftiest ideals, how soon will it be before some nation gives into temptation and weaponizes the very sky itself?"

While the greatest of pains has been used to keep the leviathans program a secret, several other nations, including the Ottoman Empire and the United States, were quick to acknowledge that they had their own leviathan programs under development, although they declined to give further information, citing national security concerns. Whether such revelations will lead to Professor Semfield's nightmare scenario or a new arms race will have to be seen.

Despite the concerns raised by the small number of guests, the overall reception to the unveiling of the leviathans was jubilant, with both children and adults watching with glee and awe as the massive airships took to the sky in glorious splendor, highlighted by the grandeur of fireworks and fluttering pennants. We can only hope that Dr. Semfield's predictions of the weaponization of aerial travel are exaggerated, and that this magnificent new technology helps to usher in the new era of peace and understanding that the Exhibition espoused.

A MONSTER IN THE SKY

Steven Mohan, Jr.

◆

The bowl of the sky was lavender with the dying night. *Polkovnik* Mikhail Kozlov's mighty vessel rocked gently at tether. A life-long mariner, Kozlov handled the ship's easy roll without thinking of it. His mind was on other things.

On this morning, the morning of eighteen October 1896, the tsar's proudest ships were moving to break the Japanese stranglehold on Vladivostok. Even now, the sleek, powerful hulls of the Baltic Fleet were slicing through the blue waters of the Korean Strait on their way to punish the Imperial Japanese Navy.

And here was Kozlov, wearing a strange uniform with a strange rank, commander of a *sky* ship, a vessel of so little importance that Admiral Rozhestvensky had declined to order out the skyfleet in support of his grand ships.

Here he was, the *polkovnik* in command of the RVS *Prince Baratinsky*, and he could do nothing. He shook his head. *Polkovnik.* A *polkovnik* was something like a colonel. Whenever Kozlov heard the title he thought "Captain."

Kozlov laid a hand on the bulk of Turret Adeen. The forward turret housed two massive eight-inch guns. If only he had a chance to show—

But, no. Kozlov inhaled a deep breath of cold air. The skyships had their uses: they could spot, and they could harass infantry, but the Battle of Port Arthur proved that three- and five-inch guns were no match for the Japanese fleet's heavy weaponry.

Would his unproven eight-inchers really fare any better against the Japanese twelve-inch guns and nine-inch-thick Krupp armor?

He lifted his hand from the turret's flank, his palm suddenly cold from the steel.

All around his vessel the fleet hung at tether, *Baratinsky*'s mate *Aleksandr Nevsky* and a score of *Berkuts*, the skyship equivalent of gunboats. They hovered a hundred feet above the earth, moored by great manila hawsers. They looked like balloons, their hulls painted a pale blue.

The Cossacks of the sky, General Ardan Tomav called them.

Kozlov had never seen anything so ridiculous in his whole life. Nor anything so magnificent.

He sighed and looked up, watching dawn break gold and yellow across the eastern sky. If he avoided looking over the railing, he could convince himself he was aboard a ship at sea. He felt the rumble of machinery through the deck, the chill morning wind tearing at his coat, the motion of a vessel battling the will of the world.

There had been a time when he'd thought these things were enough. He'd forsaken a promising naval career to sail the sky. But now he found he missed the cold spray and the taste of salt.

Missed the glory of serving the *Rodina*, the Motherland, in a way that mattered.

Kozlov's mouth tasted dry. He stood there for a long moment, just looking at the brightening sky.

An urgent, muffled call emerged from a nearby voice tube, jerking him out of his reverie: "Polkovnik *to the bridge.*"

Kozlov flew up the steel ladder that led to the port bridge wing, his mind racing. On a naval vessel, this word was passed only in the case of collision, casualty, or enemy action. Kozlov couldn't imagine what emergency demanded his presence on his bridge. He ran, his heart pounding in the cage of his chest.

He burst onto the bridge, throwing open the hatch so that it slammed against the steel bulkhead.

One officer and one noncom stood bridge watch while at tether; a junior sergeant at the wheel and the lieutenant (*nyet, poruchik*, the rank was *poruchik*) at the compass stand. The lee helm and the chart table were unmanned.

The compass stand sat all the way forward, just below the great windows that looked out on the world. The *poruchik*, in his long, black leather coat over green trousers and high brown boots (Golubev was his name), was bathed in the dawn's glow.

And yet his face was ghastly pale, his jaw hung slackly open, his eyes…lost. Kozlov had seen such a look only once before. When he'd been a junior lieutenant aboard the battleship *Retvizan*, one of his young seamen had been washed over the side in heavy seas. Kozlov had seen the very same look of despair and shock on the face of that boy's mother.

"*What is it?*" he shouted.

Golubev handed him a slip of paper, a telegraphic message. Kozlov knew with one look that it came from Admiral Rozhestvensky. *The fleet.*

PRESENT LOCATION KOREAN ST 8 MILES
NORTH-NW TSUSHIMA ISL.

JAPANESE HAVE CROSSED MY T.

Kozlov's gut clenched. "Crossing the T" was an ancient naval tactic, allowing a fleet to bring all its guns to bear while its opponent was restricted to forward guns only. It was a sure recipe for disaster.

The message listed the fleet's losses: two battleships, a pair of cruisers, and four destroyers. *So far.* Kozlov wanted to stop reading, wanted the terrible roll call to end. But he couldn't tear his eyes away. He stood there, *frozen.*

REQUEST IMMEDIATE ASSISTANCE.

The urgency—the panic—in the message was clear as daylight. Kozlov turned to the junior sergeant at the wheel. "All hands to battle stations."

"All hands to battle stations, yes sir," snapped the sergeant. He turned and pulled at the bell behind him, filling the bridge with a rapid ringing that carried throughout the ship by a network of tubes.

Kozlov pointed at Golubev. "Make preparations to get underway."

The young officer blinked. "Sir." He opened his mouth, closed it again. "Sir, we don't have orders."

"*YOU* DO!" Kozlov roared. And then under his breath: "And soon we will, as well."

Kozlov wrote out a quick message for his telegraphic operator. He addressed it to General Ardan Tomav, father of the Cossacks of the sky:

MAKING PREPARATIONS TO GET UNDERWAY.

WILL TAKE SKYFLEET TO TSUSHIMA ISL TO ASSIST BALTIC FLEET.

He handed the slip of paper to the watch messenger, then told Golubev to signal the fleet his intentions. Then he stepped back, standing in the center of tumult as watchstanders took their stations, shouting clipped reports to the deck officer.

And then silence came again to his bridge. A stray tendril of smoke found its way to him, smelling of the fires of hell. Engineering was bringing up the standby boilers. Somewhere belowdecks, stokers were feeding the fires at *Baratinsky*'s heart, sweat gleaming on their bare backs.

The messenger returned with another message.

BALTIC FLEET MUST BE SAVED AT ALL COSTS.

Which was clear enough. Kozlov was to trade the vessels of the skyfleet—*all of them, if he had to*—in exchange for the Baltic Fleet's escape. "Yes sir," he said crisply.

GODSPEED, MISHA. GEN TOMAV SENDS.

The deck officer came to attention as Kozlov looked up. "Lines are singled up, sir. Standing by engines. Deckhands are standing by to take up lines."

"Very well, Mr. Golubev. Take up lines."

"Take up lines, yes sir." The young *poruchik* repeated the order into a brass voice tube, and the order would be repeated through a megaphone to the men on the ground.

Somewhere below them, young ground conscripts were prying manila lines loose from bollards with marlinespikes. Men on the skyship's deck were rapidly hauling up the heavy mooring hawsers hand-over-hand.

A voice sounded in the brass tube. "All lines taken up, sir."

"Very well, deck officer." Kozlov turned to the petty officer—*nyet*, the junior sergeant at lee helm. "Ahead slow."

A few seconds passed, and then Kozlov heard the distant buzz of his propellers coming up to speed, great blades enclosed in aluminum cowlings beating the sky.

Kozlov pointed at the man who was the watch's lead sergeant. "One long blast."

The sergeant pulled a lever and the ship's horn sounded for precisely three seconds, drowning out all other noise and warning the assembled company that the *Prince Baratinsky* was underway. And then Kozlov's skyship—his unimportant skyship—began to move through the newly born sky.

The black smoke of battle stung Togo Heihachiro's eyes, burned them, clawed at them, until tears streamed down his cheeks and he had to lower the heavy binoculars that made his old hands ache and wipe away the tears with his dark blue sleeve. His ears—his *head*—rang with the constant report of the *Mikasa*'s forward pair of twelve-inch, 40-caliber guns. He smelled the stink of battle—steam and burning coal, the bittersweet odor of spent explosives and, because the Russian flagship, *Knyaz Suvorov*, had managed to land several blows with her own twelve-inch guns, the coppery stink of spilled blood.

It was glorious, all of it.

He stood on the *Mikasa*'s topgallant forecastle above the battleship's boxy bridge. His station was the compass stand, where he could monitor the ship's heading and pass orders down to the captain through the twin voice tubes.

But the real advantage of his station was that he could see.

See everything.

Behind him, the ship's two stacks belched smoke and steam into the blue sky, and the sea was a roiled turquoise. Three capital ships steamed in a neat line behind him, the four battleships the beating heart of his fleet. Officers clustered all around him, dressed in dark blue, wearing gold aiguillettes draped across their shoulders to mark them as his aides as they bustled about their duties.

But what really commanded Togo's attention was the signal flag overhead, rippling and flapping in the gale of the *Mikasa*'s flank bell. The flag was a square, built from four triangles, one black, one yellow, one blue and one red, the apex of each meeting in the flag's center.

What the English called the Zed flag.

Today, Togo was using it to send a special message to his fleet: *"The Empire's fate depends on the result of this battle. Let every man do his utmost duty."*

And his men and ships *were* doing their duty. *This is almost over.*

He raised the binoculars to his eyes.

The Russians were running flat out, for all the good it would do them; their remaining battleships and cruisers holding their battle line, torpedo boats and destroyers screening the capital ships' port and starboard quarters. Toho ignored the smaller vessels, intently watching the battleships.

There.

He saw a slight jog in the white wake that stretched out from the lead vessel's wake. "*Suvorov*'s showing starboard aspect," he called out.

"Enemy's turning due west," agreed Taniguchi Shintaro, Togo's flag lieutenant. "It looks like a turn together."

The boy was right. The Russians weren't turning in sequence; they had turned all at once, which meant they weren't holding their battle line. They spread out before him, running west, fleeing at best possible speed to the safety of their base at Port Arthur.

They were not going to make it.

"We can cross their T again," said Taniguchi eagerly.

Togo's fleet was capable of sixteen knots. The Baltic Fleet, its hulls fouled and its machinery taxed by the long journey to the Pacific, was capable of perhaps nine or ten. The admiral had used his advantage in speed and maneuverability to cross the Russians' T twice, with devastating results. While he could smash the Russian vessels with full broadsides, they could only answer with their forward turrets. That tactic, combined with superior Japanese gunnery, had taken a toll.

If Togo executed the maneuver again, he could send perhaps a third of the remaining Russian ships to the bottom. But for his entire battle force to pass along the T and then turn back to pursue would take perhaps forty, forty-five minutes. At ten knots, the surviving Russians would gain almost seven nautical miles.

Fourteen thousand yards.

He could send a third of them to the bottom.

But he wanted them all.

"*Iie*," Togo barked. He was silent for a long moment, vectors and times and speeds spinning in his head. When he spoke, there was steel in his voice. "We will turn in sequence in eight minutes to new course two six one. Verify my calculations and then haul up the signal flags."

"*Hai*, Admiral-*sama*," Taniguchi barked.

Togo had just committed his fleet to a flat-out run followed by a ship-to-ship battle at close range. It was a brutal decision, but looking at the Russian vessels, he could make no other.

He would have them all.

And then a lookout called, "*Leviathans. West-northwest.*"

Togo dropped his binoculars and turned to look where the boy was pointing.

He saw a cloud of the small gunboats the Russians called *Berkuts*, and two of the bigger vessels, the RVS *Aleksandr Nevsky*, and a second vessel that looked like it might be the *Nevsky*'s sister.

He felt a flutter of unease in his stomach. No commander liked the words *might be*.

"Maneuvering calculations place us on an intercept course if we turn to..." the flag navigator looked up. "Two five eight."

Togo heard the awe in the young man's voice, and allowed himself a small smile. He had been off by three degrees; he had eyeballed the enemy's course and speed and his calculation had been off by only *three degrees*.

"Raise the signal flags," said Togo. "Turn in sequence to two five eight."

"*Hai*," said his signal officer. "Raise the signal flags. Turn in sequence to two five eight."

Taniguchi stepped to his side and pitched his voice so only the admiral could hear him. "Admiral—" The boy hesitated.

"Out with it, Lieutenant," said Togo evenly.

"Sir, perhaps we should reconsider the pursuit. The leviathans—"

The admiral snorted. "Get hold of yourself, Taniguchi-*san*. The skyships are *toys*. This is the age of the gun, and their weight restrictions guarantee that the leviathans will never match our firepower."

"*Hai*, Admiral Togo-*sama*," said the boy uneasily.

"We will smash the Russian fleet and the world's interest in leviathans all in one instant." Togo's eyes found the Zed flag. "And Japan will rule the east."

This time the boy's answer wasn't hesitant. "*Hai!*"

"Sir," called out the navigator, "recommend you mark the turn in ten seconds." He held up a gold pocket watch so the admiral could see the sweep of its second hand.

When it hit twelve, Togo leaned over the voice tube. "Captain, come to new course two five eight."

"Come to new course two five eight, yes sir," came the reply.

Behind him, the flag signal officer was hauling down the tactical signal, ordering the fleet to execute the order. As each of his battleships and cruisers came to the point in the ocean where the *Mikasa* had turned, they would follow the flagship right.

In that moment the die was cast; the fate of the Russians sealed.

And then, Togo looked up. The leviathans had organized themselves into a long line abreast across his intended course, the two great ships in the center, ten or eleven gunboats on either side, stretching out like the wings of some great and terrible bird. The Russians hovered only a hundred feet off the water, a skirmish line set between Togo and his prey.

Togo studied the vessel he did not know; sister to the *Nevsky*, the size of a naval destroyer or a light cruiser, her bow massive and blunt over a forward-sloping skirt. Her bridge was set in a tower behind her forward gun turret. And her guns— This was supposed to be a sister to the *Nevsky*, but—

Were those bigger guns?

Togo watched the vessel as his battleship swept toward her at sixteen knots.

Watched it hovering *in the sky*, finding the sight as fantastic as ever. Five or six *thousand* tons of steel and coal and guns and men floating in the air as light as a soap bubble. Casting its dark shadow on the blue, blue sea. It was an abomination.

It was a monster in the sky.

Togo was going to destroy it, was going to destroy them all. Today and for always. These playthings had no place in the honorable affairs of men.

And again, Admiral Togo Heihachiro felt that light flutter of unease in his stomach.

Nothing more than unease.

Kozlov stepped to the port bridgewing. He wanted to see the Japanese coming with his own eyes, unfiltered by glass. It was dangerous on a skyship's deck when underway, buffeted by heaven's angry winds, and Kozlov had published a standing order that required all officers and ratings to clip their safety lanyards to the steel padeyes bolted to the ship's superstructure when outside.

But this was war.

Speed was important. And more was at stake than Kozlov's meager life.

As he watched, the Japanese flagship *Mikasa* fired, simultaneous with his turn. His forward guns belched billowing flame, molten orange and yellow mixed with tendrils of sulfurous black, pumping out a pressure impulse so powerful that it churned the cobalt water white; for a moment the sea next to the *Mikasa*'s hull was *hollowed out* before it came rushing back in to reclaim what it had lost. A second later, the sound came to Kozlov, the *crack* of a close lightning strike, so close you can feel the hair rise on your body and you jump, even as everything around you rattles and shakes with the terrible blow.

Holy God.

So *these* were the Japanese guns.

And if the guns were terrible, the *gunners* were even more fearsome. As Kozlov watched, white water geysered a scant twenty-five yards astern of a fleeing Russian destroyer. A near miss, fired at range, by a ship moving at flank speed *in the middle of a turn.*

The *Mikasa*'s guns spoke again, sooner than he would have thought possible.

And this time there was no escape for the doomed destroyer. One moment the little ship was sprinting for his life and the next—

The twin shells smashed into the little ship dead astern, instantly sending up a column of spray and orange fire and debris and *men.* A terrible palsy rippled the destroyer's hull. He suddenly veered starboard and then *stopped.*

Kozlov could not swallow.

Steering casualty. The little ship was not under command. The last hit had robbed him of the ability to flee.

Kozlov had grown up in Novosibirsk in Asian Russia. As a boy, he'd hunted deer with his father in the dark Siberian forest. On one such trip he'd somehow managed to become separated from his father. He trudged through an early spring snow, cold, miserable, lost, the dead weight of his old rifle cradled in his arms.

Suddenly, he looked up and saw a deer. It was a big doe, maybe one hundred-twenty, one hundred-thirty pounds, tawny coat, ears pricked, nose twitching.

Liquid brown eyes looking right into his.

Young Misha knew he should shoot the deer, but he was only eight, and not yet used to killing things. He didn't know why the doe didn't flee, but for a long time the two of them stood there unmoving, staring at one another.

And then an orange-and-black terror erupted from a thicket not six feet from where Misha stood. The tiger launched itself into the air, expending all the power stored in its legs in one leap. Its jump missed the doe, but the animal still landed a blow at the last second that broke the deer's right hind leg.

The creature tried to drag itself away, bleating with pain, barely moving but still fleeing, because that's what its instincts told it to do.

The tiger didn't even bother to run. It *loped* after the deer, brought it down.

Ate it alive.

And that was exactly what was going to happen to the destroyer.

As Kozlov watched, the Japanese battleship fired *again*, this time hitting amidships.

It took less than a minute for the little destroyer to slip completely beneath the waves.

Kozlov turned and stepped back into the bridge. If he did not act, the fleet's fate would be the same as the destroyer's. In addition to their devastating advantages in gunnery and armor, the Japanese were much, much faster than their Russian counterparts. The Japanese battle line would stab through the center of the Russian formation like a blade, battleships and cruisers firing withering broadsides until no targets remained.

The Baltic Fleet would never reach the shelter of Port Arthur's shore batteries.

Unless the skyships could slow the Japanese.

Kozlov turned to his deck officer. "Pass the signal to all ships: target the lead Japanese battleship and *fire*."

Togo looked up at the line of warships hovering over the sea, not more than four or five thousand yards from his position. He did not like having the enemy above his head, but then, they'd been there before, hadn't they? Off the coast of Port Arthur, the Russian leviathans had tried to turn the tide.

And failed.

Oh, they had damaged ship superstructures and they'd killed some of his ratings. And they'd plagued the Japanese infantry, earning the name *Rairyuuha*–Thunder Dragons. But those accomplishments were not the same as punching through the Imperial Navy's fine Krupp armor.

And if a ship's armor could not be breached, she could not be sunk.

Suddenly the leviathans' guns erupted into orange flame. Togo stood firm. If today was his day to die, he would face it like a man.

For a moment the air was filled with the whistle of falling shells, and then the sea erupted in towering fountains of white water, drenching the men standing behind him. He heard their startled gasps. Togo remained impassive.

He watched.

The leviathans were firing at range, their three- and five-inch guns barely able to reach the *Mikasa* with any kind of accuracy. The enemy could do very little to hurt him. But the reverse was not true.

Togo leaned toward the voice tube. "Captain, come to new course three four eight." His battle line was steaming directly for the leviathan line, like a spear thrust at a shield. By turning ninety degrees he was presenting his port side to the enemy, but sacrificing his pursuit of the fleeing Baltic Fleet.

Togo turned to his signal officer. "Signal 'All Ships Continue Pursuit of Enemy.'"

The officer bowed. "*Hai.* All Ships Continue Pursuit of Enemy."

Strictly speaking, the order wasn't necessary, but Togo wanted to be absolutely sure that his battle line did not follow him into the turn. His main force would continue its pursuit of the Baltic Fleet, and the *Mikasa*'s heavy guns would smash the leviathans from the sky.

A grim smile touched Togo's lips as he gave his next order.

"Captain, redirect fire at the line of leviathans. All port batteries. You may fire at your leisure."

Kozlov allowed a smile to touch his lips as he watched the *Mikasa* turn. *The Japanese are taking the bait. He is drawing them off their pursuit.*

And then the smile froze.

The second battleship *did not turn.* He watched the golden chrysanthemum on the warship's bow, the emblem of the Japanese emperor, waited for it to slide right. But the second battleship never wavered. Nor did his two brothers behind him. All three battleships knifed straight through the water and past their flagship, which was slowing and steadying on a new course.

The main Japanese battle line would not be drawn off. They were going straight for the Baltic Fleet while the *Mikasa* dealt with the skyships alone. And he could do it, too. Kozlov had twenty-two *Berkut* gunships and two *Nevsky*-class cruisers, but the *Mikasa*'s port side bristled with guns—seven six-inch 40-calibers, five three-inchers, and of course, the monsters: a quartet of Elswick twelve-inch 40-caliber heavy guns.

More than enough firepower to knock his little fleet out of the sky.

And as Kozlov watched, the great ship's guns elevated, his superior gunners taking aim.

The *Mikasa*'s guns opened up with the fury of hell itself. For a moment there was nothing—and then the sea exploded a few hundred yards in front of the leviathan's shadows.

Too high, Togo thought. *The gunners have trained their guns too high.*

His fleet had the best gunners afloat. They would determine their error.

The admiral stood stock still, enemy shells raining down all around his ship, drawing closer, the Russian fire drawing closer. An enemy shell hit amidships, the dull clank of the impact rising in the cold air. Billowing smoke and flame blossomed from the port side. Then there was another hit. And *another.* One of the enemy gunners had found the *Mikasa*'s range at last. *Clank-clank-clank.* Now the enemy shells were pounding his hull like a hard rain.

Togo drew a deep breath and ran to the ladder, climbed down, ignoring the shouts of his aides who must've thought he'd gone mad. He climbed quickly, past the bridge, hand over hand, jumping the last four feet to the wood deck and landing in a crouch. Ignoring the flash of the enemy's fire, he ran to the side of his ship and peered over the safety railing.

The black of burned paint and spent explosives streaked the gray hull. There were ugly dents all along the port side where the armor was beginning to buckle, but the nine-inch steel plates had not been pierced.

The Krupp armor had withstood the full fury of the enemy's assault. Which meant the *Mikasa* could not be defeated.

Togo stood, satisfied to return to the forecastle. As he turned, he saw the *Mikasa*'s forward twelve-inch guns lower a few degrees.

And then they spoke.

He turned back, just in time to see the massive shells hit. One moment he was looking at a *Berkut* gunship, maybe a third the size of the *Nevsky* and her sister, and then suddenly the sky was filled with fire.

It started just behind the leviathan's main guns, an explosion, orange flame leaping twenty feet into the air, debris raining into the ocean, and then there was a *second* explosion, a massive *whump* that seemed to rattle the world.

Secondary explosion, Togo thought. *Forward magazine.*

All at once the sky was gray and hazy with debris: cinders glowing bright orange and jagged pieces of wooden paneling and long, uncoiling lengths of rope, and a million fluttering pieces of paper like a flock of geese startled into the air by a gunshot.

And bodies.

Some still and falling with a dead man's weight, some screaming, some *burning*, no more than a black silhouette against the flames devouring their flesh as they plummeted toward the sea.

The ship itself, broken and burning, spiraled out of the air as electroid leaked from its hull.

All this Togo saw in an instant.

Before the next blast from the *Mikasa*'s guns.

One moment Kozlov was standing there, watching the fleet's gunners find their range, shells starting to smash into the battleship's hull. Given a few more seconds, the *Baratinsky*'s gunners would find the right angle and his eight-inchers would—

God's hand reached down and grabbed Kozlov, hurling him across the bridge and smashing him against the starboard bulkhead. The *polkovnik* lay there for a moment, stunned. He had the impression that there had been a huge noise, but in fact there was silence, total silence, and for a second he thought he might be dead.

He looked up and saw one of his junior sergeants standing over him, the left side of his face masked in dark blood from a gash just over his left eye. The man was screaming at him, his mouth wide open, muscles standing out like cords in his neck, but Kozlov could barely hear.

He touched his right ear, and his hand came away stained crimson.

Kozlov scrambled to his feet. If he *were* dead, he must be in hell. The glass in the forward windows had shattered and the blue tile deck was littered with thousands of blue-green shards of glass and streaked with blood. One of his men, young Golubev, lay on the deck.

Kozlov crouched by the *poruchik*'s still form, feeling for a pulse.

Nothing.

The boy was dead.

The *polkovnik* stood, trying to understand what had happened.

He looked out the opening on the port side of his bridge that had once contained glass, and what he saw was one of his gunships sinking through the air. The little vessel had taken position directly outboard the *Baratinsky*, no more than three hundred yards off the cruiser's port beam.

Now it was a collection of twisted and burning wreckage. The main gun turret was *gone,* just gone, and the deck after where it should've been was blackened and burning. The scorched steel had opened up like a blooming flower.

"Secondary explosion," Kozlov whispered.

The terrible explosion had also taken the ship's pilot house. As Kozlov watched, the vessel heeled over. The *Berkut*s carried two electroid spheres along their keels. The forward sphere must have been destroyed in the explosion, releasing the electroid, and with it losing the positive buoyancy needed to keep the gunship's corpse in the sky.

With its rear sphere still intact but its forward sphere crushed, the vessel fell toward the sea bow-first, like a sinking ship plunging toward the ocean floor.

Kozlov's hopes fell with the *Berkut*. This was the worst possible outcome.

He was sacrificing his skyships, but there was no chance of slowing the main Japanese force. He would lose his men and his ships *and* the Baltic Fleet.

Kozlov turned and met the eyes of the junior sergeant whose face was a half-mask of blood. "Can you hear me?" he shouted.

He couldn't hear himself, but the sergeant nodded vigorously.

"Good," said Kozlov. "Signal the fleet. All skyships break formation. Withdraw. Attack the main body of the Japanese fleet. Commanders, select targets at will. Just slow them down. *Slow them down.*"

From his perch on the topgallant forecastle, Togo watched the Russian leviathans break and *run*. It was a glorious rout, and he wished the whole world could see it. A fleet of skyships beaten by a single battleship.

And then he saw that it wasn't quite a rout. The Russian vessels were withdrawing, but they were withdrawing in good order, and they were running *toward* his fleet.

Togo's eyes narrowed. The Russian commander must be mad. Beaten by a single battleship, the man now chose to engage a *fleet* of cruisers and battleships.

No matter. Some men demonstrated difficulty in learning the realities of the world. If it was his fate to instruct them, so be it.

He turned to Taniguchi. "Signal the cruisers *Kasuga* and *Nisshin* to retrain their guns on the leviathans. All other vessels are to concentrate their fire on the Baltic Fleet."

His aide ducked his head. "*Hai*, Togo-*sama*."

This was one fight Togo didn't intend to miss. He gave new orders. "Captain, left full rudder, come to new course two four nine. All ahead flank. It is time for the *Mikasa* to rejoin her fleet."

Wind tore at Kozlov's clothes, buffeted his body, assaulted his face until tears streamed from his eyes and were carried away. The *polkovnik* wrapped an arm around the center framing of his shattered windows, holding himself up against the wind, against the treacherously blood-slicked deck, against the nausea roiling his stomach and the ice-pick agony throbbing in his ears.

"Fire!" Kozlov roared.

The *Baratinsky* shook with the recoil of his eight-inchers. Water exploded on the far side of the Japanese destroyer.

"Bracketed," Kozlov called out. The last shot had been on the destroyer's near side. His gunners had found their range.

Knowing he was doomed, the destroyer turned hard to starboard at thirty knots, kicking up a rooster-tail of white spray. The little ship's principal weapons were his twin 18-inch torpedo tubes, but he made a brave noise with his three-incher. A gray line of shells rose from the sea and shot into the sky only a score of yards from where Kozlov stood.

"Steady, helm," he barked. "I don't want this ship to move an inch."

The junior sergeant on the helm said something, but Kozlov couldn't distinguish the words. He had gone from hearing nothing to hearing muffled sounds. It was like overhearing a conversation through a closed door. It wasn't much—but he would take what he could get.

He looked at his bridge crew. They looked back at him, faces naked with fear, wanting desperately for him to somehow make it all okay.

"Don't worry about that little three-incher, boys," he said. "He's trying to run, which means he can't bring his gun all the way around *and* he's firing on the move. His problem's much harder than ours. So we're going to wait right here until our gunners find his range."

His boys all nodded. Kozlov imagined he heard a few "yes, sirs."

And then suddenly they were all pointing, their mouths open in silent yells, jumping up and down and pounding each other on the back.

Kozlov turned in time to see a great gout of flame stab high into the sky.

The *Baratinsky*'s eight-inch shells had punched through the destroyer's armor.

The destroyer's stern was down by at least ten feet and listing heavily to port.

But that wasn't what caught Kozlov's attention.

Its fourth stack was damaged, *exploded* like a joke cigar. Heavy black smoke poured from the mangled stack. In a flash of insight, Kozlov understood what had happened. One of the shells must have dropped straight down the stack, destroying the last of the four Yarrow boilers.

Unobstructed by armor.

And the *Baratinsky* had been so high that the destroyer couldn't reach up to hit him. *Why didn't I see it before?* thought Kozlov. In warfare it's always been advantageous to hold the high ground—*and what ground is higher than the sky?*

He stepped through the hole of the missing window onto the port bridge wing to take a new look at the battle raging all around him. Skyships lumbered through the heavens, trying to avoid the more powerful Japanese gunfire. The battle had devolved into twenty, thirty skirmishes, and the Russians seemed to be losing them all.

But it didn't have to be that way.

Suddenly his replacement deck officer was by his side, pulling him back inside the pilot house. The boy was pointing frantically out the windows.

Kozlov saw the damaged Japanese destroyer limping away, trailing ugly black smoke. He thought he heard the boy say: "pursue."

Kozlov shook his head. "*Nyet, nyet.*" And this time, miracle of miracles, his abused ears converted that little bit of pressure into sound. "Signal the fleet."

Overhead, one of the leviathan gunboats rocked with blows from the guns of one of Togo's destroyers. The skyship careened drunkenly across the sky.

Togo raised his binoculars and watched the wounded bird struggle to stay aloft. The Russian commander had divided his fleet, trading a fight against one battleship for a fight against an entire battle fleet. It was a desperate move—one that could only end in the Russians' destruction.

Togo shifted his view left and saw the protected cruiser *Kasagi*, harried by a pair of Russian gunships, turn sharply to port, unmasking her batteries.

The *Kasagi* elevated her guns and fired *up*. One of the gunships wandered too close to the stream of shells fired from the *Kasagi*' s lethal eight-inch guns. The *Berkut* shuddered and juked across the sky, rapidly losing altitude.

But the second gunship managed to stay out of the *Kasagi*' s line of fire, safely outside the angle to which her guns could elevate. The determined little skyship positioned her guns so her shells fell just beyond her own bow and plunged directly down toward her enemy. The *Berkut* poured down fire onto the cruiser, accepting the fact that its three- and five-inch fire that couldn't penetrate the cruiser's four-inch armor could handily smash the bridge and kill deck hands.

The gunship and the cruiser were tangled together. The *Kasagi* was like a horse trying to shake off a biting fly. The horse was infinitely more powerful, but the fly was almost impossible to catch.

Worse. The little *Berkut* had managed to lure the *Kasagi* out of the Japanese fleet's battle line. Togo's vessels were being delayed and drawn off. And every second the Baltic Fleet survived brought them a second closer to safety.

Togo pointed at the cruiser and glanced back at Taniguchi. "Instruct *Kasagi* to return to her station."

The young officer bobbed his head. "*Hai*, Togo-*sama*."

Togo raised his binoculars, watching the cruiser. The gunship fired a volley and the shells arced harmlessly over the *Kasagi*' s crow's-nest. *Toys*, he thought. *Do not bend your will to the makers of toys.*

The cruiser suddenly turned right. Togo saw the moment when her captain put on the flank bell, the screws churning the water as the *Kasagi* accelerated to her top speed of 23 knots. She raced back to her position in line, the gunship lobbing shells after her.

"Good," Togo whispered, "good."

If they kept moving toward the Russian fleet, they could not be denied.

The Russian *Berkut* fired another volley.

The Russians could not do Togo's fleet any real harm. They could only win the day if—

His breath caught in his throat.

A sound like thunder rolled across the water, drowning out the staccato *boom* of gunfire for several seconds. It was followed by a massive fireball, incandescent orange fire burning to bitter black smoke. The *Kasagi* swerved left and then right. There were men running around on her deck, some of them on fire, some of them leaping into the sea.

The leviathan had been lucky, smashing a shell into the cruiser's forward magazine and igniting a massive secondary explosion.

Except—it hadn't been luck. As he examined the scene before him, Togo realized it was a deliberate tactic. The leviathans were hovering almost directly above his ships, out of reach of his big naval guns, lobbing their shells *down.*

Tearing into ship superstructures and stacks, hitting his vessels where their armor was thinnest.

Another peal of thunder rolled across the sea. He turned to see a Japanese torpedo boat pull out of formation, bleeding acrid smoke from her second stack like a gutted man bleeds dark blood from his belly.

Rage took Togo then—rage and *fear.*

Fortunately, he knew exactly what he had to do.

Like a sea captain who lashes himself to the forward mast in the face of a hurricane, Kozlov clung to his precarious perch on the shattered bridge of the *Prince Baratinsky.* The storm raged all around him, but he thought he could see the lightening of the clouds that signaled the coming dawn.

His skyships were taking the battle to the Japanese. It was nearly impossible for a skyship to deliver a knock-out blow to a sea ship, but in this battle, they didn't have to. All they had to do was stay above the enemy's withering fire and keep them occupied.

Every minute the Japanese spent swatting at the bees buzzing around their heads brought the Baltic Fleet a minute closer to escape.

Despite the death and destruction all around him, Kozlov felt a comforting warmth in his chest. He had done the impossible. He had saved the Baltic Fleet *and* preserved his skyships.

"*Polkovnik,*" said the deck officer.

And Kozlov heard it, softly, garbled, and with only one ear, but he *heard* it.

"*Da,* Deck Officer."

The boy was staring at the sea with his binoculars.

"Sir, the *Mikasa* is approaching from the northeast."

Kozlov turned and saw. The Japanese battleship was coming in fast, the ensign at his stern, the Rising Sun, flapping madly in the breeze. The *polkovnik* raised his binoculars. The Japanese flagship was racing toward his cousin, the battleship *Fuji*, who was trying vainly to strike back at the *Aleksandr Nevsky*, hovering directly overhead.

Kozlov saw the danger at once.

The *Fuji* was swerving all over the place, his wake churning a huge swath of ocean a frothy white, turning right and then left, running in a half-circle. Coming to all-stop and drifting, then putting on a quick backing bell with rudder. Trying everything to get a clear shot at the *Nevsky*.

But the skyship was more nimble than his opponent. The *Nevsky* couldn't swoop and glide like a bird, but neither did he have to fight his way through water.

The sky cruiser was managing to keep his opponent directly beneath him. *Fuji* occasionally landed a blow, but the battleship couldn't manage the sustained barrage that would pull *Nevsky* out of the sky.

But if the *Mikasa* pulled alongside his cousin, *his* guns would most certainly reach.

Quickly, Kozlov tracked his binoculars left to right. Japanese vessels were pulling out of their battle line and forming up into pairs, an arrangement that would enable each ship to elevate his guns enough to strike at their brother's attacker.

The quiet sense of victory he had felt now turned to ash. In slowing down the Japanese battle fleet, he had saved the Baltic Fleet.

And for that he was about to pay the ultimate price.

Kozlov shouted for his signalmen to order the *Nevsky* to withdraw.

But it was already too late.

Disaster had stolen upon Togo with quiet feet. The Baltic Fleet had been in his gun sights, literally in his gun sights, and the leviathans had managed to fling themselves in his path to save their more powerful sisters.

For that they would pay.

"Right full rudder," ordered Togo into the voice tube, his voice arctic cold.

"Steady up on new course three four seven."

He was coming to a course that paralleled the *Fuji*. At five thousand yards abeam of the other battleship, his guns would have sufficient room to target the *Nevsky*. If he missed, the shells would pass harmlessly over the *Fuji*. But they would not miss for long. Togo's gunners would find their target quickly and destroy it. And if the skyship tried to run, she would find herself the target of *two* battleships' fire.

Togo had not delivered the knockout blow he had planned to the Baltic Fleet, but he had crippled Russian power in the Pacific. And now he would finish the world's flirtation with leviathans with one last, devastating blow.

He would still have a kind of victory.

"We're drawing in range, Togo-*sama*," reported Taniguchi.

"*Hai*," barked the admiral. He leaned into the voice tube. "Captain, target the Russian sky cruiser. All port batteries. *Commence fire.*"

"*Hai*, Togo-*sama*," answered *Mikasa's* captain.

Shells tore into the cruiser, flaying the light armor from her hull, ripping away the turrets that housed her three- and five-inch guns, blasting men off the ship so they fell like pieces of debris.

When Togo had been a boy, he'd gone to sea on a whaling ship. What he saw now precisely mimicked the moment when a harpoon plunged into the flesh of one of those great beasts. The sky cruiser lunged right, trying to free itself from its attacker, all the while bleeding black smoke and eteroid like a minke whale pouring its life into the cruel sea.

The leviathan drifted over the *Fuji*'s centerline, then lurched further right, and suddenly the other battleship's guns opened up. The *Fuji*'s frustrated gunners found that the *Nevsky* had wandered into their gun sights; they poured into her all their rage and hatred.

Eight twelve-inch guns and twelve six-inch guns tore into the staggering leviathan and she seemed to just *dissolve*, her burning carcass plunging toward the sea.

A jubilant cheer rose behind Togo, his men jumping up and down and pumping their fists into the air, yelling for all they were worth. And as what was left of the Russian sky ship rained down, Togo allowed himself a broad smile.

❦ ⚜ ❦

On his crippled bridge, Kozlov watched the *Nevsky* die. One minute the mighty cruiser was there, and the next it was just *not*. At that moment, Kozlov finally understood the terrible price that he and his men would pay to save the Baltic Fleet. He had always understood that price in the dry, analytical precincts of his mind.

But now he understood it in his gut.

"Helm," Kozlov barked. "Come to new course zero four six. Descend to one hundred feet. Lee helm, all ahead flank. "

"*Polkovnik*," said the deck officer, panic edging his voice. "That will take us—"

"*DO IT!*" he roared. "All battery crews, *stand by your guns.*"

"Stand by your guns, yes, sir," repeated the young deck officer, who now had a life expectancy of between five and ten minutes. If Kozlov was going to be defeated, if his men and ships were going to be destroyed, he was going to take as many as possible of the bastards below with him.

Starting with that unholy devil, the *Mikasa*.

"Answering all ahead flank, *Polkovnik*," said the lee helm crisply.

"Steady on new course zero four six," added the helm.

"Very well, gentlemen," said Kozlov, folding his arms across his broad chest. He made himself ready to meet his death as the wind howled through his bridge.

The *Baratinsky* lumbered toward the *Mikasa* to avenge the *Aleksandr Nevsky*'s death.

Togo scanned the horizon and saw the *Nevsky*'s sister turning. She was maybe ten, twelve thousand yards to the south-southwest of the *Mikasa* at an elevation of two hundred feet. The leviathan was wreathed in smoke and she was burning amidships, a yellow flame throwing a column of black smoke into the blue bowl of the sky.

But she was moving.

Togo watched her for a second.

The leviathan's squat bow was swinging *left*.

Togo's hand tightened on the binoculars. She was coming left, coming left and picking up speed.

And descending.

Togo dropped his binoculars. The *Fuji* and the *Mikasa* were bow-on to the skyship, most of their batteries masked by the angle of the ships. Togo's mouth suddenly went dry. He felt time and distance ticking away as the Russian sky cruiser picked up speed.

He leaned in to the voice tube. "Captain, forward gun mount acquire the cruiser. Fire at the cruiser."

The admiral turned to Taniguchi. The boy was watching the monster as it came for them, watching it with his mouth hanging open, his eyes wide with fear.

"*Lieutenant*," Togo barked. "Order the *Fuji* to come right ninety degrees and bring her portside guns to bear on that skyship."

Taniguchi jerked his head down in a rough nod, not even bothering to acknowledge the order. Then he ran back to order the signal himself.

The *Mikasa*'s guns opened up. Water exploded a thousand yards behind the skyship.

Togo swallowed. This was not a concern. He had the best gunners afloat.

(But the leviathan wasn't exactly *afloat*, was it?) They would lower their elevation. They would find their target. They would pull that obscenity right out of the sky.

Togo licked his lips, anticipating the next blast from his forward twelve-inchers.

Just as the leviathan came hard right.

The shells missed again, this time on range, but wide right.

And then the leviathan's guns opened up. They were not twelve-inch naval guns. But they weren't three- and five-inch popguns, either. He heard the roar of the cruiser's forward gun mounts and saw white water explode two hundred yards aft of the *Fuji*'s stern.

The *Mikasa* answered back. A smoke round traced a neat path *over* the skyship's bulk. Togo slammed his fist into the compass stand. His gun crews had failed to adjust for the beast's descent.

The leviathan's guns roared again, and this time *they hit*. Togo saw smoke and fire billow up, aft. Suddenly the *Fuji* was turning.

"What's she doing?" shouted Taniguchi.

"Her rudder's jammed," snapped Togo. The *Fuji* was four thousand yards away, but she was coming around again. Now she was stern-on to the leviathan.

And the monster was still coming.

The leviathan was close enough that Togo could see that her bridge was damaged, the glass shattered and the window framing bent. He saw a single figure hanging on to the framing. *He means to kill us*, thought Togo.

"The Russian," he whispered, "he's going to ram us." Togo gave his order. "Come about to a reciprocal course, Captain. Flank bell."

The leviathan's guns spoke like thunder. It was like thunder and a second later, Togo heard the terrible cacophony of a hit, felt an explosion rumble through the guts of his flagship. And *again*. This was not the *clank-clank-clank* of shells bouncing off his hull.

This was the horrible sound of shells punching through nine-inch armor.

This was the sound of a mortal blow.

He felt his ship— *his ship*—settle, down by the bow.

The leviathan was close enough that the *Mikasa*'s forward six-inchers were joining the twelves. And now the world was nothing but the terrible roar of big guns. It was like being *inside* thunder. The *Mikasa* was taking a terrible beating, and so was the Russian sky cruiser. He watched as a Russian five-inch gun was *torn away*. And then another. The enemy vessel was shedding armor in huge chunks, it was falling like rain, filling the air with a gray, gritty haze. The fire he had seen amidships reached out toward two more.

But the leviathan still kept coming.

The skyship's guns fired, and the *Mikasa* shuddered violently, throwing Togo to the deck, smashing his head against the compass stand. For a moment, the world faded to gray. The admiral shook his head and jagged pain jerked him back.

The bodies of his aides were scattered all around him, some of them dead and some of them dying. The heavy metallic stench of blood filled his senses.

He no longer found it glorious.

The world sloped away from him to the left. The *Mikasa* had taken on a fifteen-degree list to port. Even as he lay on the deck, he could feel the battleship slipping into the cool embrace of the sea, feel her settling into her destiny.

Her guns had fallen silent. Pointed down at the sea, she could no longer reach the enemy above.

Togo managed to climb to his feet, reached for the voice tube. "Captain," he croaked. He swallowed. "Strike our colors. Abandon ship."

"*Hai*," barked the captain and said no more. This was too painful an order to repeat back.

Over Togo's head, the Zed flag was burning. He looked up and saw the battered leviathan claw its way into the blue sky.

And at that moment, Admiral Togo Heihachiro knew that Japan would not rule the east after all.

And he knew one more thing. It was not the age of the gun any more. It was the age of the sky.

It was the age…of the leviathan.

HEROES ᶠʳᵒᵐ TOMORROW

Tyler Whitney

◆

"The whole vault? Empty?" A small, spindly boy asked in a whisper as he leaned in towards his circle of friends.

The group of six boys huddled together for warmth, hiding behind the Wingham stables as a cold wind blew ice and snow past their shivering bodies.

"Just one of them," another boy, older than the rest, replied. "There are others, I've seen 'em filled with treasure! All hidden deep below the house!"

"And how would you know!?" said a stout boy as he leaned backwards out of the group, breaking the secrecy of their circle. "How could a servant know anything about some secret treasure?"

The rest of the boys eagerly stared at Liam, eyes wide and hearts pounding.

"Not a week past," Liam spoke quietly and slowly, "in the dead of night, a pair of crimson carriages arrived. A giant, cloaked man with the look of a scarred and twisted devil exited the first carriage." The stout boy leaned back down and joined the circle again while Liam's eyes shone to his captive audience.

"With an ugly smile, he gave me his bag and gripped my shoulder to lead me through the house to the cellar. Then, through a heavy locked door, down we went, past dimly lit passages I'd never seen before. We passed room after room, filled with all sorts of treasures, till we reached a small, cluttered chamber filled with strange vials and smells."

"Who was he?" The spindly boy butted in.

"A scientist, maybe. Or some type of inventor to make secret weapons for the Lord's leviathan. A steel fortress to be more powerful than any French or German ship!" Liam's voice broke a whisper as he failed to contain his excitement.

"Did you see who was in the other carriage?!" The big boy asked excitedly. "Was it Sir Emerson Jack?"

A static charge passed through the group of shivering boys at the thought of Sir Emerson Jack arriving at the Estate: the miraculous electroid pilot who flew secret missions in the popular comic-magazine *Heroes from Tomorrow*.

Before he could answer, however, a firm voice arose from behind the group of dawdlers.

"No."

The boys jumped, and Liam paled in the towering shadow of Lord Arthur Alexander Bellicost, Earl and heir of Lord Richard Bellicost, Duke of Cantia.

"Sir Emerson Jack will not be joining us. Neither will his Russian ally, Rasputin, nor his much, *much* under-appreciated engineer Rosiland. Unfortunately, those characters are fiction." His voice was stern, but warm. He wasn't yet so old that he couldn't remember the rumors he had created of his eccentric father while a child, though neither was he so young to condone this kind of gossip.

"L-L-Lord Bellicost, I-I-I..." Liam stammered.

"Liam." The boy shrank at the mention of his own name. "This Estate demands one thing of you at all times..."

Liam's mouth moved slowly, releasing only a squeak.

"Loyalty. We are on the brink of war, and you would share the secrets of the Estate? Betray your family's benefactor? Jeopardize our home and our country? A foreign spy could be amongst us even now... Watching... Listening..." The Earl's hazel eyes deliberately moved from boy to boy, interrogating each with his penetrating gaze.

Liam's chest tightened, unable to create a sound. He wanted to run, they all did, but the February cold had suddenly gripped their bones, anchoring them in place before judgement.

A slight grin broke over Arthur Alexander's face. *Good,* he thought, *they* should *be scared; might teach them to be more careful.* "Well, if you are all to be hung tomorrow—"

An almost unified *gulp* ran through the group of boys.

"—then I might as well let you know the truth behind Lord Bellicost's airship." He knelt down to their level, caring little for the icy mud on his brand-new uniform. "Gather close lads, listen well, and, perhaps I'll find a reason to keep you all around a bit longer."

The terrified faces of six trembling ghosts before him finally made him break his character and he let out a warm, comforting laugh. *Perhaps we won't die tomorrow,* the boys thought.

"You had it partially right, Liam, though not entirely. My father *is* making a ship, a behemoth of coal and iron to dominate the skies. But to think it emptied one of his treas—"

The boys leaned in closer as the Earl paused, nearly forgetting their previous terror of the man. Arthur Alexander held back a wider smile. If anything, his maddening father had taught him that the myth of a man stands taller than any genuine likeness.

"It is true that Wingham house holds many secrets, some of which even dead men can't know." The boy's eyes widened again. "But I can tell you this: War is brewing—it has been for a long time now, and in wars, heroes are needed. To prepare, the Duke has sent out a call for his champions: extraordinary men and women from all over the globe to aid us in the fight: pilots, engineers, scientists, artists, and crusaders."

"It must have been Charles you met, boy." Arthur Alexander turned to Liam, "A legendary chemist known as Frankenstein. You're lucky he let you leave his quarters with all your limbs intact. Though of course..." He paused to think while Liam's near-death experience set in. "Lady Catherine had also arrived that night, and no doubt that she could have dropped old Frankenstein before he had the chance to harm you. Devilishly quick, that one."

Arthur Alexander smiled again as Liam blushed at the idea of needing a woman to save him. "A-A-And sir?" Liam asked, the boy's stutter now from excitement rather than fear, "Who will captain them? Our champions?"

"I will, of course." The young Lord laughed while clapping a firm hand on the boy's shoulder as he rose from the mud. "And perhaps one day, Liam, you too will join our crew to sail amongst the clouds, where only heroes dwell and fight."

STEEL, BAMBOO, AND RICE PAPER

S. M. STIRLING

—————◆—————

I

Tokyo, 1896

Togo Takeshi hurried along the narrow streets toward his home, keeping up with Tadao, his family's major-domo. He could feel the tension in the passers-by, like heat from a brazier's coals on a cold day. For three days now, people had waited for news; they knew the Imperial navy and the Russian fleet would clash soon. They paid no mind to one more young boy, for all that he was obviously of a family who were *shi*, gentlefolk. Who would know he was the son of Chūjō Togo Heihachirō: *The Fortunate Man,* the vice-admiral who held the Tsushima Strait for the Emperor with his fleet?

People awaited news with tight-lipped patience. He had heard nothing, no one had at their house, but that was to be expected. Swift news was for the leaders of the nation.

Now Tadao had come to take him out of class, and had refused to say a word. The schoolmaster had disapproved, but read the small note, crumpled it, gave a short, choppy nod of his head, and ignored him thereafter. Tadao flushed under a face as much like an iron mask as he could make it. This could not be good tidings.

Takeshi told himself to be brave, but his stomach was making strong efforts to break free and his noon rice sat like a lump inside him, as if it was a pickled plum. As they came around a corner into the small dead end street where their house was, he hesitated.

A troop of men wearing modern, western-style uniforms stood on the cobbles. And several other men, and *jinrikshaws*. Older men, senior, white-haired. The senior men were wearing *wakufu*, and old-fashioned formal *wakufu* at that; dark *kimonos* and five-mon *haori* and *hakama*, and even the two swords which were technically still illegal to wear in public.

One gestured him into the house. It was only as he passed that he realized the man was actually a *gaijin*; even at this moment that nearly made him miss a step in shocked surprise. Japanese often wore Western clothing in this thirtieth year of the modern era of Meiji, but the reverse was unheard-of.

Inside the gate, Tadao left him. His mother, Togo Tetsu, was kneeling, still as a breathing statue on the wooden deck, her face smooth and beautiful and full of overwhelming sorrow. His little sister Yachiyo was in her arms, his brother Minoru, only six this month and heartbreakingly solemn in a dark *kimono*, stood beside her. His mother wore a formal *kimono* of unrelieved black with a faint weave pattern in it, a very crisp white silk under *kimono* showing properly at the neck, and a very plain dark red obi holding it together.

Father, he thought. *This is news of Father—and bad news.* Takeshi took a deep breath to steady himself, forcing his fear and building grief far down; he was a warrior's son and could not disgrace his father with a public show of weakness. Tetsu looked at him and made a small movement of her head. He hurried to unlace his shoes and stand beside her and to the left.

As he turned, the men of honor filed in. After one startled second, he realized he was seeing the Naval Minister himself, Yamamoto Gonnohyōe, who had appointed his father aboard the *Mikasa* to keep Port Arthur bottled up. His mother bent like a willow in the wind to the men and he and Minoru bowed profoundly as was due, both to an older man and one of the most powerful men in Nihon.

"Togo Tetsu," the minister said to Takeshi's mother, his voice grave and deep. "I bring you great sorrow. I also bring you great honor. Japan mourns today the loss of the fleet. The Russians brought the new airships to the naval battle. Events...did not proceed as fortunately as we would have wished."

Takeshi kept himself still, even as he controlled the hissing, sucking breath he took in, feeling as if he had been kicked in the belly. Then his eyes fixed on the stern face before him. He could see the roiling anger behind the placid exterior and the calm words.

"We have lost the fleet. Your honored husband, our Fortunate Admiral, was able to create a new doctrine to fight the attack from the sky. Thanks to that, we inflicted much damage, but it was insufficient. Nothing would have been sufficient. Our ships were designed to fight ships, not birds!"

The Naval Minister was silent for a minute before continuing: "Togo Heihachirō held the line for as long as possible, and kept his fleet together. In the midst of battle, he devised ways to turn his guns on the leviathans, futile though it ultimately was. He is dead. His ships are dead. Most of his people, officers and sailors alike, are dead. Japan has lost face due to this, and the western powers are pressing us to an ignoble peace treaty. We will have to accept it. Our only consolation is the courage with which Togo Heihachirō and his men met their end, and the skill with which the Admiral faced an impossible situation. They died with honor."

Takeshi felt the roiling anger from each of the men before him. He ached with the desire to step forward and lay his life at the Emperor's feet through his minister.

Take me! Allow me to further my father's honor!

Next to him, he felt his mother's tension. Her high honor and great intelligence meant she understood, probably much better than the young schoolboy he was, what had happened. He raised his eyes to the stern glance of the Minister for one instant, and then looked behind him at the others. They all stared intently at the Togo family.

"These then, are the orders of the Heavenly Sovereign Majesty," said Yamamoto. "The English have made common cause with our enemies. And when we sent them the twelve young men, of whom your father was one, to learn the work of a Western Navy, they sent them to lesser schools. But the Americans have taken in many of our sons, and even some of our daughters, and treated them well, sent them to their best schools and Annapolis, their Naval school, and helped us establish schools and manufactories for thirty years, now.

"We must learn this new form of war, war in the Air, war from the Heavens. We must learn to meld it with our fleets. We must also learn to build these leviathans; not just their shells, but their engines. For that, we must also understand the minds of these people of the west. For thirty years we have studied them, but the task is not yet finished.

"Togo Tetsu, you and your children will embark on a journey to the land of the Americans. With you will go your household. You will be escorted by a man of the West who has come to love Nihon and has given himself to us, married one of ours, being adopted by her family, and who teaches in our schools. He is Koizumi Yakumo, and he will be invaluable because he understands both peoples well. In charge of a group of engineers and sailors will go Chūi Kusukabe Sadao, who was wounded by your husband's side, and will oversee the technical aspects of the design and ship building, and the security of the party. His mother and two sisters will also accompany you."

Two of the men behind him bowed as their names were said. Koizumi was the *gaijin* man.

"Koizumi's wife Setsuko will accompany you with her household, parents and stepparents. Also, you will be charged with the care of seven young men from the great industrial firms who go to learn the work of building these airships. Four of them will also bring along aunts or sisters."

Takeshi kept his frown off his face. *Why are women being sent with us?* he wondered. His unspoken question was answered next:

"Women are the heart and center of the household, as the man is the head. And women of our leaders have gone to America to learn and excel, just as our men have done. My colleague's wife, Oyama Sutematsu, was one of the first, and best of our young women scholars. She learned their ways, but did not lose our ways.

"Your children will go to school and learn naval and air warfare. The Americans have promised to open their elite schools to the men and boys we send."

Takeshi was suddenly the object of his scrutiny. "Your father faced many hardships when he went to England, alone among arrogant strangers. You are younger by nine years than he was, and boys are cruel. You and young Minoru will hold the honor of Japan in your hands as you endure what you must, and learn what is needed. This is your inescapable duty."

At last I can answer! he thought.

"Hai!" he said.

Short and sharp, standing tall, his eyes dry as befitting a warrior's son who would mourn for his father by working to avenge him, and serve as he had served. He saw the approval in Yamamoto's eyes before he glanced politely away.

"And you, Togo Tetsu. In your hand lie two tasks. Keep your sons and the rest Japanese. You speak the language of the West; you were Sensei Tsuda's best student in your years at *Joshi Eigaku Juku.* Now learn the people of the West as did the five daughters of the Samurai thirty years ago. You and Setsuko-san and the other women will be our hidden eyes and ears. The Westerners underestimate our intelligence, and even more that of our women. Eventually we...will show them that this was a serious error."

Togo Tetsu bowed again, graceful as a tree branch in a storm.

"Hai."

Her voice was neither soft nor hard, not loud nor a whisper. Takeshi's heart swelled with pride in his mother, and in the father who had died so gloriously in an unexpected trap. Grief became anger, cold and lasting.

And the Majesty has given me a great gift, the means to avenge my father! Tennō Heika Banzai! *To the Heavenly Sovereign Majesty, ten thousand years!*

He had kept the words silent in his heart, though they struggled to break free, but he thought Yamamoto read them there. The great man nodded very slightly to him before he turned to go.

II

Baltimore, 1897

Togo Tetsu and Koizumi Setsuko walked down the street, shielding their faces from the sun with the odd, heavy, black parasols used by the people in the United States. The weather was much as they would have expected this time of year at home in Tokyo, hot and damp and flavored by the nearby ocean to the east.

Their dresses—Togo's an unrelieved black and Koizumi's a rich burgundy—were, as far as their eyes could see, quite similar to the dresses other women wore on the street. Women of the better classes, of course; those the common working people wore were plainer and sometimes ragged, just as at home. The solid, dark colors popular here had the advantage that they showed the soot filling the air here less than most *wakufu* would have done. The American *gaijin* burned a great deal of the coal they possessed in such abundance, and the omnipresent fall of greasy black made it a trial to keep anything clean. So did the heaps of animal dung from the swarming horses and mules pulling wagons and streetcars and carriages and cabs, and the pigs that roamed free. Often there was so much that it dried and turned into a thick, brown dust, and urchins made a few coins by using a broom at street-crossings to help ladies cross without dragging the hem of their skirts in it.

In Japan, much of that hauling work would have been done by men, and what animal waste there was in the streets would all have been carefully swept up and carted to the paddies and truck-gardens. Along with every other scrap of the garbage the Americans left to rot and breed buzzing clouds of flies here, with an appalling lack of both hygiene and thrift.

And then they walk into their houses without removing their shoes, Tetsu thought with a shudder. *Yet this waste is also evidence of their wealth and power.*Crossing America by rail from San Francisco had been an experience that still made the eyes of her mind go wide with wonder. Hundreds of hundreds upon hundreds of *ri*, forest and mountain and plain, from the wildly beautiful to the paralyzingly monotonous, day after day...and so much of it cultivated! Granted, with a lavish lack of care rather than the painstaking toilsome gardener-neatness of a Nihonjin farm...

But what a torrent of food!

And city after city that fed from those fields, all dirty and smoky and smelly, mostly ramshackle-new, but loud with forges and factories and the hordes of workers who labored in them.

We must have such strength for our own, she mused. *The English and French* gaijin *have conquered India and many other countries to our south. And though China was the center of the world for so many centuries, now the Europeans and the Russians beat the Chinese like dogs whenever they please, and have burned their Emperor's palace and taken many provinces and cities from them. Rich country, strong army, neh?*

"Still no servants come, even though the Embassy works very hard to send us prospects," Setsuko said.

Tetsu sighed. "I wish I understood what the problem is. And I am sure it is something very, very stupid. Well, until that time, we will all have to simply put on field-hand clothing in the morning and clean and cook and wash and iron."

"What *I* wish is that these clothes fit better. That seamstress in Japan was either very badly taught, or these American women endure discomforts completely unknown to us."

Setsuko twitched her shoulders. Western clothing was common enough in Japan now, especially in public and in the bigger cities, and often mixed the introduced styles with older Nihonjin ones. But that was more true for men than for women, and even for men more in public life than at home. They had both grown up wearing *wakufu*, and the complex construction of these heavy, tightly tailored garments was irritating. They constrained the wearer to a wholly different way of moving as well, making it difficult to be graceful, and were much more difficult to clean.

Tetsu laughed softly. "I suspect, my sister-friend, that this is why Madam Oyama orders her gowns from France. Like anything else, these dresses can be done well, or badly, *neh*? And I have seen that France is where the American *gaijin* take their fashions in clothing."

"Some of the fabrics are lovely in their way," her friend agreed. "But cutting like this must waste a great deal of it in scraps. So much simpler with *kimono*, where everything is cut from whole bolts in straight lines."

Setsuko slowed her step. A pair of women, one in navy blue and another in a wine-colored dress, were drawing abreast her, and the one in navy blue had caught her eye. She smiled slightly and inclined her head in a small acknowledgement. After a few heartbeats, both women nodded back, their faces relaxing as they looked them up and down. They passed, and both parties continued on their ways.

"How rude of them. I felt like they undressed me and examined each garment." Setsuko spoke in severe accents, which was very unlike the happy, laughing last daughter of the Koizumi and the Inagaki.

Togo nodded, turning down their path and climbing the stairs to their front door. "I think that is exactly what they did. But I do not think it was *intentionally* rude, any more than the way they stare into your eyes all the time." Setsuko sighed. "You are right. It is their custom…and this is their country, not ours."

Tetsu closed the door behind them and tried to stretch her toes in the cramped shoes, before she used the bootjack—another ingenious solution to a problem that made no sense in the first place—to remove them and changed them for embroidered silk slippers. Nobody thought that excessively eccentric, at least; women here often wore such footwear indoors.

"I wonder what they—"

Her sentence was cut short by a quiet knock on the door.

Tetsu opened it to the two women who'd passed them earlier. They looked uncomfortable. The fairer skin of these people showed their blushes uncompromisingly, and both were blushing very heavily indeed. It was a social drawback she hadn't considered. A pale complexion had always been considered a mark of women's beauty in Japan—there was an ancient saying: *iro no shiroi wa shichinan kakusu*, that fair skin covered the seven flaws... but she had come to realize that it had a codicil they hadn't realized: *pale by Japanese standards*. Perhaps it was because her ancestors had had no other people to judge by except possibly Chinese and Koreans, whose complexion didn't differ very much from that of Nihonjin. This was entirely too much of a good thing.

"Mrs. Togo? I hope so... We tried to leave our calling-cards earlier today, but there was nobody home, not even a maid..."

"Yes, I am Mrs. Togo. My companion is Koizumi Setsuko, but her husband is Western, so she is also known as Mrs. Hearn. Would you like to come in and visit and have a cup of our green tea?"

Tetsu played the words over in her head. She had been taught English at school for all her years there by Japanese women who'd lived in America. But speaking with Lafcadio Hearn during their journey had taught her that while she had a good grasp on the grammar and vocabulary, the sounds she was making were not what a native speaker would expect. In fact, English seemed to have different sounds that were difficult for someone who had grown up a Nihongo-speaker even to tell apart, much less to make properly herself...and unfortunately, those included some of the most common sounds in the English language. He had focused on correcting her pronunciation, and by now she could make the necessary distinctions, but only if she concentrated to a degree that made it difficult to think about anything else.

Hopefully it was enough to get her through most social encounters. She'd been adding to her stock of social phrases, and they were becoming easier in her mouth as she parroted them to him, morning and night. She believed she had used the correct ones here.

"Thank you, thank you. I am Mrs. John Mansard, and this is my friend, Mrs. Benjamin Worley. We are your neighbors, and wish better acquaintance."

Setsuko knew the correct procedure. She stuck her hand out and gently clasped each hand extended to her and moved hers up and down once. Casting her a grateful look, Tetsu copied the action before opening the door to the back parlor and standing aside.

"Please, have a seat. I will…"

Her tongue locked for an instant. *See* as in sight and *see* as in care for and *sea* as in the ocean, and they all sounded exactly the same—

"…see to tea."

Setsuko spoke in Japanese, putting a hand on her wrist. "Stay, my sister. You know more of the language than I do. And I brew better tea than you do."

Tetsu smiled down at her friend and nodded. She walked forward, opening the windows over the back yard and smiling at seeing Setsu's clan there—Koizumi Chei, to whom she had been born, and the two Inagaki parents who'd adopted her, as well as the several uncles, aunts, and cousins who'd accompanied them—all working on a flower bed. The yard was large and barren, a fitting blank canvas that Setsu's family were having the time of their lives re-doing into a Japanese garden—and it had the potential to be a fine one. Right now, little could be seen but shoveled dirt and stakes and tape.

"Ah, you have coolies! But should you let the women work at—"

Tetsu turned to them, searching her mind for phrases she could put together without giving offense.

"I am glad my dear friend, Mrs. Hearn, left. You see her foster father and mother, her mother, her two uncles, and some cousins. They are, like she and I, nobles, *samurai*, we said in the old days before the current auspicious reign; now the law says *shi*, gentlefolk."

She left aside the ancient Court nobility, the *kuge*, who had always been a very different class from the *bushi*, the lords of sword and bow; better not to complicate matters—she could scarcely explain a thousand years of history in a few moments in an alien tongue. And in any case, for the past generation the *kuge* had officially been merged with the higher samurai ranks in the new *kazoku* peerage, *those of exalted lineage.*

"A noble is a fighter, a defender, and one thing he defends is the arts," she said instead, simplifying things. "The Japanese Garden is one of the greatest arts, and the Koizumi and the Inagaki are well known for their excellence in the design and creation of these gardens."

The *gaijin* women looked at each other, and one said, "Yes, we have heard of the beauty of Japanese gardens. Many of the prints—"

They went back and forth for a moment until Tetsu realized they meant *ukiyo-e*, woodblock prints of actors and street scenes and landscapes and such. There was a sub-genre of erotic subjects, often collected by housewives as good luck pieces, but she could already tell that Americans would probably not appreciate *shunga*. Not women, and not in public, at least.

"—many of the Japanese prints show them. In California, the wealthy often hire Japanese gardeners to copy them."

She hadn't known that, especially since they'd gone straight from the ship to the train in San Francisco, getting only a glimpse of the Bay's beauty. Some mangled names followed; it took another moment to realize that they meant Hokusai and Hiroshige. She smiled and bowed slightly, feeling more friendly than she had. From what they said, those artists were much admired among Western painters, which she hadn't been aware of before either. They mentioned names, *Degas* and *Whistler,* which she made a mental note of. Engineering was not enough, and not her responsibility in any case, and you could not truly understand a people until you knew what they considered beautiful. She had been aware that Japanese painters had picked up techniques of perspective from Western works imported through the Dutch trading post in Nagasaki.

She looked away from her visitor's faces and wandered down the length of the room, opening windows and drapes, placing her parasol, hat, and gloves on a chest at the far end.

"Please, may I take your hats and jackets?" she asked, coming forward with a serious expression on her face.

The red on their cheeks had faded as she had moved away. "I have the big question, for we are all working, working very hard. We have no servants. Nobody to come and work with us...for us!"

Setsuko entered at that moment, carrying a tray and kicking at her skirts in some irritation. Yet her exclamation in Japanese, "I hate these skirts," sounded liquid and musical: "*Watashi wa korera no sukāto ga kirai.*"

Tetsu took the tray and set it on the table and served *ocha* to her visitors. "And why do you speak to us today, yet not for many days, before?"

Once again their faces reddened. "Well, you see, Isabella Bird wrote a number of books about Japan. We did not want to see— your unclothed upper bodies."

Tetsu stiffened. Isabella's books were known to the intelligentsia of Japan, and the allegations, both lauding the Chinese and comparing the Japanese poorly to them, were deeply resented. This she had discussed with Mr. Hearn during the voyage, in English, many times. The expression he had used was *damning with faint praise*, which had struck her as eloquent and appropriate.

"Miss Bird was well treated in Japan." She paused, seeing Setsuko's faint smile had slid off her face and a stern look replaced it. "In all her books she acknowledges she was never ill-treated; never robbed, never accosted by a man of ill-repute. Yet she traduced us, traduced us to a large part of the world. I would..." She stopped, the color draining from her face. "*This* is why the men and boys have been peering into our windows? That one place in her book where she claimed the women of Japan do not wear clothing on their upper bodies? The only place she would see that would be in a bathhouse, where only women go! In a bathhouse, you *bathe!*" She could feel her voice soaring out of control, she was so angry.

Her visitors exchanged a look, and then Mrs. Mansard took a sip of tea. Tetsu could see the rigid control. *Well, so they are not entirely childlike. That is control worthy of a* samurai *lord, himself!*

"Ah, goodness! What wonderful tea this is. One can see that having a true source of the best leaf means a much better tasting brew." Mrs. Mansard smiled a small, tight, polite smile.

Mrs. Worley clicked the cup into the saucer and also smiled at her angry hostess. There was a tightness to the expression, very different from her earlier look. Tetsu had difficulty reading the grossly featured faces of the Americans, but she read a steely determination in the woman's gestures.

"Just so, Mrs. Togo; I had not realized how bad it was that even you have noticed. It will stop, this I can promise. We watched, and every day you and your...friend walk out, wearing perfectly respectable clothing..."

"Though it could fit better," murmured Mrs. Mansard.

"Holly! That is nothing to the point!"

She smiled at the two Japanese women. "We have come to the conclusion, independently, that Miss Bird misspoke about a number of things concerning Japanese customs. And both of us are interested in the arts, where Japanese things are so influential these days, so fashionable. Therefore, we determined to come, bearing an olive branch and apologizing for our...our mistakes. Please excuse our ignorance."

Tetsu took a sip. *Olive branch* meant nothing to her, but she would store the sounds and ask Mr. Hearn when he came back from the embassy. However, it was clear that a peace offering was part of the discussion. That had been a truly polite apology, one that acknowledged fault. Good manners meant suppressing anger and responding in kind.

"In fact, Myrtle, my maid Bessie has spoken of her niece, Jenny, who has trained as a cook, seeking a position." Mrs. Mansard smiled at Tetsu, that wide, wide smile that was so terrifyingly open, and said, "I think we could help with the help, if you would accept the peace offering?"

Ah, so desu! thought Tetsu. *This olive branch must be a symbol of peace, as I thought.*

"Gladly, do I look to be a friend, and have a friend. We are all so very tired of all the hard work to keep these houses clean."

"And of the clothing..." said Setsuko, her voice returning to the liquid Japanese that was so soothing to Tetsu's ears.

"My friend," she reproved. She looked over at her guests. "My companion, Mrs. Hearn, was educated at home. I had the privilege of attending one of the best girl's schools in Japan. Though I learned English, it sounds so different when spoken by people here, it is hard on my ear. So I must speak and practice it much."

The women nodded and sipped their tea and ate the sweet cakes she served and spoke of servants and children and schools and learned of the composition of the two houses where they lived.

"About the clothing," said Tetsu as the clock marked the half hour visit. "Ours were made for us in Japan, by a seamstress who advertised herself as experienced in western clothing. Yet they do not feel comfortable, nor do they look neat and fitting as the dresses you both wear. Would it be possible to ask the favor of an introduction to a...person who..."

She could not find the word she knew she wanted. It was in another language than English, and it had flown from her head; she made needle-and-thread motions.

"*Modiste!* Certainly. I was going to visit her this Friday for some underpinnings, and your underpinnings are the first problem of the garments not fitting, my dear Mrs. Togo; I was wishing to find a way to speak to you of the problem."

She managed to not wriggle her body in the very uncomfortable whalebone garment and smiled. "At what time?"

From such small beginnings we do the work the Tennō Heika *has given us to understand these people. They are simple and open, for the most part. Not unintelligent, some of them are brilliant, but rather childlike. We should be able to do better, now that we have found the poison thorn and pulled it. Though Koizumi Yakomo warns me that they will always think us inferior.*

She felt a wry amusement for an instant. Most Japanese felt exactly the same about everyone else, of course.

III

Baltimore, 1898

Takeshi hurried home from school along tree-lined roads where houses sat far back with long, green lawns in front of them; what Americans called suburbs, the shade and greenness very welcome.

Children played, rolling hoops or running with their dogs; servants pushed strollers; the odd carriage clopped by, or a slower delivery van. Now and then someone called a greeting or waved. They had been here long enough for that, and he returned the greetings in the local style. He had also been here long enough that the scene did not look so jarringly alien to his eyes, which meant he could see the details of it.

Soon, soon he would be fourteen, and able to enter the Naval Academy at Annapolis, following in illustrious footsteps of Sotokichi Uriu and others, all making the highest of marks. He was tired of Mr. Collin's Gentleman's Technical School, where Mr. Hearn had enrolled him.

But Mr. Hearn has done well by us, he thought. *Even if I have to fight these* baka gaijin *boys who do not understand what a* Samurai *is or even a* Nihonjin, *every time they call me Johnny Chink or Slant-eyes. It is a good school; plenty of mathematics, plenty of engineering. I have learned a great deal that will be of use, that will help me to serve Nippon and the* Tennō Heika.

That it was usually fairly easy to thrash the other boys—none of them seemed to have any idea of how to fight beyond hitting someone with your fist or a clumsy grapple—didn't make it any less annoying. Being mistaken for a Shina was even more so, of course. Once he'd asked another student proud of what passed for ancient lineage here how he'd like being mistaken for a Turk, and it had struck home a bit.

For a moment he was lost in dreams; dreams of the clouds seen from above, dreams of birdlike freedom. And others of raining fire on the Russian fleets, of their leviathans plunging to the earth in flames. Perhaps...perhaps receiving praise from the lips of the *Tennō Heika* himself.

The trip from Japan to Baltimore had taken three months, and in those three months Lafcadio Hearn had taught all his delegation enough English to get by. They'd practiced on the sailors for hours every day during the trip, which was an advantage over his mother and the other ladies, who of course could not do anything of the sort. As Takeshi approached the two large buildings they lived in, he grimaced.

And now I know well why Mr. Hearn prompted Yamamoto-sama to send so many women with us. It makes us like them rather, than isolated bachelors who will lose contact with their country-souls. It makes a bubble of home-ness. He understands that—it is how we caught him!

Thanks to the good offices of Mrs. Mansard and Mrs. Worley, they now had servants, or "hired help," as the local *gaijin* said. Most Americans, no matter how poor, would not work for the "damned yellow men," as they called them. Most of those they *could* hire were what the Americans called "fresh off the boat," immigrants from Europe; willing enough, but unskilled. And, to Mr. Hearn's surprise, they hadn't been able to hire from among the black people here either.

Takeshi was not sure why this surprised him, but it did; the blacks, or Negroes, or colored people to use the polite terms, were something like *eta* here. They lived apart from even the poor, shunned and loathed, and did the unclean work nobody else would. And they had been slaves until about the time the Meiji Emperor ascended to the Chrysanthemum Throne.

There have been no slaves in Japan for a very long time, he thought proudly. Though such things were mentioned in the very old stories, like the *Tale of the Heike*.

He missed a step as a thought struck him: *Unless you count girls contracted to the floating world by their parents, of course. Well, that is not quite the same thing, and what else can a poor peasant family do if they are desperate?*

Koizumi Minato and Inagaki Kinjuro enjoyed their exile by creating formal Japanese gardens. First the backyards and front yards, and now, under contract in a nearby park. Chie was Chie, a princess, and could not be expected to do anything but *be* a princess and tell them stories of the older days. But Tomi and the four women of the industrialist families frequently found themselves doing household work. Every day the technical delegation had dinner together in the large dining room of the bigger house.

That was going to come to an end shortly when the technical group moved to Pittsburgh. The collaboration between Mr. Tesla and Mr. Edison, backed by the very wealthy inventor and industrialist Mr. Westinghouse and supported politically by Mr. Roosevelt, had borne fruit, and the prototype lab had been set up in that great manufacturing city. The Americans were grimly determined to master the leviathan technology, something he could sympathize with wholeheartedly, though they approached the problem of catching up very differently from the way Japanese would, relying much more on the initiatives of private men.

Most of the men had been training in factories and on salt water sail for the past two years. Hearn was openly dubious of the American's willingness to actually follow through on their government's promises of full sharing and training. But they would know more in a few months.

Takeshi ran up the stairs through the town house door and put his book bag in his little study cubicle, removing his shoes. Most people here didn't, but some did—it was called a Dutch habit, as that type of European evidently did so too;

not surprisingly, the Dutch also had a reputation for extreme neatness about their houses.

Perhaps they learned it from us, he thought idly.

For centuries, of all the Westerners, only the Dutch had been allowed any contact with Japan, and that had been restricted to a small island in Nagasaki Harbor. Books had trickled in from there to the rest of the country, and had been translated; that was how his people had first gotten a glimpse of Western science. Possibly influences had run the other way, too.

He quickly ran to the washroom and cleaned his face and hands before entering the dining room. Food was served, and he sat at the higher end of the table, next to Koizumi Minato, the adopted father of Mr. Hearn. Discipline was strictly enforced and the flat, harsh syllables of English with its hissing overtones were all they spoke.

"*Itadakimasu,*" he murmured, bringing his palms before his face—that at least was allowed.

He accepted a bowl of split-pea soup and tucked in with a sigh for *miso* and *udon* rather than the heavy, greasy American food, though it no longer actively repulsed him, and his bowels had grown somewhat used to it. Nihonjin had never been completely vegetarian, apart from some monks and the odd strict Buddhist, and nowadays it was fashionable to eat more meat even at home, at least for the well-to-do. The *Tennō Heika* himself had done so in public, and many thought that diet had helped make the Westerners strong; certainly the youngsters here had been growing strongly, including himself. But the huge quantities of flesh had made them all fiercely constipated at first!

At least Baltimore was a seaport, and abundant fish and other ocean life was available, cheap and of excellent quality.

Tomorrow was Saturday, and on Saturday evening they ate Nihon-style and all day Sunday they dressed and spoke Japanese. It was such a relief to eat good food and dress in comfortable clothes! And speak the beautiful language that came naturally to his tongue and mind.

But for now... He returned the bowl and accepted his plate of mutton and potatoes and limp greens and a slice of bread; he admitted that the knife and fork were better for the way they served food in large lumps here. Bread was simply grain, different from rice and noodles only in that he wasn't accustomed to it. There was butter, but nobody actually used it except Mr. Hearn, who spoke of his dealings with the Embassy in Washington and the Westinghouse-led conglomerate with his usual gentle good humor.

His mother and Mr. Hearn's wife answered, seated one on either side of him. Mrs. Hearn's little Kiyoshi was but a month old, and lay in a cradle behind her. Kazuo and Iwao, her older sons, were four and two respectively, and his own six-year-old sister Yachiyo sat at their own little table in the window bay, in easy sight of the grown-ups. Minoru sat next to him, and they chatted about the school while they ate. He smiled tightly across the table at Kusakabe Sadao.

Mr. Hearn had taught them the English language and how the Western mind worked on the trip to America. He continued his lessons on Americans now, with his slightly wry acceptance of their parochial tendencies. The motivations were actually much the same, but not identical to those of his people. Men contended for power and wealth everywhere, for themselves and for their kin and their nation. It was the *ways* that were so different, and the way they put it into words; that involved some complex mental *jiu-jitsu*.

But for his lessons in physical *jiu-jitsu*, Kusakabe Sadao had no equal as a teacher. His sensei was known in the American press as "Kusanagi Sado" through a bad interpreter's attempt to pun on his name calling him the Sacred Sword of Sado in a way that was mildly blasphemous.

"I'm not even from Sado, and the Tsushima battle didn't take place near Sado!" he'd protest occasionally.

Several exhibitions of "Japanese wrestling" had made his reputation as the head of security for the *technical delegation*. Takeshi knew that his travels around to different fight venues were cover for some of the intelligence operations Mr. Hearn and the Japanese embassy were running.

And the Americans mostly don't know he carries the rank of Chūsa, commander in the Imperial Japanese Navy.

When a pause came in the conversation, he opened his mouth and forced himself to employ the American wording rather than the more formal and useful Japanese.

"I believe that Mr. Hearn and my mother may receive a visit from Mr. Collins today or tomorrow."

Sadao's eyelids wrinkled as he suppressed his smile. Takeshi shot a quick glance over at his mother and Mrs. Hearn. Their serene faces were attentive as Mr. Hearn asked: "Oh, really. What does your Dominie have to say today? Or tomorrow, as the case may be?"

"That I have once again taken unfair advantage of my special training in oriental tricks and skullduggery to injure a classmate."

"Who?" asked Lafcadio, but not as if it interested him at all.

"Metcalf. Today he scuffled with me, fell down, and hit his nose on the ground. He is a very clumsy young man. I think he may also have wrenched his arm...poor Metcalf, he has no idea of how to fall without injuring himself."

"Again!" burst out Kusakabe. "If I hit you in the mouth when we spar, I expect you to ask for a counter and learn it. I do not expect you to make the same mistake three more times!"

Lafcadio reached for the teapot and poured for himself. He would not drink coffee, claiming it upset his stomach. Takeshi agreed with him, and while tea helped alertness, coffee was like having red-hot pins jabbed into your brain.

"Well, well, well," the *gaijin*-Japanese said. "I believe, Togo Tetsuko, that I will be very busy this afternoon and all day tomorrow. I think it is time to sic a *samurai* woman onto him, or two!"

He turned towards his wife and lifted a brow. Takeshi finished off his greens and accepted a slice of pie and passed a second one down to Minoru, who was looking like he wanted to be worshipful of his older brother. He gave him a minute shake of the head—he didn't want to be admired for reluctantly chastising an ill-mannered idiot—and looked back at his mother.

She and Setsuko Hearn were communicating in that silent way they had. Two small smiles touched their lips, and Takeshi suppressed a ferocious grin. *Mr. Collins will never understand what hit him. But maybe he'll stop riding me and allowing the maths teacher to downgrade me, too.*

He waved his fork in the air. "I don't understand why Metcalf keeps on pushing at me. Partly it seems to be simple ill will that another boy is better than he. But the truth is that he is not the most competent, yet many boys defer to him. And he can't seem to learn, as *sensei* says. Not even pain and humiliating..."

"Humiliation," Mr. Hearn corrected.

"Humiliation, yes, *domo*, Hearn-*san*. Not even humiliation teach...teaches him anything; I cannot decide whether this is bravery, stubbornness, or simple lack of wits. Probably wits. This is a problem that will come back to bite him in later life."

"Yes and no," said Mr. Hearn, patting his lips delicately.

Takeshi imitated him. They *did* have table manners here, just different ones; many were simply arbitrary, like not sticking your chopsticks upright in a bowl of rice because it reminded people of the funeral ceremony. They buried their dead here, but then so had Japanese, in very ancient times before the Way of the Buddha had come.

Hearn went on: "He would have to be spectacularly inept to be other than wealthy and powerful all his life, given his father's position. Privilege will always compensate for slightly duller wits."

"Or laziness in using them," Takeshi's mother said.

"Much the same thing. They start out a little further ahead in the race. As long as they don't try to go further than they can and fall, they will always have a leg up."

"And it is not unknown in our country, either, Takeshi," said Kusakabe. "In fact, it is not even less frequent, merely somewhat differently organized."

Takeshi nodded respectfully. It was true, even in the reign of the Meiji Emperor, when unprecedented numbers of the lowly rose by their own efforts to positions their peasant ancestors could not have dreamed of a generation ago. Birth still mattered.

"You can thrash him now because we are still coasting on the tradition of sword-fighting and training, a tradition which means that all men of our class must be able to fight in open competition. As this fades, we will see more . . ." His teacher shrugged.

Mr. Hearn nodded. "And there is another problem added to the simple one of the power that this boy has exercised all his life because his father owns a very large locomotive works. And that is that the Americans despise us just as much as we despise them, and for much the same reasons."

"Dirty, smelly, foreigners?" asked Minoru. "But we aren't dirty and foreign."

"We are foreign...here!" her mother said.

He opened his mouth, visibly reconsidered, then reluctantly nodded.

Hearn went on: "Here they speak of how the black man, the red man, the yellow man and the Malay will never be the equal to the white man. Many still wish to see the black men and women enslaved. I lived here for some years, and married a black woman. It was against the law, and eventually she divorced me and married a man of her own race. I do not blame her. There was... severe unpleasantness. In some parts of this country we might well have been killed. Would have been, if I had been the woman, or if I had been a native-born white man named shall we say...Metcalf.'"

Takeshi thought about that as he polished off his plate. He thought of the horror there would be if someone like him was found to have married an *eta*; surely it could not be that bad?

"But...you, you *are* a white man, Hearn-san."

"Only by the standards of our nation. By the standards of these people...especially the Anglo-Saxons...well, I am the son of an Irishman and a Greek woman, abandoned by both parents and brought up in Ireland. It does not make me quite altogether white by their reckoning; sort of a second-rate white person. And the Irish are often despised as dirty and smelly, drunken, violent, peasant oafs good only for work in construction and mining, though less so now than in my father's time.

"The *Tennō Heika* offered me citizenship in Japan and a legitimate marriage with my dear Setsuko to convince me to come bear-leading this menagerie. A country to call my own, one I have come to love and respect. It was a great honor, a rare honor, and I am very grateful."

He smiled. "That many in Japan will always be amazed at how comparatively civilized the big-nosed hairy person has become, and that I do not gibber and scratch myself like a monkey... and that they will do so even if I lived to be a hundred and mastered the *chanoyu* more profoundly than Rikyū, and became a greater poet than Bashō..."

Everyone laughed at the droll images.

"...I find that more amusing than irritating."

"But they do smell!" Minoru's face was getting red. "They smell like oxen in the sun! And every day Mama-san reminds me to not say it to them."

Takeshi winced internally; he didn't want to hear *that* old argument all over again. "May I be excused, Mother?"

He retrieved his book bag, went to his room, and made a start of the school weekend tasks. It was no great burden, even on a fine day. The way algebraic relationships could be graphed—mathematics turned into a visual art—was fascinating. It was as if he was drawing the very underlying fabric of reality, doing calligraphy with existence. He busied himself with compass and protractor.

And if ever he was tempted to slack, there was his father's sword-set on its rack on the wall. He had not taken it to his final battle, which had been a matter of ironclads and long-range guns, and anyway the bearing of Nihonto blades was discouraged in the modern military. But Takeshi felt that they kept something of his father's soul there watching over him.

I will make you proud, father.

Saturday afternoon was balmy. Tetsu and Setsuko were in the parlor, doing the handcrafts they had been taught were proper tasks for women during visits. Tetsu crocheted and Setsuko knit. The windows were open to the back yard, where Inagaki and Koizumi senior and their wives, Tomi and Chie had created a wonderful garden, complete with ponds and a water-channel, and even some ornamental carp. A large piece near the house was covered with velvety, silky green lawn, and a wooden platform was built out from the house.

Takeshi and Kusakabe were there, drilling with both unarmed and armed combat; there was an occasional thud and harsh *kiai*-shout, or the clack of oak *bokken*, wooden swords. Minoru wanted to join them, but he hadn't finished his weekend tasks. The back parlor windows were open, letting the early spring air into the house with a scent of grass and flowers.

Tetsu kept her body relaxed and her stance approving as she stood by the window. Since the abolition of the fiefs and the old four-class system at the beginning of the current reign, many families of samurai background no longer practiced the old war-arts; many were too busy trying to make a living. Thousands had gone into the new army and navy, others had become civil servants or teachers or scholars, managed the new businesses, or even settled on Hokkaido as farmers. Some had been reduced to pitiful beggary, without the rice-stipend from their lords that their ancestors had lived on for all the long, peaceful centuries of the Tokugawa Shogunate and without any skills that mattered in the new world.

Tetsu had been taught to use the *naginata* and the short *wakizashi* sword and unarmed combat, but even in her day it had become very unusual for the women to learn such skills. She and Tomi practiced several times a week, but Mr. Hearn was reluctant to make Setsuko drill with them, and she was not interested. Her fifteen-year struggle to keep herself and her parents alive after the time of troubles surrounding the Meiji restoration had left her marked with a focused practicality that dismissed any aristocratic ideas.

Kusakabe was drilling Takeshi in a new move, one designed to get the sole of his foot high enough off the ground with enough power to knock a grown man out.

The door opened behind her, and the new maid said: "Your pardon, Mrs. Togo. Mr. Collins to see you."

"Thank you, Rachel," Tetsu said. "Please show him into the parlor."

"My dear Mrs. Togo. Thank you for receiving me. I was expecting Mr. Hearn."

The stork-like schoolmaster frowned as he handed the maid his hat and cane, and Tetsu suppressed her smile and opened her fan and waved it languidly. There was a language of the fan here, too.

What an utterly ugly person! she thought.

With his huge nose and narrow face that looked as if it had been squashed between heavy weights and his ridiculous, skinny height, he was like a caricature of a *gaijin*, or possibly a praying mantis in human form. Mr. Hearn was just exotic, once you were used to him, but this was ridiculous.

Still, do not let his appearance hide his thoughts. I must read him well. "Honorable Mr. Collins. So solly. Mr. Hearn was called to a conference over report. So I must careful be of my son's honor."

His face relaxed as she confirmed every bias he had about foolish women—not that that would have been uncommon at home—and even more foolish foreign women. That was why she had exaggerated her accent a little, and let more Nihongo forms slip over into her English. Not that there weren't plenty of Nihonjin men you could play like a *samisen* with variations of the same thing, though it required far more subtlety.

Behind her, she heard Kusakabi cry out a liquid sequence and knew they were listening; and going to practice a simple but showy drill to cover that. The schoolmaster blinked in astonishment as her son soared over Kusakabi's shoulder, hit the ground in a perfect rolling break and bounced back to his feet.

"My word! That looks very dangerous, Mrs. Togo. How can you bear for them to do that?"

Tetsu turned away from the window and looked at her visitor with a slight smile. "Is it so different from your aggressive American boys, Mr. Collins? I am sure I have heard many of the kind mothers who visit me lament each time their children indulge in yet another fight, or ride horses at great speed, or play this football game of butting with the head. And then we discuss the putting on of beefsteak on blackened eyes and liniments for bruises. They complain, but they are proud their sons are manly and brave, I think."

Mr. Collins laughed shortly. "Well, that's true. But Takeshi is entirely too aggressive and too well-trained. He is able to fight much larger boys. So far he hasn't injured any one of them, but I worry."

"I worry, too," said Tetsu readily. "Much I worry about my boy. He must avenge the honor of his father. But I see his grades each month, and they are not so good. I do not understand the grading and I hear other boys get higher grades, yet understand less. They come here, Mr. Collins, and ask my son and Kusakabe for help and drill. Mr. Collins, could you be so kind as to evaluate where my son is weak and recommend a good tutor for him? He must enter the Academy in one half year, and is still much weak in mathematics and geography, so say his grades and tests."

"My dear woman, but of course I'll check on young Takeshi's progress, and Minoru's too. It's the least I can do. But...you say avenge? Is his father dead?"

"Oh! Yes. My great sorrow. His father was *Chūshō*, you say, Rear-Admiral, I think. The Russians invaded, and they brought the leviathans to attack the Japanese ships. My husband held the line, as you Americans call it, until they must retreat. He died, fighting for the Emperor. That man who teaches my son out there? He is called Kusunagi Sado by your newspapers. He stood by my husband as his right hand, he was wounded in the same fight, and I treat him as my son."

"I had not understood you were a widow. I thought, well, I suppose everybody thought..."

"Thought what, Mr. Collins-*san*?" asked Setsuko, suddenly standing and coming to the window, a warning note in her voice.

Tetsu controlled a smirk as Mr. Collins jumped. "Good heavens, Madame Hearn, I had completely forgotten you were in the room! Well, it is just that people believe you are both the wives of Mr. Hearn."

"What a very foolish idea." Koizumi Setsuko spoke with cold precision. "How very foolish of them. Men in Japan also have only one wife."

She left aside the question of concubines—mistresses, as they were called here. Americans were a bit more hypocritical about that than their Japanese equivalents, but men were men.

Tetsu kept the smile off her face. Setsuko's move meant Mr. Collins had just placed himself at a very grave disadvantage, by local standards; he'd maligned their respectability, and to be fair he was ashamed of it, even appalled. She could see that in the way his forehead had gone a little damp, and from his expression he was making rapid reappraisals in his mind.

"I am very fond of my friend Togo Tetsu, even though our ranks are hardly comparable. Yet we are both *Samurai* women," Setsuko went on.

"I thought... I thought *Samurai* meant warrior?"

Tetsu looked out the window. Takeshi met her eyes, and she made a quick hand signal. She turned back to Mr. Collins.

"It means noble warrior, yes, just as *knight* does in your language. After all, every warrior has a mother, a sister, a daughter, or they would not live to be a class, is this not so? And the women of the *Samurai* are also trained in the martial arts. My husband was very high-ranking, and so are my parents."

Setsuko chimed in. "In England, my friend would be termed a Countess, whereas my family would be...perhaps baronet is closest. Other than my mother, who counts as a Princess. Not that it matters! The *Tennō Heika*... The Heavenly Sovereign Majesty, the Emperor in English...in his great wisdom, abolished our old system of ranks. Dear Admiral Togo is in his grave only a few years. My friend is in mourning until her daughter is fourteen."

"Well and well." Mr. Collins sound shaken. "I will review the boy's records and see about recommending a tutor for you, My Lady Togo. Madame Hearn, I bid you both good day."

Tetsu turned from the window as her son and Kusakabe ran across the gardens to the house next door. She held out her hand, glad she had not had time to offer tea, and that Mr. Collins had been so involved with his own thoughts...her lips tightened as she put aside the implication that he'd wanted what the Americans called "an affair" with her, glad he could be dismissed without the socialization that he'd eschewed up until now.

❦ ⚜ ❦

Takeshi raced into the next door garden, where the young engineer and naval cadets had their quarters. He bolted up the steps to the back door, slammed through and crashed the door shut behind his *sensei*. Barely in time, as the two met eyes and collapsed into howls of laughter. All over the house, soft, *tabi*-socked feet raced down to find out what was the matter.

When they finished laughing, Takeshi went to wash the tears off his face.

"My mother will be safe from that awful man, won't she?" he asked upon his return.

"*Hai, hai!*" answered the men.

Misubishi Jiro amplified this. "These American *gaijin* are very odd. They have no assigned titles, though one can trace an aristocracy of money and industry if one looks, and in some areas one of land. Yet they seem to have a fascination with titled people, which is prohibited by their own laws. Koizumi Setsu is a very intelligent woman, and I believe she has spiked the man's guns, well and fully."

Okura Madoka nodded. "It is late in the afternoon. Shall we work on the model house?"

Takashi hadn't realized his sister was there with Minoru, and they set up a clamor to work on the model.

As the group trooped down into the large, whitewashed, brick-walled basement, Madoka continued: "And your honorable mother has worked the man very well with respect to your grades. They will be submitted to Annapolis in just a few weeks. If they are to be altered, it must be now, before they are sent."

"*Hai!*" said Okura Shin. "And you are very advanced in mathematics, and my mother says your dominion of English in the strategy essays is very strong. There is no reason for you to place twenty-eight in a class of thirty."

Furokawa Goro led the way to the back of the basement, past the model house, to where they kept the leviathan workshop. He pressed on what looked like a light fixture, and there was a subdued *click*. The panel was carefully located in a place where no outsider could see without actually entering the room, and all the work had been done by Japanese, either themselves or helpers from the Embassy. It was amazing what you could do and how quickly you could do it with a dozen highly-skilled sets of hands.

"I have tutored you. I suspect that Mr. Collins of believing he can tutor you on his own. But I know his mathematics are deficient. I have worked with your Math *sensei*, Mr. Hollis, and also with Mr. Tesla. You have far outstripped Mr. Collins' ability. Once he sees this, you will be assigned a tutor who will be able to teach you more. And then you will teach us."

Takeshi grinned. "I am going to bring us wings!"

He looked down at the neat tables and the littered papers all written in *kanji* and *kana*. They settled down, each to their own task. Minoru was in the outer, public room. They had no doubt that the Americans spied on the Japanese mission through a variety of methods, all of them clumsy. Not to mention the Chinese, who did it much better—say what you would about the *Shina*, they understood such matters, and had invented most of the techniques of espionage at one time or another—plus the Germans, and the French. And almost certainly the Russians as well, though if so, they were being very subtle—it was so *easy* to spy here, where folk of every nation and none thronged in without supervision. And the French and Russians were allies these days, with possessions bordering the Empire, and hence both were hostile to Japan. Certainly they both knew that a day would come when the Empire sought revenge, and undoubtedly they shared information.

In the main area of the basement room was a replica of the Togo house in Tokyo, on a one-twelfth scale. Yachiyo was the ostensible recipient and owner of the model. Even at barely six years of age, she was very good at deceiving people. She was also a very neat worker with wood and paper, and had crafted many miniature kites to pose above the model. Minoru and she had also built models of the leviathans, and hung them around the model house. At the far end of the basement, on the left was a large-scale model of the Straits of Tsushima. Model ships and leviathans were also staged there, for the entertainment of more enterprising spies.

A person could catch glimpses of all that just by walking past and looking through the basement windows, which were kept helpfully uncurtained and well-washed. But the actual workroom was behind the false wall, and entirely lit by gas-lights. Even so, the notes, in a mixture of *kanji*, *kana*, and English, were coded. For two years Mr. Hearn and Sadao, often with Minoru and Takeshi in tow and several of the engineering samurai, had visited the offices of Tesla and Edison at the Westinghouse Company complex. And when they returned to the Baltimore houses, they came here to write down all they could remember.

Takeshi pulled over one of the diagrams of the stabilizers that attached to the electroid tanks and the connections to the ship's keel. Tomorrow he would practice with Sadao, again, the memorization techniques that had allowed them to study plans carelessly left out at the offices and then duplicate them from memory at home. Each of the plans they used had been reviewed and revised several times. And at least two attempts to feed them false information had been detected, though whether that was from the consortium, the American government, or third parties bribing draughtsmen was impossible to tell.

"The greatest problem," said Takeshi thoughtfully, "is the inverse square law. The models we make are very small, and do not carry significant weights of metal compared to the electroid lifting capacities. But once we scale them up, in calculations, at least, they quickly come to a set of diminishing returns that limits the size of the ships. Limits it quite severely."

Minoru had wandered in, holding a model leviathan and a newspaper photograph. He waited for attention, and Takeshi nodded at him.

"This picture and the plan you gave me do not match."

Takeshi took the model, quickly recognizing the elongated shape of the French leviathan *Ganymède*, and studied the photograph and the drawings below it.

Kusakabe leaned over as Takeshi traced a contour. "Have they added another cooling system?"

The evening passed in attempts to create a diagram of the well-known *Ganymède*'s systems to explain the odd bulge in the photograph.

Later, he wandered out to the main part of the basement and carefully whittled some more wall frames for the model house. Yachiyo measured and sliced the paper and delicately inserted it into the correct spots, using a small toothpick of ivory to roll down the edges for a good seal.

"I heard you say that as ships get bigger, they weigh much more than the smaller ships," she observed.

He cast her a sharp glance as he signed agreement.

"Why make them out of metal? Kites and balloons fly. They are silk and rice paper and bamboo; all are light."

Takeshi frowned and answered, "Because they have engines in them that can explode and are very heavy metal themselves. The heavy walls and hulls are needed to protect the ship and the airmen."

Yachiyo fingered the paper in the frames he'd just finished. "Is that what they say?" she asked. "Because Mrs. Brandon says that living in a house with paper walls is very immodest. But we are more modest than these people, Koizumi-*sama* says so. And they feel they need these heavy walls to protect them."

The child picked up the window frames with careful hands and began fitting them into their tracks. "Maybe, if there is a rock that is thrown at the ship, it would be better if it goes right through and out the other side?"

Takeshi lifted his eyes to the thoughtful faces of the rest of the students.

"We will think on your idea, Yachiyo-*san*," said Furokawa Goro with a small bow to her.

"*Sensei*," said Minoru. "What will we do tomorrow? Other than eat well and wear comfortable *wakafu*?"

"Ah! Mr. Kachman has obtained the cutter for the Embassy. We will be sailing, which means *gaijin* dress for the day. But it also means learning more, now that we have a ship worthy of the name."

A subdued cheer rang out; someone added a "*Banzai!*"

"All of you, study the lines and sheets of the ship type. We must be ready to understand Mr. Kachman very well tomorrow."

Takashi nodded and reached out for Minoru and Yachiyo. "We will go home. It has been a long day."

IV

Baltimore, 1900

Yachiyo crept down the stairs of the house that housed the industrial engineers. She had been kept home from school, as one of her classmates had been reported to be ill with scarlet fever. With little Koizumi Kiyoshi barely a year old, and Inagaki Iwao only three, it was considered safer for her to stay away for now. The eldest Koizumi boy, seven-year-old Kazuo, was away with his father in Washington.

Yachiyo set to work very quietly at the modeling table. If she made any noise, the women would find her and she'd be put to work, cleaning house. The maids had not come back this week. No one knew why. But she could remember at least three other occasions where all the hired help had suddenly decamped.

She sat at the worktable and pulled some rice paper and fine shims to her. After careful work, she had cut them with precisely angled corners and neatly glued three sets of hexagons to the paper. The first one was already dry and she carefully cut away the excess rice paper. She and Minoru had come up with a kite idea that she wanted to model. As she began to cut a series of struts out of the delicate shimming material she heard the front door open and close and frowned.

Everybody was in this house, cleaning, and nobody else should be coming in. The industrialist boys were all in Pittsburgh this week. The shoes were Western, three sets of them, coming quickly down the stairs to the basement door. Yachiyo clenched the sharp little knife and turned, just as the door was broken down.

"*Casse-toi!*"

Yachiyo gasped. Two men in rough clothes and one of the missing maids stood halfway through the splintered door.

"We were supposed to pick the locks and ghost in and out with nobody the wiser!" one said, the thin one with the small, black mustache, and his voice sounded different from the American *gaijin*.

"Hell, this is faster, and who cares about those dirty little japs, anyway?" the other replied in a hard, harsh voice like the workmen in the streets, and a big, hulking, red-faced body.

"Oh, no! Why did you bring me! If they see me, I won't—" cried the maid.

Her words were abruptly cut off when the first man turned and hit her across the face with the back of his hand.

"Shut up, *sale con!* Quick, Sean! Find the plans. We will have to take them; listen! There are people here and they heard. If there is shooting, the police will be called. *Vite, vite!*"

Yachiyo took a deep breath and screamed at the top of her lungs: "Mama-*sama!* Mama-*sama!* Mama-*sama! Supai no yōjin!*"

Then she dived under the trestles and boards holding up the scale model of their house in Tokyo.

"What the devil?"

"It's the girl!" the maid said. "The youngest of the Togo kids! Why isn't she in school?"

Over the lurching of the two men as they stumbled against the boards holding up the model, Yachiyo could hear the soft padding of *tabi*-covered feet and the sudden sound of *geta* as the women came running from all over the house.

"Shut the door!" the first of the men snarled.

"It's broken! *Vous avez le cervau d'un sandwich au fromage,* you Irish cretin! You broke it!"

The maid—Yachiyo suddenly remembered her name was Rachel—screamed and ran to the back of the basement. She crawled forward and drove the sharp work knife into the shoe closest to the boards, then scrambled back as the man roared and fell, screaming curses in a language she didn't recognize.

"Ooof!"

The trestles collapsed, and Yachiyo found herself pressed close to the floor. She could just barely wiggle. Then the man pushed on the board to help himself up, and it tilted enough for her to squirm out the back end.

Before more could be done, Setsu rushed in, holding a dripping mop, followed by Tetsu, with a *naginata*. The five aunts of the industrial-firm boys were crowded on the stairs, holding other things. The man who was fleeing fell back and pulled a revolver from his pocket. He hadn't a second to aim or pull the trigger. Like a snake's tongue, Yachiyo saw her mother flick the *naginata* forward and back. Blood spurted from a deep wound in his neck. Behind her, Rachel grabbed her, and Yachiyo went limp.

"Let me go! Or my mother will kill you too!"

Rachel's arms slackened their grip, and she yanked free. The man she'd stabbed in the foot was hopping around, his face covered with slimy, soapy water and his shirt front soaked. Setsu cornered him against the wall, crying for rope. Rachel made a run for the door, but Tetsu reversed the *naginata* and tripped her. The aunts swarmed in and they had tied up the two living invaders before they could recover.

Late in the afternoon, Yachiyo wished she'd just hid and let the men steal and copy whatever they had wanted. She was more or less corralled in a chair in the sitting room, doing her best to ignore the fat, stinking pig of a policeman yelling at her for stabbing one of the men in the foot. The gold watch-chain across his brightly checked waistcoat shook with his agitation, and his graying, ginger hair made him look like a particularly unpleasant fox spirit.

She heard the door open and Minoru's familiar steps. He was speaking Japanese with one of Kusakabe Sadao's security detachment. Then they both walked into the sitting room.

"Honorable sir! How more can my sister help you? She is so fragile, so young!"

Yachiyo knew what that meant. Her lower lip had been sticking out a little in a pout. She made it tremble, and blinked rapidly as if she was going to cry, casting down her eyes in a politeness the fat *gaijin* didn't deserve. She saw him frown a little uncertainly and sniffled a bit. It wouldn't have deceived her mother a single moment, or her brothers more than an instant, but it would do here.

"Such a terrible ordeal for her."

"You wouldn't say that, that you wouldn't, if you saw what she did to the guy's foot!"

"Most assuredly she defended herself, caught under a heavy plank. But what has that to do with her being in her own castle, as you say here, and fighting off intruders?"

Yachiyo gasped in relief, desperately wishing she could warn Minuro of her mother's peril, only to realize from his sudden glance at her that he knew all about it. The policeman turned, lifting his meaty hand, but Kusakabe interpolated his body adroitly.

"Yes, yes. I am the one you men call Kusanagi Sado! I am so glad you have come. But now, leave the child, children, for I must understand better what you have found. Come with me, and explain..."

Minoru waited until the man was completely out, and grimaced.

"Mr. Hearn has discovered that some of the police force were bribed to ignore any alarms from here. The chief is angry, but also angry at us, whom he blames for showing up his men. Mama-*sama* will be released soon; but she did kill a man."

Yachiyo found herself baring her teeth. "She had to, but mama-*sama* has said nothing to them. And I could not unless I speak with Mama, and she agrees to say that the *naginata* was left there by the boys, and that *bakayaro* spy fell into it when trying to shoot Mama."

"I like that version, little brat. Just a minute."

Yachiyo sighed as Minoru left her and went after Kusakabe; maybe the older man would listen to *him*. As a girl, she simply didn't rank anywhere in anybody's minds as someone to listen to in matters such as this. She scowled at the floor and turned her thoughts back to the kite she'd been working on when the intruders broke in.

Was there a way to make a one-person leviathan?

V

Pittsburgh, 1901

Easter week was vacation time for many, even the students at Annapolis—Takeshi had found its stern discipline almost homelike. Mr. Hearn, with sixteen-year-old cadet Togo Takeshi and eleven-year-old Togo Minoru, took the train to Pittsburgh that Friday evening, winding through the valleys under the ever-darkening pall of soot as forest and farm gave way to mine and foundry and sprawling factories.

Takeshi stared out with the combination of fascination and repulsion he always felt for this city, this place that distilled all he both feared and envied about this country called the United States. It was a place of narrow, twisting valleys and filthy rivers that ran black and sometimes caught fire and burned with ghostly, ghastly blue flames. Endless trains of coal and coke and iron ore clanked through and over the streets, more leaving full of rolls of steel and beams and girders and wire, tinplate, turbines, and engines. Every passageway was crowded with drays and wagons and a few motorcars and endless mobs of workers in their overalls and flat cloth caps and battered boots. A constant roaring of voices and wheels and grinding metal. Mansions and shacks alike were built of brick that was red beneath a thick coat of grime that made everything the same gray-black. Towering smokestacks poured more of the smoke into the lowering sky without cease. Even around the mansions of the factory magnates far away in the hills, the gardeners must toil ceaselessly to keep the gardens alive.

And on every side, the blast furnaces and converters shot red and gold flame ceaselessly through the murk, a bellow and scream through thick air that caught at the throat every time you breathed in.

It all was so ugly...but you could *feel* the power, shaking the earth with the stamp of steam hammers and the grind of machine tools and the roar of flame, making the filthy air vibrate with a hymn of might. Here the future was being built, ripped from the womb of the earth and forged into shape with hands made of hydraulics and electricity and scourging heat.

Westinghouse, Tesla, and Edison were ready to test the prototype they had named the *Pigeon*, and the Japanese engineers and cadets had been invited along to see the historic rise of the American leviathan. Takeshi and his brother and Hearn stayed the night in the boarding house with the engineering students.

On Saturday morning, all arrived at the factory and the huge testing-shed next to a vast cleared field, at an hour the Americans called "bright and early," though it was hazy here even on clear days. The watchman glared at them, a pistol at his belt and a club dangling by a thong, and a badge on his domed blue helmet reading *Coal and Iron Police*. A half-dozen more in the same gear paced around the perimeter, and several more with rifles were posted on the roof.

"Didn't Mr. Westinghouse tell me nothing about you fellas coming here without he's here first."

Mr. Hearn smiled with his usual sweet calm and said: "Well, and well. We are early and so very eager to see the prototype. But I am sure Mr. Westinghouse will be along presently."

And, in fact, Mr. Westinghouse arrived only a few minutes later; a tall, stout man with white mutton-chop whiskers and hair, scowling a little as he raised his top hat. The Japanese bowed, as was due to a man of power and position, himself an inventor of note as well as a capitalist—they had all studied his innovations in pneumatic braking systems and signaling, and he had been instrumental in the adoption of the turbine to generating alternating electricity.

Half a dozen of the guards shoved back the great sheet-metal doors, squealing as they ran along tracks set in the pavement. Takeshi blinked as electric lights came on overhead, casting a harsh, modern glare over the long shape within, at last free of the cables and cranes fixed to the roof that had swung its components into position on the slipway.

His breath caught.

The prototype looked odd to eyes used to seafaring. Its hull was the size and shape of a cutter's hull, but covered by a frame of girders with glass and steel plates inset. It was really not very large, much smaller than the leviathans the French had built for their Russian allies; hence its name of *Pigeon*.

Westinghouse clapped his hands together and ground palm against palm, a habit of his.

"The Europeans thought they could keep it secret forever. Well, you can't patent a law of nature—or keep someone else from figuring it out once you show what's possible!" he said.

"*Hai*, very true," someone murmured.

And it is true, Takeshi thought, silent as befitted a youth in the company of his elders. *And nobody will keep us from figuring it out either. But...*

"The devil is in the details you say here, do you not, Westinghouse-*san*?"

"Ah, you know the difference between principle and practice do you, young fellow?" the industrial baron said. "They're not stuffing your head with too much theory at Annapolis, then."

Some of the others gave him irritated glances; it wasn't really his position to speak, particularly among those so much elder and of senior position. He was still glad that he had. There had been approval in Westinghouse's reply. This was a man worthy of respect, *gaijin* or not.

As the Japanese technical delegation had found out over the past years of experimenting, there was a minimum size for effective power in the electroid reservoirs and stimulators. The coal-burning electrical generators were also limited by the minimum thickness of steel needed to enclose the furnaces and boilers and turbines; Westinghouse and his technicians had achieved miracles of compactness, but they could not be effectively scaled down past a certain point.

All in all, the prototype was as small as it could be made, and measured over forty feet in length and was twenty feet at its widest. A set of ballast bulges and Swan stabilizers protruded from the hull in regular, graceful curves, looking like a large pearl choker around a fine lady's neck. There were hatches, fore and aft, that opened to allow the introduction of the engines and electroid reservoirs and conduits for the thick copper cables that would excite the electroid fluid into levitation.

"Really, Mr. Hearn, I had no idea you and your crew would be here this morning!" Westinghouse said, seeming to recall himself from his own contemplation of the prototype with a start.

Takeshi and Minoru shot into the great experimental bay and clambered into the prototype. Outside they could hear Mr. Hearn soothing and babbling gently at Mr. Westinghouse.

Minoru murmured, "Amazing how he can control his bad temper when needed."

Nakajima Haruo slapped Minoru on the back of the head. "Be polite," he admonished. "Koizumi Yakumo is a good man, and his temper is triggered by personal meanness and unkindness."

Takeshi heard Mr. Westinghouse's booming tones, but he wasn't paying attention. In the rather dark area of the ship, he was using his hands to run over the newly installed containment tank. He slid sideways and let himself fall to the floor. Even as his sensitive fingers found the embossed lettering, he heard Minoru call: "Takeshi! Takeshi!"

He slid himself out from under the tank and piping. "Yes?"

Minoru was tracing an electrical circuit. "Did they decide to go for Mr. Tesla's alternating current or Mr. Edison's direct current?"

"I don't believe the direct worked as well, and Mr. Westinghouse felt that in a ship they would do better to use alternating."

"If that is so, then this circuit is wrong."

Takeshi stepped over and frowned. More than just the circuit was wrong—two connections were dangling, free, hidden behind an improperly installed ballast.

Takeshi ducked out of the cramped belly of the *Pigeon*. "Mr. Westinghouse!" he said peremptorily.

Five hands lifted to smack him for his brash insolence, and he ducked past them to stand in front of the massive industrialist with his thick mustaches so like a walrus.

He met his eyes. "Mr. Westinghouse. Who installed the components?"

His urgency was compounded by an incredible sense of wrong. There was something very wrong about the entire factory, if only he could put his finger on it.

Kusakabi Sadao came up behind Mr. Westinghouse and Takeshi could see that he was bristling like a cat scenting a fox.

Taking his courage in both hands, he said urgently: "Sir! Please, I am not playing tricks. I have never played tricks and jokes on you."

And suddenly the wrongness fell into place. "We received a letter from you inviting us to witness the launch of the *Pigeon* today at eight a.m. Yet you were surprised we were here. And there are no workers here, today. And many of the components are installed incorrectly. Not sloppy! But deliberately wrong!"

Mr. Hearn and Mr. Westinghouse's jaws had dropped. "I sent no such letter!" Westinghouse said.

"But, when was the work completed? And when did you expect it to be completed?" asked Kusakabi even as Mr. Hearn pulled out the letter he'd received and handed it over.

"I didn't expect us to begin the install until late May or early June! The memo that it was done was on my desk late yesterday. Mr. Edison and Mr. Tesla signed off on it. I had no idea they were that far advanced, Mr. Sado."

"Kusakabi," he answered absently. "If you call me Mister, you should use my family name." The head of their security was looking at the *Pigeon* with disquiet on his face.

"Sorry! I always forget that, Mr. Kusanagi." He looked down at the letter and his eyes suddenly narrowed. "I never wrote this, but that is my signature!"

"Well, as to who ordered the work, it's an easy question to answer. I'll send Harry off to roust Misters Tesla and Edison out of bed. Meanwhile, young Takeshi, show me some of these problems. Mr. Nissan, please bring me the plans for the *Pigeon*. They're on my desk and my office is unlocked."

Mr. Westinghouse's early life as a machinist was an advantage; he knew machinery intimately, through his fingers as well as his eyes on diagrams. He followed Takeshi and Minoru's pointing and quickly understood the changes, improper connections and faulty wiring. Takeshi's English didn't extend to all the phrases the older man used then, but they started with words for excrement and sexual intercourse and went on from there. *Gaijin* swore oddly, though with great force.

By the time they were out of the *Pigeon*, Tesla and Edison were both there, shouting at each other, waving pieces of paper. Edison looked a little like Mr. Collins the schoolmaster, tall and thin and white-haired, but rumpled and odder-looking, flushed red and using some of the same words as Westinghouse, though with a twanging accent, some dialect form. Tesla was smaller, slim and elegant and impeccably dressed in black and pearl-grey with an orchid in his buttonhole, and he remained calmer even in his anger, though his accent grew thicker—Takeshi knew it was that of Croatia, a country in Eastern Europe. Oddly, a servant stood behind him with a white pigeon in a wrought-brass cage, perhaps a reference to the craft he had helped to build.

All attempts to calm them down failing, Sadao got between them and pushed each one around and into one of the engineering students, who politely grappled them.

"Quiet!" he roared. "It is not time for you to cast mud at each other. This was a carefully planned and executed operation to sabotage us, and your rivalry and tempers were part of the plan!"

Okura and Nissan let go of the two men as they calmed down and turned to him, still bristling, but quiet.

"I received the memo of completion on the install last night with Mr. Tesla's signature. It had a handwritten note in Mr. Tesla's fist; it's quite distinctive, saying he'd managed to have it done much before schedule."

The darkly handsome Nikola drew himself up. "Not true! I have here, in my pocket!" he pulled out a crumpled piece of paper. "Your memo to myself and Mr. Westinghouse that we were behind the train, or leviathan, and your men had completed the install. I wondered who had given them their order this past week."

Kusakabi took the memo from Mr. Tesla and requested Mr. Edison find the memo he had received. Westinghouse stared at the three memos and the letter Hearn had received and met the eyes of Takeshi.

"You've made a very smart call, Mr. Togo. I'm glad you were inquisitive enough to be able to find the problems. I suspect you've not found them all." He chewed his lip.

Lafcadio Hearn took the four pieces of paper and pulled a magnifying glass out from his pocket. "I could use a few more everyday memos with your signatures," he suggested. "But this looks like a very professional job. So the question is, who?"

"No," said Kusakabi. "There is any number of possible enemies. The question is what to do now. Do we simply let them know we figured it out? Or lay a trap? And what was their goal? And how can we spike that?"

Westinghouse grinned, his yellowing teeth showing under the fluffy mustache. "Yeah, there's a reason they call you Sword, ya know! My guess would be the French. Right now, I don't think the English are interested, and Kitchner; well, he's a gentleman. It sounds silly, but one gets to know how far some people will go to pursue a goal."

"The French are a reasonable hypothesis," Kusakabi mused. "Or the Russians, or the Russians and French in combination. The Okhrana and the Deuxième Bureau work closely together these days."

"And the goal," said Nikola Tesla, "is to both embarrass us and possibly to abort our program entirely. Mr. Vice-President Roosevelt stands as our friend and supports the program. But he and Mr. McKinley do not see eye to eye on the need for a leviathan fleet. If it became known that there would be no orders from the War or Navy Departments…"

"Our financing would vanish like Temperance Bitters at a WCTU meeting," Westinghouse said. "I've had enough trouble with Morgan and the damned New York bankers as it is. If there's one thing they hate, it's a research program that keeps dividends down. Profits now and damn the future is their motto. My company could end up in receivership, and that would set our leviathan program back decades."

Edison and Tesla both nodded. Takeshi reflected that, rumors to the contrary, Mr. Edison and Mr. Tesla did agree on some things and worked fairly well together when they did. The leviathan project was dear to both of them. And evidently to Westinghouse too, since he was willing to endanger all that he had built.

"Honorable Mr. Westinghouse-*san*," he said. The men looked at him. "Kusakabi-*san* has said a good truth. The goal is to disrupt our work. I believe he should turn into Kusanagi now and hunt down the perpetrators. But we will do well to empty out the entire *Pigeon* and reset it completely. And do so without letting any spies know what we are doing."

Silence fell. After a few minutes Mr. Westinghouse said: "I agree, in principle, but if we bring back the work crews, the most likely thing is that at least one or two members have been suborned in some way and are passing on information to our not-friends. Passing information, and possibly more."

Sadao grinned fiercely. "That you know to be true. And I know who they are. I can arrange accidents for them."

The senior men were silent, thinking over this proposal. Lafcadio Hearn suddenly came out of his brown study. "No, no, no. Kill them without trial or defense?"

Takeshi shook his head. "Honorable *sensei*, Mr. Hearn. I honor you. And I agree with you, but for different reasons. A spy who thinks himself undetected can be given false information; if you kill him, you many not detect his replacement until too late. We need to have the flight of the *Pigeon* to happen as our enemy planned, but no errors. And to do this, we all will work under your direction, Mr. Westinghouse-*san*, and those of the great scientists here, stripping the hull down to the bare beams and re-seating all the equipment and conducting partial tests at every step. I estimate it will take possibly two or three days."

He knew that his estimate was dead on, and that giving it had just given the engineering troika a good understanding of their own spying operation. But these were their allies, and they were under attack by an unknown enemy...or enemies!

The scions of the great commercial and manufacturing families of Japan said simply: "*Hai!*" in unison.

Mr. Westinghouse suddenly laughed. "Tricky men, you are. And capable. Yes, having the *Pigeon* fly without explanation when they had paid, and probably paid well to have it crash would be the best of all worlds. Very well! Let's strip the ship. It won't kill me to get my hands on a wrench or a brazing wheel or a rivet gun again. Hell, I *invented* the rivet gun!"

Tesla looked slightly pained, then sighed and nodded. Edison laughed as well.

"No, by criminy, it won't! I started at the bottom of this business too, and I haven't forgotten how to get some grime in my knuckles. I slept on a generator housing for weeks when we put in our first central station in New York."

"Mr. Hearn," Westinghouse went on. "You and your associates clearly are well versed in espionage. Would you do me the favor of searching for evidence of who might have been responsible for these horrifying changes to our plans?"

Takeshi began to unbutton his blue cadet's uniform jacket as he looked at the *Pigeon*. And as a secondary benefit, by stripping it to the frame and rebuilding it, the Japanese delegation would solidify their grasp on the technology. Given their range of talents, it would be as good as being given a complete set of engineering drawings, or even better. Once back in Nippon, they could build their own yard, duplicate it, and go on to improved designs within a few years. By the covert glances from the others, he wasn't the only one who'd thought of that.

Takeshi straightened, blinking eyes that felt sandy and wincing at a twinge in his back. By late Wednesday the *Pigeon* had been completely rebuilt, every pipe, every containment vessel, every steam vane in every turbogenerator, every single wire, magnetic mirror and partition checked, double-checked, and cross-checked. Every lever, wheel, gear, crank had been worked, oiled, studied, and matched against the exhaustive lists Nakajima and Nissan had created off the plans.

They had kept operational security. Mr. Hearn had found a copy of the notice sent to the men, giving them the week off. One of the pigeonholes was assigned to a man who'd been home sick, and the notice left there. Mr. Hearn wandered about the city of Pittsburgh, swinging his cane, gently conversing with people and slowly becoming familiar with the nearby businesses and factories.

Early Thursday, he went to pick up George Barbee. Barbee was a horse jockey with experience in ocean sailing who'd been picked as the initial pilot of the *Pigeon*. The man was some fifty years old, and he'd held on to his fine, light body, though he'd not ridden for many years. He was a full twenty or more pounds lighter than any of the Japanese, and a good two or three inches shorter than Mr. Hearn, himself.

"I thought the test was not happening for a month or two, Mr. Westinghouse?" he said, looking up at the hull of the *Pigeon* as a bright spray of sparks fell over the side and sizzled out on the dingy stained concrete of the hangar floor.

Takeshi looked over as the man's accent caught his ear. He supposed that it came from England, but it sounded very different from other English accents he'd heard, slurred and adenoidal and dropping the initial "h" sounds.

"Ay, that's what we thought, but things changed, and we put a priority on it, Barbee. We'll need you to go aloft. One of the engineers will go with you. It's to be a short test. We won't try to find the machine's ceiling or the human ceiling this day. We want to get an estimate of the coal to range equation and also see how she handles. You've used the fake we built and know all the levers.

One of these fellas will be going with you as the fireman. Would you like a navigator, as well?"

"Now, just wait one little moment!" exclaimed the man. "Where's your crew? Why are all these Johnny Chinamen here? What's going on?"

Takeshi frowned as he backed up to the *Pigeon*. Her two cargo hatches had been closed, and only the passenger hatch next to the conning tower was opened. He climbed up the scaffolding and ducked in and let himself drop to the engineering deck, falling down the ladder with hands and feet gripping the sides.

"Minoru, how goes the boiler?"

"We're producing enough steam now to run the turbine to excitation level. Has the pilot arrived? Will I be able to stay?"

Takeshi said, "I don't know. He's calling us Johnny Chinamen, and Mr. Westinghouse got mad. His face turns very red."

An echo of angry voices came through the hull, barely audible through the steel panels. Takeshi swarmed up the ladder and poked his head out the hatch. Barbee was on the ground, being held in place by one of the men.

"Good job, Kusanagi!" boomed Mr. Westinghouse.

"Westinghouse-*san*, if *I* were trying to sabotage this project, I would have the pilot bribed if I could. As a...how do you say, second plan?"

"Backup. Or maybe we were meant to find the sabotage, and then the pilot would do the deed."

"I'm just buggered if I'll go up with Chinks in the engine-room!" the little man wheezed. "I don't know nuffink about any sabotage! Sod you all!"

Westinghouse shot him a withering look. "You're no use whether you're a traitor or just yellow."

Then he turned to the Japanese naval officer. "I'm afraid, however, that even if we keep him captive here, we don't have an alternate for the job. Which leaves us right where we began, a prototype we can't test—and right now is the only moment we can be *sure* there's no one cutting a crucial wire or damaging a valve."

Takeshi slid down again. "Minoru! Are you sure the turbine is generating enough electricity?"

"Right and tight!" his brother sang back. "Nailing the voltage with no trouble, steam flow is excellent and the Parsons turbine is running smooth. Very nice regulator mechanism."

"Minoru! That man won't go up in the *Pigeon*, and I think that means they won't be able to test the prototype. *Sensei* has him on the ground."

"So, he is probably one of the conspiracy?"

"I guess. I wonder what he said that made Kusakabe suspicious."

"It doesn't take much. Kusakabe is like the hunting hound of one of the old *daimyo*, he can sniff out tracks across mountains and water."

Takeshi worked his way down to the boiler, where his brother was using a small shovel to add measured amounts of anthracite to the fire and watch the pressure gauges and the voltammeters. Electric lights in wire cages gave a weird, hard-edged look to everything, combined with red flickers when the furnace door was opened.

Minoru grinned up at him. "Not as fun as sailing on the sea... but, if I keep very quiet, maybe the guy they pick to pilot will let us stay, thinking we are somebody else."

And in that moment Takeshi knew what he would do. "What if I pilot it, Minoru?"

A sheer, unadulterated grin spread across his brother's face. "Yes!" he said, fiercely. "Chūjō Togo Heihachirō's sons, taking up the prototype for the Japanese leviathan force! Not as good as crushing a Russian fleet, but we can do that later too! And that will be thousands, while this will be just us."

Takeshi nodded sharply. "I'm glad we winched open the sky bay this morning. Otherwise we wouldn't have much clearance."

"I'll keep the energy flowing! You go fly this little *Haiiro no hato*!"

A thought struck Takeshi. "Pigeons...well, doves...are the messengers of Hachiman."

Hachiman—the Kami of the Eight Banners—was the tutelary deity of warriors, the Kami of the bow, and the divine protector of the Land of the Gods and their Yamato people.

"So will our leviathans be!" Minoru said. "The servants of Hachiman, protectors of the Empire! It's an omen, my brother."

Takeshi leaped up to the cramped pilot position in the conning tower. He spared a one-second wish for a navigator, but then concentrated on the excitation sliders controlling the buoyancy tanks and the levers controlling the stabilizers. *Pigeon* rose, faster than he expected and he barely managed to crank the ballast tanks and kick on the pedal controlling the speed of the airscrews and clear the edge of the sky bay.

I will be forgiven if I succeed; I am not disobeying a direct order. Not if I crash!

The enclosing glass and steel made it impossible to hear anything from the ground. The dull roar of the forced-draught fans ramming air into the burner filled the cabin and the whine of the electric motors driving the airscrew, along with the smell of hot steel and burning anthracite and ozone and something else, something prickly and indefinable.

The smell of a leviathan soaring. I am the first Japanese to smell it, the first to feel the controls come alive beneath my hands. But not the last; one day our fleets will fill the sky.

"Tennō Heika banzai!" he shouted exultantly, and heard his brother's voice echo him.

His grip was precise. And the leviathan...it was a small prototype, but still forty feet long, thirty tall, and twenty wide and weighed better than a hundred tons of riveted nickel-steel plating and girders.

From the conning tower, he could see the river before him, but not directly underneath or behind. Mirrors tried to compensate for the problem, but were only partially successful. He adjusted the sliders and the ballast and kicked off the airscrew for a moment. Once they were stationary, he checked the altimeter. It read three hundred feet; the same in *shaku*, near enough, since the basic measurements were almost identical.

He dug the ship's log out and found the chronometer on the display before him.

Thursday, April 4, 1901, he wrote. *8:32 a.m., the* Pigeon *has flown for the first time. After a rapid ascent out of the bay of Mr. Westinghouse's factory in the suburb of Elliot, near Pittsburgh I am stationary...*

He reconsidered and ruled out the "I am stationary." That smacked of vanity.

...The Pigeon *is stationary at 300 feet. A serious disadvantage to this design is immediately observable. Or rather, not observable. Visibility is severely limited, even in the comm tower. Landing will be a matter of using the altimeter and the American joke of dead reckoning. In combat, there will be too many blind spots in this configuration. Redesign and war games are imperative to correcting these faults.*

8:45 a.m.: Having oriented the Pigeon, *I am using the airscrew to send us down the Ohio River to the Allegheny river. She will fly to Freeport, and I will then cut across the neck of land to the Monongahela River and return to Sheridan along the river.*

"That will be a decent maiden flight," he murmured to himself.

He closed the log and checked his dials and the automatic recording mechanism that listed wind direction and speed, light, and the amount of buoyancy and lift in the tanks and the reserve of electroid and electrical power on moving reels of paper—an invention of Mr. Edison's based on his ticker-tape telegraph, and extremely ingenious.

A deep breath, and then he engaged the airscrew and pushed the throttle forward. Acceleration pushed him backward with a large, soft hand. A little like a train pulling out of a station, but not really like anything he had felt before. Discipline kept his eye on the gauges long enough to be sure the ship was answering, and then he glanced through the observation windows. The terrain below was like a rumpled terrain model in a war game, but *alive*. A train puffed away from a siding, small as a child's toy but belching real smoke and steam. A train of barges on the river heaped with black coal inched ahead, wakes trailing backward like V's. And now he was high enough to see how the smoke hovered over the city like a brown-grey haze, and the air grew cleaner as they ascended towards three thousand feet.

He opened the speaking tube and called, "Ahoy, Minoru! How goes it?"

"Well! What does it look like topside?"

"Can you come up for a minute?"

"Yes, but only a minute."

When Minoru arrive up in the conning tower, they were so cramped Takeshi couldn't understand how they could have considered the space designed for three large American men.

The younger boy goggled about. "This is how a bird sees it," he said, more solemnly than usual. "Or a *kami*!"

"Do you have a notebook?" he asked his awe-struck brother.

With a startled glance away from the panorama, Minoru pulled one of his usual notebooks with the ribbon loop holding it closed. Takeshi took a quick look at the voltameter and pointed it out to Minoru, who promptly vanished down the rungs to the engineering station.

Takeshi quickly dated and time-stamped the first page, copied what he'd written in the log, and then turned the page. On the next page he wrote a list of things he was already sure must be changed in the design. He'd share it with Mr. Hearn and *Sensei* when they were back in Baltimore. Meanwhile, he experimented for a few minutes with the different levers. The *Pigeon* rolled a bit as he got the hang of the controls.

"Not like a sailing ship. More like a steam-launch? But—"

Something buffeted the craft, and it lurched a little.

"—but there are currents in the air! And differences in density, too. I am in the air, not riding on it as a boat does on the water. It is like a submarine, like Verne's *Nautilus*."

From the comm tower, he could see the Ohio River and using the screw and the ballasts, he navigated the *Pigeon* up river until it divided and he took the Allegheny branch east.

His grin grew wider. *And I am the first to fly so in the skies above America. Their history-books will have to record that, too!*

Each time he saw a landmark, he reckoned the airspeed, and triangulated, trying to stop directly above them and learn to use the mirrors. Bit by bit he began to achieve mastery over the *Pigeon*'s controls. *Clearly, flying and navigating are too much work for one man. It is correct to have two.*

"Can I come up?" his brother asked.

"Yes, but just for a moment," Takeshi said.

When the moment had passed, he pointed sternly to a steam repeater gauge, and Minoru yelped and dashed down again.

Takeshi wrote: *Boiler explosions are a known hazard. Men in the boiler room will lose their lives if it blows. Create a better wall between the boiler-men and the boilers. Put portholes in the boiler room; they can function as pressure releases in an explosion, too. Create breakaway bolts that encourage a boiler explosion to blow away from crew.*

He thought for a while as he took more readings and triangulated them. He took the *Pigeon* inland, watching the contours of the land, maintaining a decent height. In their mixture of *kanji* and *romaji* code, he wrote on the last page of the book:

Eventually redesign the entire ship. When in the sea, one wants to be on top of the buoyant body. But in the air, especially in battle, one needs 360-degree vision in all the planes. The main crew area should be underneath the tanks and observation posts. The bridge should be at the bow, with clear views above, below and to either side.

This is a major redesign, and one that men who are not familiar with ships would not think of. Discuss with Mr. Hearn and Kusakabe-san whether this is something we wish to share with the Americanji. In the case of boiler blowing, having the ability to jettison the damaged piece with the force of the explosion may save the rest of the crew. Consider evacuation and kites as lifejackets.

He put the book away and frowned as the lights over the dials flickered. From the speaking tube, that he'd left open Minoru suddenly called out, his voice urgent.

"Takeshi! Takeshi! We are almost out of anthracite!"

"What! We had four boxes! Why didn't you tell me when you finished off the first two boxes?"

"Because we are just reaching the bottom of the first box. The second box is clink and shale. And the third and fourth boxes, too. Same weight, with a thin cover of anthracite."

"Is there any burnable material in them?" asked Takeshi, his blood running cold.

"Yes some, but I don't know how far it will take us. I've turned down the lights in here. I can see with just one on half-power."

Takeshi nodded and flipped off the lights over the instruments and cursed quietly as he steered the most direct course back to the sheds. It was on the same circuit of the instruments and turning off the lights depowered the instruments. He flicked them back on and made a notation in the log to separate the circuits... who needs lights in the daytime?

"Minoru, what was the weight on that box? Can we trust the numbers?"

"Twenty pounds, and it felt about right. Each of the other's also says twenty pounds and feels about the same."

Takeshi busily figured how far they had come. He bit his lip and then forced himself to let it go. *I am the representative of the Heavenly Sovereign Majesty. I will comport myself as a* Samurai*! I will do this.*

They needed at least another twenty pounds to make it back, and there really wasn't any way to cut the power drain any further. He had to get over water as fast as possible and bring the *Pigeon* much lower, so that if they fell from the sky they would survive and, much more importantly, the *Pigeon* and the vital information they had secured would not be destroyed.

"Takeshi, I have sorted through the box. I think there is enough bad coal in the three left that we might have another seventy or eighty minutes of burn."

Takeshi looked at his figures. That was cutting it very fine.

"Do your best, brother!" He concentrated on his triangulation figures, cutting a larger angle across the land to the west than he'd initially planned. The need to be over water warred with the need to cut off time from the return trip. Takeshi plotted on the map, working out the distance and time.

He gasped with relief when he finally had them over the water again and could take a moment to record the time Minoru discovered the last piece of sabotage. Somebody had been very, very thorough, but it had been complete overkill. Maybe it had been two or three entities

Minoru gave him a running update as they approached the field before the cradle shed. He wasn't going to try and get the *Pigeon* inside, not with the fuel situation as tight as it was. Everyone scattered back from the field, doll-tiny figures running aside...

And then they vanished. His gaze flickered to the mirrors; impossible to judge distances that way properly!

"Brace for impact!" he shouted to his brother, and then there was a crash and a screech and something flung him violently sideways.

He flung out his arm and there was a flash of savage pain. Then everything was very quiet, until feet rang on the ladders and faces were bending over him.

"The field of visibility from this position is totally inadequate for landings," he gasped as they gently lifted him. "And there need to be restraints for turbulent weather!"

The world went away.

VI

U.S. Navy Commencement
Annapolis, Maryland
July, 1903

"Togo."

Just the one word, but one that made him very proud, though he was careful not to show it to his peers. It was the first name called. Togo Takeshi was graduating first in his class; his grades in mathematics and cartography and his work analyzing the permutations of combined water/air warfare had given him the two percentage points he needed to edge Ware, Bowels, and Grauer out of the top position. It had been close, he recognized. The four of them were the top thinkers, closest allies, and most serious rivals in their class.

He rose, did a smart about-turn and marched up to the podium. There he accepted the folded and sealed parchment and handshake from Commander Richard Wainwright. Then he saluted, very properly and walked steadily across the stage.

He could see, front and center, the Japanese delegation, politely patting their hands together, and his brother Minoru sitting stiff-faced among the plebes, the juniors, with his eyes dancing. Behind him he heard "Bowels," and walked down the aisle to the back and slid along the empty row of seats. His classmates slowly filled up the next ones in the row, and then the next row was standing and walking forward to receive their posting orders.

Togo was sure that all his classmates felt the same anxiety he did to read their orders. He was also fairly convinced that making them wait while pictures were taken, questions asked, the open air reception held was a deliberate lesson in self control. And that they were being watched.

"Hey, Johnny Chinaman," said Ware, nudging him in the ribs. "Don't you want to know where you are going?"

Takeshi shook his head, keeping his face solemn. "It is of no matter to me, or to you, Mr. Ware," he said formally.

For a fleeting second, he grinned at his closest rival. "I will take my cruise as a Junior Grade Lieutenant in the U.S. Navy, but then I will resign my commission and return to my home, as part of the escort on the four leviathans my country has bought. You, however, will do well, very well, and be promoted, and one day we will meet as commanders each of our respective ships."

Ware snorted. "I could never tell if you meant that or not," he complained.

"Of course I meant it," said Togo Takeshi. "I have my father's sacrifice to avenge. Thanks to the Heavenly Sovereign Majesty and his Naval Minister I have a great chance to do so."

"I thought you'd stay on here. Do you really want to go home? To those damp, distant islands so far from everything?"

Togo refused to smile in derision. The desire to go home ate at his heart, and he would feel joy near to weeping when he set foot on his homeland again. The exile had been long and arduous, and the rewards would be commensurate.

"Come say good-bye to my mother," he said, instead.

Ware perked up at that; he'd always been perfectly polite, but Togo knew his friend considered her a vision of exotic loveliness and mysterious grace—which showed he had good taste, at least.

Mr. Bowels and Mr. Grauer were already talking with Togo Tetsu and Togo Yachiyo, both wearing good *wakafu*. They stepped aside as Togo Takeshi approached, straight and graceful in his white dress uniform. He saluted.

His mother and sister faced him, and then they bowed. Bowed more deeply than before, recognizing him as the head of the household.

"Your father is proud, my son," his mother said softly. "Very proud."

Togo swallowed, looking westward where the sun was declining. It seemed like a pathway before him, an aerial pathway beckoning him toward deeds that would live forever.

ꟻAILURE ᴏꜰ ᴛʜᴇ ENTENTE

[*Conversation overheard in in London between two diplomats in the United Kingdom, June 1904*]

"So that's it, then? After everything we have been working for for the last four years to try to bring some peace and stability to our countries, and it is all going out the window, just like that."

"That's about the sum of it, my friend. There isn't much we can do about it now but get a drink and assume that someone will come up with a new plan."

"NO! There is no new plan—don't you get that? If we cannot settle these territorial issues with France, we will eventually be at war with each other again like in the days of Napoleon. We will beat each other senseless over piles of dirt in Africa while Germany and Russia grow stronger day after day. Eventually we will end up on the wrong side of war one of these days, and it will be all because of those bloody military wankers and their new war toys."

"I think you are really overselling the importance of this agreement. We have ruled the world for 100 years without this *entente cordiale*, and we will still do so now. What has changed to make it so important?"

"Everything. Back during the era of Napoleon our empire was kept safe because we had the strongest navy in the world—"

"Ha, but we still do!"

"But only barely now! German is building ships both on the air and at sea at an alarming rate. Italy and Austria have fallen in love with the new opportunities leviathans have provided, and

Russia alone could take us on one for one in a battle of airships. America is going at it slowly, but if they wanted to, they could join in the sky race as well. We have to start making peace with our neighbours, or we shall find all of them our enemies very soon."

"You worry far too much, my friend. Besides, we did all we could, we spoke our piece, we tried our best."

"I tried my best—"

"Yes yes, you may have put in more effort than me, but still we gave it the good swing—so what if we missed? These leviathans will bring a new era of glory to the empire, just you watch. With them we will kick the French out of Africa, and maybe even use them to take the fight to Paris itself, amazing machines that they are."

"But that sort of thinking can work both ways…if we are not careful, that very power that can bring us to the halls of Versailles can bring our enemies to the hall of Parliament."

"I see your point. I guess we'll just need to build more ships, eh? With some more ships and some good old British resolve, there is no way the future cannot be great. Now enough talk, I'm thirsty. Let us go get a pint to satisfy my throat and wash your worries away."

THE **WIND**
ʻFROM THE **SKY**

WILLIAM H. KEITH, JR.

May 18, 1904

Silent, black-robed, and invisible in the growing darkness, the raiders crept through a dense grove of orange trees beneath the villa on the hilltop. Their leader was Mustafa Hamad, a dark and angry-looking man utterly devoted to his master's service...and utterly determined that his mission this night would succeed.

Hamad raised his hand, signaling those behind him to halt. The raiding party consisted of twenty men, well-armed with a variety of European rifles—French Lebels and Norwegian Krags, for the most part—as well as curved *koummya* daggers, *shamshirs*, and even a few ornate percussion-cap pistols from the middle of the last century. They waited in the orange-blossom-scented evening, studying their objective, listening to the sounds coming from the villa above them—the bark of a dog, the low-voiced drone of conversation between a pair of Moroccan guards, the clink and clatter of dinnerware and occasional burst of laughter coming from the upstairs veranda...

The veranda...where their targets would be...

The summer villa of Ion Perdicaris rose gracefully from a low and thickly-wooded hill just outside the dusty city walls of

Tangiers. Called "The Place of Nightingales," it was a sprawling fortress in its own right, complete with high walls and its own small army of bodyguards, all locals outfitted in scarlet and white household livery. Commanding a spectacular view north across the Straits of Gibraltar, the Place of Nightingales had been transformed by its owner into a spectacular, vine-cloaked menagerie, with dogs, monkeys, domesticated cranes, and numerous other exotic animals and birds wandering freely through the ornately appointed rooms.

On the north veranda, overlooking the sea, Ion Perdicaris relaxed at the damask-covered table with his family as servants served the fish course of their dinner. At age 64, with a luxuriant, curly white beard, Perdicaris looked very much the part of the distinguished elder statesman.

Ellen Varley, lovely as always, and wearing a summery white dress, smiled at him. "And what," she asked, "did the Pasha have to say this afternoon?"

Perdicaris snorted derisively. "They had him running messages from Fez. Seems that our young idiot of a Sultan wants my help in securing a loan from the French. He probably wants another solid-gold automobile."

The ruler of Morocco was Mulai Abd el-Aziz, a 26-year-old descendent of Mohammed with a taste for Western culture...and for its toys. Reportedly, he had 600 cameras, 25 grand pianos, and several of the newfangled automobiles at his palace in Fez, including a special-order gold 1900 Smith & Dowse shipped in from England. The irony was that Morocco as yet had no roads, and travel through the country was largely limited to donkeys and horseback.

It scarcely mattered. Even gold plate would have made the auto too heavy to move.

Ellen laughed. "Doesn't he know that automobiles require *roads* to run on?"

"I'm not sure he cares. But his treasury is bare and he needs foreign cash...and quickly. I must say, Abd el-Saduk was quite put out..."

Abd el-Rahman Abd el-Saduk was the Pasha of the city of Tangiers, the local government authority and the Sultan's personal representative, but it was no secret that the man felt that he would do a *much* better job ruling Morocco than young el-

Aziz. He was ruthless, duplicitous, and treacherous...everything el-Aziz was not.

He is the sort, Perdicaris thought, *on whom one should* never *turn his back.*

Perdicaris smiled at Ellen. She was not his wife, though most people assumed she must be, and addressed her as "Mrs. Perdicaris." Once she'd been the wife of John Varley, an electrical telegraphic engineer who'd helped design the Transatlantic Cable. Perdicaris and Ellen had had a whirlwind affair three decades before, after which Varley had divorced his wayward wife, and she and her four children had immediately moved to Tangiers to live with Perdicaris.

He loved her, and could not imagine life without her.

"So...do you think the French will come through with a loan?" Cromwell Varley said, looking worried. "You know the Frogs would just love to get that kind of financial hook into the country."

Cromwell Oliver Varley, looking every inch the proper English gentleman with his enormous handlebar mustache, was Ellen's son by her previous marriage, a tough and hard-headed sort who took his duties as eldest son of the Perdicaris estate quite seriously. Like Ellen, he was still a British subject, and solidly of two opinions—that *all* golliwogs would be best off civilized under English rule, and that French colonial ambitions must be blocked at all costs. The French maintained a heavy presence in the country, though Morocco was still independent.

At least for now.

"Probably not, Crom," Perdicaris said thoughtfully as he used his fork to dismantle the delicately browned halibut before him. "I imagine they'll dangle the prospect in front of him like a carrot on a stick. They'll want their pound of flesh from the Sultan, no doubt, and they'll want him desperate enough to agree." He made a sour face. "Endless politics."

Perdicaris looked out toward the north, where night was falling across the Straits, and the Spanish coast west of Tarifa was a shadow below hilltops catching the last rays of a fast-setting sun.

To the northeast, one of the new leviathans hung in the evening sky, making her way upwind through the straits. Black smoke spilled from four stacks amidships, and gold sunlight touched her aft superstructure. Perdicaris couldn't make out her colors. She might be British, putting in at Gibraltar on the far side of the Algeciras headland…or she could be French, returning to her berthing cradle at Marseille. Potent symbols of modern technology and military might, the airships dominated current diplomatic thought. All of the colonial powers had them now, and every nation that wanted to be taken seriously on the world stage was building them at a frantic pace. They tended to cow the locals and warn aggressive rivals "hands off!"

Politics…

France now possessed at least a dozen airships, and was using them to force concessions from the squabbling, scrapping states of North Africa. She had her greedy eye on Morocco, and had only recently signed the so-called *Grand Entente* with Great Britain to secure rights to the nation in exchange for Britain having a free hand in Egypt. That news now had most of Morocco's citizens in an uproar.

Spain, too, wanted Morocco for herself. So did Germany, for that matter; they were eying Casablanca as a coaling station for their Navy. The whole world, it seemed, was teetering on the brink of the precipice, and all anyone could seem to think of in response was to build more of those damned airships.

The four of them, Perdicaris and Ellen, Cromwell and Beatrice, his wife, ate in silence for a moment. Ellen's three other adult children were elsewhere this evening.

Tangiers was a thriving, cosmopolitan city with a population of about 40,000, half of them Muslims, the rest divided between 10,000 Jews and some 9,000 Europeans, most of them Spanish nationals, but including sizable French and British communities. At 64, Perdicaris was the unofficial head of Tangiers' expatriate community, an elder statesman of considerable wealth and prestige. He'd written several books on Morocco, and knew the country—the last independent Islamic nation of North Africa— very well indeed. He loved it deeply, even while detesting the incestuous and treacherous local politics, and hated the idea of France or Spain or anyone else coming in and wringing the place dry.

But there was very little he could do about the vultures circling Morocco personally. El-Aziz was determined to modernize his country, and sought European help and advice to do so. But his need for money to fund his hobbies had built up a large foreign debt, and other European nations were only too willing to...help. For a price, of course.

Beatrice Varley sipped her wine, then dabbed genteelly at her lips with her napkin. "Well, I'm sure the golliwogs will listen to *you*, Father," she said, breaking the long silence. "Perhaps you can persuade them to look to Great Britain for help."

Perdicaris gave her a pained expression. "I *do* wish you wouldn't call them that, Bea."

"What, golliwogs? Why not? Crommy does...and that's what they *are*."

"They are a proud and honorable people, descendants of an ancient race. Their customs are different, but that doesn't necessarily mean that ours are *better*."

"Oh, Father, you can't mean that!" Beatrice said, making a face of her own. "Do you know that the other day, when Mother and I needed to take a sedan chair to the marketplace, the local Mussulmen actually *refused* to take us? They declared that they would *never* carry a dog of a Christian anywhere! We needed to get four *Jews* who were willing to take us! It was *so* humiliating!"

"Then count yourself fortunate that you could find *anyone* to help!" Perdicaris snapped. "Or next time, take one of the horses!"

"Now, Dear, don't be cross," Ellen told him. "It *is* rather tiresome trying to travel any distance in this country with no roads worthy of the name!"

"I don't care what you call the locals," Beatrice added, "they have become entirely too uppity! Why, do you know there was a *riot* in front of the British consulate today? Locals throwing stones and screaming threats—"

One of the household monkeys, a tailless, ginger-furred Barbary macaque named Mimi, shrieked agreement from the veranda railing, then proceeded to eat a pilfered handful of orange blossoms.

"That's right, Mimi!" Cromwell said, laughing. "You tell him!"

Ellen gestured to a maid standing stoically nearby. "You may serve the meat course, Dear."

"Yes, Ma'am."

"So..." Ellen continued, tactfully changing the subject, "how far do you think the Sultan will go with his modernization program?" she asked. "Roads? A railroad, perhaps?"

"Ha!" Cromwell said, leaning back as another maid removed the empty plate in front of him. He gestured toward the distant airship and its roiling black cloud of smoke. "How about one of those newfangled leviathans? A gold-plated one!"

"Good heavens," Beatrice said. "A flying battleship? Why?..."

Cromwell shrugged, pulling at one waxed tip of his mustache. "Why not? The young fool likes toys so much—"

A loud slam sounded from downstairs. "What was that?" Perdicaris asked, looking about. The sounds of yelling and wildly barking dogs were rising now from the servants' quarters.

"It must be Hildegard and Alfonse going at it again," Ellen said, rising from the table. Their German housekeeper and the French-Zouave chef were often at one another's throats. "I'll go see—"

A bloodcurdling shriek sounded from below, and Perdicaris rose. "No, Dear. This sounds like something more than a fit of temper..." Throwing down his napkin he left the veranda and started down the stairs, Cromwell and the women close behind him.

The servants' quarters opened into the villa's kitchen next to the pantry. As the family came down the stone stairs, the butler came flying through the kitchen door, closely pursued by three swarthy, bearded men that Perdicaris at first thought were household guards. That impression was immediately lost; the invaders carried rifles, and they wore black *djellabas* rather than scarlet and white. One of them struck the butler from behind with the butt of his rifle, sending the man sprawling to the stone floor.

"Who the devil are you?" Perdicaris demanded. He shifted to Jebli, the Moroccan-Arabic dialect common to the northwestern part of the country. They were clearly Berber tribesmen. "What is it you want?"

"Silence, dog!" one of the intruders snapped in Jebli. "Down! *Down!*"

One of them grabbed Perdicaris from behind and forced him to his knees. More of the raiders were pouring in from the outside. Rough hands grabbed his arms, binding his wrists tightly behind him with leather strips. Cromwell lunged forward, but an invader slammed a rifle butt against his head, knocking him down. Beatrice screamed, but one of the Berbers hit her violently with an elbow to the side of her head and she fell as well. Cromwell, stunned and bloody, tried to crawl toward her, but a grinning Berber grabbed him by his hair and held a wickedly curved *koummya* to his throat.

"Do not move, Christian," the man said, grinning through his beard. "Do not move or I will slice you ear to ear!"

Hildegard, the housekeeper had made it to the newly installed telephone in the hall and was screaming into the receiver. "Operator! Operator! Help! Robbers!" Then she, too, was clubbed down from behind, and another raider cut the wire with his knife.

Perdicaris wondered if she'd gotten through. The phone, one of the few in the country, was on a direct line to the American consulate in Tangiers. If she'd gotten a connection, Sam Gummere would hear about this.

Perdicaris had no idea what the U.S. consul general would be able to do about it, though. He was fifteen minutes away from the villa by a fast horse, and *so* much could happen in a quarter of an hour....

One of the Berber tribesmen had grabbed Ellen from behind. He laughed as she struggled wildly in his grip, pounding her fists uselessly against his arms. "Shall we bring these women as well?" he called.

"Leave them," the leader of the raiders snapped. He pointed at Perdicaris and his son-in-law. "These two. Bring them!"

"No!" Ellen shrieked. Her captor punched her hard, and she fell.

"Ellen!" Perdicaris yelled, trying to reach her, but two Moors grabbed him from either side, lifting him by his bound arms and dragging him toward the door.

The leader knelt beside Ellen and brought a *koummya* to her face. "If we are followed, your husband will die," he said in thickly-accented English. "And then we will come back and slowly cut you and your children into very small pieces. You understand?"

Ellen nodded, a terrified jerking of her head. The raider smiled, patted her cheek, and put the knife away. "Good. We understand one another."

Outside in the evening air, his captors held Perdicaris upright while more raiders came around the corner of the villa leading horses from the stable. One held the big chestnut steady while the other helped Perdicaris step up into the saddle, a difficult scramble with his hands tied. They put Cromwell on the bay as another Moor appeared riding Ellen's black, took the reins of

Perdicaris' horse, and led him toward the villa's gate. Perdicaris saw the bodies of two household guards there, their slashed throats glistening scarlet in the dimming light.

The leader had a hurried, whispered exchange with his men. Six were on horseback—on horses from Perdicaris' stables. The rest, on foot, faded away into the trees surrounding the villa. The leader gave a sharp command, and the eight mounted men began threading their way down the path descending the eastern side of the hill. This abduction, Perdicaris knew, had been carefully planned and meticulously executed by a band of men both ruthless and efficient. They'd known exactly where they were going and who to take; he was just glad the raiders hadn't taken Ellen or Bea or one of the other adult children at the villa.

And, of course, he knew what was happening. Bandits and Berber chieftains in the Rif, the mountainous region of northern Morocco, were notorious for kidnapping Europeans from time to time, holding them for ransom and for concessions from the Sultan's government. Just the previous year, an English journalist named Walter Burton Harris had been taken by a bandit named Raisuli, and released in exchange for some of Raisuli's imprisoned men. This raid was probably intended for the same sort of thing. If he and Cromwell could remain cool and collected, they should probably come through this intact.

As they rode, Perdicaris quickly became tired, his legs aching as he grasped the horse with his knees. Having his hands tied made staying balanced on the saddle difficult. He tried clinging to the cantle behind his seat, but his fingers were already stiff and swollen, making them clumsy.

"Where are you taking us?" he asked the leader, who was riding alongside his horse.

"We ride to Zinnat," the leader told him. "You will do what we say, or I myself will kill you both." He said it in a matter-of-fact monotone, without emotion. He might as well have been discussing the weather.

And what, Perdicaris wondered, *is at Zinnat, a small village in the hills nine miles southeast of Tangiers?* As a bandit hideout, it seemed too close to the city.

But then again, this was a large and very rugged country. It would be easy for a band of Berber tribesmen and their captives to simply be swallowed up.

A shout sounded in the deepening darkness off to the right. What was that...an army patrol? Perdicaris felt a stab of panic. The bandits might well kill their prisoners rather than let them be rescued.

At the leader's command, the mounted party broke into a hard, jogging trot, and Perdicaris' thighs and knees screamed in protest. The Moor leading his horse lashed his own mount with his reins, urging it forward into a gallop.

"Wait!" Perdicaris called. "Please...slow down! I can't..."

He swayed in the saddle, unsteady...and then his mount stumbled on loose and uneven ground and fell, and Perdicaris was unable to jump clear.

With a sharp, screaming white explosion of pain, he felt something in his right leg snap as he hit the ground.

"Call for you, Sir," the butler said. "It's the consulate."

Samuel R. Gummere looked up from his plate, irritated. *Why do they always call at dinner?* "Very well. I'll take it in the den." He dabbed at his bushy mustache with a linen napkin. "Excuse me, will you, Sir Arthur?"

"Of course, Samuel."

Leaving the table and his distinguished dinner guest, he walked into the next room and picked up the phone. "Gummere here."

"Sir, this is the operator at the Consulate," said the voice on the other end of the line. He sounded excited. "I think there's a problem out at the Place of Nightingales..."

He listened for several minutes, thanked the operator, then returned to the dinner table with a worried expression. His dinner guest was Sir Arthur Nicholson, the British minister.

"Good Lord. What's happened, Samuel?" Sir Arthur asked.

"Ion Perdicaris," Gummere replied. "You know him?"

"Of course. Wealthy expatriate. British wife. Something of a big noise within the expat community. And a bit of a playboy as well, I gather."

"He's been kidnapped."

"I say!..."

"We don't have any details as yet. A housekeeper managed to telephone the consulate and reported bandits. The local police went out there and found Perdicaris' wife and stepdaughter in hysterics, and the house in an uproar."

"Do we know who did it?"

"Not yet. I don't mind telling you, Sir Arthur, that this is damned serious. The locals have been thoroughly stirred up since they got wind of your Anglo-Franco entente, you know. If some bandit out of the Rif can kidnap a man like Perdicaris, no foreigner will be safe."

"Indeed. What will you do?"

Gummere sighed. "Go out to the Perdicaris house and see for myself. Talk with Mrs. Perdicaris. And then…"

"Yes?"

"I suppose I'm going to have to cable Washington."

"I do wish I could help you, here. Unfortunately, our agreement with the French rather precludes our direct involvement. You will have whatever support I can offer, however."

Leaving dinner unfinished, they hurried out into the night.

May 19, 1904

"What was that you were saying last night, Father?" Cromwell Varley asked in an acid tone that stopped just short of mockery. The band had stopped to rest, and Perdicaris and his son-in-law were leaning against a massive tree. "Something about them being 'a proud and honorable people, descendants of an ancient race?' Something about them having 'different customs that—'"

"For God's sake, Crom. That's enough."

"Sorry…"

"Up, you two," the Berber leader ordered. "On your horses…"

The pain in Perdicaris' leg had faded some, but remained a throbbing ache verging on agony and he needed help to stand. The Berber leader had splinted the break with cut branches and leather strips below his right knee, but then the nightmare ride had continued, with him perched two-to-a-saddle in front of one of the raiders.

At least he was still alive. For a few horrible minutes after his fall, he'd thought they were going to shoot him; they'd been discussing that as an option. But eventually the leader had declared that the Christian was more valuable alive than dead, and they'd put him back on a horse.

The ride continued through the night, a nightmare of pain and dread.

By early morning, they reached the village of Zinnat, a miserable place of dirty hovels and mud-brick huts. A crowd of locals had gathered about them as they rode in, a motley collection of old men and children, of bearded warriors and veiled women, and all of them, it seemed, were screaming for the deaths of the "two Christian dogs."

Christians, apparently, were not popular out here at the edge of mountains and desert.

Perdicaris was dragged from the horse, and his leg flared in agony when he tried to stand. He almost fell, but numerous hands clutched his arms and his clothing, and he was roughly pulled forward.

"Kill them!" someone yelled in the local Arab dialect. "Kill them!"

"*Stop!*"

The command in Jebali-Arabic brought instant silence to the village center. The mob parted, and a tall man in a black *djellaba*, with a bushy black beard and a fierce expression, stepped forward. The *qob*, the robe's pointed hood, was pulled up to frame the man's face, giving him the look of a high priest from Hell.

"These men are under my personal protection," the man said. He didn't shout, but he projected the words with the reverberation of an actor on the stage, powerful and sharp. Like an actor, he raised one hand in a supremely theatrical gesture. "I am the Raisuli!" he declared in English. "Chief of the Jbala, Sharif of Tetuoan, and Lord of the Rif! And you..." He made a sweeping gesture that was part bow, part welcome. "You are my honored guests!"

And Perdicaris knew they were now in the hands of Mulai Ahmed ibn-Muhammed er Raisuni.

Most English-speakers who'd heard of him knew him as Raisuli. Raisuli or Raisuni, the man had a flamboyant reputation as a Berber chieftain and, depending upon how you looked at it, as either a revolutionary hero or a bandit. He'd come to Perdicaris' attention with last year's kidnapping of that journalist, and he'd heard a lot about Raisuli since, both good and bad.

He was cousin and foster-brother to Abd el-Saduk, the Pasha of Tangiers, a man who'd tricked Raisuli and held him chained to a dungeon wall for four years. There was, Perdicaris knew, no love lost between the two. Reportedly, one of el-Saduk's emissaries to Raisuli had been tied down on a table while copper coins heated red-hot were gently placed upon the shrieking man's eyeballs.

And there were stories of even more bloodthirsty acts.

Despite this, by all reports he was a charming and chivalrous man, generous to his people and gallant toward his hostages. Nevertheless, Perdicaris knew that if he or Cromwell became inconvenient, Raisuli would not hesitate to kill them.

"Untie them!" Raisuli told his men. As their wrists were freed, the chieftain turned to face them. "I have prepared a tent for you," he told them. "You will be allowed to rest, and be given food and water. If there is anything you need, you need but ask."

"We need a doctor for my father," Cromwell said. "He fell on the ride here. I think his leg is broken."

"We have no doctors here," Raisuli said, sounding concerned. "But I will see what we can do when we get to Tetuoan. Hamad! Mustafa! Carry Mr. Perdicaris to the tent. And be gentle!"

Tetuoan? That was a large town on the River Martil, perhaps forty miles southeast of Tangiers, just south of Cape Black, one of only two major Moroccan ports on the Mediterranean. Its proximity to the sea—the place was just five miles up the river from the coast—gave Perdicaris a brief stab of hope.

Hope faded, however, as he thought about how very far he would be from Ellen and the Place of Nightingales.

❦ ⚜ ❦

"These demands are preposterous!" Secretary of State John Milton Hay threw the cable down on the president's desk.

Across the desk, Theodore Roosevelt, 26th President of the United States, stared back at him through his familiar pince-nez. "I know, John," he said softly. "The question is…what are we going to do about them?"

William Howard Taft, Roosevelt's close friend and the Secretary of War, was seated to Hay's right. "I don't know, Mr. President," he said, scratching the side of his nose. "This Sultan of Morocco…what's his name?"

"El-Aziz," Roosevelt said.

"Yes. We might, ah, *encourage* him to meet these demands."

"By all accounts, Mr. Taft," Hay said, "the Sultan is dead broke. Just how is he to come up with this kind of money?"

The latest cable from the consulate in Tangiers had listed the ransom demands of a Berber tribesman named Raisuli: $70,000 in gold, freedom for some of Raisuli's men held by the Moroccan government, safe passage for him and his men, the ousting of the current pasha of Tangiers and governorship of the city, and complete control over two of the richest districts of northern Morocco.

"Perhaps if we offer to negotiate—" Taft began.

"Damn it, William!" Roosevelt shouted, slamming his fist on the cable. "We gave the damned Barbary Pirates what for in 1805, and again in 1815! We made it clear: America will *not* pay tribute to pirates and brigands, and we will *not* tolerate attacks upon our citizens!"

"Actually, Mr. President," Hay said, "the Barbary Pirates are no more. This is the government of Morocco we're dealing with, and I would remind you that Morocco is our friend. Our very *close* friend. They were the first nation in the world to recognize the United States, remember, all the way back in 1777. We can't just go in and force them to pay ransom to some mountain bandit."

"I don't see why not!" Roosevelt growled. "We have a navy. If we park a few battleships off Morocco's coast, the young Sultan will see reason soon enough!"

Hay sighed. All he'd ever wanted to do was write literature and poetry. He was quite a good writer, he thought, but somehow he kept getting dragged into politics. He'd been one of Abraham Lincoln's private secretaries, and had stood by the great man's deathbed after he'd been shot in Ford's Theater. He'd been assistant Secretary of State under President's Hayes and Garfield, and McKinley's ambassador to the United Kingdom. Then McKinley had made him his Secretary of State, but McKinley had been shot by a madman anarchist in 1901, and his vice president had succeeded him.

And he'd continued serving as Teddy Roosevelt's Secretary of State ever since.

But he still wanted simply to be a writer. His biography of Lincoln had helped shape the public's perception of the man, and polished Lincoln's image. His anonymously published *The Bread-Winners* had been a scathing indictment of the corruption and violence behind organized labor. Damn it all, he wanted to make a *difference*...

"Mr. President," Hay said, "we have a treaty of friendship with Morocco. They are not the enemy! Our enemy is Raisuli!"

"Yes, but we may have some trouble coming the grips with the man," Roosevelt said. "Hiding out in the mountains, you know." He looked thoughtful for a moment. "What do we know about this Perdicaris fellow? Odd name…"

Hay opened a folder which contained what he'd been able to learn since receiving the cable that morning. "Ion Perdicaris, sixty-four years old. Greek-American. Born in South Carolina in 1840, son of a wealthy Greek national named Gregory Perdicaris, who was naturalized as a U.S. citizen and served as the American consul to Greece. The family moved to Trenton, New Jersey in 1846, where Gregory helped organize the Trenton Gas Company. Ion is quite wealthy…something of a playboy, I gather. He had an affair with the wife of a British telegraph engineer in the 1870s; she ran off to Morocco with him and her four children. He still has extensive properties in Trenton, in England, and in Tangiers, where he seems to be a kind of elder statesman, looking after the affairs of foreign residents there…"

"Playboy or not," Roosevelt said, "the man is an American citizen. He is our responsibility!"

"But sir—"

"Look, John, I'm not suggesting we declare war on Morocco. No, of course not! But the South Atlantic Squadron is at this moment en route to Tenerife for coaling. From there it's just eight hundred miles to Tangiers. Seven modern warships, with a compliment of U.S. Marines! That should make the sultan see reason, and warn this Raisuli fellow not to abscond with our citizens!"

"Yes, sir."

"Any ideas, William?"

Taft looked uncomfortable. "As to how to project our power? I'll have some of my people look into that. Offhand, I'd say our best bet might be to land Marines in Tangiers, first to defend our consulate there, and…well…if we need to gain leverage over the Moroccan government, we might seize the customs house on the dock in Tangiers. That would tie up a lot of Morocco's income."

"Hit 'em where it hurts, eh?" Roosevelt nodded. "Right in the pocketbook! I like it!"

"Even if we get the Morocco government to cooperate," Hay said, "that still won't give us any real leverage over Raisuli. He could take the ransom, then kill Perdicaris anyway."

"If he does," Roosevelt said, clenching his fist again, "we will crush him!"

"Yes, Mr. President. But how? We have no idea where Raisuli is holding our man."

"If I may, gentlemen," Taft said, "there *is* a possibility..."

"What is it, William?"

"One of our new leviathan aerial warships—the *Cleveland*—is in Newport right now, completing a refit. We could dispatch her to join the South Atlantic Squadron, then deploy to Tangiers."

"To what end, Mr. Taft?" Hay asked.

"As Secretary of State, Mr. Hay," Taft replied slowly, "you should know that sometimes diplomacy requires the projection of force, or the *threat* of force. Our fleet will dominate Tangiers, but we may need to proceed inland, to seek out Raisuli and punish him if he harms Perdicaris."

"I'm not sure I have much confidence in these flying battleships," Hay said.

"Nonsense, John!" Roosevelt said, beaming. "I became vice president on the strength of my personal motto: 'speak softly and carry a big stick!' A battleship is a *particularly* big stick, let me tell you! And when I became President, I swore that America's new sky fleet would 'become the envy of the world!' This will do it, by thunder. This will *do* it!"

"Are you sure, sir, that you're not gunning for the Republican National Convention?" Hay said. "That's coming up next month—"

"John!" Taft said, shocked. "How can you say that?"

"Simply an observation," Hay said. "President Roosevelt hasn't won this office on his own yet, and might not even take the nomination. It occurs to me that he might use this...this incident to garner political support."

"And what if I am, John? What if I am? One way or another we *will* get Perdicaris back, and if that happens to give us an edge politically, then *bully!*"

May 20, 1904

"Give us lift, Mr. Winnefield!"

Commander William Henry Hudson Southerland stood on the bridge of the protected aerial cruiser *Cleveland*, hull number CV-19, and felt the shift beneath his feet as the ship stirred in her berthing cradle, then moved slowly upward.

A *Denver*-class cruiser had a loa—her length overall—of 308 feet, 9 inches, and fully laden she massed 3,570 tons. Watching crowds on the ground outside cheered and hurled headgear into the air, but Southerland scarcely heard them. His full attention was focused on the ship, her attitude, and the young rating standing at the engine room telegraph beside him.

"We have positive lift, Captain," Winnefield reported.

"Helm, bring us to a heading of one-two-zero," he said.

"Course one-two-zero, aye-aye, Captain," the helm officer reported.

Southerland felt the slightest of tugs as a gust of wind caught the ship, and the stately pivot as she turned in place.

"Ship now on a heading of one-two-zero, sir."

Southerland glanced at the altitude markings up the side of the berthing tower. The bridge was now level with the fifty-foot mark, meaning they had about ten feet beneath the keel. "Take us up, Helm. Set altitude to one hundred feet."

"Altitude to one hundred feet, aye-aye, sir."

Determining a sky ship's altitude was far more art than science. At low altitudes, where precision was vital, leadsmen at the bow would actually throw weighted lines over the rail and report the distance between ground and keel, just as riverboats checked their depth on the Mississippi. At higher altitudes, barometers were used, but these depended on knowing the current barometric pressure at the surface for an accurate reading, and guesswork was as important in taking a reading as the measurement itself.

"Altitude one hundred feet, plus or minus ten, sir."

There was always some imprecision in the reading.

"Very well. Slow ahead, Mr. Cabot."

"Slow ahead, Captain, aye-aye." Cabot grasped both arms of the engine room telegraph, pulled them all the way back with a harsh, clattering ring, then shoved them forward to slow.

In answer, the skyship's powerful ducted fans aft spooled up as the engine room applied thundering power, and the vessel began gliding smoothly forward.

She will be giving an impressive show to the civilians below, Southerland thought. The *Cleveland* was long and lean, a shark of the skies, a white hull with relatively low deck houses. Originally designed as an oceangoing vessel with two sloop-rigged masts set ahead and aft of her twin stacks, she'd been hurriedly converted to a skyship with the addition of massive electroid-lift tanks and stabilizers along her sides, and the ducted screws aft that provided her motivating power. She retained her foremast and twin smokestacks, but her designers had dispensed with the mizzen. There were still men within the Navy Department, Southerland knew, who firmly believed that ships, both on sea and in sky, *must* have functional masts and a full spread of sails. After all, what would happen if the boilers burst or a screw threw a blade? He found the knowledge that the *Cleveland* still possessed—by Navy regulations—a sail locker filled with yard upon yard of canvas, vastly amusing.

The journey into the future, Southerland reflected, *is too often made in fits and starts and infuriating stops, with progress shackled by narrow minds and an abysmal lack of imagination.*

"She seems to be responding well, Captain," the ship's Executive Officer said. His name was Harvey Brandt, and he was a lieutenant commander from Topeka, Kansas, an unlikely hometown for a naval officer. He seemed competent enough when it came to aerial deployments, however.

"She is," Southerland replied. "It remains to be seen how she'll do over the Sahara. How's the crew?"

A ship's XO was primarily concerned with the functioning of the crew and internal matters, while the captain handled overall strategy and things happening outside the ship. "As well as can be expected, sir. They're still getting their sky legs."

"Meaning some of them would rather be on the water than in the clouds?"

"They're shaping up well, sir."

"Keep them at it. I want daily drills during our Atlantic passage, anything and everything you can hit them with while in flight. I want this crew *tight* by the time we reach Tenerif."

"Yes, sir. They'll do their duty."

"I want more than adherence to duty, Number One. I want *perfection*."

May 22, 1904

Ion Perdicaris had been a hostage for four days, and chafed at the loss of his freedom. His leg, still splinted, hurt like hell and had developed nasty-looking black and red bruises down his calf. He was no doctor, but he was pretty sure that the fibula—the small, supporting bone running down the outside of the larger tibia—had broken. Raisuli's court physician had examined the leg, and prescribed a green paste to be rubbed into the affected area.

Perdicaris doubted that the stuff was doing any good. At least it wasn't the tibia that had broken, or, worse, the femur in the upper leg! That would have left him completely crippled. At least he could still get around with help from a thick wooden staff.

Other than his leg, however, life in Raisuli's Tetuoan palace was quite comfortable. Raisuli was more gracious host than captor, and he seemed to be doing all he could to make his two European guests comfortable. This evening, Perdicaris was reclining on cushions in the courtyard outside, eating dates and watching the *guedra*, a traditional dance of welcome among the Blue Peoples.

"*Guedra*," pronounced, roughly "*gay*-dra," meant "gourd" or "cooking pot," and referred to the gourd with a stretched leather head used as a drum. It was also the name of the dance, of the dancer on her knees now in front of him, of the heartbeat rhythm of the drums, and of the ritual itself, which was performed as a blessing to welcome visitors to the tribe.

Cromwell reclined next to Perdicaris. His lip curled. "Why is she blue?"

"She's one of the Blue People," Perdicaris replied. "One of the Tuareg tribes. See her dark blue robe? That deep, indigo dye in her robe stains her skin like that."

"Ha! I thought she might be a woad-painted Pict. You'd think she would wash once in a while."

"In the desert? Besides, they think it's a mark of beauty." He picked up a date and examined it. "Show some respect, Cromwell.

They're honoring us with the *guedra*. See how she's constantly flicking her middle fingers and thumbs? She's flicking blessings at us from her soul. Blessings and good energy from the universe."

"Sometimes, Father," Cromwell said shaking his head, "I think you've gone native."

Perdicaris almost gave Varley a sharp retort, but held it back. If captivity was grating on Perdicaris, it must be ten times worse for his son-in-law, who knew little of Moroccan culture, and had little patience with local customs. A confrontation with him here and now would serve no purpose.

The dance picked up in tempo and in energy, the *guedra* swaying hypnotically as she leaned back on her heels and continued to flick blessings into the audience with her fingers. She'd draped the train of her robe up and over her tiara so that it hung down across her chest, and she was reaching out from behind the cloth, symbolizing reaching out from darkness, from ignorance.

Perdicaris found the presentation interesting on several levels. Raisuli, he knew, was a chieftain of the Jbala tribe which, though also Berber, was different from the Tuareg. The Jbala were not of the Blue People, and the fact that one of their women was here suggested that Raisuli had forged an alliance with them, and that was a fact worth noting. The Tuareg men were fierce warriors, more so even than the Jbala. The Tuareg were also guardians of the trade routes across the Sahel to the south and the endless Sahara to the west. That suggested the Raisuli might have forged alliances from across all of North Africa.

And that, too, was worth knowing.

Raisuli joined them, dropping to the ground next to Perdicaris. "And how are you enjoying my B'sala?" he asked, indicating the woman.

"Very much, sir. I must say, though, that I'm surprised to see one of the Tuareg here with the Jbala."

Raisuli gave him a startled look. "And I am surprised, sir, that you know the difference! Well done!"

"B'sala. Is she one of your women?"

Raisuli laughed. "Certainly not! Among the Blue People, the women are in charge! They think of themselves as the equal of men, and they even go unveiled. That one would never listen to me!"

Perdicaris nodded. He'd heard that among some Tuareg, the women did not wear the veil—a most un-Islamic custom!—while the men covered their noses and mouths. The belief, as he understood it, was that the mouth needed to be covered to protect a man from evil spirits...but women, being life-givers and strong in the magic of life, were safe.

As long as Perdicaris had lived in Morocco, he still found the peoples surprising and complex.

Raisuli seemed to be in a good mood, and Perdicaris dared to change the subject. "Is there word about the negotiations?" he asked. "Might we be released soon?"

"The negotiations continue," Raisuli said. "I must tell you, my friend, that I will be most sad if I must kill you. But I have told the government that if any attempt is made to attack me, I *will* kill the two of you instantly."

"My God..."

"You must understand that killing you would be the only means I'd have left of discomfiting that pig of a sultan," Raisuli said with a shrug of his shoulders. "Do not fear. Your death will be a swift one...and honorable. And meanwhile...why worry about what may never happen? Enjoy the lovely B'sala, and relax!"

He'd talked about killing them without expression. Perdicaris was reminded that they were in the hands of a man who would be willing to die to protect them...yet kill them instantly if they became a liability. It was a chilling thought.

The dance approached its climax, the woman's chest heaving beneath her robe, her braids snapping as she rolled her head, her hands a blur as she dispensed her blessings. The drumbeat grew faster... faster... *faster...* The crowd clapping and shouting, "*Wahad! Wahad! Wahad!...*"

And then the dancer collapsed, deep in a self-induced trance.

And Perdicaris wondered if there was any hope for the two of them at all.

May 28, 1904

Nine days out of Kingston, the *Cleveland* drifted into the port at Tenerife. Located at the northeastern end of the island, Santa de Tenerife Cruz was the capital of the Canary Islands, and an important coaling station for several navies.

The seven ships of the South Atlantic Squadron already lay in the harbor, completing taking on coal. Semaphore messages flashed between the *Brooklyn*, the squadron's flagship, and the deck of the airborne cruiser. The squadron, under the command of Admiral French Ensor Chadwick, was completing coaling operations, and would be departing for Tangiers later that night. Cleveland was to take on coal and follow the fleet to Tangiers "at the earliest possible moment."

Normally, the *Cleveland* carried 467 tons of coal in her bunkers, giving her a range of some 2,200 nautical miles at the modest speed of ten knots. Kingston to the Canaries, however, was a distance of almost 2,900 nautical miles and the orders from the War Department had said "with all available speed," so the *Cleveland* had taken on extra coal before embarkation—a full 675 tons, and even with that she'd arrived at her first waypoint with her bunkers all but empty.

Though designated as a protected light cruiser, the USS *Cleveland* was more properly a gunboat, a coastal defense craft and escort first authorized by Congress in 1899 during the build-up of the U.S. Navy in the wake of the Spanish-American War. She was designed to protect America's foreign interests in the Caribbean and in Latin America, and so far as her captain was concerned, she was not exactly designed nor equipped to serve as a projection of American power halfway around the world.

But his orders were explicit and bordered on frantic. He was to join the South Atlantic Squadron no later than 30 May, and assist in operations at Tangiers to rescue American citizens detained by foreign powers.

Southerland was an armchair historian, and had read Mahan. It sounded like the Barbary Wars all over again.

In an all-hands evolution, the *Cleveland*'s crew had attacked the mountain of coal awaiting them at the station, shoveling it into the ship's empty bunkers. Southerland had seen fanciful illustrations of "sky-ports" planned for leviathan vessels of the future, towers that could secure floating warships and load them with coal and other expendables.

The reality, however, was back-breakingly hard-labor in heat and billowing coal dust and a banging cacophony of noise as gangs of half-naked and soot-caked men shoveled black rock

from shore to dockside hoists to deck and down into the hungry
bunkers. By nightfall, they were under way once more, following
the fleet north up the coast of Africa.

Tangiers was 680 nautical miles northeast from Tenerife.

At fifteen knots, they would arrive in 45 hours.

May 31, 1904

Man and boy, Gunner's Mate Chief Gustave "Gus" Chisolm
had been a Navy man for forty years. At twelve, he'd been a
powder monkey on board the USS *Kearsarge*, and watched
the Confederate raider *Alabama* sink beneath the waves off
Cherbourg, France. At forty-six, he'd served on the *Olympia*
with Dewey at Manila Bay, when the U.S. Asiatic Squadron had
annihilated the Spanish fleet at a cost of only one man dead—a
fatality due to heatstroke rather than Spanish fire.

And now, at fifty-two, Gus Chisolm was more than ready to
retire. He'd seen the world, and decided that *nothing* he'd seen
out there could match his small family homestead outside of
Easton, Maryland. He'd lived through stunning changes in naval
service, from steam power backed up by sail to these newfangled
flying gunboats, which so far as he was concerned spelled the end
of the real navy. Life on board the *Cleveland* was much like life
on board the old *Kearsarge*...but it was strange to look down over
the railings to see the ocean's surface, and to be immune from
the battering of waves in a full gale. A storm was still no joke on
board a lev, but it made a difference not having black walls of icy
water crashing in over the bow.

Working aboard ship, though, had not changed much in
principle. Every bone in his body ached this morning after
yesterday's grueling coaling operation. Normally, a chief petty
officer worked in a supervisory position, and he'd done plenty
of that...but he'd also taken off his blouse and pitched in with
a shovel, helping to manhandle a small mountain of coal onto
the ship.

Damn, I'm getting too old for this...

"So whatcha think, Chief?" Gunners' Mate 1st Class
Lawrence Swann said, joining Chisolm at the starboard rail.
He had to shout to make himself heard. *Cleveland* was racing

along through the sky, her steam engines pounding below decks, her twin stacks belching smoke and black soot. The sere, dun landscape of the Moroccan coast drifted slowly past a few miles in the distance.

"About what?"

"This deployment. They say we have to go in and rescue some rich old guy who got himself kidnapped by bandits! How the hell are we supposed to do that in a damned *ship*?"

"In case you hadn't noticed, Swanny, this ship can fly."

"Yeah, but the rest of the squadron can't! We can't go off into the mountains alone, without support!"

"If the brass tells us to go in, we go in," Chisolm said with a philosophical detachment due more to his tiredness than to any real conviction. "We follow our orders, and we do our duty."

"That's fine for the brass, Chief. For mere mortals like us, that kind of thinking can get us *killed*!"

Chisolm was about to say something about the need to protect American citizens in foreign lands…but he held the words back and said nothing. There was a terrible, glaring problem with Swann's pessimism.

The man was *right*.

At just past five in the morning, the American squadron had slipped into the harbor of Tangiers, and Samuel Gummere breathed a sigh of relief. He wasn't entirely sure what the squadron could do, but its arrival had successfully telegraphed an important message to the local authorities. The Americans were here, and they intended to do something about the kidnapping of one of their citizens.

"This way, Mr. Gummere." His guide, the personal secretary to the Sultan's Grand Vizier, led the way down the winding, stone stairs into the prison basement. The walls to either side were sweating.

So was Gummere.

Grand Vizier Mohammad al-Muqri was the real power behind the government of Morocco. When al-Muqri had requested the presence of the American consul in the dungeon basement of Tangier's prison, there'd been, frankly, no way to politely refuse.

The dungeon was worse—*far* worse—than he'd imagined. Steel cell doors lined the walls of stone corridors. Torches lit the floor of the main room, and the prisoner stretched naked on the rack had already been reduced to bloody tatters. A bare-chested man approached the prisoner with a red-hot poker and applied its sizzling touch to a sensitive part of the man's anatomy.

Shrieks rang loud and long off the encircling walls.

Gummere closed his eyes and looked away. How was it possible for that pathetic wretch to even still be *alive* after such treatment?...

"Ah, Mr. Gummere," a tall man to one side said. "Thank you for joining us."

Mohammad al-Moqri perfectly fit the romantic western image of an African grand vizier—saturnine and dark, in white robes and with a nightmare smile. At his side was the Tangiers pasha Abd el-Rahman Abd el-Saduk. Gummere was surprised to see both men here. In his experience, such powerful figures tended to avoid dirty and unpleasant scenes like...this one.

"I...I came as soon as I got your message, sir," Gummere replied, giving a slight bow to diplomatically acknowledge the vizier's authority.

The torturer shoved the now-cooled poker back into a coal-filled and flaming brazier and selected another one. The stink—burned flesh, blood, and human excrement—was indescribable.

"I wanted you to see for yourself, Mr. Gummere, that this government is doing its best to meet the demands of your Admiral Chadwick. We captured this ruffian four days ago, one of Raisuli's men from the raid that took Mr. Perdicaris, and we have been *thoroughly* questioning him. And he has told us at last the Raisuli's location."

The prisoner watched the torturer approach with his one remaining good eye, and began screaming a rapid-fire babble of Moroccan-Arabic. Gummere didn't understand the words, but the earnest pleading and his genuine sincerity were beyond doubt.

The hot iron found another sensitive spot...a different one. Gummere winced as he heard the *hiss* under the renewed, agonized shrieks.

Turning away suddenly, he vomited onto the floor.

"Mr. Perdicaris is being held in the city of Tetuoan," Abd el-Saduk said, ignoring Gummere's reaction. "We should have known, really. He keeps court there, and it is one of his principle strongholds. He is an old enemy..."

"Why—why are you continuing to torture this man if he'd already told you that?"

El-Saduk smiled, a chilling rictus. "We need to be sure he'd telling us the truth, of course."

"You can tell your Admiral Chadwick that we have the situation well in hand," al-Moqri added. "We have plans of the Raisuli's palace, maps of the city. And you have our government's permission to use the information as you will. Just so you turn Raisuli over to us for questioning..."

June 1, 1904

"By thunder!" Roosevelt cried, appalled. "*What* was that you said?"

John Hay calmly met the President's horrified look. "I said, sir, that Mr. Perdicaris is not an American citizen." He waved the telegram he'd just received. "The Greeks just informed us through their ambassador here. Ion Perdicaris traveled to Greece in 1862 to renounce his American citizenship."

"And *why* would he do a damn-fool thing like that?"

"Apparently, Mr. President, Mr. Perdicaris, who was living in New Jersey at the time, had rather extensive properties in South Carolina. His wife's family, you understand. He was faced with the possibility that the Confederate government would seize those properties. By becoming a Greek citizen, he hoped to forestall that."

"Well...I mean...he would have renewed his citizenship after the war, wouldn't he?"

"Apparently not, Sir. The Greeks have no record of him having done so, nor do we. It seems he was unwilling to go through the naturalization process to become a U.S. citizen again."

"*Damn* the man..."

"Of course, this means there's no point in continuing the operation in Morocco," Hay said. "We don't need to rescue a *Greek* citizen—"

"The hell we don't!"

"Sir?"

"Look, Raisuli obviously *thinks* Perdicaris is an American citizen! *That's* all that matters!"

"But sir—"

"We're going to keep this news to ourselves, John. Our fleet is in Tangiers. We have Marines ready to go ashore. We *will* see this thing through!"

June 5, 1904

"Thank you all for coming, gentlemen," Admiral Chadwick said with grave formality. "We have a great deal of work to do here today and not a lot of time in which to complete it."

Including Southerland, all eight ship captains of the fleet were gathered in the officer's mess on board the USS *Brooklyn*, along with Major John Twiggs Myers, the commander of three companies of U.S. Marines attached to the South Atlantic Squadron. Southerland was standing across from Chadwick and Captain Barnes, the skipper of the *Brooklyn*, and next to Myers. Also present was Samuel R. Gummere, the American consul in Tangiers, looking curiously out of place in this solemn assembly of white Navy dress uniforms with his bowler hat and bushy mustache.

Spread out on the table in front of them was a large topographical map of the northern tip of Morocco. Chadwick dragged his finger across the paper from Tangiers to the southeast. "Tetuoan, gentleman," he said, tapping a city near the coast. "Mr. Gummere here has identified the place where they're *probably* holding Perdicaris and his son."

His emphasis of the word "probably" was not reassuring.

The hand-drawn sketch of Raisuli's palace was of equal concern. More of a villa on the outskirts of Tetuoan than a "palace," it consisted of a dozen small buildings inside a compound wall, with one tower-capped building, larger than the rest, that must be the main residence. It had massively thick walls, and getting anyone out of it was going to be one hell of a problem.

"How sure are we that this is where they've got him?" Captain Aldridge, of the *Galveston*, asked. He looked up at Gummere. "How sure are your people of this information, sir?"

Southerland thought the civilian looked a bit green. *Seasickness?*

"They're not *my* people, sir. But they...they seem convinced that this is accurate."

"The question is whether or not we should act upon it," Barnes said. He looked up at Grummere. "Washington has not been exactly...helpful."

Grummere spread his hands. "All I can do is pass on what they told me. They don't want you to attack Morocco without very specific orders from them. I fear they've been flipping back and forth on this."

"Where do we stand on the negotiations?" Chadwick asked.

"Well...the government says it's making progress. And Raisuli seems inclined to reach a settlement. The sticking point appears to be his insistence that he replace el-Saduk as Pasha of Tripoli."

"I don't imagine el-Saduk is much interested in meeting that demand," one of the ship captains said.

Grummere agreed. "Not if the first thing Raisuli does upon taking power is having el-Saduk executed. Slowly..."

"My God," Chadwick said. "Raisuli is el-Saduk's *brother*..."

"Half-brother," Grummere pointed out. "And cousin..."

"Not a problem," Major Myers said. "Those two hate each other so much that things balance out."

"Yes, well, the problem as I see it, gentlemen," Chadwick told the others, "is the abysmal and wholesale corruption in this country. Everyone is being paid off by everyone else. Everyone has their hand out. And everyone is willing to betray even his closest relative if it's to their advantage."

"Perhaps, Myers said, "we could play that to *our* advantage."

"How?"

"Set one faction against another! Tell the sultan that we'll support el-Sadak against him if he doesn't do as we say. Or we tell Raisuli will support him against el-Sadak if he releases Perdicaris."

"We can't do that!" Gummere said, shocked. "We can't interfere in local politics that way!"

"Why not?" Myers shrugged. "We don't have to follow through on our promises..."

"Gentlemen," Chadwick said, holding up his hands. "Enough. The fact of the matter is that we must have authorization from the States before taking any action. And they seem to want to let the locals sort it out for themselves."

Southerland was puzzled. It had been Gummere, Washington's representative here in Tangiers, who'd specifically requested ships and troops when Perdicaris had first been taken, and Roosevelt had been startlingly quick in sending the requested force. Now, though, they were suddenly backpedaling.

And the U.S. squadron was left hanging, unable to act and, frankly, looking foolish.

"If I may, sir," Southerland said. "We do have *some* leeway when it comes to safeguarding American lives. We know where Perdicardis is being held. We could go in and get him."

"How?" Chadwick asked. "He's several miles inland..."

"We *do* have a lev, Admiral. Inland doesn't matter."

"By thunder, *that's* the ticket!" Myers said. "We transfer my Marines to the *Cleveland* and fly in to rescue our people!"

"I'm not sure we have *that* much leeway, Commander Southerland," Chadwick replied, ignoring the Marine. "No... we'll stay here at anchor and await word from Washington."

"And what about Perdicaris?" Southerland asked.

"If he's still alive now after three weeks," Chadwick said, "He can hang on for a bit longer." He looked at Gummere. "It will be up to you, sir, to put as much pressure on the local government as you can."

"To what end, Admiral?"

"Convince them to pay the ransom," Chadwick said. "I know...I know. It grates. But it's all we can do."

"Perhaps a company of Marines ashore would help press the point?"

"No, sir. I've already authorized twelve Marines to go ashore with sidearms *only*, to protect the consulate and to look after Mrs. Perdicaris. That is all I can justify until we have further orders from Washington."

"I hope to God it's enough, Admiral," Gummere said, shaking his head. "These are people who respect *force*, not gestures of friendship."

"Perhaps," Chadwick replied. "But at the moment, we're fighting with one hand tied behind our back. That somewhat limits the force we can bring to bear."

June 12, 1904

"What...*again?*" Roosevelt threw down his linen napkin and rose from the table. "That's the *fourth time* one side or the other has backed out of a solemn agreement! What is it this time?"

"Raisuli," Hay said, dropping the latest cable onto the dinner table, "has upped the ante. He now demands governorship of *four* of the wealthiest districts of Tangiers. He has also demanded a guarantee from the governments of England and of the United States that the terms of an agreement will be enforced upon the Moroccan government."

"What...we're supposed to guarantee the behavior of Morocco's sultan? Ridiculous!"

"Yes, sir."

"This damned brigand has gone too far!" Roosevelt stalked across the White House dining room to a sideboard where several newspapers lay and opened one. "Have you seen these?"

Hay nodded. "Yes, Mr. President."

Roosevelt began reading anyway. "'All available naval forces in European waters should be ordered to Tangiers...and if these measures fail, Marines should be dispatched to make a forced march into the interior to bring the outlaw to book for his crimes!'" Roosevelt held the paper up to show Hay a political cartoon. "And this!"

The cartoon showed a very tiny Sultan and his ministers staring into the mouth of a titanic cannon sprouting from the prow of a massive American warship, the barrel decorated with stars and stripes. A sheet of paper covered the gun's muzzle, reading "Secure the release of my citizen at once," and was signed "Uncle Sam."

"They're wondering why we can't have another Derna," Hay said.

In 1805, ex-consul William Eaton and Marine lieutenant Presley O'Bannon had led a force of eight Marines and several hundred Greek and Arab mercenaries across five hundred miles of desert west from Alexandria to Derna to capture the city and help end the First Barbary War. It had been the first time the American flag had been raised on foreign soil.

"It's not that simple," Roosevelt growled, slapping the paper down. "Right now, the Rif is filled to overflowing with Berber bandits and revolutionaries, encouraged by Raisuli's antics. And if Raisuli sees our forces coming, Perdicaris is as good as dead. We also have France to worry about."

Just that morning, the government in Washington had been informed that France had just signed off on a loan of 62.5 million francs, secured by the customs income of all Moroccan ports. At the same time, French troops had reinforced their garrison there, probably to counter American influence more than to protect foreign citizens, and a French leviathan cruiser, *Le Redoubtable*, was known to be patrolling the western Mediterranean.

Morocco had become a flashpoint.

"At this point, Mr. President," Hay said, "all we can do is encourage the sultan to pay the ransom...and be certain we punish this Raisuli fellow if he harms his prisoners."

"I agree. We're too far into this thing now. If we pull out and let the French handle it, we appear weak, and every two-bit bandit and pirate in the world will be jumping on our back! If we attack, Perdicaris dies...and while we know he's not a U.S. citizen, the rest of the world doesn't. If we're seen to be abandoning him just because he's not our citizen, after all this ballyhoo..."

"That would be almost as bad, yes, sir."

"We're damned if we do and damned if we don't! I want this resolved, John!"

"Yes, sir."

"I don't care how we do it, but I want this matter *finished*!"

"Yes, sir."

It was all Hay could say...even though he had no idea how he was going to pull it off.

June 18, 1904

One month...

Their captivity had not been unpleasant. Raisuli, for all his bluster and posturing, was a decent sort. *Civilized.* He loved to read, he loved to discuss history and philosophy, and his speech was that of the educated and genteel Moors of the region, rather than that of a hill bandit.

But...something was happening. The guards seemed tense and nervous... ill-at-ease. Raisuli himself seemed distracted.

Something was happening...and it wasn't good. He wondered if there'd been another breakdown in negotiations.

"I want you to promise me something, John," Perdicaris said. He stole a glance at the open door to see if a guard was listening. For the moment, they were alone. "If this goes wrong...if it looks like they're going to kill us...I don't want you hanging back for my sake."

"But—"

"No arguments!" Perdicaris slapped his painfully swollen leg, still swaddled in a splint, and winced. He was afraid to look beneath the wrappings. "I can't travel with this. If you get the chance to run, you do it!"

Varley looked stubborn. "I won't abandon you, Father, not unless there's no other way."

"Promise me! I need you to get through this, to get back to your mother! I want you to tell her..."

"Yes?"

"I want her to know that I love her."

June 21, 1904

John Hay stood behind the lectern, looking out over the convention floor. Thousands of men filled the Chicago Coliseum, a vast and open arena beneath a high, overarching dome, the rings of theater-style seats splashed by the sunlight flooding down from the half-circle windows high up at one end of the hall. Bunting in red, white, and blue hung from metal beams overhead, and the delegates talked and glad-handed and discussed back-room deals beneath a thin, blue haze of cigar smoke.

"If I may have your attention please..." he boomed out over the crowd, but the low roar of a thousand conversations continued. He picked up the gavel left on the lectern, and brought it down three times, the cracks echoing off the curving walls of the huge auditorium. "Attention, *please*."

Reluctantly, the noise died away, and the delegates turned their attention to the lone man on the stage.

In Hay's considerable experience, presidential conventions tended to be tumultuous affairs, but this one had been almost subdued by comparison. Roosevelt had been President since

1901, after McKinley's assassination, but he'd not yet won the office on his own. He was extremely popular with the people, but so far the convention delegates had been lukewarm toward the incumbent at best.

This, Hay thought, laying the telegram out on the lectern before him, *might well change that.*

"I have before me," he shouted, trying to fill that vast auditorium with his voice, "a telegram dispatched by President Roosevelt to the American consul in Tangiers and to the sultan of Morocco in Fez. It reads, in part: '*This government demands Perdicaris alive or Raisuli dead.*'"

The response was immediate and thunderous. People stood on their chairs and in the aisles, screaming and yelling, the air filled with papers and hats flung above the delegates' heads.

With one brief line, Roosevelt's nomination at this convention was assured…his re-election and place in history all but certain. They were riding now upon a tidal wave of history.

And now, Hay thought, *all we need to do is* act.

Somehow…

Semaphore flags wig-wagged between the signal tower on the *Brooklyn* and the bridge wing of the *Cleveland*, hovering fifty feet overhead. One of the *Cleveland*'s signalmen translated the movement of colored flags to Southerland as the message came up.

"'*Perdicaris alive or Raisuli dead,*'" the man translated. "'You are directed to engage enemy forces in Tetuoan if practicable to secure the safety of our citizens.' Message ends, sir."

"Thank God!" Southerland said. "Make to the *Brooklyn*: 'Message received. We will do our duty.'"

For almost three weeks, the American squadron had been all but helpless, sitting in and above the harbor at Tangiers with no purpose and no plan, embarrassingly impotent and exposed. There'd been more riots in front of the French consulate, as well as mobs calling for all foreigners to leave the country. Grummere was frantic, as was Théophile Decassé, the French foreign minister. They feared that soon no Christian would be safe, and all Americans and Europeans would be forced to flee.

And there the affair might have remained had it not been for the *Cleveland*. Where the seagoing vessels of the American

Navy were forced to remain on the water, the little flying light cruiser could travel inland, projecting military power where it was needed. Admiral Cheswick had just told him that he was free to take the *Cleveland* into enemy territory.

The big problem remained, of course; Raisuli might well kill his captives as soon as he was aware of an attack upon his position. But the fleet commanders had worked out a plan, one that gave them a chance to get into the town of Tetuoan before Raisuli's bandits knew what was happening.

Southerland pulled out his pocket watch and glanced at it.

Two more hours until sundown...

Perdicaris made his painful way out into the courtyard, where a dozen rough-looking men sat around a bonfire. He leaned awkwardly on a crutch whittled for him by someone in the band, a y-shaped branch with a stout, four-foot stem. Cromwell walked beside him, helping him negotiate the cobblestone walk.

"Ah, Mr. Perdicaris, my friend!" Raisuli stood up and greeted him. "So good of you to join us!"

"Your man said you wanted to talk to us," Perdicaris replied. With Cromwell's help, he lowered himself onto a log set near the fire.

"Yes, yes," Raisuli said, stroking his thick, black beard in a contemplative fashion. "I am afraid our time together is almost at an end."

Perdicaris gave a start, then glanced at Cromwell. Had Raisuli decided to kill them at last? Would Cromwell do as he'd been told, and attempt to escape?

"Indeed?" Perdicaris stammered. His mouth was dry. "Is... have the negotiations broken down again?"

Raisuli lowered himself down into a seat nearby. "They have not been going well...but I have arrived at a decision. I have decided to accept what has been offered to me. It's not everything... but it will suffice. You two will be released as soon as the gold arrives."

Perdicaris' head swam, and he felt himself close to passing out. "You...You're letting us go?"

"Of course. I have enjoyed our conversations, Mr. Perdicaris, but it is time for you to go home."

The shock Perdicaris felt was enough to make him wonder what might go wrong next, to once again reshuffle his life. So much could still go wrong...

Gunner's Mate Chief Gustave Chisolm climbed the ship's ladder to the O-3 deck, then turned right and headed for the bridge. His heart was pounding very nearly as loudly, he imagined, as the *Cleveland*'s engines. What the hell did the skipper want with *him*?

As a forty-year veteran, Chisolm had learned one survival skill vital above all others stowed in the sailor's ditty bag: *Don't get noticed.* When the brass saw you, chances were your life was about to become far more interesting than it had been before... and more unpleasant.

A Marine guard announced him to the Captain as he stepped onto the bridge. "GM Chief Chisolm, sir."

"Ah! Chisolm!" Southerland said. "Thank you for coming up."

"Yes, sir." It was the safest thing he could think of to say.

"I understand you're an old hand. Thirty years?"

"Forty, sir. I came in in '64."

"As a kid?"

"Powder monkey, sir. Carried bags of black powder from the ship's magazine to the gun deck." He shrugged. "You grew up kind of fast in those days."

"I can imagine." Southerland looked thoughtful. "So...your personnel records tell me you were a sailmaker later on..."

"Yes, sir. Sailmaker apprentice, anyway. That was aboard the old *Hartford*, in '76 or '77. After that, well, there wasn't as much need for sails, with everything running on steam."

"Indeed." Southerland looked out across the starboard bridge wing. It was full dark now, and the night had engulfed the beach drifting past a hundred yards or so off the beam. He appeared deep in thought. "Chisolm, I have a special assignment for you. I want you to dust off your sailmaster's skills, pull together however many deck hands you need to get the job done, and hoist the mains'l for me. Think you can do that?"

"Yes, sir...but God, *why*?"

"Because sails on the wind are a hell of a lot quieter than steam-piston engines...Lieutenant."

It took a moment for the rank to sink in. "S-sir?"

"We're counting on you, Lieutenant Chisolm, to help us sneak up on the bandits."

"Aye-aye, Captain. But...it'll be a mite tricky steering..."

"Leave that to me, Lieutenant. Right now, you go down and tell the bo'sun's chief you need some of his manpower...as much as you need. Refer him to me if he has any questions."

"But, sir—"

"That will be all, *Lieutenant*."

"Aye-aye, sir."

Bewildered, the newly-minted lieutenant fled the bridge.

June 22, 1904

Mohammed Abd Hussain was awakened by a fearful pounding racket that came down out of the night. *In Allah's name...*

Grabbing his rifle, he stepped out into the darkness of the Berber encampment, staring up at the star-clotted sky overhead. Other members of his band appeared around him, equally puzzled, equally alarmed.

"What is that noise?" Ahmed, his cousin, demanded. The horses, staked nearby, whinnied and nickered.

Mohammed scanned the skies, then pointed. Low above the hills to the east, a...a shape, completely black, drifted across the stars, obscuring some of them. Almost magically, the thunderous pounding died away, and in the eerie silence that followed, they could hear voices...voices on the wind.

"Do you understand that?" he asked Ahmed. The voices were not speaking Moroccan-Arabic, or any other dialect with which Mohammed was familiar. Ahmed spoke French, however, and a bit of Spanish.

"Gibberish," Ahmed replied. "But it sounds European."

"Europeans!" Mohammed spat into the sand. "Foreign bastards, coming to take our land!"

"Yes...but in one of their flying ships!" Ahmed said, wonder in his voice.

Mohammed had seen the foreigners' flying ships before. The straits to the north were full of them at times, plying back and forth between the Mediterranean and the Atlantic, putting in at Gibraltar, or farther north, at Marseilles. For Mohammed

Hussein, those flying technological wonders simply represented European mischief, their blasphemous tinkering with Allah's laws, and their determination to steal all that belonged to the People.

The voices continued, distant and fragmentary in the night. A brilliant light appeared, illuminating part of the mysterious shape, which hung so impossibly, so *magically* in the dark sky.

"What should we do, Cousin?" Ahmed asked. "The Raisuli—"

"The Raisuli is twenty miles from here," Mohammed said, his initial flare of anger softening to sullen acceptance. "And he has plenty of men of his own. What can we do?"

And the Berber encampment watched through the following hours as the foreign devils worked and shouted orders to the sky.

It took nearly exhausting three hours, but Lieutenant Chisolm at last gave the final order: "Now *heave*! *Heave*!..."

Twenty men lined up along the deck railing to port and starboard pulled in on the running gear, walking aft as the sail, attached by grommets to the ship's yard, slowly squeaked and struggled up the mast. *Cleveland*'s mainmast rose directly above and abaft of the bridge, and just ahead of her forward stack. As the canvas caught the wind coming in from offshore, it billowed, then grabbed hold.

On the starboard bridge wing, Southerland felt the ship begin sliding forward, and nodded to his first officer. "Now for the hard part."

Chisolm is a genuine treasure, Southerland thought. The man— without a shadow of a doubt the *oldest* lieutenant in the United States Navy—had managed to boss forty members of the ship's deck division into putting up a spread of sail that was now, slowly but quietly, nudging the *Cleveland* ahead through the night.

The big difficulty was steering the thing. Normally, the *Cleveland*'s two massive, ducted fans high in her stern could swivel far enough left or right to swing her stern port or starboard and control her course. In the water, of course, a traditional ship would simply turn using her rudder to maneuver, but for a lev things were far more complicated. And without her fan screws, powered by the ship's massive—and *noisy*—engines, things would have been damned near impossible.

Except that Southerland had sailed a 21-foot yacht during his years at Harvard, taking the *Eleanor Q* out into Boston

Harbor, around Deer Island Point and all the way to Bass Point. Although sailboats were steered primarily with a rudder, a good yachtsman also knew how to use the wind to steer, pulling in on the mains'l or letting it luff, spilling wind to bring your bow about to left or right.

The *Cleveland* now had a very different rigging configuration—a square sail instead of the *Eleanor's* triangular fore-and-aft rigged sail—but the principle was the same. By pulling in or relaxing the rigging attached to one corner of the sail or the other, it was possible to steer, after a fashion.

The *Cleveland's* speed was picking up. She would never break any records; Southerland guessed she was making headway at about five knots, compared to better than sixteen under power.

But he'd charted a straight-line course across the desert that should bring them to their final waypoint just a mile outside of Tetuoan sometime around dawn. If the offshore wind shifted, or if it died away completely, they would go back to the pounding steam engines and *damn* the racket, but so far his scheme was working well. The generators powering the *Cleveland's* electroid tanks were not silent, but they didn't warn every desert tribesman within twenty miles of their approach, either. They should be able to reach the way point almost silently, and without literally sounding an alarm in Raisuli's fortress.

That silence gave them their very best chance of success.

The sun was not yet up, but the eastern sky was quite bright, the light banishing all but the very brightest stars, and the clear, cold beacon of Venus just above the eastern horizon.

The *Cleveland* floated hove-to above a rocky patch of near-desert, her flight brought to a halt by the simple if inelegant expedient of dropping her main yard onto the top of the wheelhouse, collapsing the mains'l into a decidedly un-shipshape bundle beneath it. Anchors had been lowered, fore and aft, to arrest her drift

Major Myers studied the clear sky above the foredeck for a moment, then snapped out the order. "Sergeant Freemantle, you may take your troops ashore."

"Aye-aye, sir," the sergeant replied. Turning, he bellowed out a stentorian "First Company, man your lines! Boots to the ground!"

Marines queued up along the *Cleveland*'s maindeck railings grasped the two dozen lines cleated to the deck and hanging over the ship's side, stepped over the railings, and began abseiling down the vessel's metal hull and onto the sere landscape below. It was a perilous debarking; the *Cleveland* had been brought down to an altitude of just ten feet between ground and keel, but she still had forty feet of freeboard and hull, more than enough to injure or kill any Marine who lost his grip on the descent line. Each man wore leather gloves to keep from burning his hands raw, and carried his rifle, ammo, water, and other campaign gear slung from his back.

It was a hell of a long way down.

"Second Company! Man your lines! Boots to the ground!"

Like ants trailing one another down strings, two reinforced companies, some 240 men, slid down the ropes and began forming up on the ground below. Thankfully, only one man fell—a lance corporal in First Section, Second Company—and he escaped with a broken ankle. Sailors on the deck rigged a bos'un's chair to haul him back up to the deck and took him down to sickbay.

As the man was coming up, Myers exchanged salutes with Captain Johnson, his executive officer and the commander of Third Company, which would be staying on-board. "I'll see you in Tetuoan!" he said, his voice cheerfully carefree as he grasped a rope and stepped over the side.

"You be careful, Major," Johnson said. He sounded worried. "The natives out there are restless!"

"Whatever happens, we have got...the Maxim gun, and they have not!" he said, reciting a poem from *The Modern Traveller*, by Hilaire Belloc. In fact, no Maxim machine guns would be lowered over the side to accompany the flying column, but there were several on board the *Cleveland*, and they would be invaluable in the fight ahead, providing covering fire for the two companies marching—O'Bannon-like—across the desert.

"*Semper fi*, sir!" Johnson said, and Myers slid rapidly down the line.

His boots hit the ground with a solid *thump* and with bending knees. Myers looked up at the impossibly huge mass of the cruiser's keel hovering just above his head, then turned and walked a few dozen paces out into the desert. He needed to get away from that steel hull to get an accurate reading on his compass.

"Sir!" Freemantle said with a crisp salute. "All hands on the ground, *sir!*"

He returned the salute and pocketed the compass. "Very good, Sergeant. Form up the men, columns of four, port arms." He pointed. "*That* way."

Another salute. "Aye aye, sir!"

If Southerland's navigational skills were on target, the objective lay one mile in that direction.

"Anchors have been raised, Captain!" his XO reported.

"What about those damned Irish pennants?"

"All descent lines have been taken back aboard, sir."

"Very well." Southerland grasped the twin handles of the engine room telegraph, shoved them from "finished with engines" to "full ahead," hauled them back, then pushed them hard once more, sounding the rattling rasp of the warning bell.

Cleveland's engines began pounding once more as clouds of sooty black smoke spilled from her pipes. The waypoint where they'd dropped off Myers and his Marines lay almost directly downwind from Tetuoan. With one sail and no rudder, there was no way the cruiser could tack into the wind and, in any case, sail was far too slow and uncertain of direction when they needed to close with the objective as swiftly as possible.

Lieutenant Commander Mason, *Cleveland*'s chief engineering officer, had kept the boilers hot and steam up during the ship's impromptu sail across the desert, assuring that she would have immediate power when she needed it. In moments, *Cleveland* was plowing ahead through the clear morning sky at an estimated twelve to fifteen knots. The sun was full up above a low ridge to the east; every damned Berber between Tetuoan and here could see them now, not to mention *hear* them…but if he'd timed this right, that should no longer matter.

"You may sound battle stations, Mr. Brandt."

"Aye, Captain!" A moment later, the ship's bugler was sounding the call to combat stations.

Belching smoke, the USS *Cleveland* steamed ahead into battle.

Raisuli was at morning prayer when he was startled by gunshots and shouting, and by the more distant dull, thumping sound of steam engines. Stepping out of his stone residence and onto the patio that gave him a clear view of the sea to the east, he held his hand up to shade his eyes from the sun. Had the American ships dared to approach Tetuoan from the water?

"Lord Raisuli! Lord Raisuli!"

"What is it, Amal?"

"The foreigners! Over here!"

Hurrying around the corner of the house, Raisuli had a clear view toward the southwest. There, just coming over the western ridge beyond the town, a smear of ink-black smoke hung in the sky.

So...they'd sent one of their flying battleships against him. Who was it? The British? The French?

Not the Americans, surely. Both the French and the British had thousands of soldiers available at their legations in Tangiers, but the Americans would have, at best, a few hundred on board their small fleet. Surely they would not dare to—

Once, in Egypt, Raisuli had heard the thunderous chugging of a railway locomotive. There were plans, he knew, for the French and Spanish to bring those metal monstrosities here to Morocco. The chugging sounded like a locomotive, and at first he assumed he was hearing the sound of the leviathan's steam engines.

But the chugging dropped in pitch as it took on a whistling tone, and the south wall of his residence erupted in a flash and a cloud of smoke and flying debris.

They were actually *shelling* him! "Quickly, Amal! Organize the men! Break out the howitzers and deploy them...there! And there!"

"At once, Lord Raisuli! If God wills it!"

"*I* will it, Amal! And that should be close enough for you! *Now!*"

What he'd just shouted was perilously close to blasphemy, but the urgency of the moment superseded all else. He would worry about the theological aspects of his orders later.

If there was a later, Allah willing...

He ducked back inside the villa, grabbed his rifle—a European Krag-Johanson—then hurried downstairs.

He needed to reach the hostages...

"*Fire!*"

The foredeck five-incher boomed, sliding back on its mount with the recoil. The gun crew yanked open the breech, pulled out the smoking spent casing, and rammed a fresh round home. The gun captain raised his right hand. "Loaded!"

"*Fire!*"

Unlike the newer and heavier battleships and cruisers, a light cruiser like the *Cleveland* did not carry turret-mounted ordnance. Her biggest guns were five-inch caliber rapid-fire breech-loaders, one each mounted on her deck fore- and aft, and four more on each side, against the hull in armored casemates, for a total of ten guns.

In most aerial gunnery, the fore- and aft-mounts were at something of a disadvantage. They could traverse a full 120 degrees, but could not depress to engage targets below the ship. The casemate guns, clinging to the vessel's considerable tumblehome, *could* be depressed, though the safest refuge from a lev's gunfire was always directly below the keel. At the moment, the forward port and starboard casemates were joining in with the forward five-incher, adding their firepower to a steady bombardment of the slowly approaching target.

Southerland watched from the port-side wing of the bridge, binoculars in hand, as spouts and geysers of dirt and sand erupted from behind the villa's walls ahead, and hoped to God his intelligence was accurate. That was *supposed* to be Raisuli's residence-cum-fortress, but if their information was wrong, they were in the process of flattening some local pasha's palace while Raisuli and his men watched and jeered from the sidelines.

Thud-thud-thud! The port and starboard casemate guns joined with the forward five-incher, their combined recoils transmitted through the deck to Southerland's feet. More geysering dust from inside the compound. Fires were burning there now, sending up pillars of black smoke.

The *Cleveland* glided gently across the city wall. Below, Southerland could see dozens of running men in Berber robes and headgear, many with rifles.

"Captain," the starboard wing lookout called. "Heavy gun ten points off the starboard bow!"

Southerland strode across the bridge and out onto the starboard wing. "Where?"

The lookout pointed. "There, sir!"

It was tough to see through the haze of smoke, but he could just make out the shape of a model 1897 French 75-mm howitzer, its crew desperately trying to elevate the weapon enough to engage the cruiser overhead. He leaned over the railing and pointed. "Mr. Jones!"

"Yes, sir!" the *Cleveland's* chief gunnery officer called back from his station above the wheelhouse.

"Take them out, if you please!"

"Aye aye, sir!"

The target was too close to the ship for even the casemate five-inchers to engage, but the *Cleveland* had plenty of other weapons in her armory—eight six-pounder rapid-fire guns and two one-pounder guns. Jones, however, dispatched a runner to take his orders down to a Maxim gun station on the forward deck starboard. As the runner descended a ship's ladder, the gun on the ground boomed and belched smoke, and the shell slammed into the *Cleveland's* heavily armored belt.

Like all modern combat ships, the *Cleveland* possessed an armor belt along what would have been her waterline had she been in the water. For an airship, that armor protected the vulnerable electroid trim tanks on both sides, as well as preventing enemy artillery from piercing the hull and wreaking havoc within. The explosion rocked the ship, sending a heavy shudder through her deck, but she righted easily enough just as the Maxim gun began its heavy, chattering clatter. On the ground, spouts of dust walked across and through the gun position, and the Berber tribesmen manning the old French howitzer pitched and spun and crumpled to the ground...or else took to their heels. A moment later, one of the *Cleveland's* six-pounders scored a direct hit, flipping the gin onto its back as wheels and undercarriage fragments rained from the sky.

The tower of the main residence rose just ahead, and Southerland ordered the helm to take the ship past it and around, circling the building at an altitude of thirty feet. Rifle bullets spanged off the ship's hull, as the *Cleveland's* sailors and Marines rained fire down into the compound. Dozens of tribesmen lay sprawled motionless in the dust, now. A robed and veiled man rode a chestnut horse out into the main courtyard wielding a curved sword nearly as long as he was tall, gesticulating as if to engage the cruiser personally, but both horse and rider were cut down by a chattering burst from one of the Maxims.

Southerland scowled his distaste for the bloody slaughter, but ordered Jones to continue firing. Had that mounted man been Raisuli? It scarcely mattered. The sheer, bloody volume of fire should end the Berbers' resistance in short order.

The starboard five-inchers began booming out their challenge one after another, as the *Cleveland* slid past the tower, sending an avalanche of sun-dried bricks and brick fragments down into the courtyard below.

Southerland knew he was taking a terrible chance of killing Perdicaris and his son with this barrage, but the hope and belief of the fleet captains back in Tangiers had been that the hostages would be either on the ground floor or in an underground basement, which would give them a measure of shelter. At the same time, it was vital that *Cleveland* lay down the heaviest possible fire, both to kill and to demoralize Raisuli's warriors and to discourage some fanatical guard from slicing the captives' throats before the American Marines could reach them. The shock and awe of the *Cleveland*'s aerial assault should pin the Berbers down long enough for the Marines to rescue the captives.

I hope…

❧ 🏯 ❧

Perdicaris and Cromwell huddled in one corner of their room as brick and pieces of ceiling rained down on them in showers of dust. It was clear to Perdicaris that a rescue was under way… though whether their rescuers would find them alive or dead in the rubble of the collapsed building was still an open question.

Holes had opened up in the story above them, admitting shafts of dazzlingly bright, white light. He could hear—between the booming thunder of heavy gunfire—the steady chugging of a steam engine, almost certainly one of the new aerial gunboats.

"My God, Father—" Cromwell began.

"Just keep your head down, Crom. We don't want—"

He stopped as two men came through the door and into the room, Raisuli, and one of his men. Both were dirty, and Raisuli had a nasty gash on his face. Both carried rifles.

"I will kill them!" the tribesman snarled in Moroccan-Arabic as he raised his rifle.

"No, Amal!" Raisuli said, reaching out and lowering the barrel of the tribesman's weapon. He gestured. "Put them *there*… in the sunlight."

As Amal nudged and prodded the two captives into the center of the room, Raisuli grinned at them.

"I told you I would free you," he said, "and I will keep my word...assuming you survive the attention of your compatriots out there! First, however, you will assist us in exacting the highest possible price from your countrymen! Now stay there...or we will shoot you!"

Perdicaris didn't understand immediately, but as he sat next to Cromwell in a pool of brilliant white sunlight streaming in from a hole in the ceiling, he realized that the two of them were... bait. Hunting parties in India would stake out a goat to attract the attention of a tiger, then shoot the tiger as it closed in for the kill.

And here Perdicaris and Cromwell were the goat. They were seated well back from the open door and slightly to its left; Raisuli and Amal were closer to the door and to the right, well out of their reach, crouching behind a shattered section of interior wall.

They were waiting for the tiger.

"Request permission to take my men ashore!" Captain Johnson said, saluting.

"Granted, Captain," Southerland replied, returning the salute. We've spotted Myers' men coming through the south wall. Be careful of friendly fire."

"Aye aye, sir," Johnson replied smartly. "I think we'll be able to recognize one another well enough!"

The five-inchers had ceased their steady bombardment, if only because most of the buildings within the compound had already been knocked down. Most of the Berber defenders appeared to be either dead or fleeing toward the protection of the city to the northeast. *Cleveland*'s six- and one-pounder guns continued to duel with snipers within the rubble, accompanied by the harsh chatter of Maxims. Another enemy bullet clanged off the *Cleveland*'s bridge armor, and a moment later a window in a partially wrecked building across the courtyard erupted in smoke and flame. Throughout the Berber compound, however, resistance was nearly at an end.

Southerland just hoped that Perdicaris and Varley had survived their rescue.

Major Myers vaulted a broken wall, his Colt M1892 service pistol in one hand, his O'Bannon cavalry saber in the other. Behind him, two companies of U.S. Marines, looking like blue-clad cowboys in their khaki campaign hats, rushed forward in line abreast, with fixed bayonets and the roar of their battle cry. Up ahead, the Cleveland drifted in serene detachment above the rubble and debris, her main guns silent, now, but her Maxims still barking out challenges and forcing the natives to keep their heads down.

A Berber tribesman rose from behind a pile of crumbled bricks, a Krag rifle in his hands, and Myers shot him with the Colt. Two more Berber warriors broke from cover, but the surging line of Marines overtook them and knocked them down, bayonets gleaming in the sun. It occurred to him that this scene must be very much like that confronting Lieutenant O'Bannon and his men as they crossed the barricades at Derna 89 years before. *Semper fi!*

Another line of men appeared through the dust and smoke up ahead...but Myers immediately recognized the blue uniforms and Stetson headgear. "Hold your fire, boys!" he yelled, raising a hand.

Captain Johnson emerged from the smoke, grinning like a maniac. "Welcome to the party, Major!" he called. "Grab yourself a dance and a piece of cake while you still can!"

"Thanks, Robby!" Myers replied. "What's the situation?"

"Resistance has mostly ceased, Sir. Still a few snipers about, but my boys are winkling them out." Turning, he pointed. "That's what's left of the main house, mostly knocked down. We think the hostages will be in there."

"Let's go get them, Captain," Myers said.

He hoped they were in time.

"You will remain very quiet, Mr. Perdicaris," Raisuli said, "and very still. Understand me?"

"Yes..."

There were noises outside the partly darkened room, and from the ceiling overhead, the thump of booted feet, the yells and shouts of orders, the screams of a wounded man. A volley of gunshots sounded, and another man shrieked, followed by the thud of a body on the floorboards and a gentle sifting of dust from overhead.

"Give it up, Raisuli," Perdicaris said. His voice shook; he fully expected to be killed at any moment, if not by his captors, then by the gun- and cannon-fire of his rescuers. "You don't have a chance!"

"The Raisuli does not run," the Berber chieftain growled in reply, "nor does he surrender. Hush, now..."

He raised his rifle, aiming at the door.

A shadow blocked the door! "On your left!" Perdicaris screamed. "Watch out—"

Raisuli and Amal both fired in the same instant as the volley from the doorway. A tall man in what looked like a cowboy hat stood with his arm outstretched, firing shot after shot from a heavy revolver. Raisuli collapsed; Amal started to run, and was cut down by shots from the door.

"Mr. Perdicaris?" the revolver-wielding shadow said. "Major Myers, United States Marine Corps. Are you two okay?"

"Yes, Major. I think we are."

"I appreciated the warning, sir. Thank you. Can you walk?"

"I'll manage."

"Is this Raisuli?" a Marine sergeant asked, prodding one of the bodies.

"That's him..." He felt as though he were adrift in a dream. Raisuli's bearded corpse lay bloody and broken on the floor.

Together Perdicaris and Varley stepped out into the building's rubble-strewn courtyard.

Hanging in the sky overhead, the *Cleveland* stood watch over a scene of near-total destruction.

Southerland looked down from the bridge wing. A signalman stood beside him, watching the flash and sweep of two flags wielded by another signalman on the ground below.

"Perdicaris...alive..." the signalman said, translating the flags, "and...repeat...*and* Raisuli dead. Message ends, sir."

"Very well." Sutherland took another look at the ship's fore deck. The Marines were coming back on board in somewhat awkward fashion, clinging to ropes in long lines, and having the rope hauled in by a steam-powered winch. About half of them were back on board, now.

Meanwhile, some of Chisolm's deckhands were hauling up the Bos'un's chair lowered for Perdicaris. A few moments later, the former hostage stepped unsteadily onto the deck, where he was caught by several sailors and gently lowered onto a stretcher. The bos'un's chair went back over the side and was lowered to the waiting Cromwell Varley.

The engagement had, against Southerland's own darker expectations, been carried off without a hitch. First reports back from the ground were of five Marines killed and a dozen wounded, which wasn't bad for the butcher's bill on an engagement this intense.

Twenty minutes later, Major Myers came onto the bridge and saluted. "Sir! All personnel are back aboard, all present or accounted for."

"You're absolutely sure, Major? I will not leave *anyone* behind to suffer the attentions of these...barbarians."

"Absolutely sure, sir. I even made sure your Navy signalman got back on board." He shook his head in mock despair. "These sailors ashore on liberty—"

"I shall expect a complete after-action report, Major," Southerland said, ignoring the jibe. "Mr. Brandt!"

"Sir!" his XO replied.

"Make all preparations for getting under way."

"Aye aye, sir!"

Steam came up, and the *Cleveland* pivoted in place. Slowly, she began moving forward, smoke pouring from her stacks and the pounding of her engines hammering at the senses. Leaving Raisuli's ravaged compound behind, she set course for the open sea, where three U.S. warships had appeared to provide support in case it was needed. Had the *Cleveland* been brought down, the *Portland*, the *San Francisco*, and the *Galveston* would have been on hand to cover the Marines' retreat to the beach and to take on board survivors.

As if eager to return to Tangiers, the *Cleveland* began pulling ahead of the other surface-bound vessels.

Admiral Jean Christophe de Montchalin stood on the weather bridge of the French heavy aerial cruiser *Gloire* and peered through his telescope. He thought...*yes! There!* A smudge on the southern horizon!

He felt the power of the vessel throbbing through her deck. The *Gloire* was a powerful, modern leviathan launched in 1900, 140 meters long and massing 9,543 tons. She'd been dispatched from Sardinia late the previous evening, when word had arrived from French agents in Tangiers that the American leviathan had departed the harbor. His orders, received over the ship's modern wireless telegraph system, were explicit and concise. *Prevent American leviathan* Cleveland *from leaving region of Tetuoan.*

The Admiralty, it seemed, was not at all happy that the Americans had hared off into the wilds of Morocco to rescue their people. Although France had not yet taken over the country formally, they were extremely jealous of anyone else making inroads, military or otherwise, within what they considered to be their sovereign territory. France had just extended an enormous loan to the Moroccan government at Fez. If anyone was going to extend military aid to the Sultan, it would be France…not the British, not the Spanish, and most certainly not the noisy and upstart Americans.

"*Monsieur* DuPont," he said, lowering the telescope. "You will prepare the vessel in every regard for combat."

"*Oui, mon* Admiral."

De Montchalin did not expect the Americans to fight…but one never knew. The little *Cleveland* was heavily outmatched by the *Gloire*, but the Americans were known for their recklessness.

❧ ✿ ❧

"What do you make of her?" Southerland asked. He was standing with his executive officer on the starboard bridge wing, looking aft.

"She's trouble, Captain," his XO replied, studying the other ship through his binoculars. "At a guess…she's a *Gloire*-class cruiser. French…half again longer than us, and three times the tonnage. Armament starts with two 7.5-inch guns and goes on from there." Brandt lowered the binoculars and looked hard at Southerland. "Frankly, sir, she could mop the deck with us."

"We haven't come all this way to mop anybody's deck. Helm! Let's give that monster some berth! Come left one five degrees!"

"Left one-five degrees, Aye aye, sir."

"Signal, Captain!" the bridge signalman announced. "'Heave…to…stand…by…to…be…boarded.'"

"The hell with *that!*" Southerland said. "Helm! Left two-zero degrees!"

"Left two-zero, Aye aye."

With a fluttering roar like an oncoming high-speed locomotive, a 7.5-inch shell hurtled across *Cleveland*'s bow and exploded in the sea a hundred yards ahead.

"Jesus!" Brandt exclaimed, involuntarily ducking his head. "I think they mean business!"

Southerland remained cool, studying the other vessel through his telescope. "So do I, Mr. Brandt." He watched the other ship narrowly. She was now almost directly astern and coming fast. She had four squat smokestacks, but in an unusual configuration, two just abaft her bridge, the other two rising quite far astern. Definitely *Gloire*-class...perhaps even the *Gloire* herself.

She was also *fast.* "What would you say her speed is, Mr. Brandt?"

"I'd guess...maybe twenty knots. A hell of a lot faster than us."

Another shell roared in, exploding alongside with volcanic fury. Spray drenched the *Cleveland*'s starboard deck.

"Captain!" the signalman called out. "Signal from the other vessel is repeating."

"Send a reply," Southerland called. "Message: we are in Moroccan waters. You have no jurisdiction here. Message ends."

"Yes, Sir! Sending!..."

Another 7.5-inch shell whistled directly overhead, followed by a volley of smaller shells—6.5-inch and 3.9-inch. *Gloire*-class heavies mounted two of the big 7.5-inch guns, one forward, one aft, in single-gun turrets. The 6.5-inchers were mounted in turrets along the sides, and in casemates on the hull, while six 3.9-inch guns were mounted in hull casemates, three to each side. She would also, Southerland recalled, carry eighteen Hotchkiss five-barreled rapid-fire guns. Those would be deadly if the French ship got in close.

Brandt was right. They *could* mop the deck with the far smaller and more lightly armed *Cleveland*.

"Mr. Jones! Return fire, if you please!"

"Aye aye, Captain!" He used the bridge speaking tube to pass the order. "Aft mount and casemates...fire at will!"

The *Cleveland*'s aft 5-incher barked, followed almost at once by several of the hull-mounted five-inch weapons. Through his telescope, Southerland marked the fall of the shot...one direct hit on the bridge superstructure just below the wheelhouse, and another on the side of the *Gloire*'s forward turret.

"Well done, Mr. Jones! Continue firing! Helm…left two-five degrees!"

"Coming left two-five, aye aye, Sir!"

A 6.5-inch shell slammed into the *Cleveland*'s aft stack, splintering it halfway up. Smoke spilled low across the ship's after deck, helping to hide the ship… but also blocking her gunners' line of sight. Southerland turned and looked forward. The *Cleveland*'s series of turns to port were bringing her over the Moroccan shoreline now. She drifted over white breakers and a sandy stretch of beach, then jinked slightly to starboard to avoid hitting a towering, red sandstone mesa. A trio of French rounds slammed into the rock scant yards to port, showering the American ship with fragments of stone.

Southerland made a quick mental calculation. "Helm! Bring us to port as we round that mountaintop! Put her in the mountain's lee!"

"Aye aye, sir!"

One advantage leviathans definitely had over ships confined to the surface of the ocean was their ability to take advantage of the local terrain. Occasionally, the tactical situation in surface combat allowed a ship to make use of an island in this way, but not often.

"Mr. Jones!" Southerland said. "Alert all gun crews. You're going to have *one shot*, understand? One chance to do as much damage to that bastard as you can. I don't know if she'll follow is around this mesa astern of us or ahead…but as soon as she appears I want you to hit her with every gun that will bear. Understand?"

"Yes, sir!" The gunnery officer turned away and began shouting orders into the speaking tube.

"Helm! We're drifting too close to those rocks. Move us out a few yards, please."

That would also give the casemate weapons on both sides a better angle to engage the enemy.

Stepping back inside the main bridge, Southerland went to the engine room telegraph, grasped the handles firmly, and moved the pointers to all stop. The ship was already moving slowly enough that she was able to come to a halt within the space of a few dozen yards.

What the hell were the Frenchies playing at, anyway? Why were they attacking an American ship? It might just be wounded pride, of course. The French could be damned touchy that way, and if they felt the Americans had shown them up by rescuing Perdicaris by themselves, if they felt they were being humiliated on the international stage, they might have simply decided to redress things by capturing the U.S. leviathan.

That didn't seem like justification enough for what amounted to a declaration of war, however.

As Southerland thought about it, he decided that the attack might actually be a purely political move, one designed to frighten the United States out of North Africa entirely. The French already had an enormous garrison in Morocco even though they didn't control the country politically as yet. It was quite clear, however, that political control was exactly what they were looking for. In that, they were competing with the British, the Germans, and the Spanish, who *all* wanted a piece of Morocco.

When the U.S. had entered the Perdicaris affair, it must have shocked both the government in Paris and the generals in Fez and Tangiers; the Americans were horning their way into Morocco! By attacking the *Cleveland*, the French would be sending a very loud, very precise message to Washington: "Morocco is *ours*, all others keep out!"

It must help, Southerland thought, *that the French probably see the United States as an easy target.* By world standards, the U.S. was still raw and young. She'd emerged from a vicious and crippling civil war just four decades earlier, and was only now clamoring at the world stage in an attempt to be taken seriously by everyone else.

If that were the case—and he was convinced he was right—then the very best thing he could do was fight back, surprisingly and with enthusiastic determination. *Bullies,* he thought, *tend to back down when their victims fail to cry and run away.*

Teddy Roosevelt, Southerland thought, *would be pleased with that reasoning...*

Unfortunately, fighting back might well mean the *Cleveland* would end up a broken hulk, abandoned in the dry Moroccan Rif.

The *Cleveland* had held all the cards in the fighting over Tetuoan—five-inchers and Maxim guns against desert tribesmen on horseback. Now, the tables were turned, and it was the *Cleveland*'s turn to square off against a far more powerful foe.

The French warship had massive armor—6.7 inches thick along her belt, thinning to 4.2 inches at bow and stern. Her main gun turrets would be protected by almost 7 inches of steel. Punching through that with a five-inch shell would be all but impossible.

There were a few possibilities, however...

"Enemy vessel emerging off the bow, Captain!" a lookout cried. "Range fifty yards!"

"Teach her some manners, Mr. Jones!"

But the weapons officer was already screaming "*fire*" into the speaking tube. The *Cleveland*'s five-inch guns, every weapon that could be brought to bear, spoke as one... and continued to speak as their crews rammed home round after round into smoking breeches, yanked lanyards, ejected casings, and rammed home fresh rounds.

Explosions walked along the *Gloire*'s superstructure, beginning at the wheelhouse and blossoming along the huge vessel's side. A direct hit on her deck-mounted torpedo tubes amidships set off a savage blast that sent chunks of ragged metal plate spinning away through the air and dropping to the desert below.

The *Gloire* returned fire, her starboard-side casemate guns firing into the *Cleveland*'s prow. Southerland and the other bridge officers crouched, shielding their eyes as the glass windows on the bridge exploded inward in a momentary but deadly hurricane of glass shards and splinters. The helmsman screamed and collapsed, hands over his eyes, blood spilling from between his fingers. Another helmsman stepped up and took the wheel, as a couple of pharmacy mates dragged the wounded man off the deck of the bridge, leaving a shocking trail of blood.

The *Cleveland* continued firing. Her starboard casemate guns were joining in now as the *Gloire* drifted across the American cruiser's bow.

Southerland stood at the engine room telegraph, hands on the indicator handles. The *Cleveland* possessed one significant advantage here, but he would only get the one chance. Massing three times more than the *Cleveland*, the *Gloire* needed a long distance to stop. She would continue drifting forward...forward... slowing, but still moving forward...

"Mr. Jones! Action to starboard!" He rammed the telegraph indicators to FULL AHEAD.

The *Gloire*'s stern cleared the mesa.

The *Cleveland*, engines pounding, drifted forward, crossing the French ship's stern at a range of scarcely ten yards. The *Gloire*'s aft turret fired, the round slamming into the *Cleveland*'s hull, punching through her armored belt and rupturing at least one of the trim tanks mounted there.

The *Cleveland*'s fire was devastating, pounding at the twin venturis housing the *Gloire*'s ducted screws. Chunks of metal exploded from the *Gloire*'s fantail, trailing smoke as it arced out over the desert and fell. Steering gear dangled from her tail, twisted and useless. The shriek and clatter of wounded screws was even louder than the pounding of the *Cleveland*'s engines; smoke poured from the damaged screw housings, and the massive cruiser slewed to starboard, drifting out of control.

The *Cleveland* sprinted forward...a slow crawl at first, but her speed picking up.

Then the *Gloire* fired a full broadside at the *Cleveland*'s departing stern, and Southerland was thrown to the deck by the shock of exploding shells aft. The deck tilted sharply to starboard, and for a horrible moment he feared the ship was going to roll... but she reluctantly stabilized with a twenty-degree list.

"Starboard trim tanks holed, sir," Brandt told him. "And our screws are gone."

The *Cleveland* had been terribly injured—as bad, or even worse, than the huge *Gloire*. The French vessel was a good half-mile off, now, continuing to fire at irregular intervals.

Both warships were crippled.

Southerland recalled that in 1893, an engagement over Corsica between the French *D'Entrecasteaux* and the Italian *Vettor Pisani* had ended with both leviathans helplessly adrift in the sky, their airscrews smashed.

They faced the same situation here. A half hour after the final exchange of fire, the two ships had drifted perhaps a mile apart... the lighter *Cleveland* pushed farther by an offshore wind. Damage control parties in the *Cleveland*'s shredded stern workings had come back with the worst possible news. The American ship's ducted airscrews were hopelessly smashed, and there was no way to make them operable again.

Southerland studied the *Gloire* through his telescope. The damage to the French vessel was significantly less. He could see working parties at her stern, clearing away wreckage. The urgency of the work suggested that they were jury-rigging something, that they might be well on the way to at least partly repairing the damage.

If the *Gloire* managed to get any propulsive force at all out of even one screw, the *Cleveland* was doomed. The two ships had drifted out of effective range of one another now, but if the French vessel could make repairs enough to manage a half-knot of speed or so, she would be able to close the range and pound the helpless *Cleveland* into scrap.

Southerland watched the ongoing repair efforts on the French vessel for a long time, then turned to Brandt. "Send someone down to find Lieutenant Chisolm," he said. "And alert the chief bos'un and the deck division."

"Sir?"

"We still have canvas, Number One, and a man who knows how to bend it on," Southerland said with a grin. "We're going to *sail* all the way back to Tangiers."

June 24, 1904

Thirty hours after the fight with the *Gloire*, the battered *Cleveland* limped back over Tangiers harbor, her deck canted at a rakish angle that forced her crew to pick their way hand-over-hand along the deck railings, her tattered flag fluttering from her fantail.

News of Perdicaris' rescue had been transmitted to Tangiers by the Portland; news of the battle with the *Gloire* had been intercepted by the U.S. fleet listening in on the *Gloire*'s own emergency broadcasts as she called Marseille for help.

To Southerland, it was obvious that the *Cleveland* had received the worst end of the deal in her engagement with the French aerial cruiser. Still, her fight with the larger *Gloire* was already being hailed as a major victory, and a thoroughgoing embarrassment for the French. When the *Cleveland* moved slowly over Tangiers, pushed silently along by her canvas sail and steered by lines of men hauling on the sail's running rigging, the bands of seven U.S. warships massed on the Tangiers waterfront had burst into a stirring rendition of Sousa's immortal "Stars and Stripes Forever." As the final notes died away, a *boom* sounded from the harbor, followed by another...and another.

The American squadron was firing a salute at the *Cleveland's* arrival.

Southerland, his hands behind his back, nodded to the white-bearded civilian standing next to him on the bridge. "I imagine you're glad to get back home, Mr. Perdicaris."

"I am, sir," Perdicaris replied. "Only..."

"Only what, sir?"

"Only...only this has all been a terrible mistake."

"What do you mean?"

"Raisuli...he wasn't a bandit. He was a...a *patriot*, fighting for his people. He'd already decided to let me and Cromwell go when your Marines came bursting in!"

"I understand from Major Myers' after-action report that it was *you* who warned him of the ambush inside that building."

"Well, yes. He was using us as...as bait, I suppose. He probably thought that the Marines would see us and immediately come to our aid, giving him and his man a chance to shoot them from ambush."

"Well, then."

"But he was defending himself! I don't know what's right any more..."

"I'll tell you what was right, sir," Southerland said. "Brigand or patriot, Raisuli challenged the United States of America. For a time, the eyes of the world were on him, watching him humble a great nation. Had we let that stand—even if you'd been safely returned—our weak response would have encouraged every would-be pirate and bandit and brigand between Tangiers and Cairo to try their own hand at kidnapping American citizens. A strong response...Teddy Roosevelt's 'big stick...' It was our only choice. Do you understand? A nation's one solemn and inviolable responsibility beyond its own shores is the protection of its citizens. I just thank God that we shouldn't have this problem in the future. Those brigands and pirates fear us now..."

"Is that what it takes nowadays? Fear?..."

"In today's world, yes. Gunboat diplomacy. Without it, the scrabbling brigands and revolutionaries might well tear down civilization itself."

"Raisuli treated us kindly..."

"While holding you captive with a gun to your head." Southerland shook his head. "Even if he *was* about to let you go, so much could have gone wrong! A falling-out with his people, a raid by the Sultan's troops, a miscalculation by the French...and you and your son would now be dead."

"I suppose so."

But he didn't sound convinced.

The man, Southerland thought, *had formed some sort of emotional bond with the man who'd had the power of life and death over him for a full month.* It was almost as though Perdicaris had, in some twisted way, come to *identify* with the bandit.

Let him get back to his home in the United States, though, and he would be fine....

June 27, 1904

Samuel Grummere raised his glass in toast to Perdicaris at the far end of the large and elegant dining table. Cromwell Varley, Beatrice, and Ellen were with them, along with a number of other distinguished guests, mostly diplomatic staff and military officers. "To you, Mr. Perdicaris! Welcome home!"

Perdicaris nodded and mumbled something suitable.

Since Perdicaris' return to Tangiers, life for the American expatriate community had been a whirl of formal receptions, dinners, and gala events. The American legation in Tangiers was quite giddy with a smugly self-satisfied and self-congratulatory bonhomie since the *Cleveland*'s return to the city. The French were sullen...though thankfully they'd elected to interpret the clash between the *Cleveland* and their *Gloire* as a mistake, a regrettable confusion of orders with a most unfortunate outcome.

Privately, Grummere thought, *they would brood...and in all probability there would be another reckoning on another day.*

Major Myers stood and tapped the side of his glass with a fork, calling for another toast. "Ladies, gentlemen..." he said. "I give you the United States Marine Corps. *Semper fidelis!*"

Grummere drank the toast...and the one that followed, from Captain Southerland to the United States Navy, long may she rule the seas *and* the sky. *This,* he thought, *could well go on all night...*

Of the *Cleveland*'s crew of thirty officers and 261 enlisted men, plus the 360 U.S. Marines embarked on board, twenty-five had been killed and another sixty-eight wounded...a shocking butcher's bill of fourteen percent. There was no way of knowing what the casualties had been on the *Gloire.* Normally she carried a compliment of 612, and her list of killed and wounded would have been at least as bad as the *Cleveland*'s. France, however, was not likely to admit a precise number.

In fact, so far as the French were concerned, the whole incident had never happened.

And that, perhaps, was the best outcome they could have hoped for. The plucky little *Cleveland* had rescued the hostages. Without the leviathan's ability to strike inland, the affair could have had a much less happy outcome...with Perdicaris and his son murdered, or at best released when the Sultan met the Raisuli's demands.

Would that have been a better outcome? Gummere wondered. He saw Perdicaris lean over and give his wife a one-armed hug.

Perhaps?... he wondered. *Was all the posturing, all the chest-thumping, all the blood and fear and confrontation really worth it?*

What about the torture in that dark and stifling dungeon?

But seeing Perdicaris reunited with his wife...

Word was that Perdicaris and his family would be returning to...not America, but to a family home in England.

Strange...

Sir Arthur Nicholson rose. *Clink-clink-clink.* "Ladies and gentlemen," he said, raising his glass. "I give you President Theodore Roosevelt...and the United States of America!"

Gummere bit his tongue...and drank the toast.

CZAR NICHOLAS II LAID TO REST

New York Times, Friday, March 10th, 1911

—

Country in Mourning after the Loss of Czar

—

Sixteen-year-old Girl to Rule Russia as Sole Survivor of Attack

—

England Blamed for the Assassination

◆

Saint Petersburg stood in quiet mourning today as Nicholas II, the deceased Czar of Russia, was paraded through the capital of his Empire one last time before he was placed with his ancestors in the grand halls of the Peter and Paul Cathedral. Alexandra Feodorovna, Nicholas's wife, who was also killed during the assassination attempt, was a part of the march through the cold streets as well, her body following closely behind that of the Czar. While almost all of their children were killed, they were not included in the Funeral procession. They were buried separately later that day, in a much smaller but still regal funeral event.

At the Funeral, Prince Vladimir Orlov, military advisor and close friend of the Czar, spoke of the deep sorrow the entire country felt for the loss of their great leader as well as the loss of his dearest and closest friend. Prince Orlov then thanked God for the safety of Anastasia Romonav, the only surviving member of the Czar's immediate family. Vladimir

Orlov promised to take care of Anastasia and do whatever it takes to protect her. It is assumed at this time that Prince Orlov will be doing much of the leading for the country for the foreseeable future.

Many people had expected to hear from Anastasia, but she was silent throughout the funeral. Anastasia, at just age 16, will be named Czar of Russia next month, but many people are questioning if she is ready. As Nicholas's youngest daughter, she has not undergone any formal training in statecraft, and no one ever expected her to need to lead such a massive country, especially after such a horrific event that took the lives of her entire family. Members of the Russian Aristocracy have even been heard wishing that the assassins had gotten her as well instead of leaving them stuck with a child to rule.

Still, not a lot of information has been obtained on how the assassins got into the palace where the family was located at the time of the attack. This, however, did not stop Orlov from blaming Rasputin, mystical advisor to the Ramonov family, and quickly stripping him of his position. Rasputin has gone into hiding, and has not been heard from since. As of yet, no evidence has been found linking him to the attack.

What is known is that there were at least 6 men involved in the attack, 3 of whom were killed in the process. One was captured while the survivors tried to escape, but two are still on the loose. The one that was captured is set to be executed in two days, as Orlov believes he has gotten all possible information from him.

Yesterday, it was announced that the assassins came in on a British vessel. That combined with the strong British accent the captured assailant is said to have is having many people point to Great Britain as the source of the attack. Diplomatic relations had already been strained over the fighting for control of the Afghan region in the last few years, sparked by the discovery of eteroid there. Many believe that if new evidence is not found soon, this event may break all relations between the two countries and push them even further into territorial competition, if not outright war in the coming years. Especially as Russia had just claimed that the Scandinavian countries of Sweden and Norway fell into its sphere of influence last month, corresponding with both minor countries having upped their own production of eteroid drastically for foreign consumption.

Only time can tell what both the immediate and long-term effects of the Czar's death will have on both Russia and the world as a whole, but one thing is certain, Russia will not soon forget this day, and hell will be laid upon whomever is found ultimately responsible for this massacre in Saint Petersburg.

Prince Orlov concluded his speech at the funeral with this: "Russia will not rest a single night until the men responsible are found and brought to this very spot, for all the world to witness, and shot like the dogs they are. Let our enemies and allies alike know that no matter how far they may try to run or how strong they may think they are, the Russian Empire's reach is farther, and our strength is greater."

MIDNIGHT WAR

Blaine Lee Pardoe

Thanks to Bryn Bills for the outline of this story and for the chance to write in the Leviathans universe again.

------◆------

"...she (Japan) is a most formidable military power. Her people have peculiar fighting capacity. They are very proud, very warlike, very sensitive, and are influenced by two contradictory feelings; namely, a great self-confidence, both ferocious and conceited...and a great touchiness..."

—Theodore Roosevelt to Senator Knox
September, 1909

July 4, 1911

Tai-so Togo Takeshi discreetly checked his pristine white dress uniform as he sat rigid in the chair of the chamber outside of Prime Minster Kinmochi's Saionji office. Next to him was *Gensui Teitoku* Gorō Ijūin, the Marshal Admiral in command of all of Japan's military forces. Takeshi was unsure why he had been summoned, but the presence of his superior officer told him that it was indeed important. The stern face of Gorō Ijūin offered nothing—he stared forward into nothingness, not even allowing a drop of perspiration to appear on his brow—so great was his self-control. It was not easy, the humidity made his own uniform stick to his body. Takeshi adjusted his round glasses, which had slid down his nose. Gorō Ijūin saw the movement of his junior officer, but said nothing. He merely adjusted his hat on his short gray stubble-like hair.

Takeshi suppressed his excitement. *My presence here means our air navy may finally be employed.* His father, Togo Heihachiro, had suffered an inglorious defeat at the hands of the Russians in the Battle of Tsushima. If it had been a naval engagement, the Imperial Navy would have defeated the Russians. They had employed their new leviathans, though. The shells of the flying warships had rained down on the Japanese and had handed the empire a staggering rout that had taken Takeshi's father from him.

That would have crushed most young boys, but not Takeshi.

He had been granted the right to study in America, at their esteemed U.S. Naval Academy. The Americans had been proud to show off their technological achievements to Takeshi, never assuming that he was doing more than studying the new technology, he was *mastering* them. To the Americans, he was a foreign visitor to be awed with their accomplishments. In reality, he was doing much more. He had been an engineering student, and had flown on the first American leviathan, the *Pigeon*. Takeshi had worked with great men like Westinghouse, Edison, and Tesla to understand the complexities of electroid, and how to use the substance to put huge warships in the skies. He had been given a great gift, to learn the technology that had taken his father from him. It was a gift that he brought back to his people and put in the skies.

The slender male secretary, wearing a crisp black suit, ushered the two officers into the private office of the Prime Minister. Kinmochi Saionji sat at his desk, jotting some notes on paper, as the two men stood at attention before him. He could smell the faint aroma of cigarettes that clung to the drapery.

Takeshi drank in the room, with its lush red carpet over the teak floors, the bookshelves lined with fascinating titles, the extreme order of things. Only a long photograph was in a small frame on the corner of the desk, set at a perfect 45-degree angle... the only personal item he could see. It told him a great deal about the Prime Minister.

Kinmochi was a slight man, his chair seemed to dwarf him. He wore his gray and black streaked hair slicked back— with a hint of lavender oil wafting in the air. When he finished writing, he set down his pen and gestured to the seats. "Thank you for coming."

"We are honored for the audience, Prime Minister," Gorō Ijūin replied slowly in his deep voice. He removed his hat and placed it in his lap. His pointed, gray goatee never wavered as he moved. "How may we serve his Majesty?"

The Prime Minister turned to *Tai-so* Togo Takeshi. "You have built a fleet of air ships that is impressive—so says his Majesty. We both feel that the world needs to see that we have recovered from the shame of Tsushima, and to prove that we are indeed a true world power."

To be summoned to the Prime Minister's office was a distinct honor for an officer of his rank...an honor that made Takeshi more than a bit nervous. He suppressed his excitement and tenseness, keeping a stern, fixed face. "I live to serve." He squirmed in his seat slightly, then caught himself and remained rigid. To be summoned for such a meeting was a rarity, an honor.

When he had returned from his studies, he had been the driving force to create their first leviathan, the Majestic-class *Mikasa*. It was the start of a fleet of airships, one Takeshi had led in building. He had tirelessly organized the training cadres, put a rigorous officer selection system in place, and had forged the Imperial Air Service from the ground up. Now there were other flying warships, the *Hayabusa Ryoushi*-class, and the new *Kuroraikou*-class Black Lightning armored cruisers...all constructed under the tightest security. *The world has no idea of the might we now have—because we have not projected it yet.*

"This report you wrote several months ago," the Prime Minister pulled out the memorandum from his side desk drawer. "You indicated that our ships are dependent on foreign sources for electroid, correct?"

He nodded. "Correct, Prime Minster. Electroid is dependent on the ore eteroid. We cannot fly without it, but are dependent on other nations for nearly seventy-five percent of our reserves." He had written the memo for Gorō Ijūin. The fact that it had reached the Prime Minster's desk was good. *It is my duty to warn of such risks to the Empire.*

"Your memo said that, and I quote here," he squinted at the report in his hands. "'In a time of war, during our greatest need, the Imperial Air Service could potentially be grounded because of our lack of a ready source of this strategic resource.'"

"You must forgive the tone of my Sky Admiral," Gorō said, giving Takeshi a quick glance of narrowed eyes. "Yet the point *Tai-so* Togo makes is valid; it is cautionary."

"There is no shame in being blunt," Kinmochi said. "I wish more of our officers would be."

"Without our own source to create electroid, our current reserves would only allow for three to four months of defensive operations during wartime—less if we were pressed into an offensive campaign," Takeshi said.

The Prime Minister nodded. "The Emperor and I see this as unacceptable. Further, it limits what we are able to do on the stage of the world. Times are changing. These leviathans are strategic weapons. They are the means to project our influence around the planet. To have this capability limited reduces our nation's power."

The Prime Minister's words were a sweet song in Takeshi's ears. He has heard whispers that Kinmochi was different—a new term, a globalist. *Clearly he advocates change, and that is good for our people.* Japan had been mostly isolationist for many years. The world was changing, driven by dozens of new technologies...from electricity for lighting and powering factories to leviathans. *Our world is getting smaller, encroaching on our people. We must be ready to cope and react to that.*

I tasked a special team of geologists in locating potential large reserves of this eteroid ore," the Prime Minister continued. "There are some in Burma, the interior of China, and a few other places that lack accessibility. One, however, has emerged that offers an intriguing potential."

He opened a drawer on his desk and pulled out a map, turning it to the two officers. His finger came down on South America's west coast—Chile.

"Chile," Gorō said, lifting his eyes to lock onto the Prime Minster. "It is halfway around the world."

"Yes. But Chile would be easier to invade than, let's say, China. The Army has been pressing that case for years, wanting to secure iron to cut our dependency on foreign supplies. Burma's supplies of the ore are so far in their interior we would spend years building railroads to reach them. Building processing facilities there would be logistically challenging given the power requirements and would require a substantial garrison force, deep in territory where it would be constantly contested by local insurrectionists."

Takeshi's eyes shifted back to the map. As an engineer at heart, he believed in organization above all—and that included organizing his thoughts before he spoke. "Prime Minister, there are four things we must consider before going further."

"Proceed, *Tai-so*," the elder statesman said with a slight bow of his head.

"Very well. First, Chile possesses leviathans of its own. They are two older British warships, technically obsolete, but still potent weapons of war.

"Second, to take Chile, we would need to transport troops to secure the country quickly. Speed will be the cornerstone to such a plan. We have troop transport-capable leviathans, but we will need immediate follow-through by the Imperial Navy." His eyes darted to Gorō, who gave him a knowing nod. *He is well aware that coordinating the Army and Navy is a delicate act of balancing egos.*

"You may continue," the Prime Minster said.

"Third, logically we cannot just send our air fleet to Chile. We will need to coal at least twice during the trip. The first re-coaling can be attributed to us being on maneuvers. The second will tip off other countries as to our destination. As such, as part of this, we will need to secure a coaling port with airship facilities at the far end of the Pacific. A place that is isolated, with little shipping traffic. Again, the Navy may be of assistance in such an operation."

"Do you have something in mind?"

Takeshi nodded. "There are several candidate locations...one that will work better than others but I need to do some research on it."

"Excellent. And the fourth consideration?"

"The reaction of the United States," Takeshi said firmly. "As you no doubt know, I attended school there, and know a number of their officers. The Americans are a people searching for a fight, regardless of the foe. We would be wise to not underestimate their resolve once their national pride or interests are injured. While we are anxious to test our Air Service, so are they. Seizing Chile might pit us against them, far from our homeland."

Kinmochi Saionji's usually emotionless face flashed a grin, if only for a millisecond. "You are astute, *Tai-so*, and wise to raise such a concern. Most military men only look to their commands, but this memo you wrote and the words you offer demonstrate your understanding of a greater service to the Chrysanthemum Throne. You have chosen your senior officers well, Gorō," he said, nodding at Takeshi's superior.

The older officer bowed his head, acknowledging the rare compliment.

"Of course, such an action will not go unnoticed," Prime Minister Kinmochi continued. "There are international laws, then there are also the policies of individual nations. I will navigate those waters while you navigate the skies."

"President Taft might very well rally his people against us, but his time is waning—even members of his own party are buckling under his leadership. In the coming year America will have a new election, and most likely a new President. Politicians would be wary of attempting to run on a platform that would plunge their nation into war. Elections are a form of controlled chaos. The timing of their presidential election will work to our advantage, give us time to reinforce our holdings in Chile."

"We are fortunate that Theodore Roosevelt is not President," Takeshi said. "His desire to wield a 'big stick' could prove problematic."

"He is out of the picture for now, off hunting and fishing," the Prime Minister said. "Which means that the United States is not likely to respond militarily. Great Britain is bound to have a negative response, but that is to be expected," he added. "They sold the leviathans to Chile, and much of the eteroid ore exported from there goes as payment for the ships. They have armed the Chileans as if they were a parent, giving them toys to play with."

Takeshi nodded, but held his thoughts to himself. *This is more than simply idle talk. This has been thought out carefully. This is going to happen.*

"Prime Minister," Gorō said, shifting slightly in his seat. "To do this, we will need time to prepare. If we wage war for our nation, even in a small way, we must do so with precision. There can be no room for mistakes."

Kinmochi looked up at Takeshi. "*Tai-so*, if you would retire to my waiting room, I would like to discuss this with the *Gensui Teitoku*."

He rose, snapped to attention, bowing his head slightly. "Of course." Then he turned and left the office.

In the waiting room he did not sit, could not. This was history unfolding, Togo Takeshi knew that. While he was thrilled to have a chance to have his fleet deployed, to erase the stigma of Tsushima and the death of his father—he was tempered by his time in the U.S. *They are a resourceful and proud people. I have seen them at their best, when innovating, but I dread them at their worst.*

A clock ticked methodically on the wall as he waited what seemed like an hour.

Finally Gorō emerged, closing the door to the office behind him. He strolled up close to Takeshi, so close he could smell his superior's breath. "The Prime Minister was impressed with you, Togo. He and I agree that you are the perfect officer to lead this expedition."

A mix of excitement and the weight of responsibility flooded through him. "Thank you, sir."

"Plan it well. You may bring in an assistant, but no one else is to know the full scale of this operation. Security is our shield. Secrecy is to be your watchword."

"You will usher us into a new age," he said in a low tone. "Do this well, and you will redeem your father and our people."

Togo Takeshi bowed his head. "I will not fail the Emperor or you."

On the Pacific Coast, *Almirante de Aire* Cristobal Rojas stood on the bridge of the *Lanza de Acero* and stared out at San Antonio. At 42 years old, he was the youngest admiral of Chile's small air service, and had already earned a reputation for daring. The navy admirals all scoffed at Rojas; they saw his tiny squadron of ships as playthings. Cristobal had been assigned as a *capitán* because of his father's influence with the President, and while his father had maneuvered to get him posted to the first Chilean leviathan, everything that followed had been built on his own accomplishments.

Many officers of his rank carried extra weight around their midsection, *their own personal armor belt*, as he referred to it. Not so with Rojas, who was determined to set an example for his men. He kept in fastidious shape, and his uniform was spotless at all times. His stature and height made him an imposing figure, which he used to his advantage when he had to. Rojas wore his hair short, slicked back with oil. He shaved dangerously close every morning, often cutting himself, but by afternoon always had a sea of black stubble on his chin.

Where most navy officers saw the air ships as a diversion of funds, Cristobal knew better, and had proved it with smoke, blood, and cordite. During a border dispute with Argentina, he had destroyed one of their light cruisers that had moved in to annex a Chilean mining operation. The newspapers had made out to be him a hero, which only made the other officers scorn him even more.

The Air Service was small. His two heavy cruisers were hand-me-downs from the British. Obsolete by contemporary standards, but Rojas had used his public relations clout to get funding for improved guns and armor. The three light cruisers were little more than castoffs from the French Air Service, one being an old training vessel. He had overseen their refit personally. Cristobal had set up a small training school for aviation and hand-picked his officers. Chile was small, but her mines produced the precious eteroid ore. He had used that as leverage with the British and French to get some of the weapons he had armed his squadron with. *The ore is what makes Chile strong. It also makes us a target.*

Almirante de Aire Rojas was not delusional about what would happen if war broke out in the world, and thought about it as he looked out over the Pacific that afternoon. *The larger countries will eventually come for us. The United States cannot resist interfering in our affairs, and the British and French also cannot keep their noses out of what we do. We are far from them on a map, but they will want to secure our resources for themselves. When they do, it is my job to bleed them—to stop them.*

War seemed far away from the seat on the bridge as he sipped his black coffee, so strong it stung his nostrils. The Europeans were constantly testing each other, always attempting to start something larger, but thus far calmer heads and diplomacy had prevailed. Rojas knew that one day, that spark of war would burst into a bonfire...one that would come right at him and his people.

And on that day, we will be ready. All of my detractors in the navy and army will look to the sky for salvation—and we will give it to them.

July 5, 1911

Tai-sa Suko Akira of the *Suifutou-Indo* sat opposite of Togo Takeshi with a look of disbelief as he saw where Takeshi's finger fell on the map. The younger man was taller than Takeshi, wiry in stature, and full of energy. He wore his hair short, almost too short for Takeshi's tastes. When he spoke, his eyes widened with vigor and excitement. "Chile. *Yūshūna!* With all due respect, my old friend, have you taken to the bottle?"

Takeshi merely smiled; he had expected nothing less from his comrade in arms. "We serve the Emperor, and this is his divine will. The task before the two of us is how do we get our leviathans and troops there?"

"My first question—how many ships are we talking about, *Tai-so?*"

"All of them."

"*Nani?* We would leave the home islands naked?"

"We can ill-afford for this operation to fail," Takeshi said. "As such, I have advocated the use of our entire air service." He slowly lowered himself into the red leather chair behind the teak desk where the map lay. Akira pulled up the lone chair opposite of it, the legs scraping across the floor as he did so.

"Very well, then," Akira stared at the map intently for a minute, saying nothing, clearly deep in thought. Takeshi could see the wrinkles form on his junior officer's brow, his eyes flaring as he studied the map. Suko was a master of logistics. He would have been stuck away in war planning if not for his desire to fly and his friendship with Takeshi. *Now I need both of those skills to come into play.*

"Our leviathans will need to replenish coal, likely twice," Akira said slowly, his eyes never leaving the map.

"I would rule out Hawaii," he said raising his gaze for a moment to lock onto Takeshi's. "They have the facilities, but the British and Americans would be more than curious as to what our fleet was doing so far from our homeland."

"Agreed," Takeshi said. "We have never sortied so far. Their wireless would no doubt put them on some sort of alert. Surprise and speed is key."

Akira nodded. "Tahiti would do." He pointed at the island. "British and French merchants use it to recoal their transports. I saw an intelligence report indicating they have ample reserves there. Also, Tahiti does not have a wireless station. The French built a small mooring for air ships as well, though it hardly gets used. It will be days, if not weeks, before word of our fleet could reach anyone of significance."

It was a stretch to get that far—*but with some recoaling at sea, it might be possible.* "That does not get us all of the way."

"No, it does not," Akira said. "A journey of this length requires many long steps. Once we get there we need one more place to recoal…" His eyes wandered across the map, looking at each tiny dot in the vast blue of the Pacific Ocean. "What about here?" he said, his finger landing on one island.

"Easter Island," Takeshi said. He turned to the files on his desk and pulled one vanilla folder out with the name on tab. "It has been annexed by Chile. Their naval port is small, but does have some coaling capabilities, most likely not enough for our needs."

"We do not have to fully recoal," Akira said. "We need enough to reach Chile and dispatch their leviathans and drop off garrison forces. Our bunkers do not have to be fully filled to do that. We just need to have enough to reach the coast and fight."

Takeshi nodded. "We could have the navy pre-position coaling ships there so that when we arrive, we are provisioned."

"Do they have a wireless?"

Flipping through his notes, Takeshi looked back up with a predatory grin on his face. "They do not."

Akira smiled as well. "Tentatively, I think Tahiti and Easter Island are where we should concentrate our efforts. It will allow us to strike at Chile more easily. Tell me, what do they have for leviathans?"

Takeshi pulled out another piece of paper. "Two heavy cruisers, three light, three destroyers," he said. "The light cruisers are older French *Liberté*-class, some of the first pressed into service. The two heavy cruisers are the old Pegasus-Class."

"Antiques," Akira replied.

"They have been refitted," Takeshi said. "While they are old, they cannot be disregarded," he slid the intelligence report in front of Akira who took a long moment to absorb all of its content. The younger man then returned his gaze to the map, sliding the report back. "Our airmen will be tired…this is a long journey."

"Yes. And this invasion ultimately requires support from the Navy."

That made Akira cock his right eyebrow. "They have always proven *so* cooperative in the past..."

That made Takeshi chuckle. The rivalry between the Army, Navy, and Air Service was the stuff of legends. "We all have our burdens to bear. While we will be carrying enough troops to seize and hold their key installations—we require the Navy to bring in the rest of our infantry. If we strike hard and fast enough, the Chileans will not have time to muster an organized response.

"Much will hang on the weather," Akira added. "Fighting storms burns coal more than in battle."

"Agreed. The logistics is staggering. That is why I brought you in. We have three weeks to produce a plan for Gensui Teitoku Gorō himself to approve."

"May we bring in staff to assist?"

"We must segment the information. They cannot know what it is for, only that they have a specific task. Secrecy is critical."

"I doubt there are Chilean spies operating here in Tokyo."

"True—but there are French, British, and Americans. We can trust no one. This is a strategic move for our people. When we are successful, it will change how the world views us. We will become a force to be reckoned with. As such, we need to move elements of our fleet to different cities so they will not be seen taking off together. Each day of confusion we buy works to our advantage."

"Does this invasion have a name?"

For a moment Togo Takeshi paused and considered the question. *My father died at Tsushima. Our nation suffered from that loss to the Russians. Revenge is a poor name, since is not a battle with our nemesis that defeated us.* Then it hit him, the perfect name. "Onryō."

"A vengeful spirit," Akira replied. "I like it."

"As do I." *It is the vengeful sprit of Tsushima, coming to wreak havoc on the world.* "Come now, I will ask my aide de camp to bring us tea. We have much to do in a short amount of time."

Former President Theodore Roosevelt sat in the wide rocker on his porch of his remote Sagamore Hill home and stared off at the lush green beauty. He drew a long sip of his lemonade, extra-sweet on his lips and tongue, then took off his glasses, and wiped the round lenses with his kerchief. The shade of the porch kept him comfortable, despite the blazing sun filtering through the maples, hickory and oak trees surrounding his home. There was just enough of a breeze to make the perspiration on his brow slow.

His second wife, Alice, took the chair next to him and watched his every move. He turned to face her. "What is it?"

"I know that look, you are anxious," she replied, sipping her own drink.

Putting his glasses back on, he turned to face her squarely. "You know what the worst job in the world is, Alice?"

"No, Theodore."

"Being a *former* President," he grumbled.

"I suspected as much," she replied with a thin smile.

"Taft isn't a Republican anymore, at least he's not acting like one. He's got Knox out negotiating with France and England. Appeasement! That's what he's doing. Selling out America... letting the Hague tell us what we can and can't do. Everything I built up to make America strong, he's throwing out the window."

"You groomed him, Theodore," she reminded him. "You picked him as your successor and even campaigned for him."

"Don't try to lay that blame on me, my dear," he scoffed. "Apparently I did a horrible job of preparing that fool."

Alice paused for a long moment, savoring the hot summer wind. When she turned to him again, she offered only a warm smile and her interpretation of his mood. "You want to run again. That's what this is about, isn't it?"

He tried to wave her off with a quick hand gesture. "Don't be silly. I can't run again. I told the American people I wouldn't seek another term."

"I don't care what you said, Theodore," she said, taking a slow sip of lemonade. "I only know what you are feeling right now. The election is next year, and I know you love being up in front of a crowd. You stepped away from the only job you were born to do. Ever since then, you have been trying to find yourself. Well I know where you belong, so do a lot of people—in the White House."

Those words brought a grin from under his thick mustache. "I do miss it, Alice. But I told the American people I wouldn't run."

"You are a politician, dear," she said. "No one expects you to keep your word."

"I do," he said.

"Since when does the man I married care about what other people think about him?"

"Bully, I married a smart woman!" he said, flashing his teeth. "If I jump into the race right now, it would split the ticket. If I do this, I need an issue to run on. Not some damned treaty with the English or French, but something tangible—something that will excite the American people."

"Like what?"

Roosevelt shook his head. "Damned if I know, but I will know it when I see it." He rocked back and forth, eyes glittering behind his glasses, and took another long drink of his lemonade.

August 10, 1911

Gensui Teitoku Gorō's office was bare, almost Spartan, especially compared with the Prime Minister's He only had a single chair opposite of his desk, and a very plain one at that. His drapes were dull navy blue, darkening the room rather than inspiring. There was not a speck of dust on the windowsills. As Takeshi stood there, awaiting his superior, his eyes fell on the few books that were in a glass cabinet. Gorō's background in the Imperial Navy showed with his books, but one stood out, the Alfred Mahan treatise, "Aerial Domination," translated into Japanese. Mahan was one of the brightest and strategic-thinkers in the United States on the use of aviation. *The fact that Gorō Ijūin even reads such works is impressive. It means he is not entirely married to the old ways of fighting wars.*

The older man entered his office, gesturing for Takeshi to sit. A lone folder sat before his inkwell and blotter on an otherwise bare desktop. "We have been reviewing that plan that you and *Taisa* Suko devised. I have shared it with members of the Admiralty, the Army, and the Prime Minster." Gorō's face betrayed no secrets, it was emotionless as always. Takeshi admired that, and knew it was something he would have to master himself.

"The Navy claimed it is too bold, too far-reaching. The Army was reluctant to commit troops for such a long aerial voyage. It is something that has never been done before, transporting troops so far and expecting them to fight."

For a moment, Togo Takeshi felt his plan begin to crumble in his mind. Gorō must have sensed it, because he continued a heartbeat later. "I informed them that this was the will of his Majesty. I told them the time had come for Japan to assert itself and show the world we had erased our past failures and were a nation to be reckoned with. As such, they have fully committed to this mission."

Takeshi tried to hide his smile, but failed miserably. "Thank you, *Gensui Teitoku*."

"There are some changes that were insisted on. Once they realized that the Emperor was behind his operation, both branches wanted a greater role for themselves. The Navy is sending a separate task force in conjunction with yours. They desire to move on the port of Puerto Montt and take it while you are engaging the destroying the Chilean air fleet."

They desire to carve out honor for themselves. "Understood. Am I required to coordinate our attacks or do I have discretion to strike whether than are in position or not?"

"You have complete authority once you cross the Chilean border to wage this war as you see fit. Full operational command is yours."

Takeshi nodded. *Good, as it should be.* He did not want to be stuck waiting on the Navy for any reason. "Are there other changes, sir?"

"The Army has insisted that these attacks be done at night. They believe that their infantry will have the greatest chance of success to strike in the darkness, to further catch the enemy off-balance."

Night fighting with leviathans was not new, but it was tricky. Searchlights could be employed, but they were often better at lighting your own ships up as targets. Finding an enemy warship in the air with a light at night was difficult at best. "My crews have trained in night fighting. I suggest sir that we strike at twilight with our aerial attacks. That will still allow the Army to deploy in darkness and gives us the best chance to ensure that none of the Chilean Air Service escapes."

"That is what I argued, and is acceptable. We want Chile to go to bed under one flag and wake up under ours."

"I see no reason why that cannot happen. This is war though, even if it is a *Mayonaka no sensō*, a midnight war. At the same time we both know that plans exist until exposed to the flames of the first shot fired. There are bound to be some surprises, things that do not go as we intended or planned."

"You will have full command, *Tai-so* Togo," Gorō replied. "It is your responsibility to fulfill this plan of yours. If this becomes a long, dragged-out fight halfway across the world, we might very well fail. Taking Chile quickly, with a lightning blow, that is the path to true victory."

"Agreed. I will not fail you or the Emperor."

"See that you do not. Your family name was tarnished once before. This is a chance at redemption. Only the honor of the nation is at stake," he said with a slight sarcastic tone in his voice.

"I will bring us Chile and secure the future for our country," he said. He knew that his father would be with him in spirit. *I will restore our name to the rolls of honor.* "Sir, all I need is time to prepare. I will want to get in some night-fighting training with the crews, to increase their effectiveness. When do we depart?"

"Soon Togo...very soon. Get your people and your ships ready."

September 29, 1911

Togo Takeshi stood on the bridge of the *Fuji* as it pulled away from the mooring gantry over Hiroshima's harbor. The fleet had been disbursed to several port cities, and would leave on staggered schedule to rendezvous over the Pacific. This way, foreign agents would not have any idea that something was afoot until the fleet was well on its way.

He looked about the pristine bridge. *Tai-sa* Hasegawa sat in the raised captain's seat and tended to matters dealing with the ship. Even the brass railings seemed to shimmer, devoid of fingerprints by the attentive crew. The *tai-sa* was older than him, formerly of the navy. He was one of the few officers that had requested transfer to the air service. He had an almost jovial face, one that transformed the moment he began operations to one that resembled a bulldog. Togo's responsibility lay with the fleet itself. *We are as prepared as we can be.* He allowed himself a moment to drink in the brilliant blue sky the surrounded him on the bridge. White wisps of clouds moved like the crests of waves off to the west. It was calming—these were the skies of home.

Some of the navy colliers had left two weeks earlier to pre-position along the long route. The trip to Tahiti required recoaling at sea, and was the longest stretch of the journey. The additional Army forces aboard the leviathans made quarters cramped, but thus far incidents between the Army and Navy had been limited.

As the *Fuji* made its turn to the south, he caught sight of Mato Hinata's leviathan *Hayabusa*. *Tai-sa* Mato's nickname of the "Falcon Hunter" was well earned, and was linked to his ship. He had been the only officer disappointed with the mission. "The only way to truly avenge Tsushima is to take our wrath out on the Russians," he had challenged. Takeshi had assured him that once Chile had been secured, Russia would be sufficiently embarrassed. "Their failure to prevent us from raising our air fleet is one that they will regret. No doubt several Russian admirals will lose their positions as a result." That seemed to be enough to qualm the fiery Mato.

The communications officer looked out with his binoculars, then turned to him. "All ships are underway, sir."

"Very well. Signal them to maintain wireless silence and follow us to the rendezvous point," he said. The communications officer bowed his head and commenced the orders to send the flag signals."

Tai-sa Hasegawa rose from his seat and stood at his side. "*Tai-so*, there is no need for you to be here. We are days away from the rendezvous."

Takeshi understood. His presence added to the tension with the bridge crew. He did not care though. *This is where I belong. They need to be comfortable with me here. Some stress is a good thing, it ensures accuracy and care.* "You have matters well in hand, *Tai-sa*, but this is my home as much as yours. I cannot lead from my stateroom. I will remain here during the day-watch during the voyage. Your crew will learn to be comfortable with my presence, I assure you."

"*Hai*," Hasegawa replied with a nod.

Takeshi grinned and reached out his white-gloved hands to the leather padded rail at the front of the bridge. Looking out he saw the blue skies ahead as Hiroshima began to drift away from his view. Below was Ninoshima Island. From this altitude he could see fishing ships in the bay—some crewmen waving as the air fleet gracefully maneuvered over them. The sampans bobbed in the water below, sails billowing slightly, caught in a light salty breeze, no doubt. The green of the Island grasses moved with the same ocean breezes, rippling towards the mainland. He remembered being in the United States and being about the *Pidgeon* on its first flight. Those days seemed so long ago, when Japan was living in the shadows of the new technology.

Now things are different, and the world will see.

October 8, 1911

From his open-air table in a small café, Barton Canter stared up in awe at the sight over Tahiti. *Nine leviathans.* Nine! *That must be their entire air service!* All flew the Japanese flag and had their distinctive forecastles and lines. It was no illusion. Canter was awestruck at the sight as they hovered over the low bay of Papeete, mooring on the simple mast that had been erected there three years earlier by the French. Only twice before had airships come to the island and used the mooring mast, now there were three tied to it, lifting bunkers full of coal in the process. Others hovered in the distance, awaiting their turn in queue.

Canter paused for a moment to regain his composure, then took out the tiny vest pocket notebook he carried and jotted down a carefully encoded message. Barton had been sent to Tahiti as a covert member of the British Foreign Service. It was far from the work of spying he had hoped for when he'd enlisted. Several times in the last two years he'd paused to reflect who he must have insulted to have been assigned to the middle of nowhere.

Now this! The Japanese air service had never been seen operating this far south in the Pacific, but here they were. This was something—something that might finally get him off Tahiti and posted somewhere else. He gulped the last of his cup of tea, then rose from the table and headed off to the wireless station.

He arrived as three Japanese officers were leaving—all eyeing him with a scrutiny he would have preferred they did not possess. Canter entered and saw Tua Amaru, the fat man that ran the wireless station. He was scooping up a handful of gold coins, sliding them off the small counter into a cigar box near his projecting lap.

Grinning broadly, Tua looked up and flashed a smile that betrayed his two missing front teeth. "Friend Barton! What brings you here today?"

"I would like to send a message...back to my mother," he said.

Tua shook his head. "I am so sorry. The wireless, she is not working."

"Not working?"

"Tube issues," Tua replied. "I will not be able to send a message for weeks."

"Two weeks?" Barton said. "Look, this message is for my mother. She is very sick—"

"I am so sorry to hear that my friend, but the wireless, she is not working."

The British spy understood now...the Japanese leaving and the wireless not working. *They paid this wanker off!* Canter leaned in over the counter and lowered his voice. "Look Tua, if it is a matter of money, I have access to quite a bit. Name your price."

The dark-skinned man shook his head. "It is not about money, friend Barton. The Japanese, they *bought* several of my tubes. They say theirs are not working. They paid a great deal. I have to order replacements—and that will take time."

Bloody hell! "Look, I will make it worth your while," he said just above a whisper.

"It is a done deal, my friend," Tua replied. "They paid me more than I make in two years here working for the French."

"I will pay you more. Go and get the tubes back," he urged.

Tua Amaru shook his head. "You no understand, Barton. Look up in the sky. These Japanese, they pay in gold. You British, you pay in promises. They have a fleet of ships here. I will not go back to change our deal. They can rain death down on us at any time and take the tubes if they want. No...the deal stands."

"When is the next merchant ship due in?"

"Three days...the run to Australia."

Three days...then another week or so to reach Australia. Damnation and hellfire! The one time something actually happens in this Godforsaken place, and I can't do my bloody job!

"Thank you Tua," he mumbled as he left the shack. *Thanks for nothing!*

As he stomped down the winding path that led back to the port, he passed under the shadows of one of the big Japanese cruisers, its brass tanks reflecting in the brilliant island air over him as winches hauled up bags of coal. Barton Canter had two questions he needed to get resolved. *One, where are the Japanese going? Two, what did I do to get stuck out here in the middle of nowhere?*

October 14, 1911

The *Fuji* settled in for a landing in the low hills over Easter Island's port of Hanga Roa as the other ships in the squadron maneuvered for their landings. Takeshi had seen the tall stone statues of the island on their approach, silent sentinels looking outward to the seas. Even from the brilliant light blue skies the statues looked formidable, warning all who approached that they protected the nearly treeless island.

The Navy had two colliers in port already and crews began the task of using burros to move the bags of coal to the fleet. *Tai-so* Togo stepped off the folding gantry and onto the ground for the first time in three weeks. The warm air, mixed with the tropical smells of the nearby town, was welcoming.

At his side was *Itto Koku* Hei Tanaka. The airman was there to translate. While Takeshi was fluent in English, Spanish was alien to him. For such an occasion, words needed to be concise and clear.

A man in a white suit came from the town, followed with a small entourage. He was not one of the natives, his skin was lighter, and he did not have the same appearance as the locals that were starting to gather around the leviathans. Sweat stains on his shirt collar showed a light brown, distasteful to Takeshi who carefully maintained his own appearance. The man seemed to be looking for someone in charge, and his eyes fell onto Takeshi.

The man spoke a long rolling sentence. Takeshi looked to his translator Tanaka. "*Tai-so.* He says he is Carlos Sepulveda, governor of Isla de Pascua. He extends his greetings."

Governor Sepulveda extended his hand, but Takeshi did not take it, he merely glanced at it for a moment, then back to the man.

"Tell him that this island is now Imperial Japanese territory, subject to the will of Emperor Meiji. Inform him that Chilean rule is over. Do so forcefully, Tanaka, I want him to understand fully that this island is ours now."

Itto Koku Hei Tanaka took a moment to gather his thoughts and composure, then relayed the message. The face of Governor Sepulveda sagged; his mouth opened, but no words came out.

"Inform him that we will not tolerate any resistance. A navy garrison will be placed here. His position is no longer necessary. We are not placing him under arrest unless there are problems with the locals."

As Tanaka translated the words, it was clear that the governor was confused...then angry. He babbled something, a long litany of flowing, almost musical words.

When he finished, Tanaka turned to Takeshi. "He says that this is preposterous. While there is nothing he can do to resist, he wants me to tell you that the Chilean government will not stand for this attack on their sovereignty."

Those words made Togo Takeshi smile. "Tell him that I am counting on that."

October 23, 1911

The sun was setting to the west, a brilliant orange orb behind a band of purple/pink clouds behind the fleet as the *Fuji* came into view of the coast at San Antonio. Through his binoculars, Togo Takeshi could make out a pair of mooring masts and the Chilean leviathans tethered to them. Two heavy cruisers, three lights, and a lone destroyer. There was only light smoke coming from the stacks, indicating they were not prepared to get underway. He counted the ships—they were all there, just as he had hoped.

Turning to the communications officer, Takeshi handed a wrapped-paper parcel. With a nod, the communications officer opened it. A Z-flag, or Zed flag, was in it, perfectly folded, its four quadrants of black, blue, yellow and red shimmering brilliantly. His father had raised such a flag during the battle of Tsushima. The flag was a message to the fleet.

"The Emperor expects every man to do his duty, to die if necessary, for the nation. I want that flag flown," he commanded. "Let the ships of the squadron see it before the sun fully sets."

"Hai," the communications officer said, handing off the precious parcel to an airman to run up.

"Wireless, break radio silence, send the following code word to the squadron," Takeshi said firmly. *"Mayonaka.* Send it twice and get confirmation."

The communications officer barked out the command and checked off each ship as they responded. "All ships report confirmation."

Then let us begin... He turned to the *Fuji*'s captain. *"Tai-sa* Hasegawa, the time has come. Take us in, concentrate our attack on their flagship, the *Lanza de Acero,"* he said, struggling with the Spanish name.

Tai-sa Hasegawa gritted his teeth. "Helm, bring us five degrees to starboard, drop the bow five degrees on a gentle glide slope. Engines, all ahead full. Gunnery officer, load for armor piercing, all turrets. Begin range-finding."

Almirante de Aire Cristobal Rojas was in his quarters aboard the *Lanza de Acero* when the orderly pounded on his door. "Enter," he said, putting the book on his small end table.

"Almirante," the clearly shaken airman said. "You are needed on the bridge."

He rose, buttoning his uniform jacket. "What is it?"

"Smoke on the horizon. It looks like a fleet of leviathans coming in from the west."

From the west? "Are you sure?"

"Yes sir. *Capitán* Morro sent me for you."

Rojas grabbed his hat and set off with the airman for the bridge. When he got there, he was greeted with a crew that was nervous to the point of near-panic.

"Situation," he commanded.

"Off to the southwest," pointed *Capitán* Morro. "I have ordered our boilers fired."

Rojas turned and saw the dots framed by the nearly set sun, their smoke showing more than the ships. He counted them. *Nine!* This was not some Argentinean ploy, they did not have this many ships. *Who are they?*

"Message to the squadron. All ships, battle stations. Clear our moorings. Head us south as soon as we get underway. I want to have us cross their T as they get close." *If they are intent on attacking, we need to be poised to deal with it.*

"It will be few minutes before we have power for the screws," *Capitán* Morro said.

"Damn it, we don't have a few minutes!" he cursed as the communications officer barked out commands. "Turret crews are to load for a mix of HE and armor piercing," he ordered. "Signal the *Toro Furioso* to fall in behind us. If you can, get a message to the Presidential Palace that we have sighted an unknown squadron of leviathans approaching from the west."

Whoever it was had caught the Chileans by surprise. *We can get underway, but it takes a few minutes to get boilers hot enough for full speed. The west...who would be coming from the west?* He didn't want to fight over San Antonio, but it looked as if he did not have a choice.

Almirante Rojas wetted his lips and rubbed his chins, feeling his evening growth of beard stubble, and moved alongside the *Capitán*'s seat, where Morro barked out commands.

"Sir, the *Toro Furioso* has cleared moorings, as have we," the communications officer called out.

"Alright then, let us go and face this mystery fleet."

"Two enemy cruisers and three destroyers are underway. They are going slow, an indication that their boilers are not at full power yet," the bridge observation officer of the *Fuji* called out as his eyes remained fixed with binoculars. "With the sun setting, we are going to lose them. They are moving to the south."

Takeshi squinted and saw their move. *They are moving south, then will swing back, trying to cut right in front of us.* "Are we within range yet?"

The gunnery officer shook his head. "Another three minutes, *Tai-so.*"

Takeshi turned to *Tai-sa* Hasegawa, "They are moving to swing back around in front of us."

"*Hai,*" Hasegawa said.

"Once they have committed, we will swing south—that will put us broadsides with them. Be prepared for the order."

Hasegawa grinned. "How close do you want us, *Tai-so?*"

"Close enough so we cannot miss in the twilight."

The *tai-sa* nodded. "It will be a tight maneuver, but possible."

"Our preparation and training called for this. Have our searchlight crews ready as well. "

"Sir," the gunnery officer called out. "We are coming in range. Your orders, *Tai-so*?"

"Forward turrets fire as soon as you have a plot."

Orders and commands made the air almost hum on the bridge as the *Fuji* closed with the enemy. "Forward turrets, fire!"

The guns roared with thunderous cordite explosions, their flashes lit up the bridge and the mighty ship rocked slightly as the massive guns sent their shells soaring at the Chilean fleet. Some shots missed, but there were flashes in the distance as some found their mark.

Almirante Rojas saw the flashes first and gripped the edge of Morro's seat, bracing for the impact. It came a few moments later, hard and savage. The *Lanza de Acero* quaked as two shells plunged into her armor belt hard. For a moment, he almost lost his balance, but somehow he managed to keep upright. *This is no visiting fleet—this is an attack!*

"Gunners, return fire!" barked *Capitán* Morro.

"We are still out of range," called the gunnery officer from his seat.

"Tell the black gang we need full speed," Rojas said, commanding the coaling crew to step up their efforts. "We are slow targets, and need to close distance to get our guns in play."

"You heard the *Almirante*!" Morro yelled at the engineering officer. "Get us to full steam or we will get blasted apart!"

"Message the squadron, fire at will. All ships fire at will!" Rojas called out. A few moments after the word went out, the *Toro Furioso*, with her German-made Krupp guns, opened fire. Her salvo was followed by his own cruiser, which rocked under its barrage.

Rojas did not watch to see if the shells hit; instead, he studied the skies and position of the enemy squadron. *We are close to our turning point, that will give us a run on them.*

"Damage?" *Tai-sa* Hasegawa called as the crew adjusted themselves from the shell that smashed into the *Fuji*.

"None, sir," called his damage control officer. "They hit armor only."

"*Hai,*" Hasegawa replied. "Gunners, keep up the fire." Takeshi admired the enemy commander for a moment. *We caught him off guard, but he has rallied and has started to put up a fight. To do so is the mark of a good leader.*

As soon as he said the words, the forward turrets roared again. The sunset made it impossible to see the shells in-flight, but Togo Takeshi tried. He saw flashes in the sky in the distance, as the enemy ships attempted to fire back—and as his squadron's shells found their mark.

"The lead ship is beginning a tight turn," the bridge observer called.

This is it. "*Tai-sa,* bring us about, parallel to the enemy, and get us close."

"You heard the *Tai-so,*" Hasegawa commanded. "Hard over, ninety degrees to starboard. Gunnery officer, bring our turrets to track as we move. Helm, keep us at one hundred meters from the enemy line of battle. Searchlight crews, do not turn on until I give the order."

Takeshi felt the mighty leviathan pitch in the tight turn. "Message to the squadron," he commanded. "Stay in line formation. All guns to bear as we pass. Searchlight crews wait for us to light them up first."

We will soon see if our training has paid off.

Rojas could smell smoke mixed with cordite on the bridge as his ship made the tight turn. It was a bold maneuver, the best he could muster in such a short period of time. The enemy shells were chewing away at the *Lanza de Acero.* The *Toro Furioso,* behind him in line, had taken a brutal blow to her superstructure, the shell plunging deep and sending a plume of flames into the early night, marking her position.

The gunners from the *Lanza de Acero* fired mid-turn, rocking the ship hard. The flash of their barrels was momentarily blinding. He saw a flicker in the distance of a hit, but there was no way to know how bad it was.

The darkness worried him. *I cannot see my enemy and we have done little training for night combat.* Cursing for not insisting that the Defense Ministry give him the funds, he rubbed his chin in angst, the stubble acting like sandpaper on his hand. *Now they may pay the price for their shortsightedness.*

The bridge observer called out, "*Almirante*! I have a bearing on the lead enemy ship," he called out. "They are turning hard west. I think they mean to pass us in-battle-line."

His words hit hard. They had nine airships, he had six—and all of his ships were older. *Whoever they are, they have planned this well. They could have attacked in daylight, but chose to do this at night. We will not go down quietly—we will give them battle.*

"Very well," he said in a grimly determined tone. "Signal the ships to prepare for a broadside pass. If these mysterious attackers want to fight, they will pay for their arrogance."

Even as he gave the orders, Rojas still wondered just who it was that was launching this attack. *Who would have such audacity?*

"Wait for it..." *Tai-so* Togo said. Out there in the blackness, was the enemy squadron, running parallel to his approaching squadron. He could make out two of the ships, barely, and they were closing in.

"Searchlights on. Gunners—destroy them!" he commanded.

The lights came on, stabbing into the night. Turning them on showed the enemy where he was, but soon the lights fell on the enemy ships. Other ships in the squadron did the same, plastering the first ship with a blinding array of hot white light.

The turrets fired, rocking the *Fuji* hard to the side with their recoil, as the full broadside slammed into the first heavy cruiser. The shells savaged one turret instantly, sending its gun barrels flailing skyward and washing the aft deck in black rolling smoke. Another blast tore into the side of the ship, punching through the thick armor belt near her stern. The big heavy cruiser fired back, shrapnel hit the armored glass of the bridge, cracking it in several places. He head a *hiss* of air from one crack, sign of a near penetration. Takeshi flinched under the explosion, but did not let it detract him.

The *Hayabusa* roared to life behind him, also targeting the lead heavy cruiser. Its forward turrets blasted the front turret of the Chilean vessel off its mount. Flames lapped along the teak decks and back to the superstructure of the ship. The *Fuji's* secondary mounts dumping streams of shells into the side of the ship, concentrating on the stern as the ship passed. The massive

Chilean cruiser dipped downward, smoke and flames roaring out from it as it began an uncontrolled descent towards the coast.

A cheer rose from the bridge crew, but was tempered by a blast from the next ship in the line, now bathed in the searchlights. His own ship rumbled under the new assault, multiple shells tearing into its thick armor.

"Concentrate fire on the next ship," Takeshi commanded, but *Tai-sa* Hasegawa was a few seconds faster, giving the same order to the gunnery officer.

Takeshi's ears ached as the *Fuji*'s main guns roared again. Explosions, hot glowing metal throwing into the night sky, told him of their hits. One of the *Fuji*'s searchlights flickered out, no doubt from incoming fire, but it did not matter to Togo, he had the enemies right where he wanted them.

The *Lanza de Acero's* plunge down had tossed *Almirante de Aire* Rojas to the deck and slid him to the front of the bridge along with two other airmen. His ears were ringing still and he struggled to rise. Looking out from the front of the bridge, he felt the ship begin to angle nearly straight down.

"We need lift!" he called out, the ringing making his voice sound muffled, merging with the chaos in the bridge. "Damage control to engineering!"

"Fires in the coal bunkers and near the aft magazine," called out one officer to his side.

Damn! If that cordite blows, we are dead!

Officers fumbled as the lights flickered off, dousing the bridge in darkness. They flickered back on as the acceleration of the ship continued.

Rojas looked up at *Capitán* Morro, sagging against the strap in his seat. His uniform was awash with blood and a jagged sliver of metal hung from the *capitán's* forehead like an arrow. In that moment, he saw Morro's face frozen, in shock—almost confusion.

Turning away from the dead man, Rojas fumbled, standing on the forward wall of the bridge as the ship plummeted downward. "It cannot end this way."

Looking downward, at the blasted bridge window, he saw the faint glow of a farmhouse below him. He braced for the oncoming impact, knowing it was a futile gesture.

A thin haze of smoke fogged the *Fuji's* bridge as one of the Chilean light cruisers tried to turn, clearly intending to ram one of the ships farther down in the Japanese line of battle.

The *Sakura* angled out of formation to meet the threat, moving almost to point-blank range with the Chilean vessel and letting loose a torpedo. The air between them was alive with flashes and explosions that lit up the night sky like a fireworks display on the Sumida River during the festivals back home.

The stern of the Chilean ship exploded—her boilers had been hit. Flames roared from the portals near the aft of the ship as it suddenly dipped downward, following the other four ships that had been already blasted apart.

The *Sakura* was unsteady in her flight path, but still in the air, flames rising from the wreckage of her aft turret. He could not fault the *tai-sa* of the ship for breaking formation the way he did. He saw a threat and responded to it. *Such daring needs to be rewarded—not punished.*

The bridge was still a hive of activity, but the sudden stopping of the guns told him what he needed to know—the Chilean Air Service was no more.

"Squadron report," he commanded to the communications officer.

The officer worked the wireless furiously for several minutes. "All ships still operational," he responded with a proud smile. "The *Fukushima* reports a fire below decks, but believes it will have it under control in an hour."

Takeshi let out a low sigh of relief. *We did it!* "Very well. Send to all *tai-sas*, 'well done.' Have them set out for their debarkation points and unload their passengers. Communications, send to the Navy force that we have met our primary objective. Let the Navy know they can begin landing troops in the port."

He moved up next to *Tai-sa* Hasegawa and patted the man on the shoulder. "Well done."

"We have given the Emperor a great victory, *Tai-so* Togo. With this, you have erased the stain on our honor of Tsushima."

Takeshi grinned. I have honored my father, and restored our family. "When the sun rises tomorrow, our flag will be over Chile," he said not just to the Tai-sa, but to the entire bridge crew who were staring at him. "The world will see Japan in a new light. This changes everything."

October 17, 1911

Viscount Uchida Kōsai, Japanese ambassador to the United States, sat in the office of Philander Knox, the American Secretary of State, his arms at his side in a gesture of respect. His summon to meet with Knox had been expected, as was the venom that showed on the pudgy face of his esteemed colleague. His desk was cluttered with haphazardly arrayed stacks of folders and papers.

Uchida eyed the circular rug bearing the symbol of the United States on the oak floor, and realized that his chair was resting on the eagle. It was oddly fitting.

Knox leaned in, his nearly bald head shimmering from the light coming in from the freshly cleaned windows. Outside the sky was gray, purplish in the distance—a hint of a coming storm. He locked his gaze on *Kōsai* Uchida and set his jaw. "Ambassador, I take it you know why you are here."

Uchida had not risen to his position being anxious. "I do not, Mister Secretary," he replied slowly in crisp English he had learned at Doshisha University. It was a lie, one he clung to for the time being.

Knox slammed a fist on his massive dark walnut desk, the distinct *thud* filling his office. "Damn it man, your people have, against all international laws, invaded and conquered a sovereign nation, Chile!"

It took a lot for the ambassador to suppress a smile, but he did all the same. "Mister Secretary, my government took actions that were necessary to preserve its strategic interests. We did so to minimize casualties on both sides. Despite that, it is a matter between us and Chile. This is of no concern to the United States."

Knox took out a handkerchief and wiped his spacious brow. "Ambassador, it is most certainly in the interest of the United States. Perhaps you have forgotten the *Monroe Doctrine?*" There was a lilt in his voice that made the U.S. policy sound as if it were a sacred law.

"As you know," Uchida replied carefully and slowly, "I went to law school. I am more than familiar with the American policy."

"Then you also know that your country is in violation of it," Knox said, leaning forward move over the wide desk.

"Respectfully, Mister Secretary, it does not apply in this matter."

"It does indeed!" Knox replied in a booming voice, clearly aimed at intimidating his visitor. "It states that no government shall interfere or seize any government in our hemisphere. Anyone doing so would be violating U.S. interests, and would be treated as hostiles."

Uchida shook his head. "That is not quite right. It specifically says it is aimed at the European nations. It was designed to fend off the Old World governments from interfering in the Americas. My people are not European, Mister Secretary." He wanted to add, *"I would be happy to show you on a map,"* but restrained himself.

"That," Knox snapped, "Is a mere technicality. It was intended to apply to all nations."

Uchida leaned back slightly in his chair, feeling the wood against his lower shoulder through his formal frock coat. "But it does not. We are statesmen, you and I. Both of us know that the art of statescraft is the subtleties of such technicalities."

"I warn you, Ambassador, the U.S. does not take such action lightly."

"Mister Secretary," he replied calmly. "My people have not violated your precious doctrine. You and I both know that. And if your nation opts to pursue war, we will respond in kind. We have reached the coast of South America with little effort. Imagine our leviathans over your beloved California, or over your precious Panama Canal." The mention of the canal hit Knox hardest. Chile was ominously close on a map to the strategic asset.

Knox's mouth hung open, but Uchida did not wait for a response. Instead, he rose to his feet and regarded the Secretary with a piercing gaze. "I suggest you consider that carefully, Mister Secretary. Japan is no longer subservient to the whims of other nations. We stand proudly...as equals."

With that, he turned and stepped off the rug, heading for the door. There would be time outside, alone, when he would allow himself to smile over his chosen words.

November 26, 1911

As *Tai-so* Togo Takeshi stood before *Gensui Teitoku* Gorō Ijūinas, the older officer pinned the Order of the Chrysanthemum onto his chest. When he finished, Gorō saluted him.

Takeshi saluted back. "Thank you, Gensui Teitoku," he said, bowing his head in salute.

"The thanks of the Japanese people and the Emperor go to you, Togo Takeshi. There will be a more public ceremony, but the Prime Minster did not wish to wait for such formality," he replied, gesturing to a seat in his office. Rather than sit across the desk as he had before, Gorō took a seat next to his Air Admiral. It was a gesture that was not lost on Takeshi.

"What happens now?" Takeshi asked.

"According to the Prime Minister, the reaction thus far has been what was expected, harsh words and condemnation for our actions. Chile's President remains in our custody, so there will be no government in exile. Thanks to you, it is now a province of our Empire. One of many yet to come."

"Will my requests for new ships be honored?"

Gorō nodded. "Politics will play out as it always does, but no one desires to refuse a national hero. Your new ships will come. We will need them—not just to hold what we have, but to secure other resources such as iron for steel and rubber. The world is changing, Togo. We can either be manning the machine of industry and technology, or be trampled by it."

"And the Americans?" Takeshi asked.

"President Taft fears plunging his people into a war with us, as anticipated."

Takeshi paused for a moment and his superior saw the concern on his face. "You are worried."

"*Hai*, I am," Takeshi said. "America is vast—a giant bear. We have come into its cave and defecated. They will not forgive or forget that. I fear we have awoken this bear, and have filled him with a great resolve."

Theodore Roosevelt tossed the newspaper onto the porch floor of his home at Sagamore Hill in disgust. The skies were gray and white, and a stiff breeze tried to penetrate the folds in his long woolen coat. The wind stirred dead brown oak leaves, the last to fall, swirling some into the air. The weather did not shake

Roosevelt, it never did. Nothing was as cold as Dakota in the winter of his youth.

He cradled a cup of coffee, letting it warm his hands. Alice dutifully picked the newspaper up before the wind did and folded it.

"'A sternly worded letter'...that's what that jackass Taft is sending to Japan. A letter? These Nips have violated the Monroe Doctrine, and he send them a letter?"

"Dear, you said yourself that the Monroe Doctrine applies to the European powers—not the far east," she reminded him.

"That fool has let another country invade South America, and he is doing *nothing* about it," Theodore replied. "I expect our British cousins to sit on their collective asses, but this is our backyard. That man lacks the balls God gave a sand-flea!"

"Theodore!" Alice said, raising her voice.

"Sorry, my love," he said lowering his tone slightly. "And to think I brokered the peace between those scheming devils and the Russians!"

"No one could have foreseen this," Alice chided him.

"You may be right. After all, it is halfway around the world. Japs in South America!"

"There's nothing you can do about it, Theodore."

He shook his head vigorously. "I beg to differ. If I were President, I wouldn't be letting the Japs get away with this stunt. Taft just dawdles, sending our ambassador to complain. Complaints won't do a damned thing. I know these people, I have sat across the table from them. There's only one thing that they will understand, and that is a show of force. I ought to go to the press with this. Tell them what I think."

"You have always maintained that former Presidents should be silent, Theodore," she reminded him.

"Former Presidents should," he snarled. "But *candidates* for President can say what they want."

She raised her eyebrows. "So you intend to run again?"

"By jingo, my dear; I intend to do more than run, I intend to win!"

BALKAN BREAKAWAY!

L'italie, Rome, July 12, 1912

—

Several Nation-States in the Balkan Pennisula
Declare Independence From the Ottoman Empire.

—

European and American Nations Recognize
the Independent Balkan Nation-States.

—

"The Empire WILL Strike Back,"
States Caliphate Representatives.

◆

Several Balkan nations, including Montenegro, Albania, and North Macedonia, declared independence from the Ottoman Empire in a stunning announcement this morning. While the Caliphate was quick to disavow the claim, stating that the Sultan and the Empire still maintain a firm hold on the Balkan region for their own safety, several nations were quick to recognize the fledgling nation-states, with more joining in on an hourly basis.

Long desired by the various countries that had been taken under Ottoman rule, the recent conflict between Italy and Turkey seems to have been a flashpoint for the nascent independence movements that had long since gone unrecognized by their Ottoman overlords.

Professor Mitchell Cezanne, of the Université de Paris, was quick to highlight the unprecedented nature of the step. "With the help of the significant rise of the various national identities in the region, as opposed to a focus upon the more monolithic structure of the Empire itself, it is hardly surprising that the various nations in the Balkan peninsula were quick to take advantage of the Empire's preoccupation with its neighbors."

The Professor was also quick to equate the sudden move towards independence with a lack of faith in the Empire following the disastrous two-month war between Italy and Turkey. "It can only be concluded that the recent Italian victories over the Ottoman Empire have had a revelatory effect on the other nations it encompasses, shattering what at one time would have been considered a towering belief in the enduring nature of the Empire. Facing off against a leviathan-armed opponent for the first time, the Ottoman Empire found itself at a seemingly-insurmountable technological disadvantage, unable to respond against devastating Italian aerial attacks. With the recent usage of 'carpet-bombing' tactics on several Ottoman military targets, the Empire was quick to sue for peace, resulting in crippling concessions whose economic ramifications will be felt for years to come."

In the wake of the announcement, several Balkan states have already begun to assume significant roles in the region, with countries such as Transylvania, Croatia, and Slovenia relying upon their comparative national stability, an impressive emerging regional infrastructure, and extensive trade links to their neighbors to move into a leadership role.

Professor Emeritus Julian Portman, of the prestigious Campbell Think Tank in the United States, was quick to weigh in upon the emerging situation on a special broadcast of *World Politics Tonight* on July 11th. "The fact that these Balkan nations have taken this grand step toward breaking with the Ottoman Empire is an incredible victory for all independent nations across the globe, standing as a beacon for other subjugated nation states the world over. Taking advantage of the temporary distraction by the Caliphate, they moved to announce their own freedom, with many nations quickly rallying to support them.

"Yet one must remember that the world is rapidly changing. One of the reasons for the recent Italian victory over Turkey was the one-sided nature of the conflict, as the Ottoman Empire has not yet equipped themselves with leviathans yet. It is only a matter of time before the various nation states seek out a new protector of their own, if they have not already, or the Ottoman Empire comes back to take what they believe is rightfully theirs."

Professor Portman's assumptions seem to have been prophetic, as within hours, a representative of the Caliphate spoke with Corriere della Sera, and was quick to reaffirm the Ottoman Empire's complete focus on protecting all of its holdings, especially those in the Balkan Peninsula. "Reports of any supposed breakaway by our loyal subjects are complete fabrications, wild exaggerations brought forth by the same rumormongers that have made claims of recent military setbacks in our recent conflict with Italy. The Ottoman Empire remains a strong, devoted partner to our subjects in the region, unfailingly devoted to maintaining stability and security throughout the Balkan Peninsula." The representative went on to say that any nations recognizing any faux nation state in the region would be courting diplomatic sanction, and that despite rumors to the contrary, the Caliphate would not take such libelous speech likely, and that "the Empire would strike back" both diplomatically, and, if necessary, with force to protect itself against any and all aggressors.

INAUGURAL ADDRESS of THEODORE ROOSEVELT

March 4, 1913

My fellow citizens, America stands at a crossroads with its own destiny. Our Republic stands facing a crisis like those in the days of Washington and Lincoln after him. Our enemies close in, testing us to see if we are as strong as we have claimed to be. Even nations we call friends show their true intentions during these dangerous times, acting against us to further their own agendas at our expense.

Many of our leaders have responded to these trials by backing down, giving into our opposition's demands to "maintain the balance and peace of things." They sell our country down the river and more importantly, they tarnish our reputation to satisfy the ravenous beast that is peace. They have backed us into a corner for peace. They say that peace is worth any price, that we should always strive for peace in all cases.

We all know the truth.

For nearly a century and a half, the greatness of our nation has proved itself again and again, emerging triumphant over all that would stand opposed. We overcame every time because every single great leader of this nation knew that the only way to show the world what this nation is capable of is by knowing when peace must give way to conflict. As our founding fathers knew when peace was no longer an option with Great Britain, as the Union would not allow the confederacy to tear apart this great country, we will no longer permit the other powers of this world to act as they do.

America must be ready to take its rightful place as a great leader of the world. As such, on this day two proclamations will be made to every citizen of this nation and to every nation of Earth.

First, we will at once both reiterate and revise the Monroe Doctrine. No nation, whether of European origin or Asian, or any other, will be permitted to interfere in the countries and lands of the Americas. Any action taken to interfere with or influence these countries in any malicious way will invite conflict with our nation. The Americas are under the protection of this nation, and any one that contests this point will feel what it is like to be opposed by a nation blessed by our Lord.

The second proclamation we make this day is a simple one. America is a great power. We will no longer allow the world to think otherwise. And with that statement comes both a promise and a conclusion to this Inaugural address. America is a great power, and someday we will be the Great Power, without equal on God's earth.

AUDACIEUX

BLAINE LEE PARDOE

---◆---

La Borget Field
France
February 3, 1914

Capitaine Travis Bellerose had only been in jail once, an unfortunate understanding with the local authorities during his cadet cruise aboard the *Triton* four years earlier. The incident was not one of his fondest memories; too much alcohol and too little common sense—all too common with cadets on shore leave.

As he entered the military jail at Le Bourget, the smells that greeted him reminded him of that time again. The mix of sweat, the tang of urine, dust, and mold mingled in his nostrils, which were still stinging from the bitter cold winds of March. Carved into the hard chalk soil, the walls seemed to hold onto everything—every bit of moisture, every feeling of despair.

Bellerose was young for a *capitaine*, one of the youngest ever in the French Air Service. That rankled some of the senior officers—and that made him smile. He had been aboard the cruiser *Cassard* on a simple patrol when a pair of German cruisers had emerged from a cloud formation near Dogger Bank. They claimed his ship had crossed into skies controlled by Germany. *Capitiane* Russou of the *Cassard* had disagreed...and it cost him his life. Bellerose had been relaying a message to auxiliary fire control when the bridge had been hit. By the time he had gotten there it was ablaze and his *capitaine* was like ground beef, blown apart by the opening German salvo.

The young Lieutenant *aérien* Bellerose took command of the ship...there was no other ranking officer that could be found at the time. He managed to savage the German cruiser *Lübeck* and to get his own *Cassard* into a thick bank of clouds. The Boche thought he had used the cover to break for home, but he had hung in the thunderstorm clouds to affect repairs. They moved to intercept him, and he waited, moving with the cloud bank itself. By the time they saw him again, there was no way for them to close and finished their ambush.

The *Cassard* limped home, and Travis Bellerose had been labeled a hero. The Air Service Board of Inquiry commended him for his quick thinking that had ultimately saved the cruiser. He did not savor the title, but he did not refuse it either. He shunned the parades and hated giving interviews to the newspapers, but he had been ordered to embrace the publicity—all for the betterment of the Air Service. Admiral Lisle promised him his own ship and promoted him to *capitaine* in a highly publicized ceremony. There was resentment by the officers he had passed over, and by those who had spent years to rise through the ranks. When it came to filling out the key positions for his ship, he found himself blunted at every turn. *They resent me...they think I am unworthy of the rank. I will have to prove them wrong.*

Command had told Travis he could choose his own crew, and gave him a list of available officers. He knew better. When *capitianes* offer up officers, it is for a reason, and that reason is often because they fail to perform. Stymied in his efforts to find seasoned crews, he had been forced to either go to the *École d'Aviation* and take raw recruits fresh out of school or get creative in his recruiting efforts. He had formulated his own list from talking to his fellow officers and from reputations. That was what had led him to the military jail today.

His escort led him to the cell, a massive wooden door with a small, iron-grated window at eye level. He stood in front of the cell window and looked inside.

The man in the cell was disheveled and filthy, but he sat rigid upright on the bench/bed that was attached to the wall.

"Excuse me, you are Lieutenant *aérien* Jacque Renard, are you not?" Travis asked.

The man rose slowly to his feet and turned to face the small window. "*Oui*. I am. Are you my appointed lawyer? If you are, I have many grievances about my treatment here."

Bellerose shook his head and ran his fingers through his blond hair. "No. I am *Capitaine* Bellerose of the *Audacieux*. I understand you were a chief engineer before your incarceration."

"*Audacieux*? I know of this ship." Life seemed to return to his face under his black whiskers—a glimmer in his eye. "Destroyer, *Grenouille* Class. I saw her in the shipyard when they dropped her keel. That class has fine lines and engines that purr—in the right hands, of course. I served as assistant chief engineer aboard the *La Gloire*, so I speak with experience. I know how to coax engines like that. So, the *Audacieux* is complete, then?"

"She pushes off in a few weeks," Bellerose replied. "I am in need of a chief engineer."

Renard moved to the door and his eyes narrowed, as if he were squinting to take in Bellerose's features. "Why come to me? There are surely other men that are more qualified? Other men who are, shall I say—" he glanced about his cell, "—more available?"

He's smart—good. "*Oui*. There are men more qualified, but their *capitaines* are not inclined to release them. Most covet their engineers, and with good reason. In fact, I have been hard-pressed to find someone with your credentials and experience."

"Unfortunately, *Capitaine*," Renard said, gesturing to the rest of the cell with his arms, "I am here, and your need is up there." He finished by pointing upward.

"The incident you were charged with...I have checked with command on it. They are willing to wave the charges if you would pay the damages. The Admiralty sees it as more of an embarrassment. Their words, not mine."

"They have kept me here for two months awaiting trial," the black-haired prisoner responded. "For a charge that, at most, would warrant a thirty-day sentence. So much for the brilliance of military justice. The embarrassment is theirs, not mine."

Bellerose shook his head. "I need an engineer, a good one. Your records show you to be such. It is at my discretion to have you released or not. If you will pay for the damages to the bar, I can have you reinstated as my chief engineer. Given your arrest, I assure you, you will not get a better offer any time soon. Chances are they would sentence you to be a deck hand or a brass-polisher."

"And why would you do differently for me—a stranger?" Renard asked.

"I have read your record and I hate to see a good resource wasted. You scored top of your class in flight engineering. You have seen battle before, albeit minor engagements. In combat, the engine room can be a chaotic place—it takes a special man to be able to keep order and calm with shells hitting the ship. Such men are a rarity, but from what I read, you are what I need...not some wet-behind-the-ears graduate who will soil himself at the first impact of a British or Boche shell."

Renard stared for a moment. "I agree to your terms on one condition, *Capitaine*."

"And that is?"

"Will you loan me the funds to pay for the damages?"

A man with such boldness was exactly what Bellerose was looking for.

Operations Planning was painted in black lettering outlined in gold on the placard on the thick wooden door. Hidden in the bowels of the French aviation base, it was where fleet deployments were planned, war plans were drawn up, etc. It was also known to be a place where officers were sentenced to serve, those that defied orders but were deemed too good to release from service. Smart men, usually too smart for their own good. It had taken him nearly a half hour to go through the security checks just for his visit. Bellerose entered the room and a half-dozen officers glanced up from their desks. He surveyed the room, found the officer he was looking for, and walked up in front of his tall desk

"Sir." The officer snapped rigid off his stool and saluted. He was a skinny man, even his uniform seemed to hang off his shoulders without touching anything on the way down.

"You are Lieutenant *aérien* Henri Delgard, correct?" Bellerose asked.

"Yes sir," he said.

"I heard about your last cruise," he added, watching for reaction.

Delgard's face reddened slightly under his slicked-back blond hair. "I, of course, have heard about you and your last cruise as well, *Capitaine* Bellerose...all of France has. My insignificant actions were far from being a secret, sir."

"The word is that you defied your captain's orders. That's why they sent you down here, to planning."

"I did what was necessary," he said sternly, without regret. "At the time, it seemed the best course of action. It saved the ship, but the cost of me getting another shipboard assignment."

"You were wrong," Bellerose said, carefully watching the other man's response.

Delgard gritted his teeth. "That was what the board of inquiry ruled. But not *too* wrong. That is why they sent me here rather than drum me out of the service."

"You would change nothing, then?" the Capitaine probed.

"I don't regret my actions," the lanky officer responded. "But now that the incident is over, I think I would have chosen a different course of action."

He has learned and is not too headstrong to admit it. Bellerose allowed himself a thin smile. "A good officer is always open to change. Look Delgard, I'm forming a crew and am in need of a first officer. If you like your job here, I won't take offense. If you want to get back in the sky—"

Delgard cut him off. "I'll take it."

Bellerose saw the gleam in the man's eyes. A chance to fly tons of steel and cordite as opposed to a walnut desk—who wouldn't want such a chance?

Bellerose's smile broadened. "Very well then," he said. "You will report to the destroyer *Audacieux* and serve under me. Get your gear together and report aboard there in two days."

Club 128
The Royal Air Service
Piccadilly, London

Captain Alistair Prentis drank the last of his glass of Plymouth Gin and embraced the warmth it gave him. Cigar and pipe smoke hung heavy in the air of the officer's club as he sat at the table and eyed his former classmate from Sandhurst, Captain Peter Banbury.

Banbury's cheeks were red and his grin was out of control, the effects of his whiskey consumption that evening. His cheek color matched his bright red hair, slicked back and shimmer in the glow of the lights. *Good old copper-nob never could hold his liquor.* Prentis rubbed his arm, which still ached. He had gotten cast off three day earlier and it was still uncomfortable. *A small price to pay for nearly losing my life.*

"I hear your ship is nearly repaired," Banbury said, slamming his empty glass hard on the deep walnut table they shared.

Prentis nodded. "She needs another few days, I'm told. The steering gear is still giving the yardmaster some bellyaches. Then again, he's an Irishman, so griping is part of his nature." Laughter rose from another table at the far end of the room, echoing off the oak floors and dark wainscot-paneled walls. He glanced over and saw the officers, a nearly empty bottle between them, and on the wall, a captured Italian signal pennant from some skirmish several years earlier.

"You were lucky to come through that scrape with the Jerries alive," Banbury said.

The worst memories of the battle were thankfully fogged by the Plymouth he had consumed. "Never underestimate the deviousness of our German cousins. They lured us in with that wireless message about a crippled ship. Bastards came out of the rising sun right at us."

Banbury nodded. "You know the saying, old boy…"

They said it together, *"Watch for the Hun in the sun."*

Prentis continued, "We *were* watching, but they still came at us."

"The reports on your engagement are classified," Banbury said. "I heard you hung back in the *Hannibal* to give the rest of the squadron time to get away."

Prentis said nothing for a moment as he remembered the orders he had barked out, and the sound of Krupp shells blasting his cruiser apart. Armored splinters stabbed at him when the bridge was hit. His arm had been broken, and he had nearly bled out there if it had not been for the swift actions of an ensign tying a tourniquet…

"Something like that," he finally responded, his mind still coping with the memories of the pain.

"So how did you do it?" his friend prodded.

For a moment, Prentis contemplated his empty glass. Discussing the incident had been forbidden, but he knew that, but at the same time the memories haunted him. Perhaps it was the gin, perhaps it was the need to talk about it. *I will not reveal much...*

"Alright old chap...now this stays with you and me, understood?"

"You have my word as an officer and a gentleman in his majesty's Air Service."

"I *did* hang back with the *Hannibal*. It was stupid of me. I swung broadsides with four levs and they tore me apart. I lost a third of my men. Yes, I bought the squadron some time to get some distance between them and the Germans, but it came at a high cost." *It is a burden I will carry the rest of my life...the men that died because of my decision.*

"I've heard that much through normal fleet scuttlebutt," Banbury said. "What no one seems to know is how you survived. The *Hannibal* is tough, I'll grant you that—but she's not a battleship. How are you still alive?"

How indeed... "We were bleeding electroid, and our engines were barely able to keep us moving. To be frank, we were crashing straight into the bloody North Sea. At the last possible moment, some of our engineers were able to get us stabilized. I came within 15 meters of hitting the water as the crew managed to level us out. Worst ride I've ever had in my entire life. We were moving like a bat out of hell at that point, way over even what a destroyer could do. Pulling out level, you could hear the hull groan at the bottom of the dive. I thought her keel might snap."

"Bloody hell! How is it the Germans didn't finish you off?"

"Fog," Prentis said, holding up his glass so that the bartender would come and refill it.

"Fog?"

"We plowed right into a big fog bank hanging off the water. I ordered the engines doused so we would stop smoking, and we lay there for a while. They could see us...the blokes probably thought we had crashed. It bought us some time to make some repairs...enough for us to limp home."

The bartender arrived and poured him another glass of Plymouth and splashed whiskey into Banbury's glass as well. "The squadron got clear, which is what matters. They thought we were dead, too. You should have seen Admiral Rife's face when we floated in at Scapa Flow three days later. Our wireless had been blasted in the fight, and everyone had presumed us dead."

"I'll bet the old boy was ecstatic."

Prentis sipped his gin and shook his head. "A mix of relief with a heavy dose of pissed off. They had started the paperwork to declare us dead. Some of the families had been notified. The Admiralty hates it when mistakes are made, you know that. He said that I had mucked things up but good, then he shook my hand and commended my actions."

The Admiral didn't want to talk about the dead men in my crew, though. 'We will take care of that Captain, nasty part of the job, but one we must all accept. You are to be congratulated for a stunning bit of command…a credit to the Air Service.' But what of my dead? The warmth of the gin in his stomach and chest did not seem to cut through the bitterness that remained.

"They didn't demote you, though…"

"No, they did not. In fact, they gave me a commendation for my actions. Embarrassing the German *Kaiserliche Luftmarine* gets you that much. It doesn't bring back the dead, though."

Prentis seemed to feel his dour mood swell. "Bloody hell, Alistair…you're a hero of the Air Service. Even the Jerries had written you off and you saved your ship in the process. We should not be wallowing in pity."

He rose to his feet, his chair scraping on the floor as he did. "I'd like to propose a toast," Banbury said, holding his glass high. "To the *Hannibal* and her gallant fucking captain, my friend, Alistair Prentis! Heroes of the Empire!"

The officers turned to their table, each hoisting their glasses skyward. "*To the* Hannibal *and Alistair Prentis,*" and "*Here… here,*" filled the air.

Flushed with humility, Prentis raised his Plymouth up and took another long swig, hoping it would numb his senses even further. If it was any other group he would have stormed out, but this was the Royal Air Service's officers. Many had faced the same sorts of challenges he had. These were his comrades in arms…they understood the internal struggle between duty, country, and death.

Prentis took his seat, accepting their salute silently.

La Borget Field
France
February 10, 1914

"So, you're the upstart they have saddled me with?" Squadron *Capitaine* Andre Laurent said as if challenging Bellerose.

Bellerose wasn't falling for the bait. It was not the first time he had encountered the hostility towards him. "I assure you, sir, I have no idea what you are talking about."

"Don't play coy with me. We both know all about you and that business with the *Cassard*."

"I did what the service required of me."

Laurent paused, filling his pipe and stamping the tobacco down into the bowl. "When they gave you to me in command of the *Audacieux*, do you know what I was told to do with you?"

He felt his face get hot. "No, sir."

The *capitaine* stepped forward and paced toward him, as if he were staking him. "Admiral Lisle told me you were a brilliant potential capitaine. But I was told to teach you what it meant to be more than that—to command a ship as part of a squadron. That means I am to make sure you are capable of thinking far beyond just your ship, but to that of a squadron, a team of men just like you."

Bellerose didn't understand at first. He felt he had those skills and had demonstrated them. "Very well, sir."

Capitaine Laurent paused in front of him, striking a match and puffing hard on his pipe until he blew a thick stinging cloud of smoke out of the corner of his mouth. "I know officers like you, Bellerose. You don't think you have anything to learn. You got promoted fast, and in reality, no one knows what you are capable of. Perhaps the *Cassard* was a fluke. To me, you are a liability. If you die, France has lost a hero. In some respects, that will make you a target of our enemies. So I will teach you, not because I like you, but because I do not want to have to deal with your death and the black publicity that would cause."

Bellerose had not considered that his status might make him a target, and it made him blush. He chose his words carefully. "Sir, I am here to learn all that I can."

"Smart answer," Laurent puffed again. "The right words will only take you so far. We'll see just how well you do when we encounter the ships of the Black Flag in the coming months."

"*The* Black Flags?"

"There is only one squadron named as such. They are the foremost British squadron in mid-Africa…a particularly nasty squadron at that. Their ships all fly a black flag on their stern— apparently they believe a flag can intimidate us. Hah! We are French, and are not cowed by the sight of a mere piece of cloth. We are forming a new squadron to operate in Africa—something to give the English pause. I have been asked to put together that unit, whip it into shape. The British like to think they rule the seas and command the skies. We have already shown them differently, and will do so now in Africa."

"And my ship is to be part of this new squadron?"

"Soon enough, yes. But before then, I want to see how you do in command of your own ship."

"I will be ready, sir," Bellerose said with a hint of enthusiasm.

"I think you are green, *capitaine*. I hope you prove me wrong."

Office of Sky-Admiral Royce Benson
Royal Air Service Headquarters
South of London

Captain Peter Banbury stood at attention in front of the massive oak desk of the Sky-Admiral. The older man was portly, his uniform buttons almost strained as his stomach thrust out. His white mustache stood out against the red blush of his skin. The Sky-Admiral was a prickly man, and he didn't look up from his paperwork as Banbury stood for two minutes before him. When he did look up, the old admiral put on his spectacles and eyed Peter from top the bottom before motioning to a chair.

"Captain Banbury," he said, shuffling through the stack of papers piled high on his left. He found one he wanted and pulled it out. "Ah, here it is. The cruiser *Hannibal*. I received word that the dockyard had a few delays, problems with your steering gear, but the dockmaster says you can launch in another week."

"Yes, sir," Banbury said.

"Well then," Sky-Admiral Benson said, "We need to find a squadron for you."

That surprised Banbury. "Sir, the *Hannibal* has been part of the Hunting Hawks Squadron since she launched. I assumed we would be returning to them."

The Sky-Admiral's white bushy eyebrows cocked momentarily as he locked gazes with him. "I would presume nothing of the sort, Captain Banbury. You serve the Empire and you go where the Empire needs you."

"Of course, sir."

"I was thinking a posting to the south," the Sky-Admiral said.

Immediately Banbury's mind went to the Straits of Dover—always a hotly contested passage. Clashes over those skies were often and almost always inconclusive. It was an honor, but it also meant a great deal of battle. *I should be happy at this posting, but I was hoping to return to the Hawks.* "If that is what you want. We will keep the Frenchies out of the Straits—you have my word."

Benson flinched at his words. "The Straits? No, you misunderstand, Banbury. I'm sending you *south*, into Africa. The *Hannibal* will be attached to the Black Flag Squadron. Sky Rear-Admiral Drake commands there. As soon as you able to get underway, you'll report to him."

The Black Flags! Banbury could not suppress his smile. Their exploits in defending the Empire in Africa were the stuff of air service legend. He said nothing for a few moments as his mind raced with excitement and a bit of nervousness. *Am I really worthy of such a posting?*

The Sky-Admiral spoke, "I trust this meets with your expectations, captain?"

"Yes sir, it does," Banbury replied.

"The Frenchies are up to something," the admiral said, pulling another page from the tall pile of papers. "Obviously this stays in this office."

"Of course, sir."

"We have received reports indicating they are planning to send ships down to reinforce the two squadrons they have operating in Africa. One even hinted that they might be sending a new squadron down there. Normally, the Admiralty doesn't give much credence to this kind of scuttlebutt. You and I only know the number of rumors our intelligence people have to wade through...still, this seems to be from a credible source. We thought sending the *Hannibal* down there to augment the Black Flags is only prudent."

"It is a prestigious posting, Sky-Admiral."

"Bloody right it is. You're going because you have combat experience and a solid crew. I will have your orders drafted and sent over to your ship tomorrow."

Banbury rose and snapped to attention. The portly Benson rose and saluted him back. "I wish you the best, Captain Banbury. The Air Service is counting on you."

Audacieux
Southern France
March 8, 1914

"New orders from the *Effronté*," Lieutenant *aérien* Delgard said, looking at the hastily scribbled wireless message. "We are to slow to one quarter and hold this position in the line while the rest of the squadron redeploys. Hold our fire until fired upon by the enemy."

Capitaine Bellerose moved over and took the message from his hands. "Only us? The opposing squadron is bearing right at us."

"Those are our orders, sir."

Bellerose frowned. *Is this some sort of punishment on the part of* Capitane *Laurent?* Five "enemy" ships were heading toward him. His lone destroyer was not a match for their massed firepower. From his position on the bridge, he glanced about. Off to starboard was a large cloud formation, dense purple, towering— but it was not drifting to his stern as the destroyer moved.

What is Laurent thinking? The other ships of the squadron were swinging around the cloud, but he was left painfully alone, exposed in the blue sky against an advancing enemy. "Very well, confirm the orders as received."

These war games had been going on for two weeks, and usually Bellerose could understand his squadron commander's thinking. Not so today. He tried to tell himself that ultimately it didn't matter. He had an order in hand and that was that. Still, there was a nagging feeling eating at the back of his mind that this was an error of some sort, or a bad call on Laurent's part. He suppressed that thought...for the moment.

"Very well, then. We do as we're told—for now. Slow to one quarter, but tell the engine room we may have to throttle up at a moment's notice. Helm, keep us perpendicular to their line if you can." He could feel the ship's speed drop, an almost indiscernible sloshing of breakfast in his stomach. In the distance, he glanced over and watched the rest of the squadron breaking off, leaving his destroyer alone against the other ships.

This is just an exercise, he reminded himself. The "shells" the ships fired were rigged with powder bursts, to mark the ships with a white powdery substance to simulate damage. While just an exercise, he knew enough to treat it as real.

The line of enemy ships didn't flinch. They seemed to be heading straight at him. *We're outgunned here. The Capitaine is sacrificing us for the rest of the squadron.*

"Sir," his first officer said. "We're coming into their guns range in two minutes."

Bellerose big his lower lip slightly. Dummy rounds or not, his performance would be noted, and he hated to be used in this way. "Hold your course, helm. Gunnery officer, forward turrets to bear on the lead ship. It was a cruiser, the *Tonnant,* a nasty beast bristling with guns. *We are outmatched.* Once the firing started, his ship would have only a few minutes of engagement with that ship alone before she was ruled by the judges monitoring the exercise as disabled or destroyed. And that was just the first of four ships bearing down on him!

"Do we have permission to release guns from the flagship?" he asked. A well-placed torpedo right now might help level the playing field, if only for a minute. Lieutenant Delgard swung around to the flagship to attempt to read the flags. The rest of the squadron was now far off, their line swinging around 180 degrees—letting his destroyer stand alone.

"No sir. Do not fire unless fired upon," his first officer replied.

We are being sacrificed. The realization stung deeply. This was not the kind of fighting he was used to. *A monkey could command a ship sentenced to die.* Anger and frustration tore at his stomach, knotting it tightly into a ball of rage. "Gunnery officer. All guns track the lead ship. Hold fire until ordered."

Sous-Lieutenant *aérien* Andre Dupont responded from his post. "Yes, sir," and immediately began barking orders into the communications tubes. As Bellerose glanced around the bridge, he could see his men were chafing almost as much as he was. *We have our orders…for now.*

"*Capitaine,*" Delgard replied. "We are now in range of the cruiser's guns."

Just as he finished, the lead ship in the exercise fired. There was a flash from the opposing ship's turrets, followed several long seconds later with the dull *thuds* of impact. The rounds used for the exercise had a significantly reduced explosive charge that shook the ship, but did no lasting damage. At least two shells went just over the superstructure, they whooshed on past before exploding harmlessly.

Finally! "All guns, fire at the lead ship. Helm, hold our position." The words were bitter in his mouth. *How long will we be able to endure this?* "I want a damage report, Lieutenant Delgard."

Delgard went over to the judge for the exercise, who stood with an odd calm at the back of the bridge. He took out a slide rule and began to move it, referencing a blueprint of the ship. He passed word to Delgard, who shook his head, then moved alongside Bellerose. "We've lost a Tesla Trim Tank assembly on the starboard side, sir."

"We'll be in range for our guns in one minute," Sous-Lieutenant Dupont replied.

"Starboard torpedo, plot and fire. Wireless—message to the *Effronté*. We're engaged and awaiting further orders." Delgard didn't have to pass on the order to the torpedo officer, Sous Lieutenant Lefevre. The bushy-haired man fidgeted with his brass calculation disk.

Again, the faux "British" cruiser opened up. This time their gunners had them in their sights and well plotted. The bracketing fire tore into his ship. No missed volleys this time. The full brunt of the salvo exploded on the *Audacieux*. Just below the bridge one of the rounds went off, spraying white powder over half of his window, obscuring their view. *Not good—not good at all.* Lieutenant Delgard darted back to the judge who was huddled over his own communication tube, validating where the shots hit.

"Loose!" Lieutenant Lefevre called.

"Torpedo away!" the gunnery officer Dupont barked out to the rest of the bridge.

The practice aerial torpedo sped away from the *Audacieux* with a snake-like contrail behind it. *That should force that cruiser to turn to avoid the shot and buy us some time.* Of course, turning would allow it to bring a full broadside to bear.

"Gunnery officer, where are my guns?" Glancing over his shoulder, Bellerose saw Delgard and the gunnery officer Dupont huddled with the judge at the back of the bridge. The lieutenant turned, his face red. "Forward turrets has been disabled, *Capitaine.*" He glared at the exercise judge, who nodded to confirm the grim result.

"We still have an aft turret. Fire at will!" A moment later, the *Audacieux* fired its own salvo. Raising his binoculars, Bellerose was pleased to see the white puffs of impact on the massive broadside of the cruiser. He knew that the judge over there would evaluate those hits, and they would not do much damage to the larger ship.

The torpedo closed with the cruiser, and Bellerose expected her *capitaine* to attempt to evade. He didn't. He was willing to sacrifice some of his crew potentially by weathering out the hit. The practice torpedo hit near the aft of the cruiser and exploded. *Perhaps that will hurt her a little more.*

The cruiser loomed closer and he had to adjust the focus to keep tabs on it. "Wireless, any word from the *Effronté?*" *Please let me disengage or do something other than float here and die.*

"No, sir," the wireless officer replied.

The cruiser unleashed another salvo—her range was best described as "intimate." The shells exploded in white powder-puffs across his vessel. Even though they were simulated hits, Bellerose could feel the ship throb with the subdued blasts. "Gunnery—get another torpedo out of the launcher and get that aft turret reloaded and firing!" he barked. Delgard huddled with the judge who dragged his pencil across the schematic diagram of the ship far too many times.

"Belay that, Gunnery," Delgard replied. "We lost the aft turret and the starboard launcher in the last salvo. We have nothing facing the enemy but our armor and our men."

He cupped his hand and pulled downward on the front of his jaw. *I have my orders, but in a matter of minutes my ship is lost.* He locked his gaze on Delgard for a moment, who seemed to sense his frustration.

His destroyer's only advantage against a larger cruiser was speed and agility. Another shell, this time from one of the other attacking ships, roared right past his bridge—sounding like a train passing by in the air. He was thankful for the miss, but knew it was a warning of impending doom if he held his position.

To hell with this! "Delgard, take us to full speed. Helm, hard to port, swing us 270 degrees. Port torpedo launcher prepare to fire as soon as we bring her to bear." *Better to disobey my orders rather than have my men die for nothing.*

Bellerose nervously stood at attention in Capitaine Laurent's cabin. The old man sat there in his chair, staring at him, but saying nothing for an agonizingly long period of time.

"So, Bellerose. Were my orders unclear? Were they in some way confusing to you?"

"No, sir." There was no point in arguing with his superior officer.

"Then *why* did you take the *Audacieux* up to full speed and swing around? Why did you then break for the cloud line following the rest of the squadron?"

For a moment, Bellerose felt like he was in grade school in the principal's office. "Sir. We had lost everything on our starboard side. Our turrets were out of action. I was worried that further damage might down us. I took the initiative to swing around so I could at least bring the torpedo launcher on the port side to engage. We were no match for the *Tonnant* and the rest of that aggressor squadron. We followed your orders until we were of no use. I managed to get off a torpedo hit and then made for the clouds for cover."

The older man said nothing again, letting his silence speak volumes. Finally: "You did so without any regard for the rest of the squadron or my orders. I was bringing us into a perfect position to drive their line. In your turn, you forced the enemy to respond to you, rather than what I wanted them to do. When we came out, they were not where I wanted them. And do you know why?"

His face felt warm with embarrassment. "Because I did not follow your orders to the letter...sir."

"Exactly. We ended up getting a draw in the exercise as a result."

"Sir, if I had followed your orders, it would have cost me my ship, sir." Exercise or not, no command officer ever wanted to lose his ship."

Laurent fumed, running his right hand back through his hair as he gathered his words. "Did it ever occur to you that your loss would have been acceptable? Or, that if you had obeyed, we would have emerged from hiding, cut their battle line and saved you?"

Bellerose felt his jaw ache under the strain of his flexing muscles. "I thought I was taking the initiative, sir."

"You did," Capitaine Laurent replied curtly. "And in doing so put my larger plan at risk." He rose from his seat and took two long strides over to Bellerose, standing only a meter away. "My plan was to swing around that cloud while you held their attention. You were my bait and they were falling for it. Coming through it in a staggered formation would have forced them to break off."

"Sir, I had no idea what your plan was."

"Damned right you didn't," snapped Laurent. "Part of captaining a ship in the *Fleet de Avion* is the understanding that you may lose your ship and crew. It is a hard and bitter reality, but one we all must come to accept. This is no game we are playing with the British out there. Someday another ship may make the sacrifice so that you and your crew will survive an engagement victorious. Part of being in command means that you must be willing to follow the orders of your superiors—*even* when they override your personal feelings and instincts. 'Initiative!' That is fine when you are out on your own on a patrol. When you are part of a squadron, you are to coordinate and fight under your commanding officer's orders."

The lesson was a bitter one, but Laurent's words were sinking in. "I understand, sir." *I failed. I failed to see the bigger picture.* In that moment he realized just how little his own life mattered. This was not something they trained you for at the *Ecol de Avion*. Following orders—that was expected. But this was not some classroom at the academy. Sacrifice was something you needed to comprehend through experience. He felt his face flush at the realization of his error.

Laurent said nothing for a moment, as if he realized his verbal salvo had penetrated the young officer. "So, you have learned from this mistake, *oui*?"

"*Oui*, sir." The words he spoke were not hollow. *He's not chiding me, he's trying to help me.*

"Everything has consequences, Bellerose. You and your crew are denied leave this weekend because of your actions. You will organize painting details and perform touch-up on your ship and my *Effronté*. You and your command crew will personally lead these details. I will be inspecting both ships on Sunday afternoon, and I expect them to be pristine. Do you understand?"

"*Oui, Capitaine.*"

He scowled slightly. "We all make mistakes. This is yours. Learn from it, or you will find yourself stripped of your command and given escort duty out over the North Atlantic in the winter. In the meantime, we shall speak no more of this incident." He paused for a moment. "Never let this kind of lapse happen again. The Steel Coqs cannot afford such mistakes in Africa."

"Steel Coqs, sir?"

Capitaine Laurent grinned. "That is our squadron's new name. I am counting on it being cursed by the Royal Air Service from this time forward."

HML Hannibal
Over the Mediterranean Sea

Captain Peter Banbury sat with his senior officers in their mess aboard the *Hannibal*. The room's fresh varnish still left a hint of odor in the air as their meal was served.

Glancing around the table, he saw his new first officer, Lieutenant Commander Alistair McCullen, flash him a grin. McCullen hailed from the lowlands of Scotland, and had served on only one tour for duty—in the Pacific. Arrogant, proud, and boisterous, it would take Banbury time to develop the kind of rapport he needed with his first officer. He found himself missing Drane Hopkins, the man that had held that post before McCullen. His body was almost unidentifiable after the *Hannibal*'s last battle, so much so that his memorial service was with a closed coffin. Hopkins' death was hard to cope with. *He practically knew what I was thinking before I did.*

Also at the table was his gunnery officer, Lieutenant Commander Robert Ash. He was nearly bald, with a thin pink scar on the right side of his scalp. That scar was a reminder of the last time he and Banbury had been in battle together. Ash had suffered a nasty head wound, and was lucky to be alive. *Hell, we all are.*

The Chief Engineer, Lieutenant Oliver Aiken, nodded as they locked momentary glances. He was short, stout man, and came from a good family; his father was in Parliament, which probably explained his commission as an officer. He too was new to the *Hannibal*, coming from service on the destroyer HML *Harken*. He was the sole engineering survivor of the loss of that ship—not to combat but to a hurricane. The short Aiken seemed almost too young to be in the service, but Banbury had read his jacket and knew he had seen more than his share of battles.

The ensigns finished serving the meal, boiled chicken. The heady smell filled the room and Banbury watched and waited for the ensigns to leave. With the click of the door shutting behind them, he lifted his glass into the air.

"Gentlemen...to the *Hannibal*."

"*To the* Hannibal," they responded, lifting their glasses almost in unison.

He sipped the wine only a little, putting the glass down and then putting the napkin in his lap. "I ordered this meal with intent, gentlemen. As you know, chicken is hardly the usual fare aboard one of His Majesties' leviathans."

Lieutenant Aiken already had his fork stabbed deep into his meal. "To what do we owe the honor, sir?"

"We are on our way to Africa, as you all know. I haven't told the crew who we are joining...I wanted to share that with you first." He reached down to the thin white box beside his chair and pulled it out next to him at the head of the dining table. All eyes fell to it as he opened the lid and pulled out a single pennant. He held it before them, a solid black triangle.

"The bloody-damn Black Flags?" Lieutenant Commander Ash said with a broadening grin.

"I'll be..." replied McCullen.

"We are to be part of the Black Flag Squadron?" Aiken asked for confirmation.

"We are," Banbury said. We will proceed to Cameroon and rendezvous with the squadron there. For the time being, we are going to maintain wireless silence...not even the daily ship reports. The Admiralty wants to surprise our French counterparts with our arrival."

The burly McCullen's brow furrowed as Banbury put the pennant back in the box. "I don't understand, sir. What does that have to do with our dinner?"

Banbury allowed himself a thin smile. "I am glad you asked. According to our boys in intelligence, the French are sending a new squadron to Africa. No doubt we will be facing up against them. They are supposedly named the Steel Coqs. Hence the chicken for dinner."

Lieutenant Commander Ash shook his head. "Cocks? You mean knobs, tallywackers, wankers? Seems like a horrible name for a squadron."

The other officers chuckled. "You don't speak French, that is clear," McCullen said. "'Coq' is French for rooster, not for your wiggle-stick."

"Ah. Much funnier my way," Ash replied, and the other officers laughed.

"Well, now that we've had our French lesson for the night. I invite you men to feast on your chicken, as well are likely to one day feast on the steel ones that the French will be sending us soon," Banbury said, waving his hand over their meal. His command staff laughed and began to enjoy their meal.

Over Algeria
Africa
May 1, 1914

As the Steel Coq Squadron crossed south into Africa, Bellerose found his mind focused more on shipboard duties than the view of the changing hot landscape below. While the continent often spun the imagination of many young men, he was in the *Fleet Avion*. For him, Africa was not an exotic land of mystery, but a place of danger. Here, far away from the constant prying eyes of government spies, squadrons of Ganys patrolled their countries' holdings. Oh, there were spies in Africa, but nothing like those on the continent. The Service was filled with stories of skirmishes being fought between ships and squadrons. Never quite enough to trigger a war, but enough to cost many good men their lives. It was a tightrope down in Africa, a never-ending balancing act between politics, diplomacy, and sheer firepower.

For the last two months, Squadron *Capitaine* Laurent had held countless exercises and drills. He paired up different ships against each other, learning their strengths and weaknesses. Other squadrons had been invited to simulate mock battles with the Steel Coqs, to test their mettle.

Capitaine Laurent had prepared the officers of his squadron as best he could. He commanded the cruiser *Effronté* and Capitaine LaRue commanded the heavy cruiser *Lion*, with the *Audacieux* and two other destroyers as escort. For a long time, Bellerose wondered if they were going to remain in North Africa. Two days ago, that had changed when Laurent had announced their first true operational deployment. "The Steel Coqs are ready and operational," the older officer had said proudly at a gathering of his captains. "It is time we show the British what we are made of."

Their mission seemed so simple—transport a regiment of troops and artillery to the southern portions of French West Africa to reinforce the garrison there. It was true that the men could have been sent by steamer on the high seas, but that would not have been a show of conviction and strength. Sending a new and fresh squadron of Ganys did more than transport troops, they sent a message of resolve to the British.

Not that things were ever that that simple in Africa. The English would want to demonstrate their resolve as well, Laurent had said so. French West Africa bordered with the British possession of Cameroon and the border clashes there were what necessitated the reinforcements. No doubt British spies noted the departure of the Steel Coqs, and guessed their destination. That being the case, the British Air Service could be expected to attempt to intervene or distract from the effort. It was an anticipated reaction, one that Capitaine Laurent was prepared for.

As they got underway, Capitaine Bellerose surveyed the bridge of the *Audacieux* slowly. The new officers had finally settled into their roles. Even he had reached the point where he could close his eyes and navigate the bridge in utter darkness—something he had practiced on the off-duty shift. Bellerose was developing a better understanding of the squadron commander as well. There had been some rough times, especially early on, but he had learned to work with the senior officer. *Capitaine* Laurent was a demanding man, precise, exacting. Bellerose had learned that the hard way. Rather than dwell on his missteps, he was determined to learn everything he could from the man.

In preparation for their mission, *Capitaine* Laurent had prepared a number of different tactical plans should they be confronted by the British. In the event of an encounter, he would transmit which lettered plan he intended to employ. Each ship in the Steel Coqs would then execute pre-designated orders. There were designations for the would-be enemy ships as well based on their position in the line of battle. The plans went through the entire alphabet, and in each of them, the *Audacieux* had a specific role to play—some more significant than others.

Such rigidity was not foreign to Bellerose, though he had envisioned having more flexibility in being able to execute orders. He had always served on independent patrols in his career, and a part of him still craved that freedom. He had retrained his thinking to be more part of a squadron, devouring and understanding fleet formations and tactics. But he had learned in the nearly fatal battle aboard the *Cassard* that independent action and skill often determined the victor. *I had been lucky that day, much more than brilliant.* *Capitaine* Laurent's plans did not offer the flexibility he craved. "There's following orders, then there's following orders according to interpretation," Laurent had coached him. "A good *capitaine* knows the difference."

Bellerose moved across the bridge and took up his binoculars, focusing them on the ground far below. There were no clouds, simply pristine air. Down below were the deserts of North Africa. Down there it was a constant struggle against heat and sand. Here, at this altitude, the air was frigid and biting. The contrast was not lost on him. The world would be a different place without Ganys and the fights in the skies…if armies were tied to the land and navies to the seas. It was not a world he liked to contemplate. *Where would men like me fit in such a world?*

May 4, 1914

Bellerose sat with his officers around the *capitaine's* table where they usually dined. He listened to the banter and offered a thin smile. Most of the talk was not about the ship or the crew, it was about ports of call, and, in the case of Bellerose, a tale about a busty female barkeep who had led to a brawl with the crew of an Italian ship also in port at the time.

For the young *capitaine*, this was the one time of the day he could relax with his key officers. Out of the view of the enlisted airmen, he could not be a rigid commander but sometimes simply a man.

Lieutenant Delgard kept the conversation serious, though. He would listen to the stories, laugh and chuckle at the jokes, but in the end, there was an air of stiffness that he could never quite shake. "*Capitaine*," he said swirling his wine in its glass. "Do you really think the British will be following our progress?" Suddenly the joy of the table was swept away and all eyes fell on him.

"I don't know for sure. If I were a gambling man, I would bet that they have squadrons out and about looking for us to make a move. That region of Africa has many important resources. Both of our countries have a stake there, and the British are the ones making overtures and calling for territorial concessions. We are simply protecting what is rightfully ours."

"If it comes down to it, will we press the issue and fight them?" Dupont asked.

Bellerose respected the man for asking the question that everyone had at the tip of their tongues. "Capitaine Laurent is no coward. That is why he has been putting us through our paces, training us so hard. If the English come with their guns raised, we will fight them. Not only that, but we will beat them."

"Do we have any intelligence on what they have down here?" Lieutenant Renard asked. "I have heard rumors with my men that the Black Flags are still operating in the region."

Bellerose sipped his own wine, a rich Burgundy he had purchased before their cruise. "Apparently the men of our own black gang in engineering should consider careers in the foreign office as spies. What your men have said is correct. The Black Flags are said to be in the area."

Lieutenant Delgard spoke up. "I heard about their battle against the *Kersaint*. They are a brutal lot, no sense of honor—"

"You did not hear from a survivor of that fight, that's for sure," Bellerose interrupted. The ambush of the *Kersaint* was something every aviator knew. It was a lesson to be learned from. It had cemented the reputation of the Black Flags in the French Air Service. There had been a public uproar of the incident, though the details of the incident were classified. France had not marched off to war as a result of the loss of the ship, but had also not forgotten what had happened.

"They said that the Black Flags circled the ship like sharks on fresh meat, literally ripping her to shreds. When *Capitaine* Brock struck his colors to save his men, the English ignored it and continued to fire until she went down in flames." There was a moment of silence after his words as each officer either uttered a silent prayer or contemplated the fate of a ship going down.

Bellerose did not have to rely on rumors like his men...he had studied the *Kersaint's* demise during the construction of the *Audacieux*. The *Kersaint* had been sent in with only one destroyer as an escort on a patrol. The destroyer had managed to make it back, battered and burned. He saw the trepidation in Dupont's eyes, and knew he had to squash their concerns. "They should have never sent the *Kersaint* without adequate support. It was a horrible and costly mistake, one we will not make again. That is why they built this squadron in the first place, to avoid the lessons of the past. We will not suffer the same fate as the *Kersaint* if we cross the Brits."

A bell rang near the communications tube. The *capitaine* rose to his feet and swiftly lifted the earpiece up. The muffled voice on the other end passed on the message from the bridge.

Bellerose heard the words and his heart begin pounding almost immediately. Lowering the earpiece, he turned to his officers. "Smoke on the horizon." *The Black Flags.* "We only have another hour before nightfall, and the range is too far. Chances are they've seen us as well. Get a wireless message to the *Effronté* to confirm our sighting." He strode to the table and stood before them with crossed arms. "I want the watch doubled tonight, Henri. I want us dark—no lights whatsoever. Third shift needs to be on alert."

Lieutenant Delgard nodded. "Shouldn't we sound General Quarters?"

Capitiane Bellerose shook his head. "If the English strike tonight, we're ready and will sound it then. I doubt they will attack though." Night-fighting is not their forte."

Night combat with Ganys was a dangerous and tricky endeavor that required specified training, something the French did much more of than their English counterparts. *They will not risk engaging us when it is to our advantage.* "I would prefer we not get the men excited and weary from lack of sleep all night for no reason. I'd rather they be rested. Odds are in the morning, we're going to need everyone in tip-top condition."

He turned to the officers at the table and scanned each one of them. "Make whatever preparations you need to tonight. Tomorrow, we see if the Brits are simply watching us or if they are prepared to fight."

HML Hannibal

"Did you get confirmation of our sighting to Rear Sky-Admiral Drake?" he asked of his wireless officer.

"Yes, sir," the Chief Petty Officer replied. "The *Grafton* confirms. I got a 'Stand By For Orders' signal after that." Banbury paced the bridge rather than sit in his seat. Somehow it was more relaxing to him.

"Did our lookouts get identification on that destroyer we saw?"

McCullen shook his head as he moved up next to him on the bridge. "They were too far to spot their name. She's *Grenouille*-Class though, that much we were sure of. Our lookouts were able to get that much."

His mind danced with the information. *Grenouille*'s were fast destroyers armed with torpedoes…the bane of every cruiser captain. The intelligence reports on the Steel Coqs said nothing about a *Grenouille* being in the squadron. *So much for military intelligence.* "Very well then. Wireless, send the information to the *Grafton*. I'm sure the Admiral will want to know."

McCullen leaned in closer to him. "It's getting dark. Do you think the Admiral will have us engage tonight?"

Banbury shook his head. "Night engagements put both sides at a disadvantage. I think the admiral will not take the risk without damned good reason."

The wireless operator spoke up. "New orders, sir. We are to turn fifteen degrees to starboard and maintain squadron order. We are to execute light management after we fall in line, sir."

Banbury nodded, then turned to his helmsman. "Very well. Helm, bring us behind the *Crusher*. First officer, it is on you to make sure we are running dark."

"Very well, sir," McCullen said.

"Tomorrow is going to be a hot day, gentlemen," Captain Banbury said to his bridge crew. "Double the watch in case the French decide *they* are willing to risk a night engagement, McCullen. The rest of you," he said sweeping the room with his gaze, "Stay sharp. His Majesty expects the most of us in the hours to come."

Audacieux
French West Africa
May 5, 1914

Dawn came to cloudy skies, but the smoke in the east showed the sky-tracks of the Black Flag squadron. They had not altered their course in the evening. Was it bravado, or had the setting sun obscured the Steel Coqs the evening before?

Capitiane Bellerose didn't care which it was. It was sunrise, and with it, the British knew the French were there. Even with his binoculars he could not make out what class of ship they were possibly facing, only their class. Two cruisers and three destroyers. Five ships against the same number of the Steel Coqs. *These are not even odds, we are French. Those poor airmen are outnumbered, and they don't even know it.*

"Wireless message from the *Effronté*," Lieutenant Delgard said. His eyes were bloodshot. No one had managed to get much sleep during the night, Delgard had been pacing the bridge most of the shift, only retreating to his stateroom when ordered. Bellerose couldn't blame him. He had only managed a few hours' sleep himself. It was the anticipation that ate at them almost as much as incoming shells.

Delgard handed him the scribbled message, and the *Capitaine* read it carefully. "'Standby for orders by flag only. We are nearing our debarkation point for our passengers. When we slow, we will see the British intentions. Laurent.'"

Indeed we shall. He was not using the wireless, not risking that the British had somehow broken the most recent code. It was also a signal, he anticipated a fight. "We have our orders. Maintain course and heading. Lieutenant Delgard, I want a watch posted to observe the *Effronté*. He will need to be watching for our orders via flag."

Delgard nodded and barked out orders and a new *Enseigne Aérien 2ème Classe* came to the bridge. The binoculars he wore around his neck were almost as tall he was. Delgard gave him his orders, and the young man's eyes locked onto the French cruiser ahead of them, watching carefully. *It is ironic, that our fate may fall the eyes of such a young man.*

Delgard moved alongside of Bellerose so he could talk without the entire bridge hearing him. "Do you think the British will make a move against us?" he asked in an almost whispered tone.

Bellerose paused, looking at his first officer. "If they are nothing else, they are British. They believe the skies belong to them. It is an arrogance you can rely on. I doubt seriously they have come a long way to simply observe us." Delgard nodded slowly.

A few minutes later, the watch *enseigne* spoke up. "Flag from the *Effronté* Capitaine. They are slowing to one quarter and preparing for descent."

"Slow us to match," Bellerose said. Delgard barked out the orders to the helm. Bellerose kept his eyes on the British. How would they react? He felt a slight surge forward as the *Audacieux* slowed her airspeed.

The British kept on course for several long, tense minutes. If they intended to attack, now would be the time. *Perhaps all of this worrying was all for nothing.*

Suddenly he saw the British ships turn, angling to intercept the French line.

He wanted to smile, but he suppressed it. Memories of his last battle swirled in his mind for a moment. "Sound general quarters!" he barked.

A klaxon sounded, and Lieutenant Delgard growled out a series of commands. Men appeared on the bridge—a firefighting crew of men, relay runners, etc. *Let us pray they are not needed.* At the communications tubes, Lieutenant Delgard validated the destroyer's readiness for battle. After three minutes, he turned. "*Capitaine*, all departments report they are at general quarters."

"Good," he said. Before he could issue another order, the watch *enseigne* called out in a young, almost squeaky voice. "Orders flag, *Capitiane!*" He squinted for a moment in the binoculars, then turned to the small booklet hanging on a metal ring at the watch station.

"Hurry up," Delgard cursed at the younger man who nervously fidgeted at the flag recognition symbols.

"Plan R," he said. "Five stars."

Bellerose paused. *Plan R.* He knew it as one of the many contingency plans. Delgard double-checked the flag from the French cruiser without having to reference the signals book.

"Confirmed sir. Plan R." Every eye on the bridge fell to the *capitaine.*

Bellerose suddenly felt the weight of the world on his shoulders. *Plan R...of all of the plans!* It called for a daring move on the part of the *Audacieux.* Her orders under Plan R were to swing around the flank of the British, then move on the largest enemy ship's in the stern, raking the rear ship if possible. The sterns of Ganys were where you could hit the engines best and where their defenses were the weakest. The risks, however, were beyond great. A destroyer could not hang in long on such an operation, especially against a British cruiser. And the enemy was bound to move in to try and take her out, get his ship out of their rear. The five stars designated their target vessel, the last in the line.

The most important part of the plan it was only applicable to the last ship in the line...the *Audacieux.* They would be going in alone, against superior numbers and firepower. Everything depended on speed and audacity on their part—and the hope that the reset of the Steel Coqs moved in and took some of that pressure off.

I have to trust my fellow squadron capitaines that they will not fail us. Resolve formed in the pit of his stomach as he felt his muscles clench. "Very well, we have our orders, gentlemen. Take us to flank speed. Get the engine room, tell them to pour it on, I don't care how hot it gets down there. Speed is our ally today! Helm bring us hard over to port. Lay us in a course just out of the range of their big guns. We'll make our run along our left, swing in behind that cruiser and tear her apart. Send a flag message for the *Effronté* confirming we received orders."

His voice was calm and even, but he was anything but that. *It was different last time I was in battle. I was a lowly lieutenant and assumed command because the* capitiane *was dead. If I made a mistake, it was out of ignorance. We were already dead, and should have died then and there. Now* I *am a* capitiane. *Any mistakes that follow will taint my name for years to come in the Air Service.*

The *Audacieux* began her turn and accelerated at the same time. The crew leaned, almost in perfect unison, as the ship listed at the apex of the long arc. The line of British ships crossed in front of them, now closer than ever. "You—watch *enseigne.* Your name."

The young man's face seemed to drain of color as he replied, "*Enseigne* Marten, mon *Capitaine.*"

"Get to the aft watch station. You are to keep your eyes on the *Effronté.* Watch for any changes in orders. We dare not send a wireless message in battle. Keep your eyes on them no matter what. If we get a change of orders, you come to me immediately. You are our eyes and ears with the squadron commander... making you one of the most important men here. Understood?"

He gathered his nerves and nodded slightly as he saluted. "I will not fail you, sir."

"On your way then," he replied. "Gunnery," he turned to *Sous*-Lieutenant *aérien* Andre Dupont. "Get the starboard torpedo tube loaded. We'll be running their battle line in a few minutes. Let's give them something to think about, eh?"

Dupont nodded. "Yes, sir!" He pivoted to the torpedo officer, *Sous*-Lieutenant Lefevre and passed the order to him. Lefevre had been aboard the *Intrépide* during her last fight under Bellerose. While the officer was a man covered with thick black curly hair and a Bohemian look about him—he had proven himself in battle. Lefevre broke out his calculating disk and began to plot the firing solution. In three minutes, he looked up. "Solution ready at the *Capitaine's* discretion."

Bellerose's eyes didn't lift from the British ships. He would not fire first, not give them the moral satisfaction of saying to the press that the French started the fight. His wait paid off. One of the British destroyers fired, not at his *Audacieux*, but at *Tonnant.* The shells went wide. *We have won the battle of the morality of this engagement, let's hope that is not our only victory.* "Torpedo, fire when in range."

Lefevre leaned over his communication tube and barked, "Fire!" Dupont looked out and saw the torpedo fire. "Torpedo away!"

Bellerose glanced at the steam-propelled torpedo streaking downrange as he sized up the British ships. From their flags and shield emblems he could make them out. The cruiser was the *Hannibal*, with the destroyers *Alacrity, Bramble, Grafton*, and he was fairly sure the farthest one was the *Crusher*. His ultimate target, the *HML Hannibal*, was a nasty brute. Classed as a Light Cruiser, she was Country Class, and more than outclassed his destroyer.

The torpedo...well, the torpedo was intended for the ship that had opened fire first. It left a white trail in the air as it moved in a long line out into the path of the lead British destroyer—the *Bramble*, he recognized her flag.

The British ship saw it and attempted to turn, leaning toward the rest of the French battle line. For a moment, he thought it was a miss, but Lefevre's calculations had been accurate. There was a flash in the distance of the explosion on the *Bramble's* superstructure, followed a few seconds later by the *boom* of the blast.

HML Hannibal

Banbury saw the last ship in the French line, the *Grenouille*-Class vessel, suddenly turn as the lead ship broke off its dive toward the ground. The destroyer turned tightly, swinging for a pass along the entire British line of ships.

For a moment, he was stunned. *What is that captain thinking?* The ship poured on speed, the smoke poured from her stacks, leaving a gray-black streak in the air.

This was Captain Atterly's fault. The *Bramble* had opened fire on the French squadron prematurely. *The Admiral will have his bollocks in a bowl for that error.* Now it seemed that the French were repaying a mistake with a mistake, sending a lone destroyer to plunge right along the line. It's arc would make it pass three of the ships in the British line before passing to their rear.

"Is he mad?" asked McCullen, staring at him.

"No—he is French," replied Banbury. "He's moving fast. Mister Ash, I want gunnery to carry that day. If he survives passing the rest of the line, I want you to blow him out of the skies."

"Aye sir," Lieutenant Ash responded, then roared a long litany of orders into his communications tube.

"He's fired a torpedo!" the ensign on the watch called out. For a moment Banbury wondered who the target was. He saw the wisp of white smoke in the air and saw it streaking at the destroyer in line before him, the *Bramble*. *Payback for you firing early, Atterly*—

The French torpedo slammed into the superstructure, shaking the British ship. A bit of flame lingered from the impact, and a new billow of white smoke mingled with the smoke belching from her stacks.

"The *Bramble's* been hit!" the watch called out, far too late. Shells arced out at the fast-moving destroyer, all missing as she passed.

That Frog is a lucky bastard. "Mister Ash, he's coming our way..." Banbury said.

"And we are ready for him, sir."

"Fire at will!" Banbury commanded.

The thunderous response of his turrets a few moments later told him that he had been heard.

Audacieux

"Good shooting," *Capitiane* Bellerose said after the devastating hit on the *Bramble*. "Reload and prepare for another, be quick about it. Our work is far from done."

As if to accentuate his point, a shell from the *Hannibal's* 4.7-inch cannons roared in front of his ship's bow. The munition exploded fifty meters off target, but still peppered the *Audacieux* with bits of hot shrapnel. The rattle of the shrapnel didn't penetrate the bridge, but it could be heard. The less experienced officers cringed for a moment. Bellerose did not flinch.

Delgard grabbed the handrail and glanced at him. "One would think they don't want us running behind them," he said with a wry grin. Bellerose nodded. The larger guns on the *Hannibal* had a longer range than his guns.

Dupont cut off any response that Bellerose might be forming. "Maximum range to the enemy cruiser on the forward turrets, sir."

"By all means, fire," Bellerose barked. A moment later the ship rocked as the two 75mm turrets sent their shells downrange. One missed the cruiser, the other slammed into her brass housings for the Tesla coil trim tanks. Arcs of electrical discharge and smoke poured out of the hole.

"Turret one scored the hit," Dupont said.

A shell came back from the *Hannibal*, slamming into the armored belt in the forward part of the ship. There was a sharp rock, hard enough to make Bellerose reach for a nearby brass support rail to steady himself, if only for a moment. Common sense said he should take his seat on the bridge, but he could not. *How can men sit in that chair in a battle? You must see what is happening to make the right decisions.*

Delgard was at a communications tube, then turned. "Minor damage, *Capitiane*. Crews quarters."

"Noted," Bellerose said. "Helm, we're going to make our run on the cruiser's aft quarter. Take us in to point blank on her stern. I want to cross her T if we can."

"She has an aft turret, sir," Delgard reminded him.

"I am well aware of that. We need to cripple her engines if we can. If not, we need to be the center of her *capitaine's* attention."

Explosions and cannon fire erupted from all the British ships as the Steel Coqs engaged them. Another shell from the *Hannibal* came in, this time on the mark. The *Audacieux* rocked hard as the shell burst. Bellerose's footing slipped and if he hadn't caught the handrail, he would have fallen to the deck. His arms ached from the pull as he regained his post. "Damage report."

Delgard was already hunched over the communications tubes. It took several long thundering heartbeats for a response. "Another blast to our armor belt sir, this time to aft," he said. "We believe it is structural damage only. Casualties—unknown."

"Thank you, Lieutenant Delgard," he said. No point in sending in damage control parties—there would be plenty for them to repair later on, especially if the plan was successful. "Helm…bring us to starboard. Put us behind the *Hannibal*. Once there, slow us to a crawl. I want to hang back there at short range, but barely move, so we get optimum advantage."

As the *Audacieux* made the sweeping turn, another shell from the cruiser exploded short of her stern. One piece of shrapnel pockmarked the aft bridge window, badly cracking the one-inch reinforced glass.

Enseigne Marten, who had been standing at the aft watch station, quickly patted his face and body for any damage. He turned slowly and looked at the *capitaine*. Fortunately, he had been spared, but Bellerose knew the younger man was badly shaken, so he gave the young man some focus. "Mr. Marten, I need you to tend to your duties. I need you to keep an eye on our flagship for any change in orders for us."

"Aye, sir," he replied, gulping down some air and returning to his station.

"Coming about, sir," the helmsman said.

HML Hannibal

There was an explosion, then a flash of electrical discharge, with blue-white lightning dancing along the hull, which was not a good sign—even if it was momentary. Tesla coils...where the electroid was storied. The coils were what kept the ship in the air. He felt the *Hannibal* dip slightly—and memories came back of his last battle. The discharge meant they were leaking some of the precious substance.

"Mister Cullen, get a damage control party to the forward coils, we've been hit."

"Yes, sir!" he responded, barking out orders to the engineering parties.

"Hit, sir!" called out Lieutenant Ash. A thin streak of white smoke snaked behind the destroyer from where the shell had slammed into her.

McCullen raised his eyeglasses. "I saw her name on the bow, it's the *Audacious*."

"So noted," Banbury replied. *She is well named, running the line the way she did.* "Helm, stand by. That Frenchie has torpedoes, and we are too close for my comfort."

His helmsman, Lieutenant Byrd, gripped the ship's wheel so hard that his knuckles looked white. "Awaiting your orders, Captain."

Another roar came from the aft turret, but the shell missed its target, if only by a meter or two, soaring off past the *Audacious* and off into the empty sky. *It's the speed—we are passing each other, and that bugger is going fast.* Still, when this was over, there would be more gunnery drills with the turret crews.

Banbury's eyes darted to the rest of the French line of battle. They were not turning to join the lone destroyer harassing him, though they were starting to arc slowly, closing their distance with the British line of battle. *What are they doing?*

The forward turrets of the *Audacious* flashed, capturing his attention. Their shells boomed against the hull of the British cruiser, making it vibrate slightly on impact. The 75mm guns of the French ship hitting him did not concern him as a much as the earlier hit on the electrode system. "Mister McCullen, what is the word on that electroid leak?" he asked, cursing the luck of his French counterpart.

"Nothing yet, sir," he replied.

Banbury didn't hesitate. "Get down there and take command of the damage control party yourself." *I have no intention of crashing...not today.*

McCullen nodded, his brow glistening with sweat. He started for the aft hatch when the ensign of the watch barked out the words no airman wants to hear. "Torpedo...incoming!"

Banbury pivoted and saw only a thin contrail in the air, seeming to stab right at him and his ship. "Helm, hard to port, take us down fifteen degrees!"

The *Hannibal* lurched hard as the helmsman executed the order...but would it be enough?

Audacieux

Captaine Bellerose called out, "Fire the forward turrets. If you would, another torpedo as well. Let's keep them dancing to our tune."

Another flash from the *Hannibal*, as her starboard batteries fired. A heartbeat later, the *Audacieux* rocked again from another hit, this time twisting slightly along her keel line as the explosion of impact merged with the *boom* of the cannons firing. The hit was to the far aft on the ship. *Capitaine* Bellerose spun and looked to the rear of his ship and saw a plume of smoke trailing from where the shell had hit.

His forward turrets fired in response. Lifting his binoculars, he swore he could see the shells racing through the air. One missed short, the other punched into the British cruiser and went off a millisecond later. Gray-white smoke billowed out of the jagged hole. In the distance, he could barely see his fellow French ships beginning their slow turn. The British line seemed to realize the danger of the *Audacieux* getting into their rear. They began to turn as well.

The torpedo whisked out of its tube straight at the *Hannibal*, boring it on it mercilessly. The hulking cruiser dipped down by the bow and started a turn away, but the torpedo crew had aimed anticipating the "dip and twist"—a common British evasion. If it had been a destroyer at this range, they might have been able to avoid the shot by virtue of their speed and maneuverability. The *Hannibal*, however, traded speed and agility for armor and firepower.

The French torpedo hit its target amidships with a bright yellow and orange flash. The concussive blast rolled over the *Audacieux* a moment later, confirming the hit. The *Hannibal* leveled out, smoke rolling from the hit. Another shot from the British ship roared past, no doubt missing because of the sudden dive. "Reload that torpedo...we are going to need it."

Lieutenant Delgard called from the first officer's post. "Word from Lieutenant Renard in engineering, sir. He says we have lost the starboard steering gear. He's got men working on it but, and these are his words, 'no promises.'"

"Understood," Bellerose said as they finished their pass of the British cruiser. "Helm, the time has come for us to fulfill our duty. Adjust our course to bring us right across their ass. When we get there, slow us down—I want to sink as much as we can into that ship."

"Aye, sir," the helmsman responded. The *Audacieux* began to turn, arcing gracefully toward the rear of the British line of battle.

"Gunnery Officer, get ready on all turrets and the torpedo tube."

As if protesting, another British 4.7-inch shell exploded against his ship. The metal under him groaned under the impact. Bellerose ignored it. Plan R assumed that the ship executing the *Audacieux's* part would suffer a great deal of damage. That was the very nature of being "the bait."

Captain Bellerose glanced out at the other British ships and saw their line was breaking, turning to respond to his presence at the rear of their line. He could barely make out the rest of the Steel Coqs, but he assumed they were swinging in on the British as well.

"Dupont—have your men pour it on—it is now or never."

HML Hannibal

The *Audacious* began her deadly turn, and instantly Banbury knew they were going to move to cross his T. *Like hell—*

"Helm, swing hard over toward him, tight turn. Do not let him get on our ass."

The helmsman spun the brass wheel with all his might. The bridge crew found themselves leaning against the turn to keep upright. The helm wheel stopped at its maximum. As the *Hannibal* swung around, the much faster and nimble *Audacious* was closing distance and at the same time, getting right to where she wanted to be…behind them.

That captain of theirs is like a tick…he bloody won't let go.

"Tell the rear turret to rig for continuous fire. They are all we have," he commanded. As soon as he spoke, the French destroyer began to bark shells into the rear of his ship. The thunder-like rumble of the hits made the entire cruiser shake. Banbury moved to the rear observation window on the bridge to get a better view.

It was then he saw the torpedo launch from his adversary. "Helm—"

Audacieux

The cacophony of noise on the destroyer drowned out all other sounds as the turrets opened up. Some of the shots missed, but most found their mark as the ship came along the port aft of the *Hannibal*. The starboard torpedo launched on a stream of white smoke. At first, it looked as if the hulking cruiser was going to ignore it. But at the last moment she turned more to port, evading the torpedo by a matter of a half dozen meters. *Damn!* Explosions from incoming French shells flashed along the *Hannibal's* aft port side.

"Hit them again with another torpedo. Helm, slow us as we cross their stern. Dupont, keep those turrets firing."

A series of *"yes, sirs"* echoed across the bridge as the *Audacieux* swung in behind the larger British ship.

"*Capitaine!*" one of the watch *enseignes* called out, pointing into the distance. One of the British destroyers, the *Alacrity*, was falling out of the formation and turning to head past the Hannibal, in direct pursuit of the *Audacieux*.

"Thank you, *enseigne*," Bellerose called out. Now it would be two against one. That was not unexpected. "They just don't want us back here." As if agreeing with him, the *Hannibal's* aft turret unleashed a deadly short-range salve that tore into the forward superstructure of his ship. The *Audacieux* throbbed violently under the hit. Smoke obscured his view, and the cordite in the air stung his eyes. From where it hit, Bellerose could see that it shouldn't have been anything vital. *As long as the turrets can still fire—we can still do some damage.*

The rear of the British cruiser began to pass at what seemed like painfully close range. He could see the black squadron flag taut as the ship passed. "Gunnery—tear that ship apart!"

Dupont bellowed out orders to the point that his voice nearly cracked. Crossing the T—firing broadside up the length of the ship—practically guaranteed that every shell would hit something. The two forward turrets fired at the same time—both shots hitting the hull of the British ship.

A blast rose from the *Alacrity* in the distance, slamming into the port side. Bellerose ignored the hit from the new aggressor. Instinctively he wanted to break off. *We have done more than enough damage to this cruiser.* His training...no...retraining took over. *I have my orders—under Plan R, we rake that cruiser until ordered to break off.*

The *Hannibal's capitiane* continued a murderously slow turn to the port. "Torpedo—fire!" Bellerose called out.

"*Torpedo away!*" Dupont and Lefevre called simultaneously. The deadly torpedo's track was measured with heartbeats. It plowed into billowing smoke from the turret hits, exploding deep into the ship. The *Hannibal's* rear funnel suddenly was pumping white smoke—proof her engines had been hit.

The *Alacrity* was still closing, he saw the flashes of her forward turret but felt nothing. It was as if he had become one with his ship. He ignored the oncoming vessel. All that mattered was the carnage he was inflicting on the *Hannibal.*

HML Hannibal

Captain Banbury remembered the explosion at the rear of the bridge. As he opened his eyes, he saw the world on its side.

Smoke filled the air as he realized he was lying face-down on the deck.

He moved, and his muscles protested, if only for a few seconds. He got to his knees and saw that only the helmsman was still in his seat. The explosion had been ruthless with the bridge crew. Reaching up, he grabbed the brass rail and pulled himself to his feet. There was a coppery taste in his mouth. Licking his lips, he tasted blood. Another low rumble shook the *Hannibal*.

One of his ears popped as the rear turret opened fire. *Good, they are still in action.* A mix of dizziness and nausea gripped at him.

"Helm, bring us hard to starboard, we need to get the forward turret to bear," he said with a cough. The helmsman, his face blackened from soot, nodded and began to swing the wheel around.

Looking aft, Banbury saw white smoke billowing from the rear funnel. French shells chewed up the teak decking, throwing bits of it in every direction as he saw the smoke and cringed. *That can't be good.*

Half-walking, half-staggering, he headed to the communications tube. "Bridge to Engine Room. Mister Aiken—status!"

It took a few moments for Oliver Aiken's ragged voice to respond. "Captain—we have a fire down here. We need a few minutes."

"We don't have a few minutes!" he snapped back. The rear six-inch turret rumbled and fired at the French destroyer. Glancing to his side, he saw the *Alacrity* swinging wide, moving in the opposite direction of his ship. Normally he would have been offended at this slight to his honor. Destroying the *Audacious* should be his honor. But the French vessel had savaged the *Hannibal*, and he welcomed the potential relief.

The heat on the bridge was stifling. Banbury removed his uniform coat and tossed it on his chair. Wiping his lips with his sleeve, he saw the streak of blood where he had bitten his lower lip in the fall. Sweat and smoke stung the corner of his eyes, but he ignored all of it. Another blast from his rear turret suddenly made the French ship drop slightly, if only a few meters.

Come on, lads…finish them off!

Audacieux

The British cruiser's aft six-inch gun barked boomed loudly at almost lethal range, sending tongues of flame raging out the barrels as he unleashed a deadly salvo into his ship. The *Audacieux* dipped slightly under the impact, forcing the bridge crew to grab ahold of anything that they could to keep balance. Bellerose could tell that this hit had dug deep into the soul of his ship, but how bad was still unknown. "First officer—damage report!"

His own forward turrets fired again, but he could not see if they had done any damage; smoke was obscuring the target. He hoped his gunners had a better view. Looking across his bow, he saw the *Alacrity* closing quickly, gracefully moving to complete its arc and come in behind him in only a few minutes. *Damn. We have our orders. I will stay here until the end.*

"Sir, we lost the starboard torpedo launcher and crew," Delgard called from his post.

Bellerose knew what that meant as a *capitiane*...good men, loyal sons of France were dead. *Now is not the time to grieve.* "Get a damage control party down there now," he said as calmly as possible.

"Engineering reports the starboard steering gear is operational," Delgard responded after he ordered the repair crews out. "The Chief Engineer says no guarantee as to how long it will work though."

It was enough to bring a paper-thin smile to Bellerose's sweating face. A bit of good news. His mind raced—the return of the steering gear gave him an option. "Helm, stand by to make a broaching turn to port. Gunnery, load the portside torpedo tube, traverse the turrets as we make the swing around."

The broaching turn was an maneuver that would put great strain on the already damaged destroyer. Called a fantail turn in the textbooks, it would spin the destroyer almost on a dime, allowing it to make another pass at the *Hannibal and* let him to put his bow toward the *Alacrity*. More importantly, when he started to make the turn, it might make the British destroyer rethink closing with him. At this point, the battle was not just with the guns and torpedoes, it was an exercise of the mind and breaking the nerves of your foe.

"*Mon capitiane*," Delgard said. "The steering gear repair may not hold up to a turn like that."

"Risk comes with the job," Bellerose replied flatly, broadening his smile. "Besides, putting another torpedo up the ass of that cruiser has some appeal, don't you think?"

Delgard flashed a grin as well, taking off his own jacket and tossing it to the floor.

"Sir," Dupont called out from his station. "What about that other destroyer? Shouldn't I have the turrets concentrate their fire at her?"

The moment he finished speaking, the *Alacrity* barked out a blast from her forward turret, sending another shell into the port side of the *Audacieux*. One shell missed entirely, roaring over his aft turret. The other didn't, making the ship quake from the hit and echoing throughout the destroyer with a sickening *thud*.

"Plan R," he responded, reminding the bridge crew of their orders. "Only the cruiser, Dupont. We follow the squadron commander's orders on this. Tell the aft turret to fire at the *Hannibal* as we make the turn." Bellerose said, fighting back his urge to go after the destroyer. He had already done plenty of damage to the *Hannibal*. His instincts told him to pounce on the *Alacrity*, but he remembered *Capitaine* Laurent's lessons. He had orders, he had to stick with them. The smoke made it impossible for him to see if the other French vessels were engaged or not. From where he stood, it no longer mattered. *I will not go rogue at this point...I will follow my orders.* Bellerose gritted his teeth and called out to Delgard. "First Officer, tell the engine room to give us everything they can. We lose power in the middle of this turn, we will bleed."

"Aye, sir!" Delgard said, barking orders into the communications tube.

The helmsman called out, "Broaching turn in three, two, one!" The men on the bridge grabbed onto anything to keep their balance as the *Audacieux* swung hard to port, her aft swinging far over. Midway through the turn, the ship made a metallic moan, her keel stressing under the demands of the evasive turn. The noise made Bellerose's teeth ache.

As the turn started, his ship's aft turret fired another shot, but the only damage Bellerose could see was that one of the smokestacks of the enemy cruiser toppled under the impact, and was now billowing coal smoke over the enemy's aft decks, making it difficult to see. *They will suffer with this as well.* As if confirming his point, a six-inch shell from the British vessel went wide of the stern, raining down somewhere into West Africa below.

The *Hannibal* had put a little distance between herself and the *Audacieux*, her own engines clearly damaged, as she was moving more from forward momentum than from actual propulsion. Despite the movement, she was still in deadly close-quarters range. Through a break in the smoke billowing from the injured *Hannibal*, he glimpsed the faint outlines of the French line of battle in the distance, sending shell after shell into the British line as the Union-Jackasses did the same.

The broaching turn was slow, agonizingly so. He watched as the turrets tried to match the pace of the turn so they could bring their guns to bear. It was going to be close. The British ship's aft turret roared again, the flames from the barrel seeming to reach out right at him. The shell hit low on the *Audacieux*, rattling his destroyer hard.

"Bring us back on her tail," Bellerose said to the helmsman, whose face was drenched in sweat after the hair-raising turn. "Dupont, I want that ship's engines taken out. Fire torpedo! Fire *everything!*"

Dupont's eyes flared with excitement. "Yes, sir!" He leaned over to Lefevre who was recalculating the shot. "Turrets one and two, fire at your discretion. Target the stern of that cruiser!"

Lefevre tugged at his dark uniform coat and showed him the calculations. Dupont nodded and the torpedoman yelled the coordinates down into the brass communication tube.

HML Hannibal

The smokestack that had been hit had collapsed up against the bridge. While it had done remarkably little damage, between the debris and the smoke it was impossible for any of the officers to get a good view of the rear of the ship to see what was happening. The impact had shattered the armored glass on the aft bridge, leaving the crew with thinner air to breathe, but also much cooler.

The helmsman had put his breathing mask, and others on the bridge were scrambling for theirs. Banbury did not—there was too much going on for that nonsense. A breeze took enough smoke away that he saw the *Audacious* making an almost textbook fantail turn.

He is not breaking off...what is with this madman? He is in a destroyer. His rear turret fired, he felt the recoil of the turret and heard the gun, but no impact explosion.

The *Alacrity* was tightening its swing toward the battle; Banbury saw flashes of gunfire, but could not hear any hits. *For God's sake man, he's damn near spinning in place. Hit him!*

The aft turret roared again, this time he heard a sickening explosion of shell against metal. It was a hit, but where? Had it taken out the enemy ship?

Through the white and gray smoke pouring out over the back of his vessel, he could make out the *Audacious*, still in the sky, its turn nearly complete. Even more sickening, its turrets were swinging around almost in unison—aiming, he felt, right for his bridge.

There, on the side of the ship, he saw an aerial torpedo launch. "Torpedo!" he called. "Take us down hard, spin us to port helm!"

The enemy's guns bellowed almost in unison, and their 75mm shells tore into the *Hannibal* as the ship dipped downward. There was an explosion and he flew back through the air and into the bridge's forward windows. His vision tunneled for a moment as he tried to get his bearings. His ears filled with a roaring, like a waterfall, distorting the voices around him. He felt a hand grab him and pull hard.

As Banbury staggered to his feet there was another massive blast. He felt searing pain in his leg and his left eye went red as he once more slammed into the forward part of the bridge.

Audacieux

The *Audacieux's* turrets roared in unison. One shot hit the thick armored belt on the aft port of the *Hannibal*, leaving a horrid black hole. The other turret's shells ripped into the rear of the ship.

Almost instantly there was an explosion that seemed larger than what a single shell could do. The *Hannibal's* six-inch turret suddenly lifted from her housing a good three meters, flames lapping up around her as she thudded down hard. Her guns were tossed a gimbal from the impact, like a child's toy that had been thrown to the ground.

The second blast came a moment later. Bellerose had never seen it happen before, but knew what had just occurred. The *Hannibal's* aft magazine train had just detonated. The explosion seared a tunnel of flames and death up into the battered cruiser's askew turret and off the ship in a column of bright orange, blue and yellow flames. The turret, consumed in fire, crashed down again, hitting the fantail of the British cruiser, knocking it so hard that the entire ship almost rolled as it began to fall from the sky.

Bellerose shielded his eyes from the blast, but was mesmerized by the sight regardless. He never even saw the torpedo launch or hit, he had only seen the result. The magazine train explosion had been so dramatic that the concussion had rocked his own ship, shattering one of the bridge's armored glass windows, raining bits of debris around the interior.

The *Hannibal* was, to her credit, still in the fight, though flames now engulfed the aft portion of the ship. She was putting distance between the two of them, diving—perhaps intentionally, perhaps from the damage. She was still operational. *She is a tough old bitch, that one.*

Another explosion tore into his ship, sending him lurching forward. Delgard swung around, scanning for their attacker. "*Merde!* It's that destroyer, sir, we took a hit in the rear."

There was more. The *Audacieux* seemed to be slowing—he could feel the ship pitch forward under his feet. The *Alacrity* was closing in now, on his own rear, tearing into him. "Aft turret—" he caught himself. He was going to call for it to fire at the approaching destroyer, but remembered his orders under Plan R. "Continue fire at the cruiser! Helm, swing us to port but keep us hanging on the aft of the *Hannibal*."

"Sir—but the destroyer..." Delgard said.

"You have your orders, mister," Bellerose countered. Delgard nodded to the weary *Sous*-Lieutenant *aérien* Dupont, who continued to call out to the gunners with his voice nearly gone.

The rear turret fired a salvo at the fleeing *Hannibal*, but the smoke enveloping the rear of the cruiser made it impossible to tell if the shots had hit or where. The *Hannibal* arced harder in her turn to port, swinging her tail around away from him. "Sir, engine room. It's Renard. We lost boiler number three in that hit from the destroyer. We're losing power."

"Tell him to get damage control crews down there. I want that boiler back up," Bellerose said. Even across the bustle of the bridge he could hear his chief engineer's swearing over the brass communications tube. "What's the word on the starboard torpedo launcher?"

Delgard shook his head. "They can't fix her, sir."

"All right, then," he said. "We'll make another run at her. Helm, take us to port in a low turn. I want to come up right on her ass again." Salty sweat stung his upper lip.

"Sir!" a high-pitched voice barked. It was the young watch *enseigne* Marten, his uniform splattered with spots of blood, his face blackened, "Flag message from the *Effronté*. Orders are to break off and head to the east."

Now Bellerose's steam was up. He had been waiting for that order long minutes ago, but now that it had come, he wished it hadn't. *The* Hannibal *is still in the air. Just a few more shots and she would go down.*

Then logic kicked in. *No—staying would mean death.* He accepted the order, despite what his heart wanted. "First officer, confirm that flag order," he said wearily. "Helm, belay my last set of orders. Break us to the east, best possible speed."

Another round from the *Alacrity* roared past the ship, missing the port side by three meters. The *Hannibal* was continuing its awkward diving turn, but was moving at a turtle's pace, wreathed in smoke and chaos.

Off in the distance, he saw a black trail of smoke heading downward. One of the British destroyers—apparently the *Grafton*, was dropping in a slow, agonizing spiral toward the ground. He hadn't seen the fighting that had taken out the enemy leviathan, but her loss must have taken the wind out of the British aviators. She hadn't hit the ground yet, but recovery was impossible. In a few minutes, hundreds of good men would be dead on some African hillside. White parachutes—far too few to account for the entire crew—opened as a handful of men managed to escape.

The *Hannibal* leveled off its dive, limping away to join the rest of the fleeing line of ships. Even the *Alacrity* broke off her pursuit and began a tight turn away from his ship.

"Confirmed, sir," his first officer called out, slapping young *enseigne* Marten hard on the back. The young boy grinned, his white teeth almost shining against the soot on his face.

"Helm, keep us on a heading away from the British ships—we've come too far to be taken out by a parting shot. Swing us on a wide arc to bring us up with the rest of the Steel Coqs." Bellerose tugged at his uniform coat, returning it to taut smoothness on his slender frame. He watched the British ships, no longer firing, move away. Smoke still engulfed the rear of the *Hannibal*, and she was lagging far behind the line of destroyers—proof he had done some damage to her engines. That sight reminded him that his own boilers had taken a hit.

Looking down at his hands, he saw they were trembling, the result of the adrenaline rush he had endured. For a long moment, he stared at them, then, with an effort, stilled them. "We're out of range of the enemy. Mister Delgard, take the bridge. I'm on my way down to the engine room."

"Sir?" Delgard seemed surprised.

"My ship has been damaged, my men injured. The time has come to tend to both."

HML Hannibal

Captain Banbury felt hands on him and heard muffled voices over him. He opened his eyes and only could see out of the right one. His entire body ached as they put him on the stretcher. Cold air cooled the sweat that soaked his uniform shirt.

"What happened?" he managed to say, he barely heard his own voice as he spoke.

Lieutenant Ash leaned over him, his shirt soaked with sweat and blood. "Our aft magazine blew," he said, his voice muffled to Banbury. "We've stabilized our descent and broken off contact with the enemy. You are badly wounded, sir. We need to get you to the infirmary."

"McCullen," Banbury managed. "Where's my first mate?" He wanted to give the executive officer formal command of the bridge before he was taken off.

"Dead, sir!" Ash yelled, leaning above him. "So is the Chief Engineer. Most of the crew is fighting the fires. We have to dump coal, or risk the fire getting out of hand. We are out of balance right now, listing to port."

The magazine had exploded and his ship was still in the air…it was a miracle. Thoughts of Alistair McCullen and Oliver Aiken being dead washed over Banbury, as if someone had laid a wet blanket over his face. For a moment, it was is if he couldn't breathe. That damned Frenchie had done this…killed his crew and crippled his ship. How would he explain this to the Admiralty? What could he tell them that could explain how that ship had run down the British line and had so badly savaged his vessel? Shame washed over him as he finally got his breath.

"Mister Ash, the ship is yours…" he said before the darkness overwhelmed him once more.

Audacieux
Three hours later

Bellerose's shirt was drenched in sweat as he pulled on the massive wrench. Every muscle in his body ached, but he ignored the pain and continued with the work.

The engine room of the *Audacieux* was a shambles. Piping that normally would be aligned perfectly was a twisted jumble. The deck was three inches deep in hot water from the blasted boiler. Temporary patching kept the room at relative pressure, but Travis Bellerose's ears had popped long ago, and he felt lightheaded as he pulled. The air stung of oil, grease, the sickly-sweet smell of electroid, and a half-dozen other chemical aromas.

Lieutenant Renard was in the middle of the pile of piping along with three of his engineers, barking commands. If Bellerose was hot, Renard was boiling. The loss of one boiler had cost him eight men—a fact he reminded his *capitaine* of several times. Metal could be repaired—lost lives wore heavy on his officers. *As it should…*

As Bellerose pulled on the wrench, he felt a hand on his shoulder. Turning, he saw *Capitaine* Laurent standing behind him. Immediately he let go of the wrench and looked around for his uniform jacket, which he had shed hours ago.

Laurent saw his momentary nervousness and waved a hand. "No need for formality, *Capitaine*. How is your ship?"

Before Bellerose could respond, Lieutenant Renard barked, "Who said to stop pulling that wrench, sir?"

"Lieutenant Renard," Bellerose said, feeling his face flush. "*Capitaine* Laurent is present."

"Good. Tell him to grab the wrench. You sure were not making any headway with it!" he called back from inside the twisted metallic wreckage.

Before Bellerose could respond, Laurent tossed off his own coat and grabbed onto the wrench. Bellerose joined him, and the two men managed to turn it a half twist before Renard called out, "that will do…sirs. *Merci*."

Bellerose turned to Laurent, who pulled out his pipe and began to pull tobacco to put in it. "You must forgive me, sir, I did not know you were aboard."

"I'm surprised you didn't send your first officer down here for this."

"I wanted to see first-hand." He glanced around the engine room. "It is my first ship, I would hate to lose her."

"How bad is it?" Laurent asked tapping the tobacco into the bowl of the pipe.

"We've lost a boiler, that will take a shipyard for repairs—as will some of the damage to the hull. We should be able to get her flying trim, or close to it, according to my chief engineer—but that will take a day or so. I've lost twenty-two men, and have another ten in the infirmary."

Laurent smiled. "We are going to drop off our passengers tonight and swing along the coast heading home. We all took some damage, especially the *Effronté*, but you seemed to bear the lion's share. We'll match your speed so you are protected until we make port. We Steel Coqs need to take care of each other."

Renard came out of the pile of piping, half-staggering. His shirtless body was stained with sweat and grease. He stopped next to Bellerose and nodded to both officers. "Sir, I've rigged a bypass for the damaged electroid valve. I should be able to get us trim in a few hours."

"Good work," Bellerose said.

As Laurent struck a match, Renard reached out and put it out with his fingers. "No, sir. No open flames right now, *Capitaine*. I have just started rebuilding this engine room, the last thing any of us need is for you to blow it up."

Bellerose wasn't sure how his senior officer would respond, and for a long tense moment, Laurent seemed to glare at the chief engineer. "You have brass, Lieutenant."

"*Oui*. In my line of work, sir, it is a necessity."

Laurent smiled. "Then let me take your *Capitaine* up to the bridge. I want a full briefing and we need to get out of your hair."

"Yes, sir," Renard replied—with a hint of sarcasm in his voice. Bellerose looked over at him and saw the rough-and-tumble engineer flash him a quick wink before turning and bellowing orders to his repair crew.

Laurent turned to Bellerose. "You learned your lesson well, *Capitaine*...very well."

Courtroom One
Royal Air Service Headquarters
South of London
June 11, 1914

Captain Peter Banbury stood at attention before the Royal Air Service Board of Inquiry. He only broke his stance to reach up and adjust the eyepatch worn over his left eye. Surveying the room with his remaining eye, he stood in abject humiliation before the Sky-Admirals and Captains that were assembled before him.

The *Hannibal* had made it back to Britain and was in dry dock. From what he had been told, it would be five months or more of work to get her repaired. There was talk of decommissioning her entirely, the battle damage had been so horrific. Some of the bodies of the dead were still being found, hopelessly trapped in the areas gutted by the magazine explosion and fires. So many funerals and letters to loved ones...each one seemed to take a bit of his soul.

For two days, he and his surviving officers had recounted the events of the battle to the Board—a battle that had lasted only a few minutes in real life. They had faced a verbal barrage from the officers who could not understand what had gone wrong. *They were not there...and they are looking for someone to blame.* If there is one thing that the Air Service disliked it as a disaster...and the battle in Africa fit that bill.

Rear Sky-Admiral Drake, commander of the Black Flag squadron, offered the cold facts of the matter, but he sat on the board, rather than face it himself. I am to be his sacrificial lamb.

The *Hannibal* had hit the enemy ship numerous times, but had failed to land a killing blow. It was bad luck, like a bad dice roll at a casino. The Board of Inquiry did not want to hear that. They wanted to blame long dead gunnery crews for failures, or the shipyards for the design of the fireproof doors on the ammunition train.

Or her captain...

Rear Sky-Admiral Drake seemed to look at him with contempt as he prepared to inflict the judgement. "Before we pronounce our verdict, would the officer in question care to make a statement to this board?"

Banbury nodded and tried to gather his thoughts. "I was the captain of the *Hannibal*. As her master, I alone must bear responsibility for what happened. It doesn't matter of it was a lucky shot on the part of the French...the ship was mine, so the accountability for her crew and to the Air Service is mine to bear. I accept full responsibility for the loss of the men that were under my command. I have answered all of your questions to the best of my ability."

He paused for a moment. "The one question none of you asked is, 'Would I have done anything differently?' I think it is important to have been asked. I will answer it for you, so that you know my thinking on the matter. Then you can pound your gavel and pass judgement on me.

"I would have done nothing differently. Nor would you. You won't admit it, because you were not there. You didn't see what I did. You didn't experience what I did. That ship, the *Audacieux*, she should have blown up more than once. She didn't. It wasn't about training or skill or design—it was a matter of fate and luck.

"Given everything that transpired—even the loss of my eye—I would have done everything as I did before because it was the right thing to do."

There was a long awkward silence, followed by several members of the board of review muttering to each other.

"Very well," Sky-Admiral Drake said. "In the matter of the HML *Hannibal* and the action on five May, in the year of our Lord, nineteen hundred and fourteen, this board of inquiry rules the following..."

Le Bourget Field
Office of the Admiralty

In his office, Admiral Lisle looked at the after-action report and allowed himself a satisfied smile. Capitaine Bellerose, the man he had taken a chance on months ago, had come through. He had proven himself in battle as master of his own ship. The British were once more clamoring for reparations for their lost destroyer—proof they had lost the fight, as far as he could tell. The Black Flags had been handed a defeat, and were still infuriated by it. *All of which is good for France.* Britain may have owned the seas for generations, but it was not the king of the skies. Not today.

The ever-rigid Admiral Gravois entered Lisle's office, his own copy of the report crumpled in his hand as he walked. That made Lisle even happier.

"You can wipe the smirk off your face Baston—you know why I'm here."

"My pet project—Bellerose."

The red in his colleague's face was all the answer he needed. "He was lucky—nothing more."

"I beg to differ. As does the squadron commander of the Steel Coqs, Andre Laurent. He's put him in for a commendation. You know Andre personally, as do I. Would he put in any officer for a commendation that had not earned it?"

"No," Gravois responded. "Andre is a rigid commander. Perhaps this Bellerose earned his medal. You cannot argue that his actions left the *Audacieux* in fairly bad shape. His ship is going to be in the docks for at least a month getting repairs."

"Given that he hung his destroyer off the fantail of a British cruiser at point-blank range, I'd say he did remarkably well. We build the ships for battle, and that was what he used her for. Some damage was bound to occur. That is the nature of our service."

"Bah!" was all Lisle got in response. It was all he needed.

"In fact, I think we should let this leak to the press," Lisle said wryly. "Imagine the story…'Hero of France once more defends our great nation.' The newspapers—and the people—will love it."

Gravois frowned. "We did that last time with that impertinent officer. You want to puff him up even more? Consider this—the more you make him a hero, the worst things will be if he fails at some point or worse, is killed in action."

Lisle grinned. "That time has not come yet. And if you recall, our recruitment numbers reached an all-time high when he toured after his last victory. Now our brave hero has returned victorious once more. I say we leverage his time at home to make him an even *bigger* hero to the public at large. Let the press know what happened, and of the English protests and demands."

"Baston, I have known you for years. You are taking a great risk. Such a man, if lost, could injure our efforts as much as he has helped. You are creating a legend that will cost him acceptance by other officers who will see him as an upstart."

"Perhaps. At the same time—I am giving them an example to follow. That cannot be a bad thing. Besides, Bellerose will have an important duty to undertake if war does come with England or Germany. And you know my stand on that. War *is* coming. It must. These skirmishes may trigger something bigger, or some political event is going to unfold that sparks it. And when it comes, we will need all of the *Capitaine* Belleroses we can find if we are to have any chance of winning."

"You're not considering him for...that...thing you have the shipyards working on?" Admiral Gravois's voice quaked with surprise.

"We shall see," Lisle said, leaning back in his padded leather chair and steepling his fingers in front of him. His mind raced to the future, to a war that he knew was coming. *Bellerose, I am counting on you not failing me before then...*

GENERAL ACT OF THE SECOND BERLIN CONFERENCE ON SWITZERLAND

January 21st, 1912

———◆———

{Excerpts}

SIGNED BY THE REPRESENTATIVES OF GERMANY, FRANCE, ITALY, AUSTRIA, RUSSIA, AND THE UNITED KINGDOM

GENERAL ACT OF THE 2ND CONFERENCE AT BERLIN OF THE PLENIPOTENTIARIES OF GERMANY, FRANCE, ITALY, AUSTRIA, RUSSIA, AND THE UNITED KINGDOM RESPECTING: (1) THE USE OF RESOURCES IN THE ALPS; (2) THE DIVISION OF LAND OF THE ALPS; (3) THE DEFENSIVE AND OCCUPATION OF THE ALPS; AND (4) THE CONTINUED PEACE OF THE MEMBER COUNTRIES IN EUROPE

IN THE NAME OF GOD ALMIGHTY

—

Article 2

The country of Switzerland is to be dissolved immediately, its land to be divided among the great powers. Any country that attempts to keep diplomatic relations with any part of the current government of Switzerland after the passing of this General Act shall be considered an enemy of all member states of this General Act.

—

Article 3

The people of the former country of Switzerland are to be treated fairly and humanely as full Christians and members of their new countries. Any county found in contempt of this article shall be considered at odds with all members of this conference and formally condemned by all members for their actions in relation to their treatment of the former people of Switzerland

—

Article 6

The entirety of the Alps is to be divided between the Powers of Germany, France, Italy, and Austria. The division of land is to be outlined in the following articles, the division having been agreed upon by the Member countries following natural claims to the regions involved in this General Act.

—

Article 12

Austria-Hungary is given full claim to the Country of Serbia on the condition that electroid is found within the region with sufficient quantity to justify their need for the region's supply. Austria-Hungary may not lay claim to the country without electroid being found in the region.

—

Article 13

The regions having been put under the charge of the Great Powers shall not have any military fortifications built with the capability of holding more than 5,000 men and with no more than 10-gun batteries. No training grounds or general military quarters are to be built in this region.

—

Article 21

All member states of this General act are to uphold the new territorial claims of the other member states as to maintain a peace on the European continent. Any country found in violation of the territorial claims as they have been laid out in this Act, either in claiming the region of another power or ceding land back to the people of Switzerland, shall be found in contempt of this General Act.

—

DONE at Berlin, the 21st day of January, 1912.

LAST FLIGHT OF THE SWAN OF THE EAST

HARRY TURTLEDOVE

◆

The *Swan of the East* hung at anchor above Tsingtao harbor. From his perch on the bridge, her skipper, *Luftfregattenkapitän* Karl Friedrich Max von Müller, could not see the stout iron chains leading down into the summer-warm water of the bay, nor the stouter anchors attached to them. But the SMS *Emden*'s steadiness in place proved they were there.

Karl von Müller smiled to himself, the expression fighting for room on his long, lean, aristocratic face. The son of a Prussian colonel, he'd been intended for the army himself. But he had just turned five when Rychnowski discovered electroid and turned the world on its ear. Leviathans instantly became the coming thing in matters military, and now, a year past forty, Müller commanded a *leichte Luftkreuzer* rather than a regiment of ground-pounders in *Feldgrau*. He did it with his father's blessing, too, which made him a luckier man than perhaps he fully realized.

The electroid controlled in the *Emden*'s containment tanks had no trouble lifting her more than 4,200 tonnes of mass. But moving that bulk took steam power, steam and airscrews. So did holding it in place when such was needful. If you didn't want to burn through your coal keeping the world's winds from blowing you where they would, anchors in a medium more resistive than air were needful.

Fondly, Müller set a hand on the polished brass rail of the bridge. He was proud of his *Luftkreuzer*. Launched in 1908, the *Emden* had had a busy term of service in the Kaiser's Far East Squadron. She was everything her designers had hoped she would be and more besides. Her ten 105mm guns threw shells uncommonly heavy and long of range for their caliber. With full power, she could make thirty knots. For showing the flag, for intimidating the heathen Chinese, she was a nonpareil.

Of course, the Royal Sky Fleet's newer armored air cruisers had thicker steel protecting their vitals than the *Emden* boasted. Worse, they mounted 150mm guns, even if they called them six-inchers. Against a leviathan like that, the *leichte Luftkreuzer* wouldn't—couldn't—last long.

But such worries were foolishness, moonshine, vapors. Germany and England had been at peace ever since Bismarck brought unity to the *Vaterland*. Germany followed England on the path to empire. As England had Hong Kong as a base from which to exploit China, so Germany held Tsingtao farther north. Green hills rose up behind the settlement. The brewery on the edge of town made the best beer in the Far East.

For as long as he'd lived, *Luftfregattenkapitän* Müller remembered what had been going through his mind just before a commotion behind of him made a flashover of his thoughts. He turned away from the green hills and towards a rating who had just come up onto the bridge. It was Schatzeder, one of the men from the wireless shack. He carried a folded sheet of flimsy paper and had the most appalled expression on his face. So did the young noble *Oberleutnant zur Luft* who'd just allowed him into the skipper's presence.

Müller affected not to notice any of that. "*Ja*, Rolf?" he said, as calmly as if Schatzeder were smiling from ear to ear. "*Was ist los?*"

What is wrong?

"*Mein Herr...*" The wireless operator thrust the sheet into Müller's hand. As he did, he blurted, "*Mein Herr*, some Serbian maniac has murdered Crown Prince Franz Ferdinand of Austria-Hungary in Sarajevo! His poor wife, too!"

"I hope Austria teaches the damned Serbs a lesson they never forget!" *Oberleutnant* Hellmuth von Mücke, the first officer, burst out. "They've been asking for it for a long time. Who do they think they are, assassinating people who never did them any harm?"

Von Mücke had close connections to neither Austria-Hungary's royal house nor to Germany's. But he was a good patriot and a good officer. Müller unfolded the paper and read the despatch the wireless operator had given him. "Franz Joseph's government has sent Belgrade a sharp note, it says here."

"Good, sir," Mücke replied. "I bet the government there was in things up to their eyebrows. They feed those crazy people money and guns through back channels, then try to pretend their hands are still clean."

Strange to think how a killing halfway round the world had echoes even here. In musing tones, Müller said, "I wonder what Russia will do if Austria-Hungary punishes Serbia with war. And I wonder what we will do if Russia looks like fighting Austria-Hungary."

"We'll smash the stinking Slavs!" The first officer had no doubts.

Wishing he didn't, either, Müller replied, "They're very good with leviathans. Ask Japan if you don't believe me." The Japanese were still licking their wounds after the hiding the Czar's flyers had given their old-fashioned seacraft. Pausing only to light a cigar, the skipper went on, "If we have to fight the Russians, we'll be fighting France at the same time."

Hellmuth von Mücke asked the question also uppermost in Müller's mind: "Sir, what do we do if...if England comes into the war against us?" He had to try twice before he could bring it out.

It was a terrible thought. Long had Germany and England had been on friendly—even intimate—terms. The British had allied themselves with Prussia a century ago in the great war against the Corsican Fiend—Europe's last great upheaval.

After Napolean's defeat and Germany's unification, the two nations had only grown closer. The two royal families were thoroughly intertwined. Why, King George V of England's family name—von Sachsen-Coburg-Gotha—was *German*.

Surely the English wouldn't turn against their German brothers...

One could hope not, but the madness that threatened to wash across the Continent might drown them all in the end. Müller did not care to guess what dark tidings the future held.

But he couldn't tell *that* to his officers and crew.

"There is no war yet, *danken Gott dafür*, and if the Lord stays kind, there will be none," Müller said, dancing around the question without answering it. He went right on dancing as he continued, "Even if, heaven forbid, war should come, surely England will find no reason to involve herself in a purely continental quarrel."

"Surely you're right, sir," Mücke said with hope and relief in his voice. He didn't want to face the facts, either, and who could blame him? As Müller had been thinking not long before, in a fight, the Swan of the East—the *Emden*'s nickname because of her graceful lines—wasn't likely to last long.

For that matter, neither was the Kaiser's Far East Squadron as a whole. Its two strongest leviathans, the *Gneisenau* and the *Scharnhorst*, were armored cruisers with far greater striking power than the *Emden*'s. But they were no match for the Royal Sky Fleet's flying battleships—and England also had close to a dozen cruisers that could match them in this part of the world.

"Another question to consider, sir, is what will the Americans do?" Mücke observed.

"Indeed," Müller said slowly, eyeing the first officer with startled respect. Yes, behind those innocent-seeming gray eyes lay a brain that shot fast and straight.

Yes, the Americans descended from English stock, but many other nations had sent sons and daughters to live in the United States. That distant land was peopled by Irishmen and Poles, Jews and Italians, Chinamen and Africans—even *Germans*. The behemoth on the far side of the Pacific would not necessarily follow Britain's lead.

Even if Great Britain finally decided which way it was going to go.

Müller hoped the Americans' independent streak might keep them neutral. At the same time, he feared his hope was too optimistic.

"As I said just now, there will be no war if the Lord stays kind," he said. "If one should come, that will be the time for us to concern ourselves with foreign powers' choices."

"Just as you say, *mein Herr. Aber natürlich.*" Hellmuth von Mücke was a model of subordination. He sounded as if not a drop of aristocratic blood coursed through his veins.

But, even if not a royal, he was as much a noble as Müller himself. A photograph of an apple was not an apple, however much it looked like one. You would find out the difference in a hurry if you bit into a photograph. And you were liable to find out in a hurry what kind of blood ran in Mücke's veins if you were rash enough to cross him.

Along with steam and coal and electroid and guns, a leviathan skipper worth his stripes had to keep such things in mind.

As crow or leviathan flew, it was something like eight thousand kilometers to Berlin and Vienna. Karl von Müller and the rest of the *Emden*'s complement got their news of the Powers' *Totentanz* toward war by the wireless' clicking Morse. It was like watching *Hamlet* or *Faust* from a high balcony—and through the wrong end of a powerful spyglass. Everything seemed even farther away than it really was.

Near the end of July, an old Austro-Hungarian *Luftkreuzer*, the *Kaiserin Elisabeth*, flew into Tsingtao. The *Emden* was a light cruiser, but a modern light cruiser. The *Kaiserin Elisabeth* dated from the 1890s, and from the early 1890s at that. She'd seen hard use in the generation since. A new gunboat would have given her a run for her money.

Polite as a cat, Müller said nothing of that. He wined and dined her skipper and the rest of her officers. Her CO, who wore bushy gray muttonchops and a waxed handlebar mustache of rococo splendor, said, "We'll kick the Serbs back to the Stone Age—not much of a boot, when you get down do it. After that..." When he scowled, Müller saw he was much older than he looked at first glance. Knocking back his brandy, he finished, "After that, *mein Herr*, it's anyone's guess. I wonder if even God knows what comes after that."

One of his officers and one of the *Emden*'s crossed themselves to hear such blasphemy. Karl von Müller was inclined to agree with the Austrian, though he never would have said so out loud.

The next day, Schatzeder brought Müller the text of Austria-Hungary's ultimatum to Serbia (actually, Vienna called it a timed note, but the Austrians could have called it a bouquet of geraniums, and it still would have been an ultimatum). When he finished reading it, the skipper whistled softly. "Well, we're two days away from war," he said.

"Yes, sir," the wireless operator agreed. "No country could accept such demands without being gelded first."

"Which is bound to be what Austria-Hungary has in mind," Müller said.

Being only a rating, Schatzeder did not presume to discuss grand strategy with the skipper, any more than Müller would have argued about Germany's foreign policy with the Kaiser's foreign minister. The man from the wireless shack would obey whatever orders Müller gave him...and Müller, as readily and unthinkingly, would follow whatever orders he got from his own superiors. If a military man owed his superiors anything, he owed them ready, unthinking obedience.

He studied Austria-Hungary's timed note once more. slowly nodding to himself. If the Serbs accepted it, they took the scalpel to their own crotch. If they rejected it, they gave Franz Joseph a *casus belli* every state in Europe, even Russia, would have to respect.

Or so the skipper thought, till word of Serbia's response flashed across the aether and reached the *Emden*. The men who ruled in Belgrade might be—were—nasty, murderous connivers, but they were also clever. They had swallowed as much as they could, far more than Müller had ever dreamt they would. Five of Vienna's ten demands they accepted outright, and four others with reservations. Only the sixth, in which Austria-Hungary insisted that its agents "help" the Serbs investigating the plot and bringing conspirators to trial, did Belgrade reject as an infringement on its sovereignty.

The reply would not be enough to satisfy Vienna. Müller was sure of that. Nothing but full acceptance would satisfy the murdered heir's uncle and his government—and they'd written their demands so as to make full acceptance impossible. But Serbia's soft answer was much too likely to keep her friends willing to fight the Austrians on her behalf if she was invaded. It was likely to lead to the general European war everyone had been dreading and getting ready for since the turn of the century, in other words.

In the wardroom at dinner, his junior officers seemed as gloomy as he felt. "I wish we were back in home waters, sir," Mücke said, washing down Chinese-style spicy lamb with a mug of beer from the brewery in Tsingtao. It wasn't a great pilsner, but it was a good one.

The first officer went on, "As part of the Grand Admirals *Luftflotte*, we might accomplish something. By ourselves?" He shook his head. "Doesn't seem likely."

No one tried to contradict him, regardless of how hopeless he sounded. Hopeless or not, what he said seemed all too obviously true. After a moment, Karl von Müller responded, "We are where we are. We have to do what we can. Everything depends on England now."

Hellmuth von Mücke's nostrils flared. "Who could imagine the English going to war over Serbia? It's a worthless little country. They don't know anything about it. Chances are, half their ministers can't find it on a map."

"More than half," Müller agreed with similar scorn. He raised his own mug; like Mücke's, full of the local brew. "All the same, here's to victory! May our soldiers go home in triumph before the leaves fall!" *And may we go home at all*, he added, but only to himself.

"To victory!" Without hesitation, each and every officer in the wardroom drank the toast. If any of the others had doubts and worries like their skipper's, they also didn't reveal them. They too, were professionals.

Dominoes. Old men played the game with the little ebony tiles inset with ivory markings like the pips on dice. Sometimes it was for cups of coffee or mugs of beer at the tavern. Sometimes the stakes got higher.

Sometimes boys played with their granddads' dominoes. Karl von Müller had, when he was a tyke. He hadn't played dominoes, exactly. He'd played with dominoes, lining them up so that, when he knocked over the first one, it would take out others that flattened others still, till column after column fell over. Running out of dominoes was all that limited him.

Now the assassination in Sarajevo had toppled the piled dominoes in Europe. Austria-Hungary declared war on Serbia. Franz Joseph's gunners bombarded Belgrade. Franz Joseph's leviathans flew above the Serbian capital and dropped explosives on it from above. (King Peter's cannoneers promptly shot two of them out of the sky, but that news appeared in no bulletin the *Emden*'s wireless picked up.)

Russia declared war on Austria-Hungary. Germany came to her ally's defense and declared war on Russia. France came to *her* ally's defense and declared war on Germany. Dominoes tumbled, one after another.

Germany knew she couldn't beat Russia quickly. No one could beat Russia quickly, as Napoleon had discovered to his sorrow a century before. The thing to do, the Kaiser's generals had decided, was to defend in the east while the Czar got everything he deserved and a little more besides.

The Japanese had entered the war on the side of Germany and Austria—not out of any love for the Teutonic peoples, but to prevent Russia—the nation that had defeated the Rising Sun in battle only the decade before—from swallowing much of the Pacific.

The United States soon declared hostilities, siding with France. Washington had been drawn into the conflict by the same fears as Tokyo—except America's fears were directed at Japan.

Only Britain among the great powers remained stubbornly neutral.

Though Müller wasn't sure how much forbearance neutral Britain would accord foreign warships poaching freighters in her own backyard.

A principle he thought he might be forced to explore in the near future.

The *Emden*'s skipper sighed and buried his face in his hands for a moment when Schatzeder brought him another of the terrible despatches that explained how the dominoes were falling and what it would mean for their poor benighted world.

"Will the Americans attack, sir?" asked the sailor.

"Why wouldn't they?" Karl von Müller said gloomily. They have the strongest wet navy and leviathan fleet south of Japan anchored at Subic Bay in the Philippines. Tsingtao's just sitting here, a ripe plum on the tree. Of course they'll pluck it."

"Perhaps the Japanese—" began the sailor hopefully.

Müller shook his head. "The Imperial Japanese Fleet has its hands full with the Russians. And the British will stay out of it."

"What will we do, sir?" Schatzeder asked.

"Whatever Admiral von Spee requires of us, of course," the skipper answered. "If he thinks our guns can best defend the town here, we'll do that. If he has other orders, we'll follow those."

He didn't want to join the foredoomed defense of Tsingtao, which didn't mean he wouldn't do it. The fortress and the wet-navy craft and the leviathans here could keep the *Amerikaners* busy for some time, and tie up a lot of Japanese resources, but they had not a hope of holding.

It turned out the despatch *was* from von Spee.

The message from *Konteradmiral zur Luft* Maximilian *Graf* von Spee was encoded, naturally. Schatzeder handed Müller a couple of lines of five-letter groups that might have been in Finnish or Kalmuk or Swahili for all the sense they made. Müller herded the wireless man out of his little cabin and, after locking the door, took the code book from the safe hidden behind the medicine cabinet.

Proceed to Pagan in Marianas Islands chain, he read. *Raid enemy commerce, but do not violate British neutrality pending war declaration.*

Müller nodded, more pleased than otherwise. He wouldn't be stuck like a rat in a trap, anyhow. The American Civil War had shown that commerce raiders had a strictly limited life expectancy. But it had also shown that they could make damn nuisances of themselves while they lasted. The skipper steepled his fingertips. He quite looked forward to it.

Night had fallen when the *Emden* pulled away from Tsingtao and out over the Yellow Sea. The *leichte Luftkreuzer* was brimful of coal and food and *Luftmarinen*, having taken some from the old Austro-Hungarian cruiser, some from a German seagoing liner, and a few from Tsingtao's garrison. They might not all be perfectly acquainted with the *Kaiserliche Luftmarine*'s quaint and curious native customs, but Müller was sure the petty officers would knock them into shape well before the *Emden* reached the Marianas. That was one of the things petty officers were for.

Also aboard were three Chinese laundrymen. They jabbered in their shrill native tongue and pointed back toward Tsingtao. They wanted to go home. But if they did, who would keep the Germans' linen clean? Karl von Müller gestured invitingly over the stern rail.

They were a thousand meters up, with nothing but ocean under them. That first step would be long—and final. The laundrymen quieted down in a hurry. From then on, to Müller's surprise, they became excellent shipmates. If they couldn't go home, their attitudes said, they might as well settle in. He wished more people were so sensible.

It was war. The *Emden* flew with all lights doused and all portholes closed and covered with black cloth. All the same, her star-blotting bulk would be visible to fishing boats and warships on the Yellow Sea. Worse, the coal smoke belching from her three funnels shouted *Here I am!* to the world.

That was one reason she'd left Tsingtao by night. When darkness ruled anyhow, smoke trails mattered little. Müller stood on the bridge, enjoying the sweet night air and steering by the stars and the radium-painted compass needle. All the guns were manned, the crews ready, if not eager, for whatever fate might bring them.

"Leviathans ahead!" a forward lookout cried. "Crossing our bow, and above us!"

Müller snatched up the Zeiss binoculars from a stand by his bridge station. There they were—three long, lean shapes eclipsing the stars as they drove across the sky. Each was half again the size of the *Emden*: they were real cruisers, full cruisers, not a lighter vessel suitable for little more than overawing natives. They were—they had to be—part of the Royal Sky Fleet's formidable Far East Squadron.

Not a light showed aboard any of the English leviathans, not so much as the flare of a match or the gleaming coal at the tip of some deckhand's cheroot. Admiring the Britisher's discipline, Karl von Müller hoped the men under his own command could match it. The *Emden*, of course, presented herself bow-on to the English. That gave her a smaller silhouette against the sky than they showed. If discipline and luck held, they might not notice she was there.

And they didn't. They flew on, oblivious to him and intent on whatever business their orders assigned. Müller allowed himself the luxury of a long sigh of relief. Here in the sheltering darkness, no one could see him do it, and he kept the sigh as quiet as he could.

Had the English spotted him, they would have issued him challenge using their signal lamps. If he had answered them, they would have interned his ship and crew. And if he had *not* answered them?

The British leviathans would have turned and destroyed him...and the *Emden*'s career as a commerce-raider would have ended before it really began.

As things were, he and his leviathan lived to fight another day, in the most literal sense of the words. Before long, the *Emden* passed through the smoke trails the English war leviathans had left behind. He coughed once or twice, and heard some of his men doing the same. Leviathans were wonderful inventions, but no one could accuse them of being inconspicuous. That they so often traveled by night and rested during the day was anything but accidental.

Müller slept for four hours, going to his cot well after midnight. When the clatter of his alarm clock shocked him awake, twilight was giving way to dawn. He shrugged on his jacket, slid into his shoes and tied them, and hustled back to the bridge. A silent steward handed him a roll and a cup of sweet coffee white with milk. He made quick work of the breakfast while scanning the sky around them for smoke trails.

He couldn't see what lay right below the *Emden*, of course. A junior officer down near the steering gear kept an eye on that. Wet-navy warships these days had learned their lessons from the Japanese: they all mounted guns that would bear on targets overhead. Even some freighters packed surprise stings in the tail. You had to watch yourself. The world was a nasty old place, and no one would do it for you.

A brazen voice came from the speaking tube connecting the lower observation post to the bridge. Brazen or not, Müller heard the words clearly: "*Mein Herr*, we're coming up on a nice, fat merchantman. If it belongs to the enemy, it would make a fine prize."

"We'll find out," the skipper replied. He used another speaking tube to bark orders at the electroid engineers. They lowered the voltage in the coils surrounding the *Emden*'s trim tanks: the leviathan's equivalent of a U-boat's letting seawater pour into its ballast tanks. As the cruiser's buoyancy decreased, it sank toward the Yellow Sea.

Müller soon got a good view of the steamship chugging east. He muttered unhappily to himself, for the freighter flew the *Hinomaru*, Japan's red rising sun on a white field. Nor was it a ruse, a trick played by some canny English or French skipper hoping to protect his ship and cargo. Müller's field glasses showed that the sailors crowding the freighter's deck and pointing excitedly at the *Luftkreuzer* uniformly owned black hair, narrow eyes, and high cheekbones. They were Japanese, all right.

The merchantman dipped her flag in salute to the German leviathan. Gravely, Karl von Müller ordered the courtesy returned. War made for strange alliances.

He worried all morning about the English leviathans that hadn't spotted him. He ordered the black gang to make as little smoke as they could. That meant slowing to under twenty knots, so the English would have a smaller area to search. But the *Emden* would be harder to find within that area.

Several *Luftmarinen* with field glasses scanned the sky in all directions. The cruisers from the Royal Sky Fleet might be hard to spot, but the trails they scribed across the heavens wouldn't be.

And, not long before noon, one of the German lookouts raised a shout: "Smoke! Smoke to the south!"

Müller used his own binoculars to study the trail. A single smudge was all it was, not the three from the night before. Undoubtedly, though, it came from a leviathan, not an ocean-going ship.

"We shall pursue," he declared. "If it's a fast freighter, we'll capture it and put a prize crew aboard. If it turns out to be an enemy war-leviathan...Well, in that case we'll turn away and hope we're fast enough to make our own getaway."

Half an hour later, the other leviathan came into sight. She was indeed a fast freighter, flying the Czar's colors. The *Emden* piled on the coal to keep her from reaching Chinese airspace. She would be safe there.

Before long, the bridge telescope let him read the name blazed on the Russian leviathan's stern: *Rjäsan.* "Fire a warning shot," he told the gunnery officer.

"*Zu Befehl, mein Herr!*" the junior officer replied. One of the *Emden*'s forward 105s bellowed. Only a dead man could have ignored the fiery tracer that passed a few hundred meters above the *Rjäsan.* Her skipper didn't. He put on more speed, still trying to get away.

A runner came up from the wireless shack. "She's broadcasting, *mein Herr*," he reported. "We don't savvy Russian, but it's bound to be about us."

"Jam her frequencies as best you can," Müller said. Word of the *Emden*'s departure from Tsingtao *would* get out, but he hoped to delay it as long as he could. Saluting, the runner hurried off to relay his command.

"Give him another one," Müller ordered. "If that doesn't change his mind, give him a couple of live rounds. If we can't take him, we'll wreck him."

The second warning tracer only made more black smoke spurt from the *Rjäsan's* stacks. They flew south over the Yellow Sea, the Russian vessel trying to cheat west, the German vessel trying to force her east. If the freighter could reach a Chinese-held islet...

Then both forward 105s bellowed, nearly in unison. The projectiles burst close to the fast freighter, probably close enough for fragments to bite her. They might slice men into sausage-meat. They might also damage the electroid tanks that held her aloft. Unlike war leviathans, civilian vessels weren't armored against such disasters.

Through the telescope, Müller watched the Czar's ensign come down from the staff at the stern, and a white flag replace it. More to the point, the airscrews reversed, braking the *Rjäsan*. That was a slower business than it would have been against more resistive water, but the Russian leviathan was no longer trying to flee.

"Stand by to be boarded!" a petty officer shouted in German and French. "And quit sending your SOS, or we will resume fire without warning!"

A moment later, Schatzeder emerged from the wireless shack with right thumb upraised: the *Rjäsan's* set had fallen silent. The *Emden* came up alongside the fast freighter. Under cover of her guns, rifle-toting German *Luftmarinen*, some skilled with steam and electroid, slithered down ropes onto the *Rjäsan's* deck. Riding a breeches buoy, the Russian skipper glumly rose to the *Emden*.

Speaking fair German, he asked, "What will you do with my ship, *mein Herr?*"

"Fly her back to Tsingtao, I believe," Müller replied. "Armed and crewed, she'll make a fair commerce raider herself."

"The Americans will take Tsingtao away from you," the Russian said.

The Americans, Müller thought. He had lived all his life among Englishmen, and Russians, Frenchmen and Austrians, Italians and Turks. But Americans were separated from the civilized world by two vast oceans.

Even their English cousins regarded the Americans as half-clever—and half-crazy.

"Are you really so sure you know what the Americans will do?" asked Müller softly.

The Russian captain was unable to conceal a look of unease. The Americans might be his putative allies, but apparently he didn't understand them any better than Müller did.

The base commandant didn't seem overly worried about an American attack on Tsingtao. He toasted Müller's return and his captured ship with schnapps. Armorers set to work mounting guns on the *Rjäsan*. Maybe, instead of raiding over the Yellow Sea, the fast freighter would help defend this embattled Chinese city.

"How long do you think you can hold out?" Müller asked in a tone of clinical curiosity.

"A few weeks," the commandant answered cheerfully— almost gaily. "We'll give the damned Yankees enough of a fight to make them remember us—you can count on that. Since you're back, will the *Emden* stay and help us hold 'em off?"

Müller sounded as diplomatic as he could: "Much as I'd like to, *mein Herr*, Admiral von Spee has ordered my leviathan south. I wouldn't have returned if I weren't delivering my prize."

"Well, that's a damned shame," said the officer in charge of Tsingtao.

Diplomatic still, *Luftfregattenkapitän* Müller did not reply. Getting trapped in this losing fight—and what else would it be, with reinforcement and resupply impossible?—was the last thing he would have wanted. He would have done it had Spee so ordered. *Zu Befehl, mein Herr!* held him no less tightly than any other German officer. But he was glad that cup had passed from him.

He flew away from Tsingtao for the last time the next morning. He didn't know what plan Spee had in mind for the German Far East Squadron, whether all the ships would go to war together or whether they would fight separately. He also didn't much care what the *Konteradmiral zur Luft* and the other skippers who outranked him decided. Anything at all was better than staying here.

Bright August sun blazed in his face as he guided the *Emden* southeast. Whatever he wound up doing, he would do it in the freedom of sky and sea, not trapped over one ultimately indefensible place.

Though the end might prove the same either way, with these orders he would enjoy himself more while reaching it.

While the *Emden* flew toward Pagan, the German wireless station on the island called Yap, fifteen hundred kilometers farther south, suddenly fell silent. That had to be an American attack, and reminded everyone on the cruiser what kinds of odds the Germans in this part of the world faced.

At Pagan, Admiral von Spee's squadron included his two heavy cruisers, hulking leviathans that dwarfed the *Emden*. When Müller repaired aboard the *Gneisenau* to confer with the squadron commander and the other skippers, he found Spee grim.

"I had planned to send the whole squadron into the Indian Ocean to do what harm we could, but I fear we wouldn't last long," the admiral said. "That ocean is a British lake, or might as well be...and where would we coal?"

With several large, hungry vessels to feed, that was an important—a vital—question. But Müller asked, "What other choice have you, *mein Herr?*"

"Chile is neutral—and, unofficially, friendly to the *Reich*," Spee answered. "We could refuel there and try to round the Cape and reach European waters. Also, the enemy has not so many war vessels on the sea or in the sky in the eastern South Pacific."

Müller found himself nodding. America held no colonies in that part of the world, and so needed no great military presence there. "Am I to accompany you there, *mein Herr?*" he asked.

The squadron commander's face was stern and white-whiskered, the kind of face any service's senior officers might be expected to own. All the same, Müller would have sworn Spee's eyes twinkled for a moment. The expression vanished almost before he was sure he'd seen it.

"I think not," the *Konteradmiral zur Luft* replied. "You, I think, *will* go to the Indian Ocean. One leviathan can stir up almost as much trouble and do the enemy almost as much harm as the full squadron might. And one leviathan, especially one not so large, may prove harder to hunt down than the whole squadron."

And one leviathan, especially one not so large, won't be such a great loss to the Kaiserliche Luftmarine, thought Müller, who had no trouble reading the writing on the wall. "Just as you say, *mein Herr*," he replied, the very image of subordination...unless his eyes sparkled, too.

Perhaps they did, for Admiral von Spee's flinty features briefly lightened again. "And, *Luftfregattenkapitän*, it strikes me as the kind of business where an enterprising young officer might have almost more fun than he knows what to do with. Get under their skivvies, Müller. Get under their skivvies and bite 'em in the *Arsch*."

"*Mein Herr*, I look forward to it!" Müller exclaimed, startled out of the usual formalities between officers of such vastly different rank.

He would bedevil French and American freighters passing between the Suez Canal and the South China Sea. Only...

"Do you think the British will stay out of our way, *Konteradmiral?* I worry they will feel we are giving the British lion's tail a hefty yank."

"Stay out of British waters, *Kapitän*," von Spee said. "As long as you do that, then they have no cause to complain."

Neither he nor the admiral said what they both knew, that the English considered the whole of the Indian Ocean—from Muscat in the west to Singapore in the east—to be their waters.

"Be careful, young Müller," said the flag officer softly. Admiral von Spee's eyes twinkled no more. He went on, "Of course, when the lion turns around, the other end has the teeth. Chances are you won't last long, I fear. We do the best we can for as long as we can. Past that, no man can ask."

He held out his age-spotted hand. Müller clasped it. The admiral had grown old, but his grip held its strength.

The rest of the Imperial German Far East Squadron flew farther east yet the next morning: the *Gneisenau* and the *Scharnhorst*, three light cruisers not too different from the *Emden*, a few destroyers and scouts to protect the bigger leviathans, and lightly armed colliers and supply vessels.

Along with a single collier, the *Markomannia*, the *Emden* remained at Pagan another couple of hours before heading southwest toward the Indian Ocean. As the admiral had said, she was off to make as much trouble as she could. But she was heading into trouble, too. Only a fool could have thought anything else. And fools did not command leviathans in the *Kaiserliche Luftmarine.*

The *Markomannia* carried about five thousand tonnes of coal. That could keep the *Emden* flying for a month, maybe a bit longer. Her own bunkers held another eight hundred tonnes. If she was going to carry the war to the enemy, she would have to do it with captured coal and whatever she could get at the neutral ports in the Dutch East Indies.

Germany also had a network of seagoing steamships from which her leviathans could draw coal in time of war. They could... if they could find the steamships on the vastness of the ocean's bosom, if they could do so before the American leviathans and warships swept those steamers from the sea, and if they could get the coal from a steamer into their holds.

Leviathans floated above the water, not on it. That was the chief complication. Gravity worked against them when their men and winches had to haul tonne after tonne of coal aboard. After a coaling like that, the hands would be exhausted and the *Emden* would need a thorough cleaning. But if there was no other choice...

The men in the wireless shack reported signals from a German mail steamer. Müller ordered them to arrange a rendezvous. But the *Princess Alice*'s skipper told him, "I'm sorry, but I can't help you, *mein Herr.* We are low on coal ourselves, and two of our boilers are giving us trouble. We're bound for Batavia, in the Dutch East Indies. Maybe we can coal up there and make repairs and then go on. Or maybe the Dutch will intern us." He shrugged. "Either way, I have to protect my ship."

Müller wondered whether the man cared more about his firm's property than the German war effort. All he said, though, was, "I will give you some despatches to take to the consulate there." The coded despatches would, with luck, arrange for colliers to post themselves along the route he planned.

With no great enthusiasm, the *Princess Alice*'s skipper accepted the despatches. The mail ship steamed away, her wake scribing a thin white line across the Pacific's vast tropical blue.

Oberleutnant zur Luft Mücke fumed. "We ought to drop something on his stupid head," the young first officer grumbled. "You could tell he was lying."

"Maybe he was, maybe not," Müller answered. "His worries are different from ours. We're fighting for civilians, too, not just for the men like us who wear the uniform."

"And a fat lot of thanks they give us...*mein Herr*," Mücke replied. Since the skipper had no comeback to that, he left it alone.

By the twenty-fifth of August, the *Emden*, cruising slowly and economically, had reached Timor. Portugal held the eastern half of that island; the rest was an eastern part of the Dutch East Indies. A collier should have been waiting for the leviathan near the northern shore of the Dutch portion. The ocean, though, was bare of ships. Müller took on several hundred tonnes of coal from the *Markomannia*.

While the work went on—not so bad when the other leviathan could lower coal to the cruiser—Schatzeder popped out of the wireless shack to report, "*Mein Herr*, I'm getting strong Dutch wireless signals. We may have company before long."

Which they did. Not half an hour later, a leviathan that dwarfed the *Emden* flew out of the west. She was the *Tromp*, one of Holland's colonial-defense craft. Slow but heavily armored, she mounted a pair of 240mm guns and half-a-dozen of 150mm. Her secondary armament, in other words, packed more punch than the *Emden*'s guns. The German leviathan could outrun her at a pinch, though.

It didn't come to that. Everything was most polite, most diplomatic. Captain Umbgrove of the *Tromp* spoke perfect German. "Yes, there was a collier near here," he told Müller. "I sent her packing—she stayed in Dutch territorial waters too long. Our neutrality proclamation says belligerents may coal only one day in three months within our possessions."

He didn't want to offend Germany, which lay next door to his homeland. But he was also wary of the intentions of the still-neutral England, which could cut the lifetime between Holland and the Indies. And he didn't want to offend either the Japanese or the Americans who sometimes looked toward these islands with covetous eyes. The *Tromp* and her two sisters—styled battlewagons, but really well-armed heavy cruisers—were as powerful as they were because of the Japanese, not the natives here.

"You are...punctilious," Müller observed.

"Things being as they are, it is necessary," Umbgrove replied. "Would you care for another glass of beer?"

"Thank you, but no," Müller said. "I should get back to my own vessel. After all, you're going to hustle us out of your airspace, too, aren't you?"

Captain Umbgrove spread well-manicured hands in apology. "Sometimes we do not do exactly as we would wish to do. Sometimes we do as we must do."

The *Tromp* followed the *Emden* and the *Markomannia* until they passed the five-kilometer limit. Müller held a course to the southeast till the Dutch battlewagon, satisfied, turned back. Only then did he swing west, and by then night was falling. He had to assume Umbgrove would blab. But the Dutchman couldn't testify to what he hadn't seen.

That evening's wireless intercepts brought word from a Dutch transmitter of a four-funneled British leviathan somewhere farther west. When Müller casually mentioned it, Hellmuth von Mücke's face lit up. "*We* ought to be a four-funneled leviathan, *mein Herr!*" the first officer exclaimed.

"Perhaps we should," Müller said dryly. "But God and the Kaiser's engineers saw fit to give the *Emden* only three."

"*Jawohl, mein Herr,*" Mücke replied. "But if we rig a false fourth funnel, people will have trouble telling who we are from any distance."

A slow smile stretched across the skipper's narrow face. "You're an enterprising one, aren't you? That *could* be amusing. Go ahead, then. See what you can come up with."

The false stack was made from poles and pipes and canvas and paint. It rose aft of the last real one. It was two-dimensional. From the broadside, it looked convincing—so the *Markomannia*'s crewmen attested. From astern, though, it might as well, not have been there. "With more time, we'll improve it," Mücke said. But even this will make people wonder." He paused. "Some fresh paint wouldn't hurt, either."

"True," Müller said. The *Emden* still wore the Far East Squadron's color scheme: creamy white above and dark brown below. It was distinctive, and was meant to be. Now, though, distinctiveness was the last thing the *leichte Luftkreuzer* needed or wanted. The skipper went on, "Have we got enough gray to cover the whole machine?"

"I think so, *mein Herr*," the first officer said. "That and the false stack will make us look English. Where we're heading, it's just what we're after."

Broad grins on their faces, the crew worked with a will. They'd seen plenty of British leviathans in Far Eastern skies. They understood at once what the change was for. "We'll call her the *Chameleon*," Müller heard one of them say as he wielded a long-handled brush. "We have to change color so we can sneak up on whatever we hunt."

No great skill was needed for the lying coat. Every rating not on duty worked on it. Men who actually did have some skill painted two red rings on each real smokestack and two red lines on the false one. The Royal Sky Fleet identified vessels within a class by varying the number of rings on the funnels. If the *Emden* was going to play the chameleon, she needed to play it well.

She flew above the Sunda Strait under cover of darkness. No one painted then; all hands were at battle stations. If she'd been spotted, someone unpleasant might be listening for her motors or scanning for a smoke smudge that dimmed the stars.

Someone might be—but no one was. Sumatra to the north, Java to the south...and the Indian Ocean opened out ahead of Müller, nothing but water to the west as far as the eye could see—and much farther than that.

"Now we go hunting," he said.

Fregattenkapitän Müller kept the *Emden* well away from the shore as he cruised northwest off Sumatra. The fewer people who spied the *leichte Luftkreuzer*, the better off he would be... and Holland ran a leviathan route for important passengers and freight between the northern tip of the island and Batavia, the capital, near the northwestern tip of Java.

There were good reasons for the *Emden* to patrol the Indian Ocean. Müller could attack enemy shooting without having to worry about the French leviathans homeported in Saigon, or the American Sky Fleet stationed at Subic Bay.

But he would have to step quickly around the British.

It was after ten on the night of September 5th when a watchman spotted a steamship on the sea below. The *Emden* swooped down on it like an owl gliding after a mouse. At Müller's orders, the forward guns fired two warning shots. He used Morse with the signal lamp to say in English *Stop at once. No wireless.* The steamship proved to be the *Pontoporos*. Since her registry was as Greek as her name, she was a neutral. But the coal she carried for the U.S. government was contraband of war.

Crewmen from the *Emden* and the *Markomannia*—and, under the guns of their captors, the *Pontoporos'* sailors—transferred as much of the coal to the German leviathans as they could before sunup. The ship's engineer proved to be an American citizen. He was taken prisoner and put aboard the *Markomannia*. The *Luftmarinen* also took food and cigarettes from the freighter. The Greek skipper looked unhappy, but sensibly chose not to quarrel with Mausers.

The next morning, lookouts spotted another freighter. This was no neutral: the S.S. *Kentuckian* flew the Stars and Stripes. The false stack and new paint scheme showed their worth. As the *Emden* overhauled the freighter, sailors waved as if to friends. Then Müller ordered the German ensign raised and fired a warning shot to stop the ship.

She obeyed orders not to use the wireless, but burning papers flew out a porthole near the stern and into the sea. Her skipper was getting rid of his secrets. In his shoes, Müller would have done the same thing.

When Müller boarded her, she turned out to be bound for Cebu in the Philippines to unload French guns and horses for the defense of the American territory. Again, the Germans took foodstuffs and tobacco and spirits. The men drank some of the beer aboard on the spot. They also took several dozen cases of soap. They had been low, but were no more. And Müller took all the old newspapers they could find. Those would let him know which ships had sailed from the various Indian ports, and when.

One of the newspapers he had managed to acquire was a week-old copy of *The Straits Times*, an English-language broadsheet printed in Singapore. He studied the paper thoroughly, and discovered a small article written by the representative of a British manufacturing concern who had been in eastern Siberia a week before and had observed Russian leviathans assembling at Vladivostok.

The piece was no more than a few hundred words long and written in a straightforward prose style that offered not even the smallest rhetorical flourish. Nevertheless, the article sent a chill wriggling down Müller's spine.

Because he could read *between* the lines.

The Czar's Pacific Fleet was planning a strike against Japan. If the Russians won that battle—as they had won their last battle with the Japanese, ten years before—then the little *Emden* would soon be contending with Russian leviathans, in addition to the French, the Americans, and the irritated British.

And if the Japanese somehow defeated their Russian enemies? Even then, the situation would be little better. Müller wouldn't have to worry about Russians, it was true. But he also wouldn't be getting any help from his putative allies. Surely a victorious Japan would press its advantage, meaning to do as much damage to the Russian fleet as possible.

No, the *Emden* was still on her own, no matter what happened in the Far East.

Irritated, he tossed aside the copy of *The Straits Times*.

Under the Germans' guns, the glum crew were put aboard the *Markomannia*. "Pretty soon, she'll carry more prisoners than Germans," Mücke said.

"I hope so," Müller answered. "That will mean we've done well."

His men opened the *Kentuckian*'s seacocks to sink the ship. To hurry the job along, and to give his gun crews practice, he also fired half-a-dozen shots into her. She slid beneath the waves not long before sunset.

They crossed the equator again that night, this time from south to north. All that happened was that the skipper logged the fact. No one had the time or the energy for the horseplay that usually accompanied a crossing.

The small island of We lay off the north coast of Sumatra. No electric lights or gaslamps illuminated the town on the island: only fires. It must have been a settlement of fair size, though. Müller could see them from well out to sea. He kept the *Emden* and the *Markomannia* as dark as possible, to stop the natives and any Dutchmen who might be there from spying them.

Up into the Bay of Bengal soared the cruiser and her accompanying collier. They came across another enemy freighter the next day. The *Marseille*, like the *Kentuckian*, was bound for the Philippines. And also like the *Kentuckian*, she never got there. The *Emden* sank her in the same way after putting her crew aboard the *Markomannia*. Mücke's joke looked as if it might come true after all.

To make sure it didn't, Müller emptied the collier of enemy citizens after stopping the *Minnesotan*. The freighter was also of American registry, but her cargo was bound for the port of Rangoon. Because the goods were the property of owners in the neutral British Empire, under the laws of war the *Emden* had no right to sink the ship carrying them. Müller unloaded his prisoners on the *Minnesotan* instead, and sent her on her way after smashing her wireless set.

"We got ourselves a seagoing *lempensammler*, so we don't have to use the *Markomannia* that way for a while," Müller told his first officer.

Hellmuth von Mücke laughed. "A rubbish collector, yes! And a fine load of American and French rubbish we dumped, too."

"Easier to let someone else worry about them," Müller said. "They can't cause us any trouble down there, either."

"We would have handled whatever they gave." Mücke spoke with the sublime confidence of youth. Grinning, he went on, "This is *fun, mein Herr!*"

"*Aber natürlich*," Müller agreed ironically. "How much fun it will seem when they start shooting at us, though... That may turn out to be a different question."

"They can't even find us!" Scorn filled the first officer's voice.

"They haven't found us *yet*. It's not the same thing, no matter how much I wish it were." Müller knew too well that the Americans were on the prowl after the *Emden*. The airwaves had been howling for his blood ever since the *Pontoporos* made port, and brought word he was on the loose over these waters.

And it wasn't just the Americans.

The English were after them, too. Merchant traffic through the Indian Ocean had been delayed, cargos going undelivered, and Lloyd's of London was suffering mightily. Insurance rates had risen so much that many neutral-flagged vessels could no longer afford it. French and American vessels couldn't buy it at *any* price.

The *Emden* was no longer only a problem for Germany's enemies. The British were feeling the pain, too. If the American Sky Fleet were the first to find the *Emden*, it would try to blast her out of the air.

The British wouldn't. The British would only intern Müller's crew and leave his ship to swing at anchor while she was tended by a cold-iron watch.

Either way, Karl von Müller would be out of the war.

There were ways to minimize their presence. During the day, he brought the *Emden* and the *Markomannia* down almost to the surface of the sea. That way, their smoke trails also stayed low, as if they were steamships. The trails didn't seem scrawled across the sky, the way leviathans' exhaust commonly did.

By doing that, of course, Müller gave any enemy leviathans that did stumble across him the advantage of height. But they were likely to have so many other advantages—more speed, bigger guns, thicker armor—that he failed to see how yielding one more would make much difference.

After darkness came down again, he ordered the *Emden* to rise while he studied a chart. Müller had taken many a prize in these waters, which was well enough, but there was a dark side to his success.

"Well," the skipper said in musing tones, "they won't have much doubt now about where we are."

"Which means we'd better not stay here much longer," Mücke said.

"That's exactly what it means." Müller bent his head to bawl into the brass speaking tube that led to the engine room: "All ahead full!"

"All ahead full—*zu Befehl, mein Herr!*" The metallic answer came back at once. Müller would have been astounded if it hadn't. The black gang gave new meaning to good, old-fashioned German precision and obedience.

Then Müller told the steersman, "Set course to 125."

"Do I hear you correctly, *mein Herr?*" the rating asked in surprise. "Did you say 125?"

"You do, and I did." Müller condescended to explain: "The British will look for us to head west, to raid the shipping lanes that join the Red Sea to the ports along the west coast of India. So we'll do the opposite and go east, toward Burma."

"I see, *mein Herr.*" The steersman swung the wheel. "I am setting the course at 125."

"Excellent." The skipper turned to the petty officer at the signal lamp. "Give the *Markomannia* the new course. We'll leave her behind—we have more in the way of legs than she does. But she can catch up to us tomorrow. Make sure she repeats and acknowledges." Müller didn't want the collier's skipper taken aback the way the steersman had been.

"*Zu Befehl, mein Herr!*" The signalman worked the lever that opened and closed the shutters on the lamp to send Morse. Long practice let Müller read the clacks as readily as if they came from a telegraph key—he hardly even noticed he was doing it.

He read the return flashes from the *Markomannia*'s lamp as automatically. "Repeated and acknowledged, *mein Herr*," the signalman said after the collier signed off.

"Thank you. I saw it, too," Müller told him.

He kept the engines on full power for an hour and a half, then took them down to the much more economical cruising speed. Since he was heading in the last direction his foes would expect (well, almost the last. If he'd felt more suicidal, he might have taken the *Emden* over land), he reckoned that put enough distance between the leviathan and the scene of the crime.

Not long after slowing, he spotted another freighter on the sea. He intended to go low soon anyhow, to make his smoke less conspicuous. If he could send one more ship to the bottom, so much the better.

The freighter's crew was alert. They doused their lights and tried to run when the *Emden* came up on them. Only a live round that kicked up a great plume of seawater made them heave to.

"What ship?" Müller bawled in English through a megaphone.

"We're the *Clan Matheson*." The reply came back in the same tongue, and sounded almost as guttural as his own words.

Wanting to be sure of his quarry, he asked, "You are English?"

A long pause. Then a grudging, "Well, British. We're out of Glasgow."

Müller chuckled. Scots were touchy that way, like Bavarians mistaken for Prussians. They were parts of the same larger nations, but they acted as if it wasn't their fault.

The *Matheson* wasn't on course for Rangoon or any of the Indian ports. No, she seemed to be en route to the Strait of Malacca, the passage that threaded its way between the Malay Peninsula and the Island of Sumatra. The freighter *could* be bound for Singapore—or one of the Malay ports.

But the strait was also the route a ship would take if she were headed to the Philippines.

Müller's orders were to respect British neutrality, but an idea prickled at the back of his skull. America was a nation of peoples from a hundred lands.

How many of them were Scots?

"Very good, Britisher," he said. "Stand by to receive boarders."

What the boarders found was a wonderful, valuable cargo— and one useless to the *Emden*. Bound for Rangoon—or so the ship's master claimed—with goods plainly assembled before the war began, the *Clan Matheson* carried locomotives, motorcars, typewriters, and other expensive precision machinery.

They also found an American ensign carefully folded and cased in the Captain's stateroom, hidden under his bunk. Along with the Stars and Stripes were papers that indicated that *Matheson* was an American-flag vessel.

The fine cargo all went to the bottom, along with the steamship.

Down to the bottom with her and the expensive machinery also went a Thoroughbred racehorse sent out to one track or another in India. A *Luftmarine* from the boarding party shot the horse, which never knew anything was wrong till the moment it died. There were worse ways to die; when Müller heard the news, he reflected that he and his crewmen were much too likely to find some of them.

Even so, he wished they could have kept the horse alive. But, unlike the *Clan Matheson*, neither his cruiser nor her collier had any space in which to care for such a large animal. They also lacked fodder and straw and the other necessities of equine life. It was a shame, but that *Luftmarine* had done the right thing.

The one thing Müller *didn't* send to the bottom was the freighter's American flag. "It is a filthy trick to pretend you are something you are not," he said as he returned the ensign to *Clan Matheson*'s captain.

The man said nothing, but he did cast a meaningful look at the *Emden*'s British paint job before taking his leave of the cruiser's bridge.

After finishing the *Clan Matheson*, he swung to the point where the steamer route between Rangoon and Madras and the one between Calcutta and Singapore met. If he was going to find easy pickings, he hoped to find them there.

But the only ship he encountered on that stretch of ocean was the *Dovre*, a Norwegian neutral. A check of her manifest showed no contraband. So did a quick check of her holds. Müller paid her skipper a hundred Mexican silver trade dollars to take the crew of the *Clan Matheson* to Rangoon. The man was so glad to get the money, he even agreed to delay his arrival to the next day to give the *Emden* time to disappear. He also warned that American, French, and English leviathans and warships had begun to search for the German light cruiser.

"Did you see the American vessels yourself?" Müller asked him in English, the tongue in which they had the most words in common.

"No—I heard from a friend they were coaling in Phnom Penh," the Norwegian answered, "a hundred miles inland from the Gulf of Siam where the Mekong meets the Tonlé Sap."

"*Ach, ja*—Phnom Penh." Müller nodded. "I know of it." The seed of an idea might have been planted there. But that seed would have to wait to grow. Other business still needed attending to.

Müller ordered the *Emden* and the *Markomannia* south till the *Dovre* vanished over the horizon. Then he turned them east, away from the coast of India. By that time, wireless stations in both India and Burma were shouting about the Germans. Some of the shouts were furious. Some sounded admiring, in a way: he was a damned nuisance, but he played by the rules.

"Nice to be a law-abiding damned nuisance, isn't it?" he remarked from the deck chair on the bridge where he'd come to spend most of his time when not actually conning the leviathan.

Hellmuth von Mücke was the officer of the watch. "Nice to be a nuisance any which way."

"Well, yes." On his lap, Müller had a thicket of papers: old newspapers from the captured freighters, more wireless intercepts, and a map or two. "And I have a way to make us, with luck, a very large nuisance indeed."

Interest and excitement sparked in the first officer's eyes. "I like that, *mein Herr*! How shall we make the Yankees hop like fleas on a hot griddle?"

Tapping the map, Müller answer, "Not far from Saigon sits a collection of oil storage tanks owned by the *Compagnie française des pétroles*. If we shell them and set them on fire, we hurt England.

We make her look foolish, too. And I think we can do it without causing the natives any harm."

French Indochina was restive. Anything that made it friskier yet could only harm Paris and help Berlin.

Mücke saw the same thing Müller did. "If the people of Southeast Asia rise up, France will need to keep more soldiers here to show them what-for. Better those soldiers should shoot at the men in these parts than at our brothers and cousins back in Europe."

"That's how it looks to me, too," the skipper said.

He had to plan his approach with care. A British cruiser and an American vessel were hunting him, and wireless intercepts showed the American leviathan had orders to cover the South China Sea. But then someone reported gunfire off the Burmese coast. The American cruiser flew off to investigate. Müller had no idea what that alleged gunfire might have been. He knew it didn't come from the *Emden*. Meanwhile, the British leviathan seemed to be lingering in Ceylon, probably taking on coal.

Her hunters thus diverted, the *Emden* crossed the long north-south run of the Malay Peninsula in darkness, careful to pass over neutral Siam rather than risking antagonizing the British by coming anywhere near Singapore.

The small country below glittered with modest lights in the darkness. When the handful of lights gave way to total darkness, Müller knew he had passed from Siam to the Gulf of Siam.

Once he was again over open water, he steered a careful southeasterly course angling out of the Gulf of Siam and into the South China Sea.

Müller hardly dared breathe as his ship drifted through the darkness. All of French Indochina lay to the north as he rounded the Mekong Delta. The American Philippines were to the east. And neutral—but unfriendly—Britain was at his back. Even neutral Holland to the south would inter him if he tried to make port in the Dutch East Indies.

Müller's vessel was trapped in a maze of peninsulas and archipelagic islands, every passage to open water blocked by someone who would be happy to capture—or *destroy*—it.

His officers and sailors seemed to understand this as well as he. No chatter filled the long, dark hours of the *Emden*'s dangerous transit.

The bridge seemed to be filled with a substance as heavy and oily as electroid itself. But *this* fluid didn't flash off to nothing after a few frantic heartbeats. And it wasn't the magical liquid that made warships float.

No, this dark substance was as sticky as tar and his men were all caught in it. Müller knew well what filled his bridge and held his officers and crew in its black thrall.

Fear.

In war, fear was as unavoidable as death and horror.

High above a hostile world, the *Emden* slipped stealthily through the moonless dark.

The inlet of the South China Sea called Vinh Ganh Rai was defended by forts mounting six-inch guns. That kind of weaponry wouldn't hold off a dreadnought of sea or sky, but it handily overmatched the *Emden*'s 105s.

He couldn't fly in at noon, work his will on the helpless oil tanks, and sail away on the breeze, then. He approached the port around 2000 hours. Saigon was lit as brightly as if it were peacetime. The authorities might worry about the *Emden*, but they didn't *worry* about her.

They should have. Müller brought the cruiser within three kilometers of the shore. "Light the searchlights!" he commanded. The arc lamps blazed blue fire. He didn't want to shoot blindly and hurt the natives he was trying to incite against France. The beams of light, focused by the reflectors behind the arcs, probed the seaside.

There! Those stubby white cylinders south of the city had to be what he was after. Müller shouted the order to commence firing. The gunnery officer relayed it to his crews, and the leviathan's five-gun broadside rang out again and again. Fire stabbed from the 105s' muzzles at every shot.

Under the searchlights' glare, Müller could see smoke and dust rise as the shells slammed home. The first few salvoes gave the gunners the range. After that, they started scoring hits.

Men from the *Emden*'s bow to her stern whooped and capered when tanks caught fire and poured thick, black, greasy smoke high into the sky. Müller shelled the tanks for about ten minutes, then took the *leichte Luftkreuzer* north to bombard some of the ships berthed in the harbor.

He didn't have everything his own way. One of the harbor forts started shooting back with commendable quickness. It could fire only a few shots, though, before the *Emden* pulled out of range. The closest burst a couple of hundred meters astern of the leviathan: not near enough to be dangerous, but plenty near enough to make a thoughtful man wonder what might have happened had the French gunners had better luck.

Mücke stared back toward Saigon through his field glasses. "Might as well be a carnival," he reported. "Everybody and his granny seems to be running to find out what we did."

"We wounded the French, that's what," said Müller. "Now we need to get clear before half the world is after us."

"They haven't caught us yet." By the way Mücke said it, he was confident they couldn't. Müller, older, knew too well that, in a sentence with *yet* in it, time would run out sooner or later. He still aimed to make that as late as he could.

They *would* catch up with him. Time was anything but on his side. Still and all, he had three million square kilometers of ocean above which to hide. At need, he could also go overland; in many of these benighted countries, wireless senders and even telegraph clickers were few and far between. But that would add to his risk, and he did not care to do it unless he found himself without other choices.

Rolf Schatzeder brought him a wireless intercept. "*Main Herr*, the French report that *Graf* von Spee's leviathans have shelled Tahiti! It must have happened about when we were striking Saigon!"

"That's wonderful news!" Müller said. "Let the whole crew know. We're not in this fight alone, by heaven! The whole world's at war."

Surely French leviathans were now racing to answer Saigon's panicked bleats, the burning oil tanks a bonfire in the darkness. Still others would move to secure Hanoi to the north and patrol the long Amman coastline.

American vessels would spread out from Subic, a pack of baying hounds trying to catch his scent over the South China Sea.

Aggrieved Britain would close the back door, the Royal Sky Fleet guarding the Strait of Malacca.

Müller decided to cut northwest, using the last dregs of night as cover until he could climb high enough to conceal himself in Southeast Asia's low cloud cover.

French Indochina was a narrow land. Barely a thousand kilometers separated Hanoi from the Bay of Bengal to the west. Müller skillfully slipped between Hanoi and Vientiane before cutting west across helpless Siam.

Before long he found himself crossing the coast, his vessel once again over the Indian Ocean.

Every leviathan east of Tehran and west of Tokyo was looking for him, and *still* he had managed to slip free.

As the cobalt sea spread out before him, Müller felt exultant, *invincible.*

Then the broad smile slowly faded away.

Every leviathan west of Tehran and east of Tokyo.

That is not an exaggeration.

Up until now he has been bold.

And *lucky.*

But it would only take a single small mistake to change all that. Only a single piece of ill luck.

His mind sober and his countenance grave, Müller ordered his vessel west to harrass allied shipping lanes while his enemies searched for him in the wrong ocean.

For now.

The *Markomannia* following sedately behind him, he flew the *Emden* south, staying off the east coast of India and then off that of Ceylon. He had thought the *Königsberg* was operating in the western Indian Ocean, but he'd seen no reports of her in the papers or in the wireless intercepts his operators gave him. Deciding she was nowhere nearby—perhaps she was marauding along the East African coast—he thought he might swing south and west himself. These were busy sea lanes, full of freighters moving between India and England. The pickings ought to be rich.

Sure enough, fifty kilometers southwest of Colombo he overhauled and sank the S.S. *Hewitt*, an American freighter flying the Stars and Stripes in the confident expectation she would run into no enemies in these waters. The *Emden*'s boarders showed her skipper, a man named Harris, his mistake. They seized provisions from the steamship and made the *Hewitt*'s sailors join them in hauling coal up to the *Markomannia*. Then the merchantman went to the bottom, and her crew joined its pilfered fuel aboard the collier.

It was dark by the time the *Hewitt* turned turtle and sank. Far off in the distance, searchlight beams stabbed up into the sky. Müller smiled. Colombo was alert, even if he didn't intend to raid the harbor there. Soldiers and sailors and flyers would be standing at alert. Chances were they'd be standing at alert at ports from Rangoon all the way to Karachi. The strike at Saigon was certainly distracting every port in the Indian Ocean. What more could a commerce-raider want?

Over the next few days, the *Emden* seized several more freighters. One was a French collier with a cargo of top-quality fuel for the warships and leviathans operating out of Hai Phong. That made looting her doubly delightful. Some of the cheap coal they'd pilfered from merchantmen gave only about two-thirds of the power the steam engines drew from the good stuff. The junk would foul the boilers, too.

The flimsy that Rolf Schatzeder brought Müller turned out to be a diplomatic cable from the German Embassy in Tokyo. The report was brief, and did little to change his *leichte Luftkreuzer's* tactical situation.

The German Embassy reported that the Japanese had defeated the Russians in a fleet action. This conclusion was arrived at by conversations with sources within the Tokyo government and Japanese sky fleet.

Müller felt glad that of his allies' victory. And he was always happy to see someone strike a blow against the Russian animals.

But he knew the Japanese victory would do him little good. The Japanese high command was sure to press their advantage. Which meant he had little hope of Japanese assistance down here in the South China Sea.

Müller let a Dutch steamer go on about her business: she was a neutral without contraband aboard. A couple of hours later, Schatzeder carried some fresh wireless intercepts up to the bridge.

"You're grinning," Müller said. "Have you got something good?"

"See for yourself, *mein Herr*." The wireless operator handed him the intercepted messages. An American freighter westbound out of Colombo had asked the Dutch ship whether any raiders were in the neighborhood. *Refuse to answer on grounds of neutrality*, the Dutch skipper had answered tartly.

Nobody on the *Emden* spotted that American merchantman. Her officers must have been smart enough to take a hint. But, as Müller had with him, the Dutchman played by the rules. One could hardly ask for more. All too often, one didn't get nearly so much.

A drunken brawl broke out aboard the *Markomannia* between captured American sailors on the one hand and the Arabs and Chinese who helped fill out their crews on the other. It wasn't just fists—it was knives and crowbars. No one got killed, but not from lack of effort. After German *Luftmarinen* broke up the fracas with bayoneted Mausers, Müller declared prohibition against his unhappy guests. No doubt they loved him less after that, but they showed better sense.

Sitting in the deck chair and poring over the newspapers his boarders had brought back from the captured steamships, Müller let out a pleased grunt. It was loud enough to make Hellmuth von Mücke turn his head and ask, "*Was ist los, mein Herr?*"

"There are more warships in and over the Bay of Bengal these days, but fewer freighters," Müller said. "The chap writing this piece expects the price of rice to go up on account of it."

"We really are hurting people where they live, then—and I mean that literally." The first officer sounded amazed that he should.

"We are," Müller agreed. "And we're making the French and Americans send heaven only knows how many men and warships and leviathans after us and keep watch against us. We're like a bumblebee buzzing through a crowded railway car with all the windows shut. The commotion the bee stirs up is all out of proportion to its size."

"*Bzzz!*" Mücke said. It was beneath the skipper's formidable dignity to imitate a bug, but Müller found himself tempted.

He took the *Emden* south, not least because the Bay of Bengal was still boiling with enemies. The papers also told him that the Allies were shipping Filippino and Indochinese troops to France.

If he got astride the route between Aden and the Strait of Malacca, he might sink some returning troopships. They probably wouldn't have escorts when they weren't full of men and horses, either.

He didn't stumble across any troopships. But the quiet time in untenanted waters let him get on with some running repairs his men simply hadn't had time to handle while they were seizing freighters.

He came to Diego Garcia on October 9. The atoll, not far from the center of the Indian Ocean, raised coconuts and little else. An Englishman and his half breed assistant ran the plantation. They came to the beach waving their hats in greeting when the *Emden* and the *Markomannia* neared. Müller ordered them hoisted aboard the *Luftkreuzer*.

They happily drank his beer. Since he'd taken it from captured ships, that seemed only fair. He soon realized they had no idea the English were hunting him. "Does Diego Garcia boast a wireless set?" he asked.

"No." The Englishman shook his head. "Don't want one of them newfangled things, neither. Don't want nobody thousands of miles away telling me what to do."

"I don't blame you." Müller felt more than a little sympathy for that point of view, even if his professional responsibilities didn't let him share it. "Excuse me for a moment, please."

He stepped out of his cabin and—*auf Deutsch*—warned his men not to inform the pair from Diego Garcia of the true world situation. As long as the locals thought all was peaceful, all would be...here. And he could use a couple of days of peace to coal and let his men stretch their legs on dry land. Diego Garcia boasted no taverns or loose women, but it was beautiful, and it wasn't fashioned from steel.

His one really awkward moment came when the Englishman asked for news from the outside world. After reporting the death of Pope Pius X, Müller ran dry. Luckily, the plantation manager didn't press him.

With almost five hundred tonnes of fresh, high-grade coal filling her bunkers, the *Emden* flew east, back toward the real world. Hellmuth von Mücke peered sternward, watching Diego

Garcia shrink behind them. The first officer heaved a sigh. "It's still 1914 there," he said, "or maybe 1614."

"And are we better off for knowing how things are, or is that Englishman because he doesn't?" Müller asked.

Mücke had no answer for him. Come to that, he had none for himself.

Once out of sight of Diego Garcia (force of habit there—the plantation keeper was most unlikely to tell anyone else which way he'd headed in time for it to matter), Müller swung the *Emden* north again. He took her up toward Ceylon and India east of the Maldive Islands. Soon he found himself above more traveled waters once more.

He sank a French freighter after his *Luftmarinen* took coal from her, as well as several live beef cattle, a quarter of a million cigarettes, and all the beer she carried. He also sank a dredger wallowing along at four knots in heavy seas. Her skipper, bound for a French Indochinese port he feared he'd never reach, jumped for joy on her rolling deck at being captured. He and his men cheered when the *Emden* sent her to the bottom. They turned out to have been paid in advance, so losing her bothered them not in the least.

An hour before midnight, another American steamship was spotted, overhauled, and sunk. The next ship the *Emden* found was a Spanish vessel with no contraband in her holds. Müller sent the neutral skipper on his way. Then, only a couple of hours later, lookouts spotted a large cargo liner steaming east. Müller had to fire warning shots to make her stop.

She was the S.S. *West Cobalt*, bound for the Far East from Mombassa with tin, copper ore, and rubber aboard. There was little to be salvaged from the freighter's capture save for Yankee discomfiture. Müller's *leichte Luftkreuzer* could scarcely carry away such a heavy cargo. He ordered the boarding party to set scuttling charges and return to the *Emden*.

So the captain was surprised when he heard Mücke's static-ridden voice over the wireless. Müller was even more surprised by what his first officer—and the boarding party's commander—had to say.

"Forgive me, *Herr* Captain," said the younger officer, his words barely intelligible. "But I think there is something down here you need to see."

West Cobalt's main cargo hold was a filthy cavern lighted by nothing more than a square shaft of sunlight admitted by an open deck hatch. The space's bulkheads were coated with rock dust and old coal smoke. Müller was certain he would grow filthy just by standing in such a grimy space.

Just by *breathing* in such a grimy space.

"*Was ist los, Herr Mücke?*" he demanded, his voice stiff with irritation.

Müller did not like being down here, but it was not the dim and dingy hold that had shortened his temper. The tension that tightened the muscles at the back of his neck came from being away from the *Emden*.

He never debarked during a boarding action. What if a more powerful leviathan came across his *leichte Luftkreuzer* while he was not aboard? It would be difficult enough for the little *Emden* to survive an encounter with an American or French warcraft if he were present.

Without him there would be no chance.

Mücke did not flinch at his captain's stern words. He merely handed Müller a *taschenlampe*.

The captain swept the device's beam across many tonnes of ore the dull-yellow color of old brass. "Chalcopyrite," said Müller after a slight hesitation. He'd had to search his memory for the word. "So? It is a copper-iron sulfide, *ja?* The freighter's master told us he was carrying copper ore. Chalcopyrite is quite common. Why is this important?"

"I did not think you would believe it, Captain," said Mücke. "I thought I must *show* it to you." He stepped forward and wrenched a piece of ore up and tossed it aside. Then he reached for another. He worked quickly, sweating freely in the dark, stifling space.

"The copper ore is not important, *Luftfregattenkapitän*," said Mücke, breathing hard. "It's what's *under* the chalcopyrite that's important."

His first officer stepped back and jerked his chin at the divot he'd created in the copper ore.

The beam of Müller's *taschenlampe* caught something *not* the jaundiced color of old brass. The rock beneath the yellowish copper-iron sulfide was a dull gray. Müller was no geologist, but it looked ordinary enough.

He turned a questioning look on the *oberleutnant zur luft.* "It seems the *Amerikaner*'s supplier cheated him. Some of the weight of this shipment was made up with ordinary stone."

Mücke shook his head. "*Nein, mein Herr.* Not *some* of the shipment. *Alles.*" He pointed at the little depression in the rock beneath their feet. "That is the sixth place I've checked and in every case there is only a thin layer of copper ore. Always there is something else beneath the chalcopyrite. There has to be hundreds of tons of this stuff aboard the freighter. Do you believe the American officers and rating are such fools that they failed to notice their vessel was being loaded with worthless stone?"

"*Nein,*" said Müller softly.

"Nor I," said Mücke. *This* is the real cargo. I believe the copper ore is only camouflage."

Müller nodded. He knew *exactly* what his first officer was saying. He thought for a moment and then crouched down and unscrewed the *taschenlampe's* face cap, revealing the bare bulb. He carefully tapped the glass part on a rock, shattering it.

Then he touched the bulb's live electrodes to the pedestrian gray stone, administering a small electrical jolt.

After a minute he touched the rock.

His fingers came away greasy. When Müller went down into the engineering spaces where the air was freighted with atomized mineral oil, his fingers felt like this. *Oily.*

And there was something else—the mild tingle of electricity. It was so small that the captain almost wasn't sure it was there.

Almost.

And then it was gone, the greasy feel, the mild shock, all of it. There was nothing on his hand.

It was like it all had been a dream.

"Electroid," breathed Müller. "This 'common' gray stone must be eteroid."

"This is what I thought as well, *Luftfrigattenkapitän.*"

Müller turned to the young man. "You found this?"

The younger officer nodded.

"How?"

Mücke looked over at the shaft of blinding sunlight piercing the darkness.

"I was up on deck, *Herr* Captain, and I happened to glance down through the open hatch. I wanted to make sure none of my men were still down in the hold. Some of the copper ore must have shifted during transit, revealing the rock underneath. It didn't look...right."

"So you investigated?"

"*Ja*, mein *Kapitän*."

Müller stood and clapped the *oberleutnant* on the shoulder. "*Sehr gut, Herr* Mücke. *Sehr* gut."

The young man looked away, embarrassed by the praise.

A moment of uneasy silence passed between them.

The *oberleutnant* bent down and picked up a piece of the dull gray stone the size of a hen's egg. Mücke hefted the rock as if checking its weight. Then he slipped it into the pocket of his trousers.

Even officers take the occasional trophy, Müller thought.

"What did the *West Cobalt*'s captain say when you confronted him with the discrepancy in the stone?" the captain asked.

"He pretended outrage that he'd been cheated by the supplier of the copper ore."

"His charts?" Müller asked.

"Burned," said Mücke gravely. "The ashes scattered on the sea."

"Unusually thorough," said Müller dryly.

No doubt the American ship had been travelling a great circle route that had taken her from Mombassa east across to the Strait of Malacca and finally to the Philippines.

What Müller didn't understand was why the American vessel had risked that long crossing of the Indian Ocean, every centimeter of it under the threat of a German marauder's guns.

Why hadn't the *Cobalt* headed north to Band el-Mandeb, the gateway to the Red Sea and the Suez Canal? Surely that would have been a much safer voyage than heading for the distant Philippines. The freighter could have made port in Algiers or Marseilles or even Casablanca and sold her cargo of eteroid on to America's French allies.

So why had the ship's master taken her *east?*

What had that wily American been thinking?

At last, Müller recovered his boarding party from the freighter and ordered the vessel sunk.

He wasn't sorry to lose the tin or the copper ore or the rubber. But he was very sorry to send the eteroid ore to the bottom of the Indian Ocean.

The freighter's skipper, an arrogant American named George Long, barely tried to hide his fury. For one thing, he'd swerved south trying to avoid the *Emden*, and instead had blundered into her path. For another...

"Damn you, sir," he said, scowling at Müller as scuttling charges sent his ship beneath the waves, "you've cost my firm three million dollars. They won't thank me for that."

"Three million dollars," Müller murmured. That was more than thirteen million marks: easily enough to build two light cruisers. He wouldn't win the war singlehanded with the *Emden*, but he'd make bookkeepers back in New York howl.

The American stomped off, allowing his anger to strip away his courtesy.

Müller ignored Long's atrocious manners. In truth, he barely noticed them.

Instead, he studied the white scar the freighter's death had left on the ocean's cobalt surface. He stood watching that mark on the sea until the *Emden*'s course carried the fading wound out of sight.

One more American merchantman proved to carry a cargo of cotton cloth bound for India. Since that was on its way to a neutral port, Müller let her go on after disabling her wireless, and after using her as a rubbish collector: he unloaded the crews from his recent captures on her.

Then a lookout spied yet another plume of smoke rising from the sea. The *Emden* flew off to investigate. The French collier *Massif du Jura* carried fine coal shipped from Nord-Pas de Calais. By now, the *Emden* and the *Markomannia* held enough for close to six weeks of steaming above the sea, all of it courtesy of France and America.

Müller finished the busiest day his leviathan ever saw by sinking the *Îles de la Société*, en route to Hai Phong. Before scuttling her, he had his *Luftmarinen* plunder her provisions and her doctor's equipment. His crewmen would eat better and stay healthier because of her.

He swung out of the sea lanes, heading west but staying well south of Ceylon.

When the ships he'd sunk failed to report in, the French, English, and Americans would take a look at their charts and start looking for the *Emden* in the eastern Arabian Sea.

Müller planned to be long gone before his pursuers reached this part of the Indian Ocean.

The *Emden* was less than lovely these days. Crewmen who'd left farms to serve the Kaiser tended to the cows and pigs and chickens and ducks on the deck. Coal dust fouled the *leichte Luftkreuzer*. Men slept in hammocks rigged on deck: they were cooler than the sweltering bunkrooms. When it rained, everyone stripped naked and bathed. Rainwater and prizes were the only sources of fresh water the *Emden* had.

On the twenty-second of October, the crew paraded and the gunners fired a twenty-one-gun salute to celebrate the Empress' birthday. Three days later, with the *Markomannia* impersonating a foe, Müller drilled his men in aerial combat.

Meanwhile, the leviathan kept heading west. Müller had raided Saigon, the jewel of French Indochina. Now he aimed to call on Phnom Penh. The *Dovre*'s skipper had reminded him about the place. Hitting it seemed to him an ideal way to make the French have even more kittens about him than they already were.

As he crossed the Gulf of Siam, he ordered the *Emden* to jog north, to ensure that her smoke wouldn't be spotted from Cambodge. If he were not careful, Müller might get a warmer welcome at Phnom Penh than he really wanted.

And so he took that jog. War was a chancy business any which way. Some of those chances, no one could avoid. Getting rid of the ones you could kept you in business longer.

France had held Cambodge since 1863. The city of Phnom Penh, located at the junction of two of Indochina's most important rivers, did a booming business. *Soon,* Müller hoped, *it would be booming in ways its designers hadn't planned for.*

If his charts and reports were right, the city was fortified against attack from the south and the west. Attack from the north? As far as he could tell, the French military engineers hadn't worried about that. Not much defensive work had been done on the place since the age of the leviathan had dawned.

The *Emden* reached Phnom Penh at about 0230 hours, half an hour after moonset. Almost all of the natives in the surrounding villages would lie sleeping. Anyone who did chance to look up at the sky would take the *Emden* for a French vessel...Müller hoped. How likely was a German interloper here?

Not very likely, evidently. Hellmuth von Mücke pointed south, toward sleeping Phnom Penh. "Look, *mein Herr!*" the first officer said. "They're lit up like a Christmas tree! They don't know we're within a thousand kilometers!"

"They don't yet," Müller answered. "Pretty soon, though, they will." Till then, he'd been flying without a flag, to make it less obvious what the *Emden* was. Now he called, "Hoist the ensign!" The German battle flag rose on the mast.

A lookout with field glasses exclaimed, "*Mein Herr*, there's a leviathan in port, and not a small one, either!"

"*Donnerwetter!*" Müller's own glasses leaped to his eyes. Had the French set a trap for him after all? But the leviathan's lines told him at once she was no French or American vessel. She was, pretty plainly, an older machine. A moment later, the city's streetlights let him spot the Czar's ensign fluttering at her stern.

"She's Russian!" he shouted. "Change course to 180 to present the starboard broadside and knock her out of the sky!"

As soon as the *Emden* reached a decent firing position, the five-gun broadside spoke, again and again. Shells burst all around the Russian leviathan. Then flashes and fires told Müller the 105s started scoring hits.

Aboard the Russian cruiser, men taken by complete surprise ran this way and that, as if wild beasts were chasing them. No return fire came from her. Müller could see that one hit had knocked a boat onto a gun that might have borne on him. From a well-run leviathan, even one caught off guard like this, he would have expected some kind of resistance. But since there was none...

"Fire a torpedo!" he yelled. "Let's finish her off!"

He hadn't used a single torpedo in all the time he'd harried French and American merchant shipping. Gunfire, bombs, and scuttling charges had done his work for him against civilian steamships. Torpedoes were air-to-air weapons, designed to pack a bigger punch than guns could and to take it farther. They carried enough electroid to make them buoyant, and were powered by steam engines so overstressed that they would tear themselves to pieces inside of two minutes...unless the infernal device scored a hit first.

Whoosh! Trailing smoke, the Austrian Luppis torpedo roared away from the *Emden*. Müller breathed a silent sigh of relief once it cleared his leviathan. Torpedoes were nearly as dangerous to the men who launched them as to the ones they aimed them at. And, a proper Prussian, he never fully trusted devices manufactured under feckless Vienna's auspices.

But this torpedo flew straight and true. It struck the Russian cruiser—Müller thought he made out the name *Zhemchug* near her stern—amidships. The blast pierced her light side armor. The aether vortex and the associated transformers to at least one of the Russian's buoyancy tanks were lost, so the electroid flashed over: that is, it returned to the ordinary electricity from which it was born. Shorn of her lift, the *Zhemchug* tumbled in ruin from the sky.

Men aboard the *Emden* whooped and waved their hands and cut capers at the blow they'd struck against their foes. Müller felt like cutting a caper or two himself. He didn't; his sense of an officer's place forbade it. But the impulse remained.

Down below, in the convulsing city, someone had the presence of mind to start shooting at the *leichte Luftkreuzer*. This was not a neighborhood where a sensible man wanted to linger.

"All ahead three-quarters!" Müller called to the engine room. To the steersman, he added, "Set course to 045 till we're well clear of the city, then steer due east."

He thought that would quickly solve his problem. Enemy gunfire persisted, though, far longer than he thought it had any business doing so. Peering astern and down through field glasses, Hellmuth von Mücke said, "Bugger me blind if we haven't got a *verdammte* seagoing destroyer on our tail!"

The *oberleutnant* was right. In their flight from Camboge, the *Emden* had cut across the narrow width of Amman and found herself over the South China Sea, just south of the Gulf of Tonkin.

Most leviathans traveled through the air faster than most warships steamed atop the sea. But a few navies built fast, light ships expressly designed to go leviathan-hunting with their long-range guns. Karl von Müller hadn't known one of those was cruising off the Annamite coast south of Huê. But he wasn't especially alarmed about it, either. Those ships had severe limitations. They carried only a couple of guns and no defensive armor: a sacrifice on the altar of speed.

He swung the *Emden* to present her broadside to the surface ship, as she had to the Russian leviathan. Her guns boomed. Brass shell casings clattered as they fell from the 105s' breeches. The shooting was excellent, perhaps because the gun crews were already in practice. The *Emden* left the bold surface ship behind her, afire and sinking.

In European waters, where they were likely to encounter leviathans far more ferocious than the *Emden*, some of those fast ships sported a pair of 300mm guns: they were monitors with rabbit legs. This one had been a baby of its kind, just as the *Emden* would have been nothing to speak of in the crowded skies over the North Sea.

Here above the South China Sea, the *Emden* was doing exactly what she'd been designed to do. Thinking of that, Müller smiled. After all, how often did such things happen?

The Emden *at Phnom Penh... The* Emden *at Phnom Penh...* For as long as they could, the men in the German cruiser's wireless room jammed the frequencies the French commonly used. When they finally gave up the effort, in the middle of the morning, the *Emden* was no longer at Phnom Penh, but heading northeast as she hugged the Chinese coast, giving American Luzon a wide berth. Müller expected to make it into the East China Sea by the following morning.

"Take her down to fifty meters," Müller told the steersman, who saluted and obeyed. Again, the skipper was doing his best to keep from scattering betraying smoke across the tropical sky. Even if he wasn't at Phnom Penh anymore, French men-of-war would converge there by air and water. He didn't care to advertise his position any more than he had to.

He also slowed the *leichte Luftkreuzer* to fifteen knots: by leviathan standards, a lazy amble. That also helped lessen the smoke the *Emden* belched forth. And it let the *Markomannia* catch up with him. In the dash across the South China Sea and the rush to get away, Müller had left her behind. Unlike the French, though, her master would know what his escape plan was.

Sure enough, she came up behind the *Emden* a little past noon. Like a man and his faithful hound, the two German leviathans went on together.

No enemy leviathans or warships spotted them. On the vastness of the ocean, even leviathans sank below flea size in relative terms.

When he reached Formosa, Müller turned the *Emden* and the collier to the east, wanting no trouble with the Chinese. So far that immense Asian nation had offered him no hostility, and he wanted to keep it that way. And he did not wish to fly above the Formosa Strait, hemmed in on either side by leviathans of uncertain intentions. So he headed east into the daunting sun, and put the Chinese mainland behind him.

It was a decision he had a chance to regret not more than an hour later.

The brass speaking tube on the bridge suddenly bellowed with alarm. "Bridge, forward lookout. Leviathans twenty degrees off the starboard bow!"

Müller, who had been half-dozing, was up and out of his captain's seat in a single frantic beat of his heart, his spyglass pressed to his eye.

Sure enough, the lookout was correct. Müller spied multiple dark silhouettes against the painful brightness of the morning sun. The leviathans, painted black by the sun's blinding light, were impossible to identify. But he could still *count*. He made out eight ships, most of them destroyers or frigates or colliers, but at least one of them a light cruiser like the *Emden* herself—and one of them was a battleship.

Müller's heart sank.

Judging by their relative size, they were no more than fifty kilometers distant—and well capable of catching him with their superior speed.

And although he could not see more than their silhouettes, he knew who had they had to be.

The British were searching for the *Emden* in the Indian Ocean. The French no doubt had their leviathans patrolling Indochina, after Müller's twin attacks there. That left only one possibility.

Die Amerikanerin.

The Yankees had finally come for him.

As he watched through his spyglass, he saw the Yankee squadron come right, their aspect changing from beam to, to bow on.

Already the chase had begun.

Frantic thoughts ran through Müller's mind, though they did not disturb the grave expression on his face.

The nearest safety for him were the islands of Japan, twelve hundred kilometers to the north. But if he tried to fight his way through the American squadron, he would certainly be destroyed.

He could run to the South, hoping to reach neutral Dutch—or even English territory—and accept the possibility of being interred rather than destroyed. But it was unlikely he would be able to outrun his American pursuers. And even if he did, surely the French leviathans based in Tonkin and Annam and Cochinchine would be warned by their American allies and would come out to greet him. He would not make it to Singapore or Batavia.

His best—and only—option was to run for the Chinese coast, hoping the neutral Asian government would give him a comfortable cell in which to sit out the war.

But even that was unlikely. The Americans would surely gun him down before he reached Chinese airspace.

Nevertheless, he turned and ordered the steersman, "New course 270. All ahead full."

He felt the movement of his *leichte Luftkreuzer* as she came about in a tight hairpin turn.

He never took his eyes off the American squadron, hoping to deduce their course. Heading west was a good approximate course. But if he could guess the Americans' heading and distance, he could call out those numbers to *Oberleutnant* Mücke. The boy would get out his protractor and parallel ruler and calculate a refinement on Müller's westward course that would open the distance between the *Emden* and the Americans to the maximum extent.

They would play this game again and again over the next many hours, Müller adjusting his course slightly to gain greater distance, and the Americans adjusting their course in turn. Back and forth they would go, the Germans trying to draw away, the Americans trying to draw near.

If Müller played the game well, he *might* reach the safety of the Chinese coast.

As he watched, a winking light began flashing against the dark silhouette of the American squadron's lead ship.

No doubt the enemy was offering him humane treatment if he hove to and laid down arms.

Müller translated the flashing light in his head. "*Emden.* Come about and plot an intercept course." He snorted. Of course.

It would be a cold day in hell before he surrendered his vessel. If he had to go down, be would take as many of these American devils with him as he could.

"This is the captain of the Japanese battleship *Shikishima*," proclaimed the flashing light.

Was? What?

As the pursuing vessels completed their course changes and slipped free from the blinding light of the sun, Müller saw the red sunburst on the white field of the ensigns that hung from the vessels' jack staffs. Of course, this was not absolute proof that the squadron was made up of friendly ships. Hadn't the *Clan Matheson* tried to hide that she was an American trader? And even Müller himself was not above such chicanery.

Why were the "Japanese" not up north, fighting the Russians?

It was at this moment, that Schatzeder brought him a flimsy, the message encoded. Again, Müller had to use the five-letter groups to decipher it. The first part of the message read, "From *Shikishima*, to the *Emden*. Now that we have pulled the Russians' fangs, we intend to take the fight to the most dangerous enemy fleet remaining in the Pacific.

"The Americans.

"We propose you assist us."

A slow, grim smile cut across Müller's face. It seemed he would have at least one more chance to do some damage to the Americans, after all.

While travelling south, Müller had promoted three dozen men who'd served well aboard the Swan of the East. He toasted their success with sparkling wine taken from a British freighter. They lifted mugs of beer removed from some another prize.

The next day, a sooty albatross crash-landed on the *Emden*'s deck. From everything Müller had heard about the long-winged birds, they were marvels in the air, but spavined on dry land. This one certainly seemed to be. It flapped and skrawked and thrust with its formidable beak when *Luftmarinen* tried to approach it. But when a cook set some boiled beef on the deck the albatross waddled over and ate with good appetite. It took off almost as badly as it had landed, but managed to gain the freedom of the skies once more.

Müller watched its visit with less enthusiasm than most of his men, who were glad of anything to break up the monotony of the cruise. "People say those birds are bad luck," he murmured.

"Bad luck for the Americans we're going to visit." Hellmuth von Mücke always looked on the bright side of things.

"Well, I hope so," was the best Müller could do.

The Philippine Islands were green and brown dots against the blue sea, each one ringed by the turquoise of shallow water. The Philippines was an archipelagic nation, a sweep of islands laid out across the sea.

By official count, there were 7,107 of these little malformed dots on his charts. But Müller was skeptical of the official count. He didn't think that anyone knew for sure how many islands made up the Philippines. He suspected that 7,107 was just a guess.

A *low* guess.

As the *Emden* drifted across the sky, Müller studied each and every last speck of green and brown through his spyglass intently.

Japanese intelligence had determined that the Americans were mining etoroid out of the Sierra Madre, the territory's longest mountain range running from the northern edge of Luzon, nearly all the way to the island's south.

The Japanese planned to blockade the Philippines to prevent the Americans from shipping all of that ore back to the United States. Eteroid meant electroid, and electroid meant flying battleships.

The Japanese meant to dry up the Americans' Pacific source of eteroid, limiting them to what they could pull out of the Rockies and Appalachians.

It is good strategic thinking, Müller thought.

But he was troubled by his encounter with the freighter *West Cobalt.*

That American vessel had been carrying eteroid disguised to look like copper ore.

And she had been heading *east.*

If the Americans had managed to purchase a consignment of this valuable material from an African country, perhaps originating from a mine in the Atlas Mountains, why had they shipped it *east?*

If the source *were* the Atlas Mountains, why did the American freighter not load up in Algiers or Casablanca and either head across the Mediterranean to Marseilles—or cross the Atlantic to New York or Savannah?

Müller did not understand.

Unless the Philippines was not *only* a source of eteroid ore.

Unless they *also* had a secret refinery hidden among the seven thousand Philippine islands.

The Japanese did not believe his mad theory, but Müller was happy to let their blockade draw the attention of the United States Sky Fleet while he searched the Philippine's backyard for what he reasoned had to be there.

Then he saw it.

A long concrete pier extended out from a jungle-green island like a finger sticking out from a hand. The long run of concrete nestled between two parentheses of rock that served as natural breakwaters. Jib cranes mounted on towering columns reached out over deep water.

Müller wondered *how* deep? How deep a draft could the quay accommodate? There was *some* reason the Americans had chosen *this* island.

"Is that it?" Mücke asked, standing beside his captain and studying the pier through his spyglass.

Müller nodded. "It has to be," he murmured. "It might be possible to hide a refinery in a jungle. But it is quite another thing to hide a pier large enough to accommodate commercial shipping."

Looking down on that small blot of land with its inexplicable concrete pier, Müller couldn't help but remember the sight of *West Cobalt* foundering, her decks awash like a diving U-boat.

Except the American freighter would never see daylight again.

Müller wasn't sure why the death of *this* freighter had stuck with him—unlike all the other ships and leviathans he'd ordered destroyed.

Maybe it was because he hadn't stepped foot aboard any of those other vessels. Somehow the American freighter was more *real* to him than the others.

Somehow, *West Cobalt* was *his*.

In his dreams, Müller found himself standing in the freighter's pilothouse as she slipped beneath the waves, a cold, liquid darkness closing over him.

The darkness seemed wrong somehow.

In a world where ships were raised into the sky, the darkness that had closed over *West Cobalt* seemed *wrong*.

But that didn't change the way the dream ended, night after night.

As they descended toward the nameless island with the pier, Müller ordered the wireless operators to do their damnedest to jam the local transmitter. This time, their damnedest didn't prove to be quite enough.

Wearing an unhappy expression, Schatzeder came to the bridge and reported, "I'm very sorry, *mein Herr*, but I'm afraid they managed to get off a few signals. *Strange leviathan nearing harbor*, they sent, and then *SOS—the* Emden *here*. We've stifled them now, but..." He spread his hands in chagrin and regret.

"We'll have to work fast, that's all, and hope no enemy is close by," Müller said. "You haven't picked up any signals to make you think we might have unwelcome guests, have you?"

"None from closer than a couple of hundred kilometers, *mein Herr*," Schatzeder said.

"That gives us more than long enough to do our job and disappear." The skipper turned to his first officer. "Are you ready to take charge of the party landing on the island, *Herr* von Mücke?"

"*Jawohl, mein Herr!*" the younger man replied, saluting.

"Good. I will leave that to you, then. The wireless sender first, and after it the cable station," Müller said.

The *Emden* came down close to the ground near the wireless antenna. Ropes let Mücke and three dozen *Luftmarinen* descend to dry land. Any foes with rifles could have given them trouble. Any foes with the smallest field gun could have made the *Emden* very unhappy. But no one offered the slightest resistance. The Americans at the transmitter and the cable station must have fled into the jungle that prevailed everywhere neat rows of coconut palms didn't. Two well-placed sticks of dynamite brought down the antenna. A *Luftmarine* with a torch set fire to the shabby little hut next to it.

Mausers in hand, Maxims on wheeled carriers ready, the Germans moved on to the cable station a few hundred meters away. Müller hoped the Yankees wouldn't have had time to burn or carry off records of the messages they'd received before they ran off to hide. Their books might give him precious intelligence.

Then a lookout at the *Emden*'s stern let out a horrified shout: "*Mein Herr!* A smoke smudge to the southwest, *mein Herr*, coming closer very quickly. I think it's another leviathan!"

"Oh, damnation," Müller said, so quietly that no one but a lipreader was likely to have understood him. A leviathan was almost sure to be a warcraft. And any warcraft approaching now was almost sure to outclass his own cruiser, too. The *Emden*'s luck had just run out. Maybe it was the albatross' fault.

Whoever's fault it was, Müller was damned if he'd go down without a fight. "Take us up to a thousand meters, course 240," he told the steersman. To the engine room, he ordered, "All ahead full! Emergency power as soon as you can give it to me." He let out one more shout, intended for everyone aboard: "Battle stations!"

The *Emden* rose and swung. The landing party was still on the ground. He'd worry about those men later, if he had the chance. *And if I'm still alive to worry* also flashed through his mind, but it vanished a split second later. He had no time to dwell on anything except the fight ahead.

His field glasses told him the other leviathan was an American-built light cruiser, a member of the *Omaha*-class, unless he missed his guess. There was a white number painted on the ship's sleek bow. He raised the spyglass to his eye: "6." This was CL-6, which made her—he searched his memory—the *Cincinnati*.

Sure as the devil, 150mm guns. They threw shells that weighed forty-five kilos apiece, more than three times as heavy as the ones that burst from the muzzles of his leviathan's 105s. The *Cincinnati* had more and thicker armor, too. Taking her on hardly seemed a fair fight.

When you got right down to it, it *wasn't* a fair fight. But it was the fight Karl von Müller had.

❦　⚜　❦

Sunlight filtered through the jungle canopy filling the world with a translucent green light. The air was thick with heat and water vapor. There were bugs everywhere, biting, stinging bugs. Mücke saw a gecko clinging to the trunk of a palm tree, its small triangular head oriented down towards the jungle underbrush. This place wasn't the *Vaterland*.

It wasn't even Tsingtao.

This was a whole different world.

Mücke led his small contingent of saboteurs up the dirt road that climbed away from the dock. It was not especially wide, no more than ten meters across, and rutted by the wheels of trucks. Someday, it would have to be paved. But not in the near future.

After Mücke and his men were done, there would be no need for *any* kind of road.

For twenty minutes they crept through the jungle, moving parallel to the road, near enough that they could see its dusty brown color through the trees, but not so close that they couldn't immediately take cover if someone drove by.

The party moved quietly—or at least as quietly as a group of *Luftmarinen* unused to conducting stealthy operations on dry land could move.

It was their good fortune that they were not discovered.

At last, they came to a great sprawling structure whose walls were fashioned from cinderblocks and corrugated steel siding. So this was the place where the Americans transformed eteroid into electroid.

It *had* to be.

The road led up to a loading dock. To the north of the factory was a field where the jungle had been cleared. A massive pile of scree fifteen meters high filled this space. The rocks looked utterly ordinary, like the kind of thing you would dig out of the soil of your front yard while gardening. Mücke thought he had never seen any set of stones so boring.

Except once.

His hand stole into his right trousers pocket, and he fondled the small, smooth stone he found there. It was the size of an egg and completely uninteresting. It was the stone he had taken from the hold of the *West Cobalt*, before his charges sent the freighter to the bottom of the Indian Ocean.

And he did not have to take it out of his trouser pocket to know that it looked exactly like the pile of stone in the cleared field to the north of the factory.

But the clincher was the enormous copper spheres that sat in steel cradles on the concrete apron outside the gaping maw of the open factory door. There were six of them, each five meters in diameter. In and of themselves, the copper spheres were strange enough, but what really convinced Mücke was the soft, almost subliminal humming originating from the spheres.

He couldn't really be sure he was hearing that unnerving noise with his ears. But he *was* certain he felt that irritating sound vibrating the fillings in his back molars.

There was refined electroid in those copper spheres, all right.

"Should we set our charges on those spheres, *Oberluetnant?*" asked *Luftmaat* Franz-Walter Beyer, a tow-headed Bavarian boy who demonstrated unusual bravery and cunning.

Mücke liked the lad.

He thought long and hard about the *luftmaat*'s suggestion. The young officer knew if electrolyte were suddenly and catastrophically released from a containment vessel it would flashover, transforming instantaneously into an electrical charge. Such an incident would cause plenty of damage—as well as destroying part of an electroid shipment. That would no doubt be irritating to the Americans. But the damage would be concentrated on the outside of the factory. Mücke wanted to destroy the specialized equipment *inside* the refinery.

Also, people were going to die when that much electroid was suddenly released.

Mücke was an officer of the Imperial German Far East Squadron, and he was committed to killing the Kaiser's enemy as need be. But he did not like the thought of taking the lives of workers from this small, poverty-stricken American outpost. The men working in the refinery had never done him or any of his countrymen any harm.

For a long moment, he lay there staring at the dark opening in the factory's side, his mind working fast.

Müller felt like a boxer in the ring against a foe who outweighed him by thirty kilos and was all over muscle besides. If he didn't land a lucky punch—or a whole bunch of lucky punches—he'd get his head handed to him.

Had he been facing Royal Sky Fleet men, he would have known they were as well trained as his own *Luftmarinen*. With Americans, though, who could tell for sure? Maybe he could hurt them early enough to take the starch out of them.

"What's the range?" he asked the gunnery officer.

"Coming down to eight thousand meters, *mein Herr*," that worthy answered.

"Commence firing!" Müller ordered. If he could knock the *Cincinnati* back on her heels, so to speak, he might be able to loose a torpedo. One of those could wreck even a superior leviathan if anything he had could.

His first two salvos were clean misses. The third, though, did some damage to the enemy vessel. Through his glasses, he watched debris fly up at her bow and stern. He also watched one of the *Emden*'s shells strike her flank and spark away without penetrating. She had a 50mm belt of hardened steel warding her there, and it showed its worth.

Then she started shooting back. Her guns fired one by one, not in salvo; his hits must have put paid to her fire-control system. But when they started to strike home, they would smash him like a bug under a falling brick.

And he couldn't close the range on her. Besides being stronger and better protected, she had two knots on the *Emden*. Müller ordered a torpedo launched, but more in despair than in hope of hitting the *Cincinnati*. Sure enough, it flew wide and low, and kicked up a great waterspout when it burst on smashing into the sea.

The bridge thundered as if in an earthquake when the *Cincinnati* scored her first hit. Schatzeder staggered out of the wireless shack, his face all over blood. He was limping, too. Müller hoped he wasn't too badly hurt, and that not too many men had been killed outright.

Mücke took five of his men—including the irrepressible *Luftmaat* Beyer—and sprinted through that large open door. He left the rest of his boarding party outside, covering the door so they could get back out again.

The factory was dark compared to the sun-drenched shipping dock. It smelled of soot and the burnt electrical stink of ozone. Mücke tasted grit on his tongue. He was surrounded on all sides by boilers and lozenge-shaped pressure vessels, all of them bigger than a ship's boat.

To his right he saw a dancing light cast up against the factory's cinderblock walls, and heard the stuttering *crack crackcrack crack* of an arc welder. All around him machines bellowed and roared. He heard the whine of pumps running at full speed, and the hiss of steam racing through pipes.

And underneath it all, there was the *hum* of electricity twisted by humanity's mad genius into something nature had never intended.

Ja, there was no doubt. *This* was the place.

Mücke dispatched his *luftmarinen* to find the electroid storage area and set their charges. Then he found some oily rags on a workbench, bundled them up with some greasy papers, and stuffed them into a sheet steel rubbish bin. He struck a sulfur match and dropped it into the cylindrical container and soon dirty gray smoke was roiling out of the ad hoc incendiary device, greedy yellow flames licking at the air. It was not enough to do any real damage to the factory.

But it might be enough to get the workers to flee to safety.

It was not long before a dark-skinned man dressed in blue denim trousers and a gray workshirt rushed by. Instead of hiding from the man, Mücke grabbed him by the arm. "*Alarm!*" he shouted. "*Alarm, alarm!*"

The Filipino worker looked at him with wide eyes.

Mücke tried to remember the English or Spanish word for fire, but couldn't. He used the German word, and hoped it would be close enough. "*Feuer,*" he shouted, pointing at the column of dirty smoke. "*Geh weg. Feuer. Geh RAUS!*"

The worker stared at him for a moment, and then broke and ran.

Mücke found and accosted another worker.

At last, he found one who must've had the courage to follow the refinery's safety directives, because a shrill, angry buzzing filled the air. Then he no longer needed to approach the Filipino workers.

At the sound of the alarm, they were already fleeing.

It was then that Beyer and his comrades approached. "It is done, *mein Herr*," the boy said. "All the charges are set. We too must leave."

Mücke nodded and clasped the boy's shoulder. They moved towards the open door, following the factory workers out.

Mücke was never sure what happened next. His guess was that one of the mechanical timers was faulty—or incorrectly set. He chose to believe the mechanism was faulty.

He did not want to believe one of his brave sailors had made an error.

Whatever the cause, he heard the muffled *whump* of a small explosion, and suddenly blue lightning forked through the factory, live electricity dancing all around them as it branched and sizzled and sputtered. A bolt of lightning hit one of the overhead lamps and popped its immense light bulb, showering the shop floor with tinkling glass and a cascade of glowing sparks.

Other electrical bolts found the steel pedestals on which machines rested. Lightning raced along the corrugated steel walls. One jagged spear of electricity found an iron welder's mask, making it hop and dance until the electrical charge finally dissipated and the mask fell on a workbench sitting in a puddle of melted iron glowing a sullen red.

All of this terror and destruction lasted no more than a few frantic heartbeats. His men instinctively sheltered behind the nearest large piece of equipment—in this case a steam boiler. They crouched low, seeking to escape the seemingly random lightning bolts.

Keeping low and hiding behind something big and solid was a good strategy if you were trying to survive an artillery barrage. But it wouldn't save you during a flashover event—especially if the big thing you were hiding behind was built out of enormous steel plates.

There was nothing to do but get out as fast as they could—and pray to Providence that they would make it. Cowering would not save them.

Mücke grabbed Beyer by the arm and hauled him to his feet. "*Raus, RAUS!*" he shouted over the shriek of imminent death. He shoved the boy roughly toward the rectangle of sunlight cut into the refinery's wall.

Then he did the same with the next man. He was none too gentle. *Mücke* was terrified, too. He wanted to flee.

But not before he got his men up and running.

It couldn't have taken Mücke more than thirty seconds to get them on their feet and headed for safety, but it felt like a lifetime.

The *oberleutnant* ran after them, the hair on his arms and the back of his neck and even his head standing straight up, and his molars singing with exquisite pain. His nostrils were filled with that wretched ozone stink, and Mücke was sure his nose hairs were standing up straight, too.

The whole time he was running, he was *sure* he was going to die.

The world was bright flashes of terrible blinding incandescence and the whipcrack *boom* of near lightning strikes.

Somehow, he managed to stumble out of the refinery, the last of his little team to escape danger.

He and his men moved among the milling Filipino factory workers. The presence of German *luftmarinen* should have roused a cry from the workers. But they were so frightened and disoriented by the catastrophe, that they didn't even notice.

"Get into the jungle, *schnell!*" Mücke told his men.

Surely there was a company of U.S. Marines stationed somewhere on this island to protect this hidden factory. Mücke did not know how close their barracks might be, but he wanted to be gone before they made an appearance. He moved quickly towards the jungle, again the last of his men.

It was then that the factory exploded, lobbing huge chunks of cinderblock at them. Wedges of jagged steel spun through the air. A piece of cinderblock fetched Mücke a glancing blow, smashing into his hip and then bouncing away

Thank God it didn't hit my head, he thought.

And then he looked up in time to see one more tendril of lightning flash by him and catch young Franz-Walter in the back, just as he was climbing the hill to where the rest of the landing party hid.

The boy crumpled to the ground, smoke rising from his back. Mücke ran too him, rolled him over, but the moment he saw the lifeless eyes, he knew there was no hope of life.

He was the first one out, he thought. *He was supposed to be safe.*

But perhaps in this new and terrible war, no one was safe.

❧ ⚜ ❧

Another 150mm shell slammed into the *Emden*'s engine room, making the whole ship tremble. Smoke and flame and shrieks rose to the uncaring heavens.

The *Emden* slowed. She began to sink toward the South China Sea.

"Does she answer her helm?" Müller demanded of the steersman.

"*Ja, mein Herr*...after a fashion," the rating answered.

"Well, guide her back toward land if you can." Müller looked around. "If they take out an electroid tank, we'll drop a lot faster than this. I'd rather not go into the drink if I can help it."

"*Zu Befehl, mein Herr!*" the steersman said. Even in the midst of chaos and death, he saluted. He was a good German.

Despite the chaos and death, the *Emden*'s gunners kept banging back at the *Cincinnati*. After the first couple of hits at long range, though, Müller couldn't see that they were doing a pfennig's worth of good. He might as well have been fighting the American cruiser with flyswatters as with the 105s. Had he had a moment, he might have tipped his hat to the foe. The Americans might not have been so smooth as their English cousins, but they had courage enough and to spare.

And they had a superior leviathan. That counted for more than everything else put together.

As the *Emden* took hit after hit, she sank toward the sea. She almost made it back to the island, hitting a reef a hundred meters from the coral-sand beach. Fires grew on the part of the leviathan still above the seawater.

"You may abandon!" Müller shouted. "Make for land and save yourselves!"

"What about the ensign, *mein Herr*?" a petty officer asked.

"Haul it down and run up a white flag." The words tasted bitter as wormwood in Müller's mouth. He brought them out anyway. He had an overwhelming reason for doing so: "It's not as if we can fight any more."

Instead of finishing the *Emden* at once, the *Cincinnati* flew off. A few minutes later, her big guns sounded again in the distance. *That's the* Markomannia *getting smashed*, Müller thought miserably. The collier had been through a lot with him. Now it too was paying the price.

Luftmarinen were dragging the wounded and dead up from the bowels of the *Emden*. The wounded, they tried to get ashore for whatever treatment the doctors could give. They laid the dead in neat rows on the deck. Müller's eyes stung—oddly, all the more when he spied the corpses of the Chinese laundrymen. They'd stuck to the leviathan, and to their posts, as long as they could... and this was what their loyalty had won them.

Back came the *Cincinnati*. In spite of the white flag, the guns from her forward turret bellowed once more. Both big shells, luckily, missed, but they kicked up plumes that drenched the men still aboard the shattered *Emden*. Müller pulled a white handkerchief from his pocket and waved that—anything to make the enemy realize he could do no more against her.

The firing stopped. Through a megaphone, a leather-lunged American petty officer shouted, "Do you surrender?"

"Yes!" Müller yelled back. "Please help us!" He wanted to say something like *What do you think we're doing while we're wrecked here?* He stifled that, though, fearing the enemy skipper might not understand sarcasm, or appreciate it if he did.

After that, the Americans did lend a hand. Their hoses helped bring the fires under control. Their medics gave the *Emden*'s doctors a hand with the wounded. And they took Karl von Müller to their skipper, Sky Captain John Glossop.

"You fought most gallantly, sir," Glossop said—in English, for he seemed to know no other language. "Unfortunately, the difference in power between our two leviathans was too great to let you hope for success."

"Most unfortunately," a tight-lipped Müller agreed. He would have needed luck and complete idiocy from his foe to win the fight. Luck he hadn't had. By the way Glossop seemed, he'd missed idiocy from the man by less. But it was all over now. He asked, "What will you do with me, sir?"

"Well, I believe you and your men will be confined at Pearl Harbor. No hope of escape, but the quarters are not too bad."

"Yes, it could be worse," Müller said.

"We have all your survivors now?" Glossop asked.

"You see what remains of us." Müller didn't use the lie direct, but he evaded as best he could. So far as he knew, Mücke and his landing party remained at large on the island, a few kilometers away. They might be able to manage something. If they couldn't, they would surrender to the next warship or leviathan calling here. Müller spread his hands. "We gave you Americans a run for your money, anyhow."

"A long run." John Glossop nodded politely. "But it's over now."

Müller thought of the gallant *Emden* falling from the sky, and the men who had trusted him with their lives lying dead on her decks. For a moment he was reliving his nightmare, standing alone on his bridge.

Darkness closing over him.

A searing agony sliced through his middle, the pain as sharp and cruel as any blade. Müller never knew anything could hurt half so much.

He just hoped it had been all worth it.

"*Ja*," he whispered, "it's all over now."

Oberleutnant zur Luft Hellmuth von Mücke stared in something close to despair at the burning wreckage of the *leichte Luftkreuzer* lodged on the reef.

Beside him, a hard-bitten *Oberluftmaat* named Klaus Breitenstein spat disgustedly. "That's that," the petty officer said, his words and tone brooking no contradiction. "The *Emden* is washed up." Then he added, "Anybody got a cigarette?"

One of the *Luftmarinen* handed him a Lucky Strike looted from one American freighter or another. He scraped a match on the sole of his boot and lit the coffin nail. Mücke fired one up, too. If he turned around—and if the coconut palms let him—he could also see the *Markomannia* afire. It wasn't just the *Emden* that was washed up. It was the entire German presence in the Indian Ocean.

Blowing out a stream of smoke, Breitenstein asked, "What do we do now, *mein Herr*? Come out with our hands up and surrender to the goddamn Americans?"

That had to be the only logical thing to do. Logic, however, wasn't what stiffened Mücke's stubborn spine. Tied up at the palmwood pier in front of the wireless station was a schooner that looked big enough to carry the whole thirty-man landing party. If they could sail over to the Dutch East Indies, they might be interned for neutrals, or even manage something better than that rather than being taken prisoner or dying in battle against what was bound to be a superior force of Marines. If...

Nothing ventured, nothing gained. Pointing toward the schooner—her name was *Following Sea*—Mücke asked, "How many of you *Luftmarinen* know anything about being *Seemarinen?*" To his gratified and astonished relief, half a dozen men raised their hands. Some had served on tramp steamers, others on the herring boats that plied the North Sea and the Baltic. "Them was all scows next to this here beauty," one of them said in a singsong, half-Danish accent that showed he came from Schleswig-Holstein. "With her, you can go places."

"Can you show a bunch of lubbers like the rest of us what we need to do so we can all go places?" Mücke asked. The place he most wanted to go was Padang, the main port on the west coast of Sumatra. It lay southwest of where he stood now.

"Expect so, *mein Herr*, if folks does like we tell 'em to," answered the Holsteiner—his name was Jens Rasmussen. "Don't know much about navigating, though."

"I can handle that," Mücke said. "It's the same for sky or sea. If there's a sextant aboard, I'll do fine. Even if not, we can find north by stars and sun. That's what we have to have."

"We'll take supplies from the Americans?" Breitenstein asked.

"You bet we will," Mücke said. "We'll leave them enough so they don't starve—"

"Better than they deserve," the *Oberluftmaat* broke in.

"It's what the skipper would expect of us," Mücke said. That silenced even the fierce Breitenstein at once, as the *Oberleutnant zur Luft* had known it would. Everyone aboard the *Emden* venerated Karl von Müller; he'd held the crew together when they were the only Germans carrying the war to the enemy in these parts. Now Mücke had to do the same job for the handful of *Luftmarinen* who stayed free. He made himself smile. "Come on, boys. Let's go fetch and carry, hey?"

They lugged cases of tinned beef, crates of hardtack, and barrels of water from the storehouse behind the wireless station out to the schooner. They soon broached one of those barrels; under the tropical sun, the work was hot. But they went at it with a will. After fighting so long and so hard, none of them could stand the notion of hanging around and waiting to give up.

To make the *Following Sea* seem more like a warship—more like the S.M.S. *Following Sea*—Mücke had them mount one of the Maxim guns they'd brought down to make sure no one here did anything stupid at the schooner's bow and the other at her stern.

In the captain's cabin, he found a sextant, a few maps (smaller than he would have liked), and some sailing tables that looked to have been printed around the time of the French Revolution. He might be able to use them all the same...and, if and when he reached the Dutch East Indies, he might be able to get some real cash for them from a rare-book dealer.

His own nautical experience was limited to afternoons on pond and stream, the more pleasant ones with a pretty girl along for company. He let the *Luftmarinen* who did know what they were doing boss the others around. Jens Rasmussen seemed to know more about the business, and about how to show ignorant men what they needed to do. Hellmuth von Mücke remained skipper of the *Following Sea*, but Rasmussen became her master.

Everybody cheered when they raised the sails and watched them fill with wind. They cast off from the pier, and the breeze carried them into the lagoon. The Americans they'd chased away from the transmitter and the Filipinos who had worked in the refinery came out of the jungle to watch them go. One fellow circled his finger by his ear. His friends nodded. They thought the Germans were crazy. Mücke wasn't so sure they were wrong.

A few minutes later, Rasmussen walked over to him after coming up from below. "We've got some water in the bilges, *mein Herr*," the fisherman reported.

There was a problem leviathanmen didn't need to worry about. "How do we fix that?" Mücke asked.

"We have two pumps down there," Jens Rasmussen said. "We need to put some men on them."

"See to it, then." After a moment, Mücke found another question: "What happens if the pumps can't keep up with the leaks?"

"In that case, *mein Herr*," Rasmussen answered bleakly, "we sink."

But they didn't. A little water slithered in between the *Following Sea*'s planks, but not a lot. The pumps had no trouble sending it up and over the side.

Mücke tried to steer as close to southwest as he could. Everything seemed to move very, very slowly. Aboard the *Emden*, he'd got used to traveling at twenty or thirty knots. As best he could figure, the *Following Sea* made four or five. They were more than fifteen hundred nautical miles from Padang—closer to some of the smaller towns farther down the Sumatran coast. They would be a while on their way.

They turned out to take twice as long as Mücke had guessed. They made their paltry four or five knots only when the wind blew from the proper direction. When it didn't, they stood still. Water ran low. When it rained, they used pots and pans and spare canvas to gather the precious fluid. They stretched and varied their food by pulling fish from the sea.

Rasmussen happily ate raw fish. "They're not herring, but they're not bad," he said. Mücke agreed with the first part of that; with the second, not so much. He supposed raw fish beat starvation, but it was close. Most of the *Luftmarinen* were on his side, but a few followed the fisherman. The galley did boast a stove. They had scant coal to feed it, though. With tinned beef, that didn't matter so much. With fish, it did.

Above all else, Mücke dreaded a tropical storm. Those could rattle a leviathan. What they'd do to the *Following Sea*... Every time clouds piled up, he shuddered. He got a taste of one when sheets of rain pelted down and lightning filled the sky. Waves tossed the schooner like a toy boat in a rambunctious five-year-old's bathtub...and then the squall blew over, the sun came out, and the sea calmed again.

Mücke felt proud of himself when the *Following Sea* reached Siberoet Island. He would have been prouder—and less hungry—if she hadn't taken more than two weeks to get there. He guided her into the Seaflower Channel, which separated Sumatra from the small islands to its west, and made for Padang. He went ahead with great care; in those shallow waters, he needed better charts than the ones he had.

A leviathan—that Dutch fast freighter, not too different from the *Rjäsan*—paused to look the schooner over. A few hours later, another Dutch leviathan, this one a destroyer named the *Lynx*, came out to guide the *Following Sea* to port. The *Lynx* ended up towing her into Padang harbor, because the current ran strongly against her.

As they neared the harbor, a young officer at the *Lynx*'s stern called, "Purpose of your visit?"

"We are a German warship," Mücke answered proudly—it wasn't as if the Dutchman wouldn't have noticed those fore-and-aft Maxim guns. "We need some refitting."

Once tied up, he paid a call on the *Lynx*'s skipper, another on the harbormaster, still another on the official with the awkward title of neutrality officer, and one more on the German consul in Padang, Horst Schild. The neutrality officer didn't want to let the *Following Sea* have anything that could aid her, even food, money, or better charts than the ones Mücke had used to come this far. He also laughed at the idea that the schooner was a warship.

"Would you care to stand in front of her Maxims, *mein Herr*?" Mücke asked politely. "You may pick your range—anything out to a thousand meters."

The neutrality officer, a very pink fellow, turned red. "You are being deliberately difficult!" he spluttered.

"Not at all," Mücke said, meaning *Of course I am.* "As a belligerent in a neutral port, I have the right under the laws of war to resupply for twenty-four hours and then sail away. That is what I aim to do, so long as you quit hindering me and let me go about my business.

"You are a fool if you don't let yourself be interned here and sit out the rest of the war," the neutrality officer said. "The Americans will sink you. And the French will sink you if the Americans don't. And if *that* doesn't happen, the English will scoop you up. Most of the *Emden*'s crew is already dead or captured. Do you want to make it a clean sweep?"

"I want to get on with the war. I don't have the luxury of being neutral," Mücke said, and the Dutchman flushed again. Mücke finished, "Please, *mein Herr*, you are not my superior officer, to order me around. Will you let me go on?"

Although the neutrality officer made handwashing motions Pontius Pilate might have envied, he did. Consul Schild slipped Mücke enough German, French, and English money for him to buy food (including a dozen live shoats) and other supplies from the local merchants. German skippers whose freighters were interned at Padang showered the *Following Sea* with clothes, more tinned food, and beer.

That evening, Hellmuth von Mücke slept the calm sleep of a successfully stubborn man.

And, come morning, a steam launch from one of those freighters towed the *Following Sea* out to the harbormouth.

Consul Schild waved to the schooner from the launch's rail. The German sailors on the small steamer saluted and sang *"Die Wacht am Rhein."* By the looks on their faces, they thought Mücke was a maniac.

Some of his own men might have, too. Jens Rasmussen quietly asked, "Excuse me, *mein Herr,* but are you sure leaving this way is a good idea?"

"No." Mücke shook his head. "But I think we can make it work."

"How?" Rasmussen asked, then hastily added, "Uh, *mein Herr?*"

Hellmuth von Mücke smiled what he hoped was his most carnivorous smile. "I'll tell you how, Jens. Ever since the *Emden* flew out of Tsingtao, we've been good little boys, and we've always played by the rules. Now? Now we turn pirate!"

Two mornings later, a lookout on the *Following Sea* pointed northwest. "Smoke!" he shouted. "Smoke in the sky!"

Mücke followed the *Luftmarine's* arm and index finger. Sure enough, here came the Dutch civilian leviathan, bound for Batavia.

"Get ready, boys!" he called, feeling as if he ought to be wearing a three-cornered hat and talking around a cutlass clamped between his teeth. He took a deep breath to steady his nerves, then nodded to Klaus Breitenstein.

"Zu Befehl, mein Herr!" The *Oberluftmaat* struck a match and tossed it into a bucket half full of waste oil and kerosene. The bucket sat on a couple of bricks so it wouldn't ignite the deck planking.

When the inflammable mix caught, a column of thick black smoke rose straight into the clear sky: a miniature, as it were, of what the *Emden* had done to the storage tanks at Saigon. *Luftmarinen* ran this way and that, waving their arms in the air and doing their best to show that they feared for their lives. Mücke thought they were overacting like nobody's business, but he wasn't the audience they were trying to impress.

That Dutch civilian leviathan was. Surely the crew would notice the smoke pouring up from the *Following Sea.* Surely, they would turn glasses on the schooner and spy the panicked, inexperienced

Germans aboard. Surely, they would take pity on them and come close to lend a hand against the fire...wouldn't they?

They would. They did. They approached on the side where the oil was burning in the bucket. Before they drew too near, Mücke had a man pick it up with iron tongs and another man move the bricks so the cabin shielded the source of the smoke from close inspection.

The leviathan's name—*Meester Cornelis*—was blazoned in large letters on her flank. Mücke had no trouble at all reading it, for she came up within twenty meters of the *Following Sea* and no more than five meters above the sea. A Dutchman wearing military-looking blues shouted to the schooner in fair German: "How can we help you?"

From the rail, Mücke answered, "You can see that we have two Maxim guns covering your vessel. You can see we also have riflemen ready to open fire along with the machine guns." The *Luftmarinen* had stopped playacting and grabbed their Mausers.

Waving to them, Mücke went on, "You are our captive. We will shoot you down if you try to fly away or if you use your wireless set." The *Following Sea* had no receiver, but the Dutchman didn't know that. "Come closer. Lower ropes. Let us board you, and no one will be harmed."

Eyes big as saucers, the Dutchman said, "You must be out of your mind! You can't get away with this!"

"No, eh?" Mücke nodded to the two *Luftmarinen* at the forward Maxim. They fired a burst that flew just forward of the *Meester Cornelis'* bow.

After that, no one seemed inclined to argue with the Germans on the schooner. As meekly as anybody could want, the leviathan approached. Ropes came down. *Luftmarinen* scrambled up them. They took charge of the bridge, the engine room, the wireless shack, and the electroid tanks. Then they set the leviathan's crew to work bringing up supplies from the *Following Sea*.

The *Meester Cornelis'* skipper was a bald, gray-muttonchopped fellow named Peter de Graaf. "If you and your men give your paroles, we'll treat you the same way we treat ourselves," Mücke told him. "Otherwise, we'll have to keep you closed up and run the leviathan ourselves." He wasn't sure he had men with enough different bits of skill to do that, but there was one more thing he kept to himself.

After plucking at those bushy side whiskers, de Graaf said, "I will give mine. I will urge others to give theirs, but I cannot force them. If they refuse, that is between them and you."

"Good enough." Mücke hadn't been sure he would get so much.

All the crew but two agreed to cooperate with the Germans. So did all six passengers, who luckily included a doctor. Perhaps more luckily still, the *Meester Cornelis* carried no women this trip. That would have complicated Mücke's life. He ordered the two obstinate crewmen confined to a stateroom, and posted a guard outside the door and another outside the porthole.

Though the Dutch wireless operator denied it, Mücke had to assume the *Lynx*, back in Padang, had gotten an SOS. Maxim guns would be useless against her cannons. He set the course to the southwest and piled on the coal. He wanted to get out of Dutch airspace as fast as he could. He didn't think the *Lynx* would follow him over international waters. If he proved wrong... well, that would likely be his last mistake.

"What in damnation are you doing?" Peter de Graaf demanded.

"Going back toward territory the Central Powers hold," Mücke answered calmly.

"You fornicating lunatic!" the Dutchman said. "We haven't got coal or food or water to cross the Indian Ocean!"

"Not yet," Mücke said. "After we run across a steamship or two, though, we will."

De Graaf fell into Dutch to say what he thought of that. Mücke understood only bits of his opinion, but it seemed heartfelt.

Finding some dark gray paint that matched the *Meester Cornelis'* base coat, the Germans painted over the leviathan's name. Mücke would have been content to leave her anonymous, but one of the Dutchmen volunteered to paint on something new. Casting around in his mind for English towns, Mücke came up with *Duluth*. Even without stencils to help, the Dutchman neatly and legibly put it on both sides of the leviathan and at her stern.

Mücke took her up to almost three thousand meters. She was more visible that way, but the lookouts could also see much farther. The German *Oberleutnant zur Luft* knew they would have to find freighters to rob or else run out of fuel, run out of electricity and electroid, and fall into the ocean.

Once out over open ocean, he steered toward the sea lanes the *Emden* had also haunted. He found them crowded again. With the German cruiser wrecked, American skippers assumed they had nothing more to worry about. He proved one of them wrong, swooping down on the *Jacob H. Gallinger* in the middle of the night. Machine-gun tracers were plenty to make her stop in a hurry.

Down came the *Luftmarinen* to wreck her wireless, to pilfer as much coal and fuel and potables as they could, and to dispose of the two Dutchmen who hadn't paroled themselves. The *Gallinger*'s skipper, a Mr. Drinkwater, grumbled, "Confound it, they told me the *Emden* was all smashed to pieces! Bunch of lying hoptoads, is what they was!"

Realizing the Englander thought the little Dutch leviathan was the *leichte Luftkreuzer*, Mücke had all he could do not to guffaw. "Well, you can let them know we are still in business," he said. His English was worse than Karl von Müller's, but he could make himself understood.

The Germans did a proper job of smashing the wireless set and any parts that might be used to repair it. The *Jacob H. Gallinger* couldn't report her sad encounter till she made port at Mangalore three days later. Then the wireless seemed to explode. Newsmen claimed the *Emden* hadn't been shot from the sky after all. The U.S. Sky Fleet bellowed at the tops of their lungs that she had so. It sounded to Mücke very much like an argument on a kindergarten playground.

Little by little, something closer to truth emerged from the welter of confusion. As if happened, neither Dutchman released from the *Meester Cornelis* spoke much English. The Britishers in Mangalore, like so many of their countrymen, had trouble with any language not their own. They needed a while to understand the Dutchmen's story, and longer still to put the pieces together so the puzzle looked right. Getting from the *Emden* to the *Following Sea* to the *Meester Cornelis* to the *Duluth*, from the Philippine Islands to Sumatra to the waters off southern India, wasn't easy for them, but they eventually managed.

By the time they did, Mücke didn't worry about it so much. He was a great many kilometers west of the waters off southern India by then, and putting more kilometers behind him every hour. The Royal Sky Fleet and Royal Navy had stepped up patrols in those waters. Again, that didn't bother him a great deal. Where he was, no armed leviathan would stumble over him except by accident.

What did bother him was that he would have to strike again before he got where he was going. Right now, the English had no idea where that was. If they got a report that he'd attacked another ship, though, they were liable to figure it out.

Well, no help for that. The *Emden* and now her detached crewmen had been running on raw gall as long as they'd been running on coal. And so, not long after sunset on the night of December 24, the hijacked Dutch leviathan fired a burst of machine-gun bullets ahead of the *Savannah's Pride* and warned her by signal lamp not to use her wireless.

Down came the *Luftmarinen*. They ruined the freighter's wireless gear and smashed her signal lamp. For good measure, they pitched every electric torch, kerosene lamp, and candle they could find over the side. They aimed to keep her from signaling for as long as they could.

Then it was hauling coal and tinned food and beer up to the *Duluth*. The Germans and, covered by their rifles, the *Pride*'s sailors, worked through the night to replenish the leviathan's bunkers.

"Who in blazes are you, anyway?" the freighter's skipper called up to Mücke as the plundering neared an end.

"Don't you know? I am Saint Nicholas in my sleigh. My reindeer are hungry," Mücke answered. It was starting to get light. He could see the American's wide-eyed, staring face. He didn't laugh in it. Karl von Müller wouldn't have approved, and Müller's good opinion still mattered to him. Instead, he waved cheerily. "Happy Christmas!"

When he flew away, he took care to set his course to the southeast till *Savannah's Pride* was well out of sight. Then he swung back to the west once more. The *Duluth* went on, and on, and on.

She was passing north of the English-held but barren island of Socotra when word of her latest exploit finally splashed across the aether. Not everyone seemed willing to believe the leviathan that had stopped the *Savannah's Pride* was the same one that had robbed the *Gallinger*.

This time, Hellmuth von Mücke did laugh. The Americans might understand Occam's Razor, but they didn't want to shave with it. What were the odds of *two* small, piratical leviathans running loose above the Indian Ocean at the same time?

❦ ⟁ ❦

With the Arabian Peninsula to the north and the Horn of Africa to the south, the Indian Ocean narrowed into the Gulf of Aden. The city of Aden, a British protectorate and base, sat near the southern end of the Red Sea, warding that approach to the Suez Canal. Here in that confined space, the sea seemed full of ships.

Under cover of darkness, the *Duluth* became the *Mogadiscio*, at least if you believed what was painted on her sides. Like Holland, Italy was still neutral in the great war. (She should have joined the Central Powers, but she hadn't.) Mücke hoped to be taken for a fast freighter flying out of Italian Somaliland. He didn't know whether any leviathans actually did that, but with luck, anyone spotting him would be just as uncertain.

No matter what new disguise he traveled under, he stayed clear of Aden and of the Bab al-Mandab, the southern opening to the Red Sea, till the following night. He slipped north bare meters above the water and out in the middle of the strait. French-held Djibouti, on the African side, was almost as big a danger as Aden.

Then they *were* past. Hellmuth von Mücke hadn't known how tense he was till some of that weight slid from his shoulders. North of Aden and its surrounding territory lay what was still the southernmost tendril of the Ottoman Empire, reaching from Yemen up through the holy cities of Arabia to more thickly settled parts of the Middle East. And the Ottoman Turks were allied to Germany and Austria-Hungary.

Hodeida was the closest port in Ottoman-held Arabia. Once the Germans reached it, Mücke was confident the Turkish officers and their Arab soldiers would convey his *Luftmarinen* and him north toward something resembling civilization. Once they got to Constantinople, reaching Austria-Hungary and then Germany itself should be easy.

Like any leviathan that traveled over water, the *Meester Cornelis*-turned *Duluth*-turned-*Mogadiscio* carried boats to save crewmen and passengers in case of aerial disaster. Mücke got his men—with their rifles and Maxim guns—into those boats just outside Hodeida.

Before he slid down a rope into a boat himself, he sketched a salute to Peter de Graaf. "Well, *mein Herr*, I give you back your leviathan," he said. "I thank you so much for the use of her."

"Never a dull moment with you aboard," the Dutch skipper said.

That wasn't exactly true. Long stretches of the flight across the Indian Ocean had been dull as dull could be. All the same, Mücke understood what he meant. The *Oberleutnant zur Luft* asked, "What will you do with her now that you have her back?"

"I won't stay around here," de Graaf answered at once. "Even by night, this is an evil-looking place. Are you sure you want to go ashore? If the men are as bad as the town, they'll slit your throats for whatever coppers you have in your pockets."

Mücke had more than coppers in his pockets. He had gold: less than he would have wished, less than a proper pirate would have stolen, but enough, he hoped, to grease whatever palms needed greasing. And... "Two Maxim guns make excellent persuaders. You've seen that yourself."

"Good luck," de Graaf said. "I think you'll need it." Mücke went down the rope hand over hand. He and his men began the short row into Hodeida harbor. The *Meester Cornelis* flew away. He never saw her again.

Six months later, Kaiser Wilhelm himself pinned the Cross of the Royal House Order of Hohenzollern on the left breast of Hellmuth von Mücke's uniform tunic.

The All-Highest's own uniform seemed to be about half-and-half, ordinary blue wool and cloth-of-gold. Ten kilos' worth of decorations were splashed across his narrow chest; Lord Nelson might have envied his bicorn *Grossadmiral zur Luft*'s hat. Despite the hat, Wilhelm was eight or ten centimeters shorter than Mücke had expected.

"I congratulate you, *Luftkorvettenkapitän* von Mücke," the Kaiser said.

"Thank you very much, your Majesty," Mücke replied as the watching dignitaries applauded. He'd got the promotion from mere mortal officers of the *Luftmarine*. They'd also presented him with the Iron Cross Second Class and the Iron Cross First Class.

He knew he was a stand-in for Karl von Müller here today. When Müller got free of English captivity, he had a *Pour le Mérite* waiting for him: the Blue Max, Germany's highest honor. But chances were he wouldn't see the *Vaterland* again till after the war was won. Mücke hadn't commanded the *Emden*, but he had come back to German soil once more.

It was summer in Berlin, warm and muggy. Mücke and the rest of the landing party had needed from January to May to make their way from Hodeida up to Constantinople, though they'd gone from Padang to Hodeida, across the whole Indian Ocean, in far less time.

He'd ridden on a camel going through the desert. He'd ridden in a dhow, sailing up the Red Sea. As far as he was concerned, the dhow made the *Following Sea* seem like a luxury liner in the class of the *Berengaria* or the *Titanic* by comparison. He'd lost whatever liking he'd once had for camels, too.

And he'd lost whatever liking he'd once had for Arabs and Turks. They made Chinamen look honest, something he hadn't imagined possible. They were all bandits, out for whatever they could steal. One or another of their chieftains might well have cut his throat, and his men's, if they hadn't hung on to their Mausers—and to the Maxim guns, which scared the stuffing out of the brigands infesting the Arabian Peninsula. Occasional judicious bribery hadn't hurt, either, even if the Arabs and Turks called it *baksheesh*.

Wilhelm brought him back to the here-and-now by saying, "Come with me, *Luftkorvettenkapitän*. We have a fine luncheon laid on."

"Thank you once more, your Majesty," Mücke murmured.

Sure enough, the luncheon was very fine indeed. Course after course went by. The baby shrimp stuck out in Mücke's memory. So did the ham, and the casserole of eggplant and a rainbow of peppers. Every course had its own wine, all of the finest vintages.

Mücke would have enjoyed it more if he hadn't seen how hungry the Entente's blockade was making most Germans. They ate cabbage and potatoes and turnips and black bread that tasted as if the flour were stretched with sawdust—probably because it was. No one complained. People were glad for whatever they could get, when they could get anything at all.

He did wonder whether the All-Highest and his courtiers had any idea how ordinary people here lived. By the way they ate and drank and laughed, Mücke doubted it. Their bellies were full. Why should they worry?

His belly soon filled, too, which stifled revolutionary thoughts. He couldn't remember the last time he'd eaten so well. He wasn't sure he ever had. This beat the devil out of the boiled sheep's eyeballs and stewed camel's udder he'd downed in the desert. It beat the devil out of endless tinned beef and hardtack, too. And it beat the devil out of nasty black bread and sauerkraut.

As if to prove the point, the kitchen help carried in on a silver platter a magnificent saddle of venison roasted with squash and onions. After carving off a slice thick enough to feed a poor family for three days, a *Generalleutnant* whose mustaches were waxed to points even sharper than the Kaiser's turned to Mücke. and said, "So tell me, young fellow, now that you've come back across all those countless kilometers, what will you do here in Germany?"

The newly-minted *Luftfregattenkapitän* cut himself a rather thinner slice of venison before replying. Then he said, "*Mein Herr*, next week I report to Wilhemshaven. I am to take command of the Fifteenth Half-Flotilla of *Luftflotilla* VIII, operating against air pirates over the North Sea."

"*Ach, so.* Very good," the senior officer said. "Give them the hardest knocks you can. They're damned nuisances."

"That's what I'll be there for, *mein Herr*." What with everything he'd been through, Mücke wondered whether any mere European service could get him more than lukewarm. But wherever they sent him, he'd give it his best shot. He had to.

Karl von Müller would expect nothing less from him.

LEVIATHANS
THE GREAT WAR

For more information about the Leviathans tabletop game, visit the link below to go to Catalyst Game Labs' website.

You'll find quick-play rules downloads, announcements about the upcoming Kickstarter campaign, expansions, fiction, and much more!

WWW.CATALYSTGAMELABS.COM/LEVIATHANS